EVER DARK

M VIOLET

This book is a work of fiction. Names, characters, places, and incidents either are products of the author's imagination or used fictitiously. Any resemblance to actual events or locales, or persons, living or dead, is entirely coincidental and not intended by the author.

EVER DARK
M VIOLET

All Rights reserved. Except as permitted under the U.S. Copyright Act of 1976, no part of this publication may be reproduced, distributed, or transmitted in any form or by any means, or stored in a database or retrieval system, without prior consent and permission of the publisher.

Copyright 2025 by M Violet

Cover Design by ARTSCANDARE.
All stock photos licensed appropriately.

Edited by Kat Wyeth (Kat's Literary Services)

Formatted by Champagne Book Design

For information on subsidiary rights, please contact the publisher at authormviolet@gmail.com

A NOTE FROM THE AUTHOR

Ever Dark is a why choose dark romance about monsters, villains, unhinged psychos, and the woman they will destroy everything for. Ever Dark is for 18+ adult readers only.

This book is dark and chaotic, romantic yet brutal. It's messy and depraved. Sweet and vile. Just like love. These characters are not redeemable. They fall hard and fast. They don't make rational choices. And they do whatever the fuck they want.

There are no boundaries, no polite sentiments, and no logical explanations for their behavior. But they will take you on a dark and lovely ride through the most sinful places if you let them.

Please check the CWs on my website before diving in. There's a lot of them.

WELCOME TO THE WORLD OF MELANCHOLIA

Reading order:

Good Girl (Wickford Hollow Duet, Book 1)

Little Fox (Wickford Hollow Duet, Book 2)

(Wickford Hollow Duet omnibus contains a bonus chapter in Riot's POV, and sets up the next book)

Pretty Little Psycho (The Devils of Raven's Gate, Book 1)

Dirty Little Saint (The Devils of Raven's Gate, Book 2)

Nox (The Ever Dark Journals of Mia Harker)
A free short story when you sign up for M Violet's Love Letters

Absentia Mori

Ever Dark

For all my dark romance besties who crave the thrill of the chase.

Who want to be told to shut up and get on their knees.

This is for all of you.

My beautifully depraved good girls who like getting caught being bad in the dark.

Because getting caught is the best part.

"Deep into that darkness peering, long I stood there, wondering, fearing, doubting, dreaming dreams no mortal ever dared to dream before."—Edgar Allan Poe, The Raven

PLAYLIST

Prologue: trouble—Camylio

Chapter 1: I've Got a Darkside—X V I & Nocturn

Chapter 2: Evidence—Letdown.

Chapter 3: Villain—RIELL

Chapter 4: Lady Parts and Mannequins—mehro

Chapter 5: Dark Side—Iris Grey

Chapter 6: Will You Love Me When I'm Dead—Amira Elfeky

Chapter 7: Fuck Me Like You Hate Me—Jutes

Chapter 8: Crash—DeathbyRomy

Chapter 9: Contemptress: Reincarnated (feat. Maria Brink)—Motionless In White

Chapter 10: Numb—Noise Machine & Blue_Eyed_Darkness

Chapter 11: SOMETHING IN THE WATER—Kami Kehoe

Chapter 12: bite—Ellise

Chapter 13: MONSTER IN ME—Nocturn & SPELLES

Chapter 14: Dusk (Unbound)—Chelsea Wolfe

Chapter 15: Burned—Britton

Chapter 16: Claws—The Haunt

Chapter 17: what is my body worth?—hazel

Chapter 18: Bones—In This Moment

Chapter 19: Over and Over—Echos

Chapter 20: I Choose Me—Roniit & Amanati

Chapter 21: Perfect Crime—Chrissy Constanza

Chapter 22: Dangerous Game—Stellar & Camylio

Chapter 23: let me fall—Ex Habit & Bury

Chapter 24: You are what you fear in me.—Banshee

Chapter 25: QUIET, IN YOUR SERVICE—Echos

Chapter 26: Insanity—Maryjo Lilac

Chapter 27: If Only—Elizabeth Lentz

Chapter 28: I Would Die for You—In This Moment

Chapter 29: Hell Is Empty—Memphis May Fire

Chapter 30: The Whisperer (feat. Sia)—David Guetta

Chapter 31: Don't You Want Me?—Desire The Unknown

Chapter 32: Red Velvet (with Ari Abdul)—Jutes & Ari Abdul

Epilogue: The Lighthouse—Halsey

EVER DARK

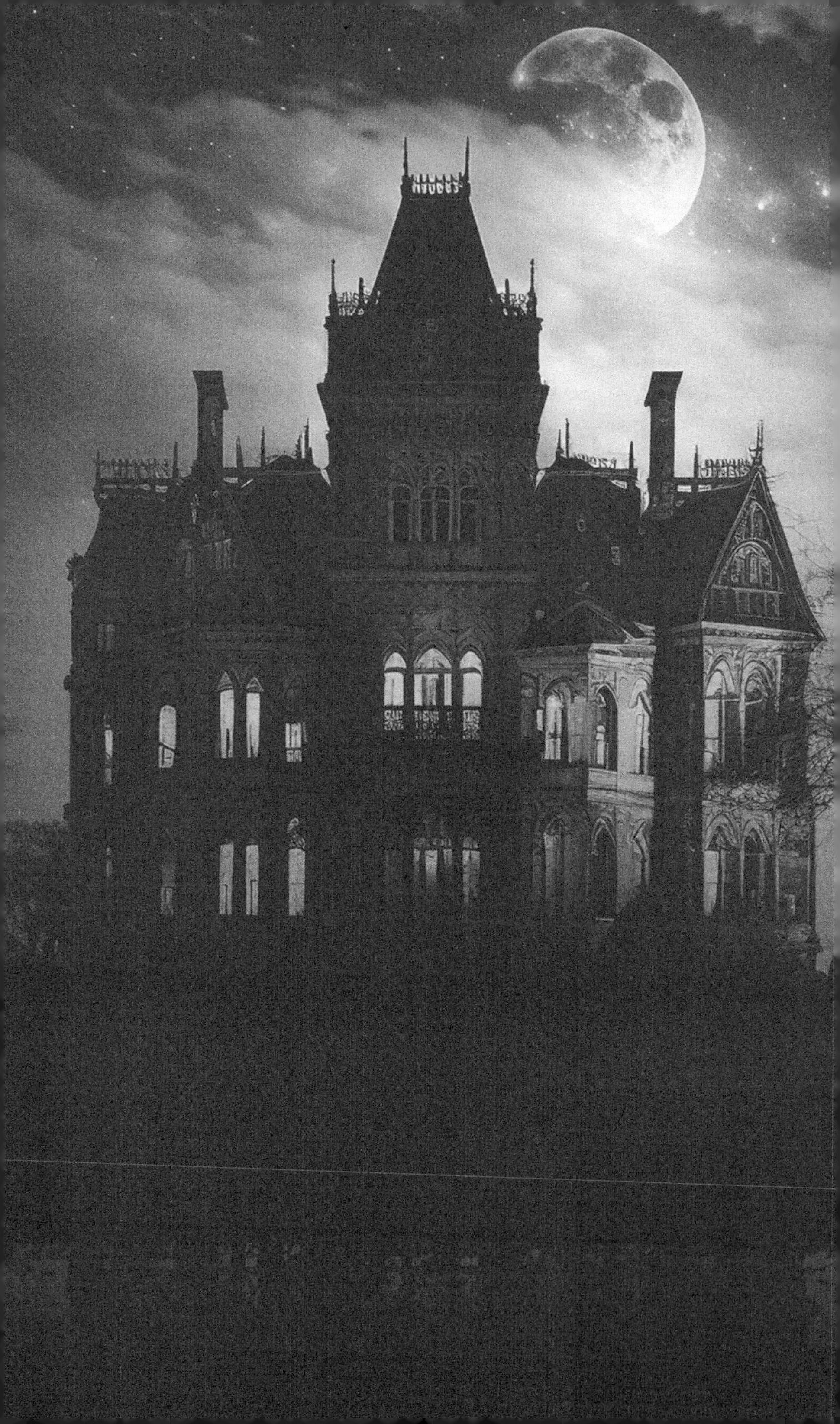

PROLOGUE

Draven

When the matriarch of an empire dies, most heirs fight to the death to stake a claim for it. Not my family. No one wants the chaos that is the Blackwell Gin Company. So since everyone eligible has refused the inheritance, the burden falls at my feet.

I never wanted it. But the second I saw my grandmother's lifeless body slumped over her favorite velvet chair, I knew. *I do fucking want it.* Some say monsters aren't born, they're made. In this family, it's both.

After going through the documents Penny Blackwell left for me, I now know why. There are far more dangerous things in these woods than me. But I don't give a fuck. The devil may have a hold on Ever Graves, but so do I. And I have no plans to give up control.

"You good, man?" Bones flips his lighter in the seat next to me.

I don't look at him but instead keep my gaze focused out the tinted window of the limousine. "I just want to get this over with. I have meetings scheduled for the rest of the day."

Aries snickers. He sits across from me, blond and godlike. "On the day of your grandmother's funeral? I'm sure you can reschedule."

I grip the edge of the leather seats, my palms sweating. "I don't *want* to reschedule. Someone has to clean up this mess of a company before we all end up broke as fuck."

They both shut up at that. My two best friends care about self-preservation just as much as I do. Plus, they know better than to push me when I'm in this shitty of a mood. It's not sadness or loss. Just fucking inconvenient. I actually don't remember the last time I felt anything other than apathy, darkness, and fucking misery.

The only things that bring me even a sliver of pleasure are ice-cold glasses of Blackwell Gin, hand-rolled cigarettes laced with nightshade, and getting my dick sucked by women who don't ask me any fucking questions.

Even then, the joy is fleeting—temporary euphoria that ends up making me more miserable because it's faker than the last pair of tits I had in my mouth.

There's already a crowd of a hundred people gathered around my grandmother's coffin when we arrive. She was the richest person in this town. As much as the locals fear and despise us, they also have to show us respect. My family owns most of the land in this town. Every one of these pathetic fools pays rent to us for either their homes, businesses, or both. Fuck me over, and I won't forget.

The three of us step out of the limo in our crisp, black suits, looking very much the part of the town heathens. *Super fucking rich and powerful heathens.* It's no secret that the men in this town seethe with jealousy every time we show our faces. Mostly because all their women want to fuck us so badly they can barely walk past us without clenching their wet thighs.

Bones snickers as he looks out at the mixed expressions glaring back at us. He chews on a toothpick, unfazed, as it rubs against the cut on his lips. It took a miracle to get him into this suit, but even with his neck tattoos and scarred knuckles, it works for him. It makes him look even more dangerous.

"Are we late, or are these ass-kissers fucking early?" Bones is always itching for a fight. Anyone. Any time. It's like he's always high on adrenaline.

I grit my teeth a little too hard and wince as a sharp pain shoots up my jaw. "I honestly don't give a fuck. Take note of anyone who's not here. We'll pay them a visit later."

Aries runs a hand through his pale-blond hair, admiring himself in the reflection of the car window. "As long as no one finds out *who* put your grandmother in that coffin, I don't give a shit who turns up."

"Of course, no one's going to find out. It's family business," I snap. There's only one person who means more to Aries than us, his twin sister Libra. She may have been the one to finally put an end to Penny Blackwell, but I paved the way. Libra was owed justice after Penny had her locked up in Absentia Asylum, and I needed my grandmother to leave me the fuck alone. It's a win-win in my eyes. As sick and fucked up as that sounds.

We stalk over, our leather shoes sloshing through the wet grass. The autumn equinox has brought more rain and humidity than usual this year. In my twenty-seven years in this town, I've never gotten used to my clothes clinging to my skin. But the scent is intoxicating. Another one of those little slivers of enjoyment I periodically savor.

I take my rightful place at the head of the coffin just in time to catch the scowl on Father Peter's face. I glare back at him, forcing his gaze to the ground. *I'll fucking slit your throat, priest.*

Bones clenches his fists at his sides, picking up on my feral energy. One nod in his direction, and he'll slaughter whoever holds my ire. No questions needed. Aries and I would do the same for him.

The crowd collectively bows their heads as Father Peter rambles on about endings and new beginnings. I tune him out as the three of us keep our heads upright, fixated on all the superficial tears and forced expressions of remorse. Waiting. Watching. For one of these motherfuckers to step out of line. *Give me just one sign of disrespect, and I'll gladly ruin a life today.* I'll add that to my list of joyful slivers as well. Like bittersweet slices of shit pie I choke down.

By the time he's done with his torturous soliloquy, we're drenched. It seems even the rain wants to cleanse Penny Blackwell from this world. But no one dares move unless I do, and I'm stoic as fuck.

I will make these sheep stand in the rain all day if I feel like it.

I have a sick, perverse lust for the sight of the whole town shivering and wincing under the marble-size raindrops. It gets my dick hard. It's the power. The control. I'll get off later tonight thinking about it.

Aries groans, snapping me out of my crude fantasy. "You made your point, Dray, *and* you've ruined my suit. Can we hurry this the fuck up now?"

Always the delicate pretty boy. "I'll buy you another one."

Bones cocks an eyebrow at me. "Fuck the suit. I need a drink. Let's wrap this up."

I sigh, nodding as I stalk toward the pile of black dahlias on the ground. *My grandmother's favorite flower.* I pick one up and place it on her chest. Despite the coroner's feeble attempt to make her look presentable, the flower matches the color of her lips. I shudder as I look upon her one last time.

I lean down and whisper in her ear, hoping my words reach her wherever she is. *"Even in death, I have no love for you."*

I wait for Bones and Aries to drop their flowers before slamming the coffin shut. The crowd flinches at the loud bang. They can leave their flowers in the dirt where they belong.

As the three of us traipse back to the limo, tiny gasps and whispers echo behind us.

Fuck them.

I hold my finger up, pointing back toward the shocked crowd. "Take note."

They both nod. "Bones and I will sort it out."

I run a hand through my wet hair, slicking my black strands back off my forehead. I get a glimpse of myself in the tinted window, my golden eyes glowing like fireflies in the reflection of the headlights. Eyes like burnt honey, I'm told, but there's no warmth inside. No sweetness. Just another tool I can use to my advantage. To lure in my prey.

I don't wait for the chauffeur and instead yank the limo door open myself. "Fuck it. You're both right. I can reschedule the meetings. I need a drink."

Bones claps me on the back in excitement. "Thatta boy. Let's go get into some trouble."

Aries laughs as we pile into the limo. "That shouldn't be a problem. Trouble always finds us."

The bar is packed tonight. I welcome the noise of high-pitched laughter, glasses clanking, shitty rock music blaring from the speakers, and the clack-clack of pool balls right before a fight erupts between drunk douchebags who accuse the other of cheating. Just a typical night at Duff's.

The bald owner is behind the bar, taking up most of it with his massive frame. He gives me a nod and slides three shots of Blackwell gin toward us. "First round's on the house, boys. Just keep your tempers under control."

I scowl at him. "You must have us confused with another group of devastatingly charming men."

Duff arches an eyebrow. "You all broke three bar stools and my back window last time."

Fucking hell, I'm already annoyed. "And *you* were compensated above and beyond for it, Duff."

Bones points to the speakers. "You even got a new sound system out of it. Quit crying like a little bitch and keep the shots coming."

He shakes his head but stalks off, conceding. No one wants to start a war with the three of us. We make far better friends than enemies.

Aries bursts out laughing. "It's not my fault the bar stool went through the window. The fucker ducked," he shouts after him.

I sigh and tap my cigarette against the bar before lighting it. "Seriously, though, no brawls tonight. Burying one body was enough for me today."

I scan the room, taking note of all the new faces. Another batch of outsiders are here to indulge in our fall festivities. The entire town square of Ever Graves becomes a haunted playground for paranormal lovers from all over Melancholia. Even Duff makes up these silly little ghost-themed cocktails. I told him I'll turn him into a headless bartender if he ever tries to give me one.

Aries squeezes my shoulder. "Relax, Dray. Loosen up. You just became the richest fucker in Ever Graves today."

Bones lifts his hands, a shot of gin in each one. "All this is yours now, my friend. Let's drink to owning this fucking town."

They're right. I need to let go of some of this tension. I can still feel the rain on the back of my neck. Still smell the black dahlias on my fingers. It's time to numb it all.

I wave Duff over. "Give me the bottle."

He sighs and sets it on the bar with three fresh shot glasses. "Fuck it. You break anything, you buy it."

I smirk as I line up three more shots. "Keep taunting me, Duff, and I'll buy this whole fucking bar out from under you."

His eyes widen before he dips his head. "Holler if you need anything else."

That's what I fucking thought, asshole.

With each shot, my shoulders relax. The knots in my back dissipate. I take off my tie and stuff it in my pocket. The heat in my chest rises as I eye all the pieces of ass surrounding us. All those short fucking skirts designed to be lifted for easy access.

Aries and Bones laugh and banter with several girls, all of them practically drooling over the attention. We're a striking group. None of us has to do much to get laid. They come to us. But it lacks creativity.

I want to hunt. To stalk and trap. Fuck. My erection grows against my perfectly pressed black pants just thinking about it. But there's no one worth chasing in this town. These chicks here tonight are so fucking thirsty. All I have to do is look in their direction. And I will. I just need to find one who isn't going to bore me to death. I prefer them buzzed but not too obliterated that they can't give me a decent blowjob. And the less chatty, the better. *If I could find a mute one, my night would be complete.*

Fuck, I'm such a fucking asshole.

After six more shots of gin, my head tingles, and my cock is at full fucking mast. I undo the top three buttons of my white dress shirt and lean back against the bar. A stumbling blonde catches my eye. She giggles as she falls against the pool table. She might have to do.

I down another shot before stalking over. I'm three strides away from her when someone barrels into me, knocking me from behind. I stumble into a barstool. *What the actual fuck?* I spin around, fists clenched.

My breath hitches. The culprit is the most gorgeous fucking brunette. I stare at her hips and work my way up, speechless. Short skirt, check. Natural breasts, double-check. Thick lips that would look insane around my cock. Check, check, check!

"Fuck. Sorry. I think some asshole pushed me."

I glance behind her, searching for Aries or Bones. I wouldn't put it past either of them to throw this woman at me. But I spot them on the other side of the room, taking turns throwing darts.

"Hello? Did you hit your head?"

I look back at her. "I'm good. Let me buy you a drink."

She wobbles to the side a bit, her cheeks flushing. "Um, I think I've had enough."

"I haven't. You can buy me one, then." I'll never let her pay, but my foul mood is back.

"Wow. You're a real charmer, aren't you? Sorry again for bumping into you. Have a good night." She turns and starts to walk off.

Fuck. Now I've got a fucking chase. I grab her wrist. "Wait. It was a joke. I have plenty of money."

Electricity sparks between us. I feel it tingling in my fingers as her pulse quickens.

She gazes up at me, and my breath hitches again. Her eyes… they're different colors—one blue and one brown. Or I'm just really fucking drunk.

"Oh, charming and humble. What a winning combination," she teases.

A challenge. Fucking finally.

I rub my thumb in light circles on the inside of her wrist. "You're trouble, aren't you?"

Her cheeks flush. It's probably the alcohol, but I tell myself it's because of her irresistible attraction to me.

"No, but you're relentless." She shakes her head and tugs her arm back. As she tries to walk away again, I swoop in front of her.

I tip her chin up. "You're beautiful… I don't really want to buy you a drink."

Her throat bobs. "So you just want to stalk me through the bar then?"

I scrape my teeth across my bottom lip before tilting my head to her ear. "I want to fuck you," I whisper.

She shudders, and her eyes are wide when our gazes lock again. "Well, that's fucking direct. Who are you?"

The mystery girl is trying to be good, but every sign points to her need. Her racing pulse, her flushed cheeks, the way her chest heaves as she fights to control her breath…

"A charming and humble man who wants to give you the best orgasm of your life." Something tells me she doesn't come to places like this often. She's out of her comfort zone.

"You're not used to hearing no for an answer." The blush on her cheeks spreads to her chest.

I flash a grin. "How long are you in town for? A night? A few days? Have fun with me tonight. We'll never see each other again, but you'll have a great story to tell your friends back home. Wherever that is."

She licks her lips. I can see it in her eyes. She's conflicted. The alcohol, impulsivity, and the force of fucking nature, which is me, are convincing her.

I wait, patient like a wolf.

We stare at each other for five whole fucking minutes. I know because two song changes happen during this.

But I don't break eye contact. I'm not letting her walk out of here without fucking me.

She lets out a deep breath. "One drink."

My cock twitches. That's a yes. I'd prefer to skip the drinks, but I don't want to spook her now that I've got her on the cusp of bending over for me.

I'm not even annoyed by how slowly she sips her whiskey. "What's your name, beautiful?"

She licks her lips. "No names."

Fucking hell, this couldn't be working out more perfectly if I dreamed it up myself. I flash her another grin. "Trouble it is, then. Come with me." I reach my hand out to her.

She downs the rest of her drink and takes my hand. Her skin is warm and soft. "Lead the way, Slick."

I can't help but chuckle. She has no idea. I tuck her arm through mine. "See, we even have cute pet names for each other already."

Every word, every touch, works on breaking down her defenses. I almost gag from my own performance. I've never had to work this hard for pussy before. But I want a real release. The tougher the challenge, the sweeter the reward. So I channel Aries, mimicking his words and demeanor. I've seen him in action a million times.

But I have to be careful not to let the mask slip. Not until I get what I want. *What I need* so I can sleep tonight.

She relaxes against me. I can feel her need is as strong as mine. Maybe more so. This girl has so much pent-up sexual tension inside her; she might fucking cum the second I touch her.

I lead her down the neon-lit hallway toward the bathrooms—Duff's private bathroom that I convinced him to give me the key to. A fair trade for some extra cases of Blackwell gin that he doesn't have to pay for.

I open the door, pull her inside, and lock it behind us. "Don't be nervous…" I cup her face in my hands. "Turn around and face the mirror."

Her breath hitches, but she does as I say. *Good obedient little slut.* I brush her hair to the side and plant a soft kiss on her neck. "Good. Now, lean forward."

She whimpers as I run my hands up her thighs. I push her skirt up over her ass. *No fucking panties.* "Fuck, you are trouble," I rasp. I unbutton and unzip my pants with one hand.

"Just so you know, I'm not a slut."

I don't care. I trail my hands up higher. "I know, baby. Neither am I. Go on and spread your legs for me." I rub the tip of my cock against her pussy.

"Oh, fuck," she whispers as she widens her stance.

"Mmm, I should be calling you Slick." I grab her hips and anchor them up as I thrust my cock inside her.

She lets out a yelp.

"You have the tightest fucking pussy I've ever been in. Fuck." I still myself for a second so I don't explode. She's so warm and wet, and her insides are literally trembling around me.

"Why did you stop?" Panic riddles her voice.

I chuckle. "Because I don't want to cum too soon. Relax and hold on to the counter."

She grips the edge and bites down on her lip as I start to slide back and forth. Fuck, she feels good. Her scent is intoxicating. With each thrust, it wafts up to my nose—jasmine—sweet and seductive like new money.

A deep growl erupts from my chest as she clenches around me. Fucking hell. I burrow in deeper, hitting all the way to the back.

She lifts her head, her mascara running, and lets out a deep moan. "Harder," she begs.

I drive into her, pinching her hips between my sweaty fingers. We lock eyes in the mirror, and I almost cum. Her gaze is haunting. Broken. Provoking me to tear her apart.

"Fuck," I grunt out.

She jerks back, then forward, as she rubs her clit against the bathroom counter. "Yeah… right there," she breathes out.

My cock swells as the blood rushes forward, my belly fluttering. I feel sick with need. A strange chill rolls up my spine as spasms shoot down my shaft. It's her eyes. She keeps them glued on me.

"*You fuck like a slut.*" I don't know why I'm so angry, but my fury threatens to consume both of us.

My degrading words don't seem to faze her. She gasps. "I'm… cumming." Her body writhes against the counter as she grinds her pussy on the cold ceramic tiles. Her cream spills out, cradling my cock like a warm cocoon. It sends me over the edge.

I let out a moan as I cum inside her, riding her hard as I unleash. I can taste the jasmine on my tongue now.

With her beautiful eyes still on me, she squeezes her pussy around my cock so tight, it makes me hard again. Fuck. I can't take this anymore. "*Don't look at me.*" I grab her by the hair and press her face down on the counter.

I slam into her harder this time and grind in circles, fucking her like an animal. "Oh, fuck. *Ahhh.*" The fucking pressure… fuck. I explode inside her again, my cock trembling and twitching against her folds. I can't stop. I rock into her as I ride one of the longest orgasms of my fucking life.

My cum fills her so full she can't contain it in that tight pussy of hers. It leaks out and runs down her thighs. I thrust again as I milk myself, desperate to stretch it out for as long as I can. I don't want to fucking leave this pussy. Fuck.

She whimpers against the counter, her legs shaking. "Holy… fuck."

I can't listen to her anymore. I can't look at those eyes. No. I need to get out of here. My cock hardens again as I slide out. I lick my lips, and all I taste is jasmine. Sweet fucking fragrant jasmine, like a fucking drug that I would actually snort off her pussy if I could.

I let go of her head and put myself back together, cock and all. As I look at myself in the mirror, my anger grows. I came in here to fuck her so that I could numb myself. Now I'm angrier than I was when I left the funeral.

I pull her skirt down, my hands lingering on her hips for a second. "I hope I gave you a good story to tell… See you around, Trouble." *I know that I won't.*

Before I'm halfway out the door, I hear her murmur, "*See you around, Slick.*"

I wrangle Bones and Aries away from the pool table before they get accused of hustling for the third time this month. Which, of course, they are. Aries has a pool table in his house. We've been playing since we were eight.

They follow me without protest. Once inside the safety of the limo, I let out a deep breath. I roll the window down, relishing the feel of the cool autumn breeze on my face as we head back to Blackwell Manor.

Bones taps his lighter on my knee. "So, who'd you fuck in the bathroom?"

I wipe the sweat off my brow with my sleeve. Fuck. She's still on me. Jasmine. It's all I can fucking smell. All I can taste. I shrug as I slip back into the apathetic version of Draven they're both accustomed to. "Just some random out-of-town slut."

Bones lets out a hearty laugh. "Ever the gentleman."

I grit my teeth. "That, my friend, I am not."

When we pass Harker Mansion, my fury grows even more. Emma Harker finally croaked. She had no heirs. No family except for that imbecile nephew, Dorian, a professor at Tenebrose Academy over in Raven's Gate. It was supposed to be easy. I'd swoop in with a generous offer and a few threats.

But the granddaughter we all thought was dead showed up to claim the land that I want.

"Where do we stand with the Harker girl?" I growl.

"Mia Harker hasn't returned any of my calls. I'll pay her a visit tomorrow." Aries pulls out his phone and begins typing away.

I smack the door with the side of my fist. "We need that land. It's the only place that grows baneberry. Double our original offer."

Gin isn't our only empire. We're also the leading purveyors of poison. Aries's family controls most of it. And I control the rest. But if I can get my hands on the baneberry fields at Harker Mansion, then I'll hold the majority.

Bones cracks his knuckles. "What if she refuses to sell?"

The darkness that flows in my veins spikes my adrenaline. I light up a cigarette. "Then we'll make her life hell. Mia Harker will wish she never came back to Ever Graves."

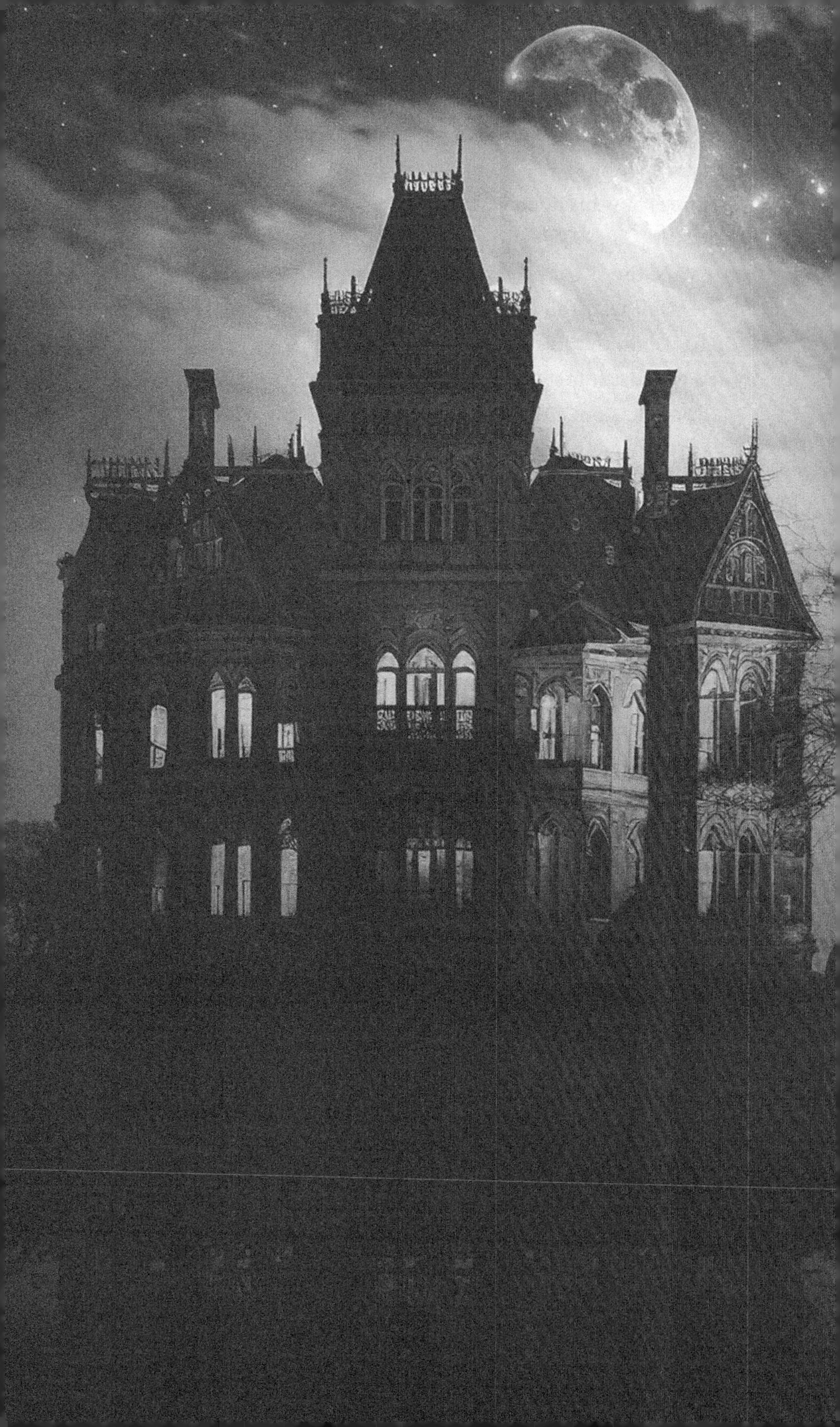

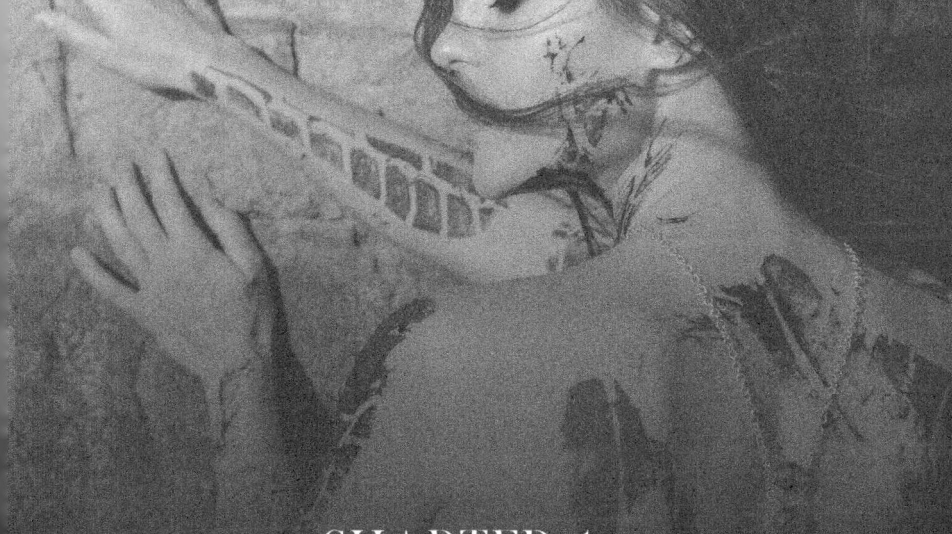

CHAPTER 1

Mia

*R*EMEMBER WHAT HAPPENED THE LAST TIME, MIA...

I toss and turn, tangling in my crumpled sheets. "It will be different this time, Nox," I murmur.

Caught between sleep and consciousness, I reach for the darkness with one hand and claw at the light with the other. But my monster always wins. Nox always gets his way.

"Surrender to me, dark one." His voice is louder in my ear, pulling me deeper into his realm.

I lose my breath somewhere between my lungs and my throat. A weight slams into my chest. I feel his claws around my wrist, securing me to the bedposts. "Mmm," I moan even though I want to break free. I know what he does to me. How he makes my body feel. I can't ever resist it.

"Open yourself to me, dark one. Spread those thick thighs and welcome me home." Nox's forked cock slithers against me, tickling the folds of my pussy. I'm dripping with sweat, still somewhat anchored to reality. I feel the sheets around me, damp and hot. But it's fleeting as Nox teases my entrance, pulling me back to him and his twisted game.

I arch my hips to allow him access. "Just this once, then you have to let me wake up."

He hums in my ear. "You can wake up anytime you want, dark one. You're here because you crave this as much as I do." *Thrust*

A gurgled cry escapes my throat as the force of his enormous cock plows through me. His two tips twist and tangle around each other while they work against my inner walls. I grab onto his horns for leverage and sink into the mattress, letting him destroy me like he's done almost every night since I was eighteen years old.

Seven years.

The things I've fucking lost for him… The people I've pushed away for his sinful pleasure.

"You are mine, Mia. Do what you must when you are awake, but down here, you are all mine." He hits a spot so deep inside me that I almost black out. His cock swells to a full eight inches, stretching me, destroying me in the most exquisite way.

When his unholy body is inside mine, I'm more of a monster than he is. I feel the darkness growing, promising to consume me and whatever sanity I have left.

I buck and writhe on his smooth hard cock. The veins in his shaft protrude out and push against my folds, pulsing with need. I clench around him, desperate to milk every inch of him.

"That's it, my dark beauty. Use me. Fuck me until you're too tired to even breathe."

His voice is my trigger. My comfort and my torment. He's been haunting me since I was a child. *Since I was born.* My beautiful, twisted monster.

"Nox," I whine. "Please…"

An animalistic growl erupts from his chest as he drives in deeper, harder, faster, as we claw at each other. He leaves scratches on my skin. I yelp as he bows his head to my chest and sinks his sharp teeth into my collarbone. "*Mine.*"

"Yes. I'm cumming. Fuck." I squirm, clenching around him as the ecstasy transports me. It's a deep rumble, sparked by filthy claws, coaxed by his forked tongue and forked cock. The spasms roll through me like waves crashing onto a barren shore.

I scream and cry and dig my nails into his massive frame, knowing that I can't ever hurt him. My nightmare man. My Nox. He's unbreakable and relentless, crushing my resolve over and over again. I can't escape him. He's my curse, my sickness. And because of him, I've destroyed everything good that I've ever touched.

I cum hard, my juices soaking his cock. But my eyelids are heavy and weighted. "Let me sleep now, Nox. Please."

He kisses my forehead, his tongue darting out to lick both of my brows. I shudder as I try to fight the urge to beg for more. I know what that tongue feels like inside my traitorous pussy. But I need rest. I have to keep these boundaries, or his love might actually kill me.

"Yes, my love. My dark one. I'll set you free for tonight. Sleep well. I'll summon you again soon."

And like a flip of a switch, I'm freefalling back toward home. Toward my bed at Harker Mansion. Back toward hot and sweaty crumpled sheets.

I jump at the sound of the tea kettle whistling. My brain is still foggy as I try desperately to ground myself in the present. It never gets easier. Shame fills me when I see the scratches on my wrists. Real-life marks that can't be explained with any logical reasoning. I used to think I inflicted them on myself. Until the morning I woke up with teeth marks on my neck…

I clench my thighs together, my pussy sore and missing the sensation of his monstrous cock. My cheeks burn with indignation. The priest's accusation echoes in my mind—*you're sick, Mia. We need to get the sickness out of you.*

They didn't believe me. Not the priest nor the nuns at the orphanage, not even my ex-fiancé wanted to listen. I *can't* get Nox out of me. This is why I'm better off alone. It's exhausting enough to be ensnared by Nox every time I sleep. I don't have the energy to explain where I go when I close my eyes. Not when I don't even understand it myself.

"Fuck." I zoned out again. I pull out the tea bag and add another scoop of sugar to balance the bitterness. I need the extra caffeine anyway. I'm determined to stay up for at least three days this time. I still have boxes to unpack, and I need to find a room in this enormous house to set up my easels. It's been weeks since I've painted anything. The suppression of creativity threatens to kill me more than Nox's torment. More than the lack of sleep that I'll need to combat it.

I sip my tea in eerie silence. It still hasn't really sunk in. I have so many questions, ones I've carried my whole life. Why did my family give me up when they had all of this? I look around the commercial-size kitchen. It's bigger than my last apartment in Raven's Gate. I wish I could ask them myself. But there's no one to ask. They're all dead.

The only family I have left is that quirky professor from Tenebrose Academy, Dorian Harker. I'm grateful he got me out of Absentia Asylum, but then he just disappeared. He won't return my calls or texts. I'm at a loss. But they couldn't have hated me that much if they left me everything they owned.

I'm not even sure what to do with all this space… Not to mention the money and the assets. When I first found out how rich my family was, I was angry. I had nothing my whole life. After I left the orphanage in Wickford Hollow, I was on the streets. Safety and security came in spurts and never lasted long. I starved some nights and almost froze to death on others. But Nox was always there. I let him become my crutch. My comfort. He likes it when I need him.

But now… my anger has faded into genuine curiosity. I want answers. And I feel like somewhere in this house, or in this town, lies the truth of who I am. Of *why* I am the way I am.

The first peek of the sun streams through the front window, drawing my attention to the enormous stretch of property that surrounds me. It's all mine. So why does it make me feel more alone than ever?

I sigh as I remember the stack of letters on the counter. Someone named Draven Blackwell has made three offers on this house and the surrounding property. *I just fucking got here.* Selling is the last thing I want to do.

I'm told he's some big shot here in Ever Graves. This land is just a cash grab for him. He doesn't understand the emotional attachment, the need for me to be here. It's the only connection I have to a family I've never known. People like Draven Blackwell don't get it. They don't know what it's like to be abandoned and penniless.

The money isn't important to me, although it's nice to have it. It's the energy here. I feel the ghosts of my past all around me. Like they're trying to reach out and tell me something.

Ugh. I wish I could put my finger on it. I wish I could touch something tangible for once.

And that's why I got drunk at Duff's the other night. I wasn't planning on fucking one of the locals in the bathroom, but after a few drinks, my loneliness was suffocating me. That man was gorgeous, devilish, and slightly feral. *Slick.* My pussy tingles just thinking about the way he bent me over the counter. He was rough and impatient, and I loved every second of it.

I remember how he looked at me in the mirror. We took whatever was eating at us out on each other. I just hope it isn't too awkward if I ever run into him again. I sort of led him to believe I didn't live here. Well, technically, I didn't until that night. I think a part of me was still thinking of selling everything and making a run for it.

He didn't strike me as the clingy type though. He was gone before I could even stand upright. I was still smeared across the bathroom counter when I heard the door shut behind him. If anything, we'll give each other a little smirk, or maybe we'll pretend we don't know each other. Hell, we were both so tipsy that I might not even recognize him.

I can't help the smile from forming on my lips. It's been a really long time since I let someone fuck me outside of my nightmares. Like a real man in the flesh. It felt amazing. And I think I want more. Just not the complications that come with it. I can't be in a relationship like a normal person. I'm too damaged, too fucked up, and too broken.

I reach for the first envelope on the stack and pull out the letter inside. This has been the most troubling one of all. It's the only message I have from beyond the grave. The only thing my grandmother Emma Harker left me with. It was sealed with her initials, dipped in red wax, when my uncle Dorian handed it to me at the asylum.

I've read it a thousand times since—in between packing, at various rest stops from Raven's Gate to Ever Graves, every night when I wake up and stand in this kitchen over a cup of tea...

Dearest Mia,

It pains me to write these words because if you are reading them, then I am gone from this world. I know you don't remember me. You were just a baby when you went away.

You must have many questions. Questions I will no longer be able to answer. Especially not in this letter. For I fear this may fall into the wrong hands. But what you seek is in this town. In Ever Graves. In these very walls of Harker Mansion.

Between the living and the dead, secrets abound. I pray you have your father's cunning and your mother's heart. I will leave you with this, my final gift to you:

> Roses bring Thorns
> Night is ever Black
> When the shadow comes
> The Crane will attack
> Heads will roll
> When the nightmare roams
> Stick close to the well
> Of broken Bones

Your ever-loving grandmother,
Emma Harker

It's a riddle I can't decipher. But I'm determined to figure it out. I will search every nook and cranny of this entire estate if I have to. Even if it takes forever.

It's only been a week, but from what I can tell, this house has three floors, an attic, and a basement cellar. There are staircases everywhere, and I've gotten lost several times. So far, I've counted at least twenty guest rooms, ten bathrooms, a library, three sitting rooms, and two kitchens. The second kitchen is much smaller, so I'm assuming it was once used for servants.

I've never even had a personal assistant, so the thought of an entire staff of people waiting on me is mind-boggling. *I wonder what happened to all of them.* There are traces of their former existence all over this house—name tags, neatly pressed uniforms, and even photos of them posed in the backyard at what looks like some kind of massive party.

My head pounds as the sun streams in brighter, announcing that a new morning has come. It's going to be another crisp autumn day in Ever Graves, judging by the dew hanging off the orange and brown leaves that lie scattered all over the grounds.

I head out to the back veranda and plop down in one of the cushy chairs so I can watch the sun fully rise while I finish my tea. A strange scent assaults my senses. It's unfamiliar and appears to be exuding from the endless rows of colorful bushes that stretch out as far as my eye can see.

I'll have to take a closer look at the deed and files that Dorian gave me. I'm curious as to what my ancestors were growing and why there is so much of it. Do I have to maintain it? I don't have a green thumb, so I'd hate to see all of it die just because I moved in. I make a mental note to look into hiring a gardener or two.

The quiet and stillness are a nice change from the chaos of Absentia Asylum. I didn't belong there. But then again, no one does. That place is worse than hell. I slipped deeper into Nox's nightmare much more there. It was my only refuge. I owe him a lot for getting me through that dark time. But he got too used to me always being with him. So now that I want to stay awake longer, he's more determined than ever to keep me asleep.

I can't survive like that though. And now, more than ever, I *have* to survive so I can find out who I am. Even if I don't like what I find.

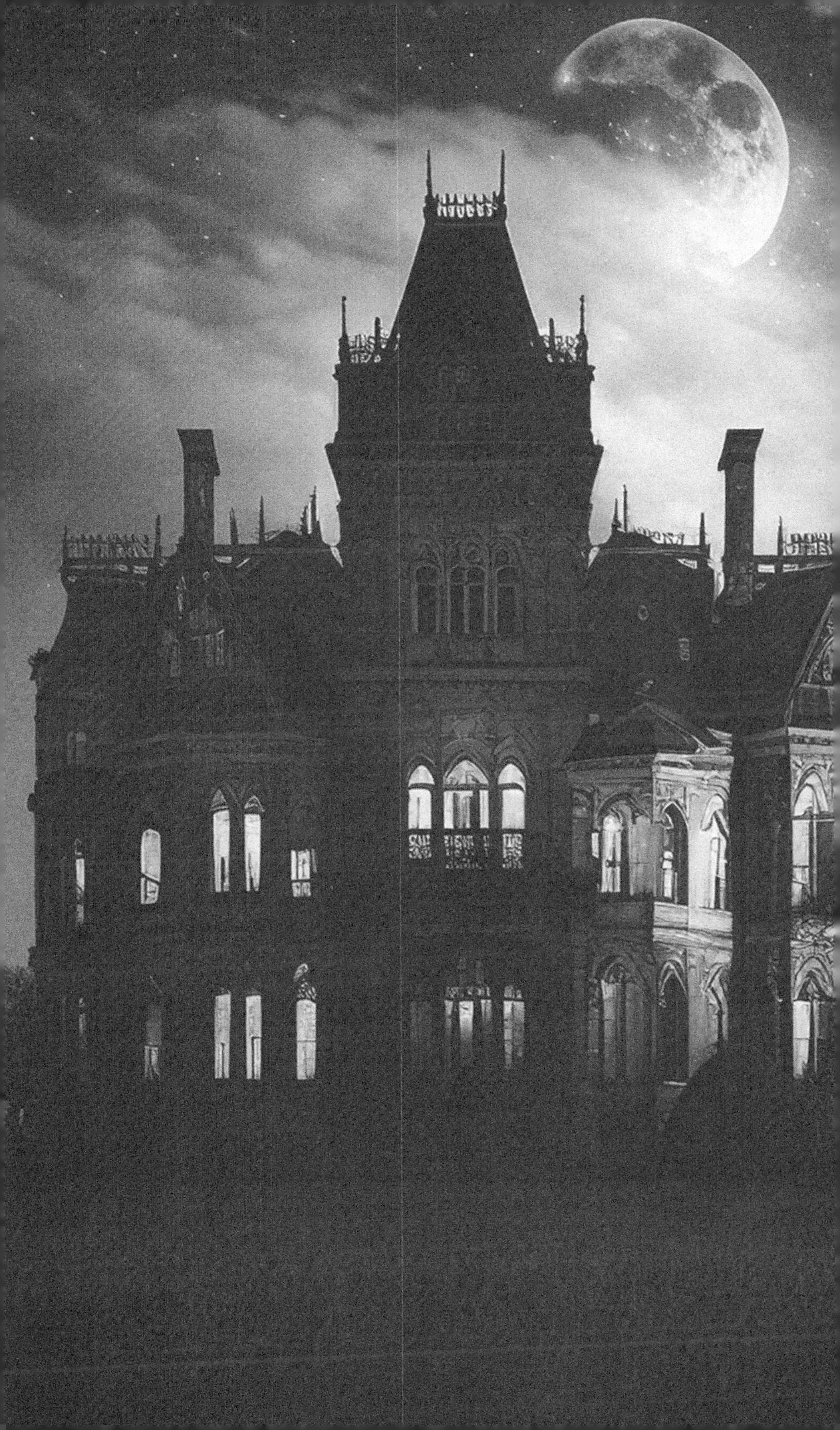

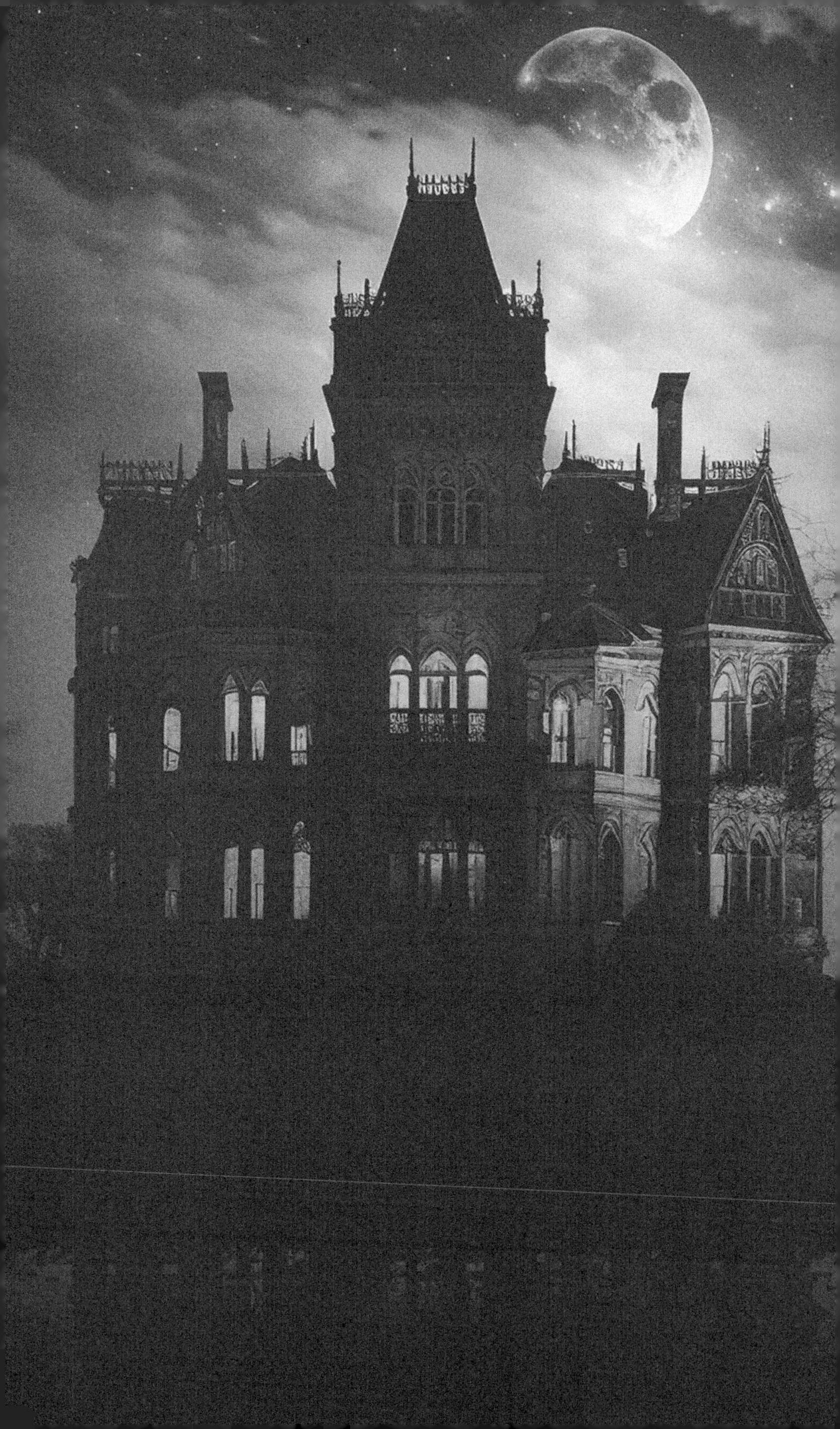

Chapter 2

Draven

"Find out everything you can about Mia Harker. I want to know where she came from, what she does for fun, what she fucking eats for breakfast. Don't call me back until you have something useful." I end the call before my sorry excuse for an investigator can respond. The lack of competence is infuriating.

Six months ago, I had instructed him to find a loophole in Emma Harker's will. Our families took part in a treaty centuries ago. We agreed to equally split the poison fields until the family line died out or someone refused the inheritance. Dorian Harker wanted no part in this war. He was happy to stay a boring as fuck professor in Raven's Gate.

So when Mia Harker resurfaced after twenty-five years, I put my entire team on proving her invalidity. She was given away for adoption, for fuck's sake. That alone should make her claim null and void. But Emma Harker was a sneaky old crone. Her will was ironclad. Now I have to resort to other measures. If this bitch doesn't sell, I swear to the fucking raven, I'm going to bury her alive in the middle of the baneberry fields.

I loosen my tie before downing a vial of nightshade. The fiery liquid trickles down, burning my throat with its bittersweet sting. I lean my head against the leather seat of my limousine and close my eyes while the toxin works its way into my veins.

These days, it's getting harder and harder to take the edge off. No amount of whiskey or poison or jerking myself off seems to work. But I still try. I have to, or I'll fall off the deep end again. And no one wants that. My destruction is unstoppable once it begins.

"Take the long way home, and don't disturb me until I call on you," I tell my driver.

I close the partition and lock it before he can respond.

The poison heightens my senses. Everything feels more intense. I unzip my pants and pull out my cock. "Ahh, yeah. Now I can breathe."

I roll my thumb over the tip, coaxing my pre cum out in circles. The weight of my issues feels a little lighter already. Even as they lurk deep inside my subconscious like a monster hiding under my bed.

I spit in my hand, then smooth it over my shaft slowly, fingering every veiny ridge, savoring it like it's my last supper. "Fuck, that feels good," I rasp to myself.

I spread my legs wider and press back against the seat. The poison winds its way through my fingers, elevating every tingle and spark of pleasure. I rock my hips up as I stroke harder, squeezing my cock tight inside my palm.

As a deep spasm courses through me, I see her face.

Fuck.

Not again.

But it's too late. I'm too hard to get off this fucking ride now. Fuck.

I see her eyes—one brown, one blue, haunting—staring back at me in the mirror of Duff's bathroom.

"Uhhh," I cry out. My cock swells, stretching so tight my muscles may rip open while I bleed out.

I flash back to the memory of her perfect fucking ass. The smoothness of it as it pressed against my belly while I fucked her pussy raw.

Fuck, I can't breathe. The heat in my neck and chest becomes an inferno as I pump my cock hard and fast. I pretend I'm back inside her tight pussy with the taste of jasmine on my tongue.

"Fuck!" All the blood shoots down my shaft and rumbles, sending every nerve afire. I pant for breath as my orgasm unleashes. I jerk my wrist furiously, sliding my palm up and down faster and faster. I cover the tip of my cock with my free hand and unleash a deep guttural growl as my hot milky cum spills into it.

"Mmph," I mutter unintelligibly. I bite my lip hard as I rock my hips. The mystery girl's eyes flash in my mind again. She licks her lips in the mirror at me. "Oh, fuck." Another burst of spasms grips me. I cup my balls as I continue to grind against my hand.

I almost hyperventilate. Fuck. My chest heaves as I try to center myself. As I try to steady my racing pulse. "Fuck," I whisper.

This has never happened before until her. I don't fantasize about girls I've fucked in seedy bathrooms. But this one… I can't get her out of my fucking head, and it's enraging. It's masochistic.

I have zero interest in anyone else. I don't even have a real interest in *her*. That's not the kind of man I am. I don't care about *any* women. But her eyes haunt me. And every time I get a whiff of jasmine, I'm spinning around looking for her. It makes me want to drive my head into a brick wall.

Bones and Aries are starting to wonder what the fuck is wrong with me. I haven't fucked anyone since her. They know that's not like me. I keep telling them I'm stressed about my grandmother's estate and acquiring the baneberry fields. But they know I'm full of shit. I'm only grateful that they don't press me on the issue. My fuse is so fucking short these days, I'm tempted to burn the entire Harker estate down out of spite.

But ashes don't make poison or money. And I really fucking love both.

I clean myself off with my monogrammed handkerchief and stuff myself back into my pants. I pinch my eyes shut for a moment and take a deep breath. I try to blow out the shame that fills me for letting myself give into this fantasy for the third time this week.

I glance out the window and sigh when I glimpse the stone-cold walls of Blackwell Manor. The partition opens when I press the button. "Change of plans. Take me back to town."

"Yes, Mr. Blackwell."

I shoot Bones a text on the way there. *Time to go trick or treating.*

He responds with a thumbs-up emoji.

There's only one thing that will make me feel better right now. Power. Because whenever I think of that sinful brunette from the bar, I feel like I'm losing control.

Crack.

Bones's fist flies into Clive's jaw, snapping it out of place. He's bare-knuckling this one. It gives him more of a rush. He's the only man I know whose cock hardens when he's beating the shit out of someone.

"I just need a few more days, Mr. Blackwell," Clive slurs. *It's kind of hard to talk with a broken jaw.*

I snicker. "That's what you said three days ago, Clive. We've been more than agreeable. Now it's time to pay up. Poison doesn't come for free."

He leans forward in his chair and spits a glob of blood out on the ground. "You have plenty of money. Business has been slow this week. Would it kill you to give me just a few more days?"

Wrong answer. I don't even have to nod at Bones.

He flashes Clive a sadistic smile before delivering another blow.

Crack.

Clive cries out in agony as his nose bursts open.

"Would it kill me? Is that what you seriously just asked me?" I snarl. "No. But it might be the fucking death of *you*. You think I got rich by letting every motherfucker who owes me money take their sweet fucking time paying me back?"

A stream of urine trickles down his pant leg. "N-no. Fuck. All I have is in the register. Take it. I can get you the rest by tomorrow night. Please… I'm begging you."

Bones yanks on the register drawer and shakes his head as he counts the bills. "It's only half of what he owes."

I let out an exasperated sigh. "Twenty-four hours, Clive. Not a second more. Or else I'm going to let *him* break every bone in your body. Right before he cums all over your mangled flesh."

Clive's eyes widen. He looks to Bones, who waves back at him like a psycho. "I swear. Thank you, Mr. Blackwell."

Fuck. It's not enough. I'm not satisfied.

I suck in a deep breath. "One more for good measure." A sliver of darkness sparks inside me as I raise my foot and bring it down hard on his ankle.

Crack.

"Fuck!" Tears stream down Clive's bloody face, but he doesn't dare look at me. He doesn't dare say another fucking word.

Bones arches an eyebrow, and I shrug. "What?" I straighten my tie. "See you tomorrow, Clive."

I cringe at the bell that jingles when I push the shop door open. I need quiet and stillness. I need release. But I can never find it. Only for that split second I was inside… No. I will not allow a piece of ass to bring me my salvation. No fucking way. I will not feed that monster.

"You all right?" Bones puffs on a joint, his knuckles bloody.

"I have a lot on my mind. I'm fine."

"It's just... you never get your shoes dirty. Not since we were kids. And that's all good. But you wanted to hurt him. I saw it in your eyes."

Bones is tough, psychotic, unhinged, and physically addicted to pain. But he's also incredibly smart, intuitive, and sensitive to other people's emotions. He's like a sadistic fucking empath who feels everything all the time.

I can placate him for a while, but eventually, he's going to call bullshit and force me to open up.

But it won't be today.

I flash him one of my famous grins. "He needed to feel it from me. I didn't like the way he was insinuating that I'm just some rich guy." I grab Bones by the shoulders and give him a gentle squeeze. "They need to fear me as much as they do you. If not more. Otherwise, I'm nothing but a cock in a suit."

He chuckles, satisfied with my answer as he pats me hard on the back. "Thatta boy. We should fuck up people together more often."

I nod and light up a cigarette. Cool as a fucking cucumber, even though I'm shaking inside.

He loves fighting. He gets off on it. I do too. But the difference between me and him is I won't be able to stop myself once I get going. I was playing with fire today, even doing what I did. If Bones hadn't been there to witness... Clive would've been nothing but a pile of bloody mush.

I wave him off and flick my cigarette into a puddle before hopping back into my limo. "Home now, Rodrick. Slow down when we pass Harker Mansion. I want to enjoy the view."

I roll down the window and bask in the crisp autumn breeze. I take a big gulp of it deep into my lungs. We wind through the dark dirt roads away from town. The tree line gets thicker, the leaves and branches shading the road like a sinister force. Rodrick slows the car when we approach the outer edges of Harker Mansion. From here, I can see the lights of the house glowing from every window. A shiver rolls through me.

Locked behind thick iron gates, it sits like an ancient tomb. Surrounded by poison and shrouded in darkness where the particles of light don't reach. This has become the purpose of my existence. The very disease that works its way into my bones, rotting away my flesh. I will not rest until I get my hands on that fucking baneberry.

"Deep breaths, Mr. Blackwell. Like we practiced," Rodrick coaxes.

I nod and count to ten as I inhale and another ten on the exhale. "You know you can call me Dray when no one's around," I quip. "I've been telling you that for years."

Rodrick has worked for my family since before I was born. He was just a boy when he came to Blackwell Manor. Now, at the ripe age of fifty, he's the epitome of professionalism and loyalty. But at times, he was like a father to me. And he's coaxed me out of more than one panic attack over the years.

He clears his throat. "You're not a boy anymore. You're Mr. Blackwell. That's what I'll call you. Sir."

I chuckle. "Whatever you say, old man."

His smile reaches his eyes in the rearview mirror. "With all due respect, sir. I am fifty years young."

I laugh out loud at that. And sharp as a fucking whistle. "That you are, my friend."

I take one last glance at Harker Mansion before it disappears on the road behind us. The farther we get, the calmer I feel. I know my reprieve won't last, but now that Rodrick has guided me down from the ledge once again, I will sleep a little better tonight.

Well, after I polish off a bottle of gin and jerk myself off to the memory of my mystery girl again. Fuck me.

There is no true rest for the wicked. No hope for the depraved.

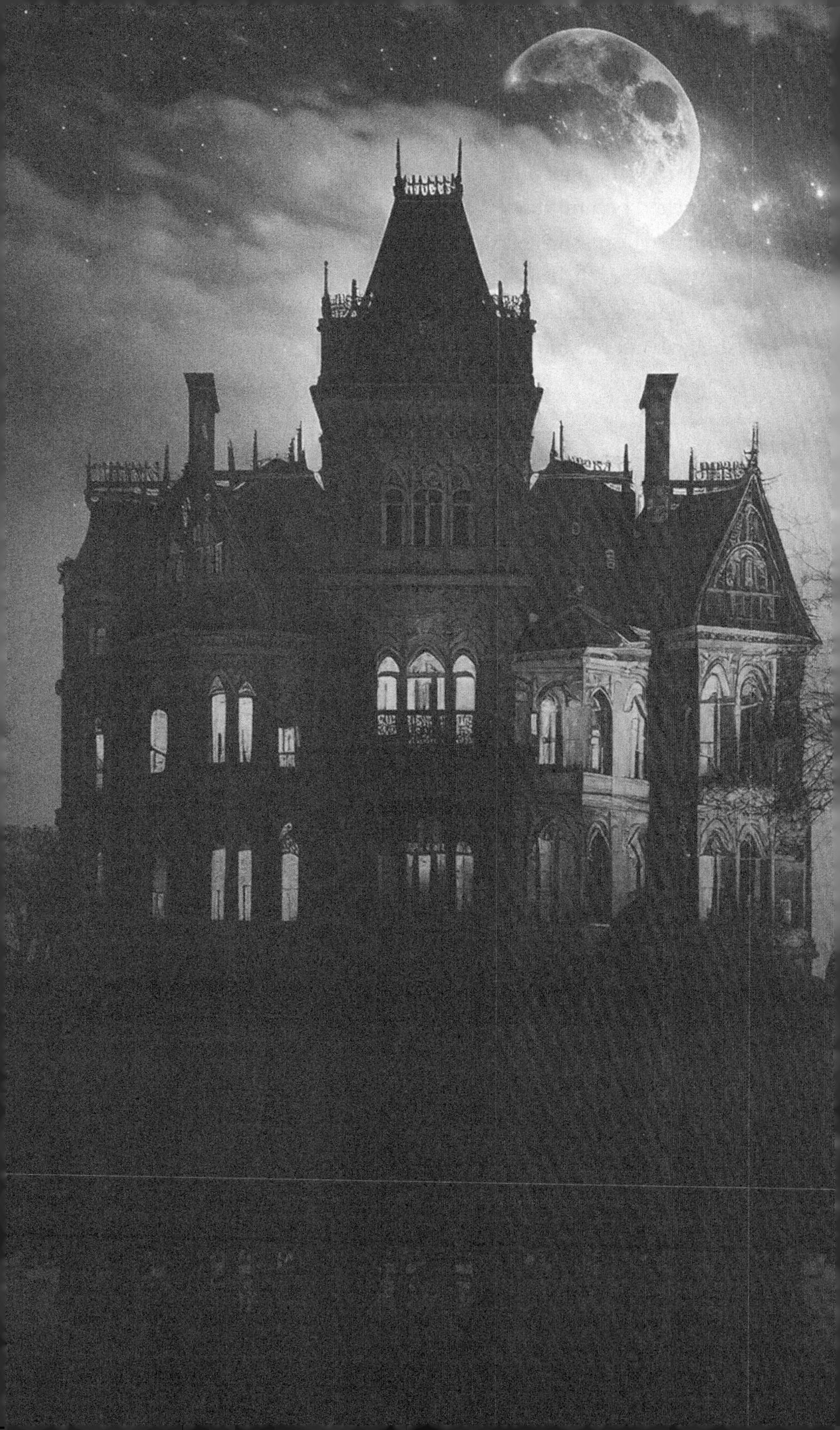

CHAPTER 3

Mia

When I open the door, my breath hitches. Standing on my porch is the most angelic-looking man I've ever seen. With ice-blond hair slicked back off his forehead, still showing off the wave of it, and blue-green eyes that sparkle like two lagoons, he could make anyone melt on the spot. He towers over me by at least a foot and a half. I gaze down the length of him, taking stock of his broad shoulders and thick arms held snug inside his expensive designer suit. My heart flutters when he flashes me a grin.

"It's Mia, right?" He sticks out his hand. "You probably don't remember me. I'm Aries Thorn."

I feel my cheeks flush when his hand clasps around mine. "I… um. No, I don't remember anyone here. I was just a baby when I left."

He grimaces, remembering something about my past that I don't have any recollection of. "Such a tragedy what happened to your parents. I'm sorry for your loss."

I shrug, but I can't tear my eyes away from his. "That's okay. I never knew them… Is there something I can help you with?"

His charm falls right back into place. "May I come inside? I'd love to discuss an important matter with you."

I shouldn't let a stranger into my house, but his name is synonymous with Ever Graves. His family is rich, powerful, and well-respected in Melancholia society. I step back and motion for him to pass. "Of course."

I catch a whiff of something familiar as he walks past me. Something sweet and heavy and pungent. It lodges in my throat and makes me cough for a second. I've smelled it before.

"I'd offer you a drink, but I don't have anything stronger than tea or coffee." It's only the afternoon, but I've heard how the Thorns like their booze before brunch.

He winks at me. "Have you checked the cellar? That's where your grandmother kept the good stuff."

I laugh, forgetting that the people in this town knew her better than I did. It didn't even dawn on me until now that he's probably attended parties in this house. This estate is so big, I haven't even seen half of it in the week I've been here. "Show me where that is. I'm still getting the lay of the land."

He licks his lips, and for a split second, I think I see a ring of light swirl around his pupils. "I'll lead the way."

I swallow down the lump in my throat. Between the guy I screwed in the bathroom at Duff's Bar the other night and now this flawless Adonis in front of me, I'm starting to think that Ever Graves only allows beautiful men to live here.

Aries leads me to a door underneath the sweeping staircase. The wood creaks when he pulls on it. He flashes me another grin before descending yet another staircase. "You have no idea what you're getting yourself into."

Butterflies dance in my belly at the tone of his voice. He's polite yet suggestive, like a man who is doing everything in his power not to let the mask slip. The hairs on the back of my arms prickle as I follow him down the dark passageway.

"Is this the part where you murder me and hide my body in one of the wine barrels?" I'm only half-joking.

He reaches back for my hand, another gentlemanly gesture so I don't slip, but his grip is a little too firm. "I hadn't thought of that. Thanks for the suggestion."

I freeze on the stairs, my palm sweating inside his. "Um..."

He bursts out laughing. "Relax, little lamb. Murder is a bit too messy for me." We reach the bottom of the stairs—I know because he flicks on a light, knowing exactly where the switch is located. It illuminates the room and his face, which is now just inches away from mine. "I'm more of a bury you alive type of guy."

If it weren't for that devilish smirk on his face, I'd question if he was joking. He's playful and charming, but something sinister creeps at the edges of his lips, something dark pulls at his eyes.

I lick my lips, my mouth suddenly dry. The cellar is musty and cool and smells like old library books. "How thoughtful," I tease.

When I finally tear my eyes away from his face, I gasp. "There must be a thousand bottles down here."

He wipes the dust off the nearest one and presents it to me. "This is a 1982 Chateau Lafite. It's worth about ten grand. There are a few thousand others in here just like this one. Different vineyards and years, but all worth about the same and higher. And it's all yours."

What in the actual fuck? Now the back of my neck is sweating as well as my palms. "That's insane. People actually pay that much for wine?"

Aries dips his head to the side, a seductive move that lands its intention. A tiny trickle of moisture leaks out of my pussy. He caresses the bottle in a way that makes me want to *be* the fucking bottle. "People will pay anything if they want something bad enough." There's a hint of ache in his voice.

"What is it that *you* want?" I ask, my fingers trembling at my sides. I'm overwhelmed by the scents of this room and him and the heat of his stare on me.

He fingers a few more bottles before landing on another and pulling it out from its home on the rack. "To drink this very expensive bottle of wine with you while I tell you exactly what I want."

It's strange how Aries knows his way around my kitchen. He pulls out the exact drawer that the wine opener lives in before crossing to the cabinet that holds a set of crystal decanters. I wonder just how much time he's spent here…

"You have to be gentle with these old corks." He carefully twists the wine opener into the cork. "They're fragile and can disintegrate if you don't get the right angle."

Despite the fact that it's just a little after noon, my mouth salivates for a taste. This wine, this moment, is the stuff from fiction. These scenarios don't happen to girls like me. *Not to dirty little orphan girls who can't even dream because their sleep is possessed by nightmares.*

With the cork safely out and in one piece, Aries sets it on the marble counter. "Now, no matter how gentle you are, there's always going to be some sediment at the bottom. So that's why I'm going to pour it into here." He winks and rolls up his suit sleeves before reaching for the crystal decanter.

The veins on his forearms protrude around his chiseled muscles as he grips the bottle. I clench my thighs together as every single one of his movements turns me on. *Fuck, I'm such a whore.* I feel my cheeks heat when we lock eyes. He knows I want him. Fuck. But I'm sure this man is used to everyone wanting him. He's universally hot.

"Where did you learn how to do that?" I ask like an idiot.

After he finishes decanting the bottle, he reaches into another cabinet and pulls out two goblets. "My mother taught me when I was six. She loved showing off that trick at dinner parties."

I nearly choke on my first sip. "Six years old? Holy shit."

He smiles, but his lips are tight. "There's nothing holy about my life, darlin.'"

I nod and swirl the wine around in my mouth. I remember seeing someone do that in a movie once.

He holds up his glass. "Look at the legs on that. Fuck."

I nod again, but I am so out of my league right now; it's painful.

"See how the wine teardrops down the sides of the glass? This one's been fermenting for a long time. Higher alcohol content—which means we're going to get fucked up." He laughs.

I don't usually drink much, so after a few more sips, I'm already feeling buzzed. I lean against the center island, thankful that it stands between us. Aries looks and sounds like a very bad idea. He's not only sexy as hell, but he's also rich, powerful, and charming. Where I come from, that combination leads to devastation and ruin.

He cocks his head to the side. "You don't talk much, do you?"

Not when I'm flustered. "I-I'm just tired. There's still a lot of unpacking to do. Sorry."

He undoes the top button of his shirt, revealing swirls of ink across his collarbone. "Don't ever apologize, little lamb. You're too pretty to be sorry."

I swallow down the lump in my throat while my traitorous pussy pulses with need. "Um, thanks." The last time I checked myself out in the mirror, my dark circles were more prominent, and my face was paler than usual. An unfortunate side effect of forced insomnia followed by coma-like sleep spells that can pull me under for days.

He furrows his brow. "I guess we should get down to business, Mia."

His shift in tone snaps me out of my sex-with-a-stranger fantasy. "Right. Yeah."

"This property is special. Aside from it being the largest estate in Ever Graves, it's the oldest. And it's a lot for one person to manage." He doesn't take his eyes off me as he swirls his wine in circles on the counter.

Something prickles the back of my neck. Fear? Uneasiness? "It's a bit intimidating, but it already feels like home. My grandmother left me a lot of money. Once I get settled, I plan on hiring some people to help out."

He winces, his lips pursed. "That's the thing, Mia. No one is going to want to work here."

I set down my glass and push it away from me like it's going to bite me suddenly. "What do you mean? Why?"

"Do you know who Draven Blackwell is?" He grips the stem of his glass so tightly that I think it might snap in half.

Fuck. *So this is why he came.* "I don't know him personally." There's a chill in the air between us.

He takes another big swig of his wine. "Well, I do. Draven Blackwell runs this town, Mia. He has forbidden anyone to work for you. Trust me, you don't want him as an enemy."

I grip the edges of the counter to steady myself. My stomach knots, and my knees shake. "I think you should leave," I rasp.

Aries reaches into his jacket pocket and pulls out an envelope. "We are offering you three times what the property is worth. You can go anywhere you want in Melancholia. Fuck, you could buy ten houses with the money we're giving you."

A quiet rage begins to fester in my bones. The fucking audacity of these people. "This is Harker Mansion. And *I'm* a Harker. My grandmother wanted me to have it. So with all due respect, fuck you and fuck off. I'm not selling."

He creeps around the center island, stalking toward me. My breath hitches as I back up against the wall. "You need to leave," I repeat.

He rests his hands on the wall, boxing me in between his arms as he glares down at me. "Such foul language from such a *quiet* girl. I think you were just biting your tongue before to hide all that filth." He leans in closer. "This property is covered in baneberry. Its mere existence infringes on our poison territory. You can either sell it to us or become our biggest competitor. The latter option is a whole lot messier. And as I mentioned earlier, I don't fucking like messy."

I catch another whiff of his scent and know why it's familiar. It's the same scent I smelled on the veranda yesterday. I take a deep breath and force myself to hold his gaze. "Are you threatening me?"

He licks his lips. "We're beyond threats, little lamb..." He steps back and adjusts his sleeves, rolling them back down and buttoning them at the cuff. "I'll leave this here for you to look over. My cell number is at the bottom. Call me when you've signed, and I'll make sure you have the funds in your account before the ink is dry."

I snicker, my cheeks flaming, but not for the same reason as before. "Get out before I call the sheriff."

A devilish smirk takes over his mouth, and this time, he doesn't try to hide the rings of light swirling around his pupils. "No need. I don't want Sheriff Moss distracted during our golf game tomorrow. He's a terrible swing as it is."

Fucking hell. My chest heaves as I watch Aries back away toward the front door. Ever Graves is my chance at a new life. To start over. I'll be damned if I let the town bullies take that away from me.

In the past, I've always backed down. Ran away. Conceded. But for some reason, this time, I want to stay and fight. For the first time in my life, I want something more for myself.

I follow him out and stand on the porch, watching him climb into his black SUV. He rolls down the window before he pulls away. "I expect a call from you soon, Mia."

"Don't hold your breath," I call out. But he's already driving away, laughing as he speeds through the open gates.

"Fuck," I murmur. The wind howls around me, sending shivers down my spine. I look to my left toward the skeleton trees that line my property. I spot row after row of pink and white flowers. I charge toward the closest cluster. The bushes are full of bright, beautiful berries. *Fucking poison?*

I take a deep breath to try and calm my nerves, but the scent of the toxin lodges in my throat, and I almost cough up a lung. I stumble back to the porch, angrier than ever. I have no friends, no allies… Just a bunch of old money that doesn't mean shit in a town full of people who have just as much. Fuck me. What the hell am I supposed to do now?

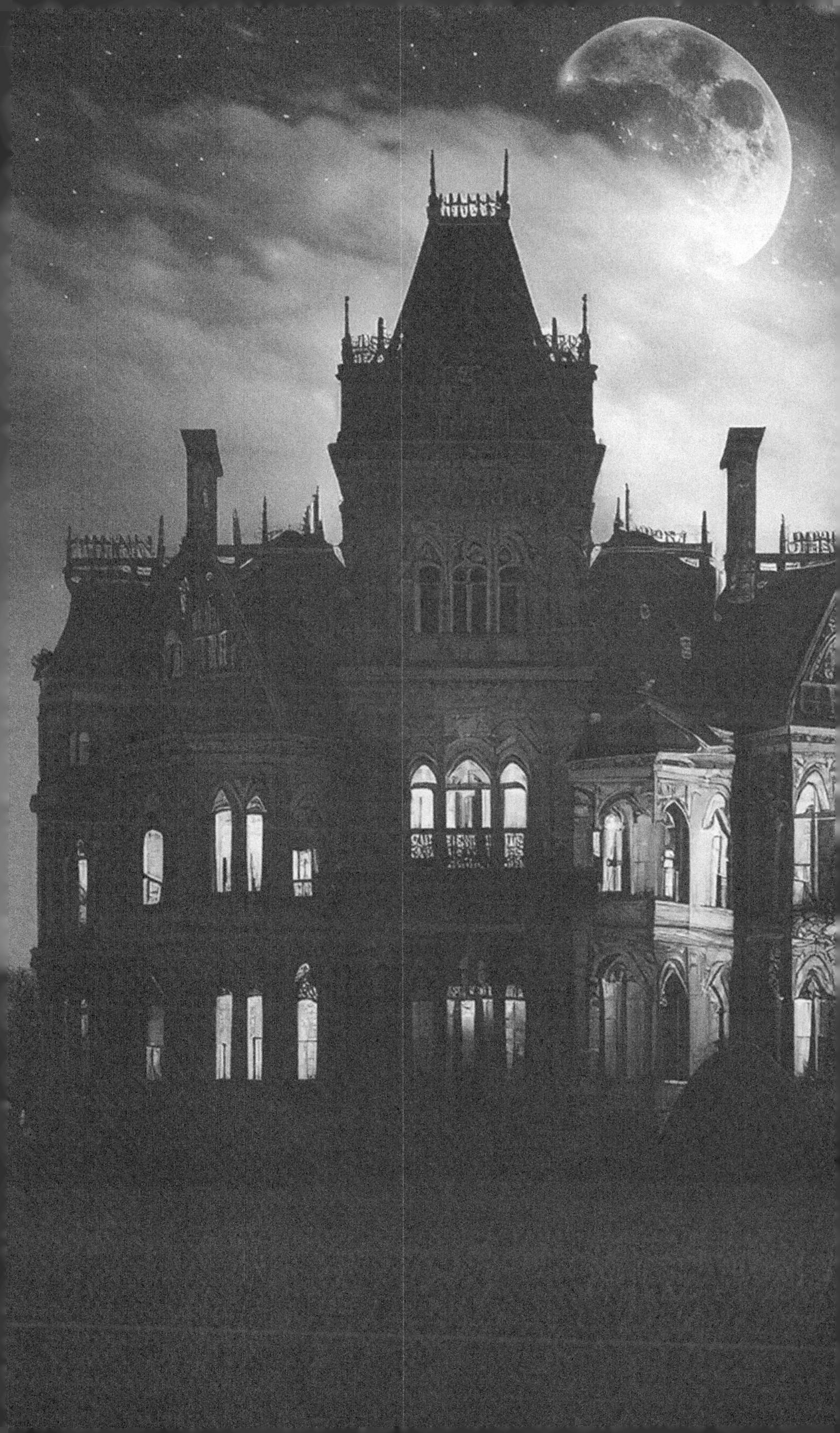

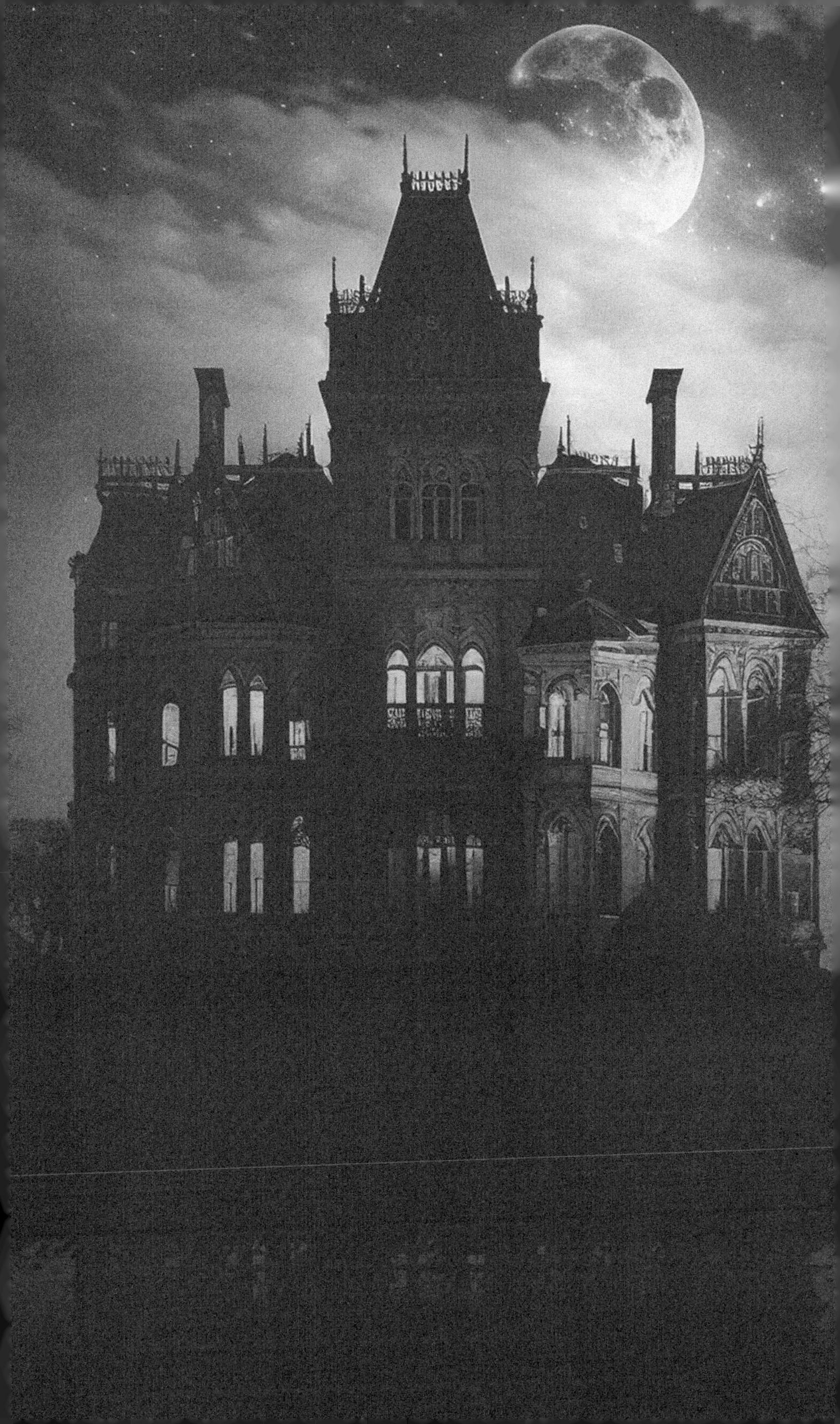

CHAPTER 4

Aries

Mia Harker is fucking gorgeous. *Dammit. It's a shame we have to run her out of town.* I could have fucked her so easily in the wine cellar. She was clenching her thighs together like she hadn't had a cock between them in years. She was practically begging for it. I imagine how loud she'd moan, bent over a wine barrel with her panties around her ankles, my cum dripping down her legs... *Fuck.*

"Anyone home?" Bones snaps his fingers in front of my face. "You zoned out for a full minute."

I grab my cock and readjust it before sitting down next to him in Draven's office. "Sorry, I've had a long day."

The door swings open, and Draven saunters through in a cloud of darkness so heavy that I can feel its weight on my chest. The air always thickens when he enters a room.

He plops down at his desk and glares at me. "Why don't I have the deed to Harker Mansion in my hands, Aries?"

Fuck. Here we go. "She refuses to sell." I learned a long time ago that the best way to deliver bad news to Draven Blackwell is to just come out with it. Rip off the fucking bandage.

He leans back in his chair in dramatic fashion, sighing as he taps his fingers on the desk. "That's unacceptable." He throws Bones a familiar look.

"You want me to try?" Bones cracks his knuckles, and fresh blood seeps out, saturating the gauze.

Draven's smirk doesn't reach his cold, unfeeling eyes. "We're going to make Mia Harker want to get the fuck out of here so fast she runs screaming with just the clothes on her back."

I flex my jaw. "You want me to go back and hurt her?"

Draven shrugs. "If necessary. I want you to scare the ever-loving shit out of her. Let her know she's not safe. That she's not wanted here."

Bones nods and smiles. "This is going to be fun."

Fucking sadistic bastards, all three of us. I wouldn't wish us on my worst enemy.

I clear my throat. "She's petite, timid, and way out of her league. It shouldn't be too hard to scare her. I'm also pretty sure she wanted to fuck me before I presented her with the papers."

"Everyone wants to fuck you, Aries. You're just so fucking pretty," Bones taunts.

I roll my eyes. "I barely had to do anything, and her nipples were as hard as my cock. That means she's vulnerable. Needy. We can use that to our advantage."

Draven arches an eyebrow. "Sounds like *you* want to fuck *her*. I can hear it in your fucking voice. Is that going to be a problem?"

Fuck. The last thing I need is Draven thinking I'm compromised over a piece of ass. "Nah. I'm good. She's not my type."

He stares at me for a few seconds longer, studying my face, my breath. "Good. The sooner we get that cunt out of Harker Mansion, the sooner we can start expanding the business. I've already had several calls for the baneberry."

"Maybe we shouldn't get ahead of ourselves," I interject. "What if she doesn't sell?"

Draven's gold-flecked eyes darken. "Then we'll kill her," he mutters.

Fuck. I don't know if I have the stomach for any more murders.

"You okay?" Bones squeezes my shoulder.

"Yeah, I just need a drink. Like I said, long day." I rub my sweaty palms against my silk suit pants, not caring if I streak them. I can buy more.

Draven's eyes soften. "You two should go down to Duff's and have a few before Bones heads over to Harker Mansion tonight. You both need to burn off a little steam."

"You're not coming?" I ask.

He shakes his head. "Not tonight. I have too much work to do."

Which is Draven's code for *I'm going to wallow in my own self-loathing while fisting myself.*

I stand up to leave. "Try not to break your wrist jerking off this time."

He snorts. "You both know I broke my wrist from the fall. Fuck off."

Bones laughs. "Yeah, because you made yourself cum so hard you crashed my fucking bike."

I burst out laughing as we both get death stares from Draven. "Out *now*. Fucking heathens."

"So, how hot is she?" Bones's eyes glaze from his third whiskey. He licks the rim of the glass, savoring every drop.

I shudder, annoyed that I showed any sign of weakness in front of them. "She's pretty. Not hot. There's a difference," I lie. With one brown eye and one blue eye, dark silky hair that cascades down her back, Mia Harker is hot as fuck. But she's also shy, boring, and unsure of herself. If Bones doesn't give her a heart attack tonight, I'll be shocked.

He arches an eyebrow at me. "Bullshit. Come on, *Ries*, tell me. Dray isn't here to scold you." He chuckles.

There's no fucking way I'm saying shit. "Let it go, Bones."

He shrugs. "I'm gonna find out tonight anyway."

"What's your plan?" I'm almost envious that he gets to go instead of me. I bet she looks even hotter with fear in her eyes. I think my little lamb has a dark side too. There was something about the way she looked at me when I had her cornered.

He grabs a cherry from the bar tray and pops it into his mouth. "None of your fucking business unless you tell me how hot she is."

I let out a frustrated grunt. "Forget I asked then." Bones is going to fucking rip me a new one later after he lays eyes on her himself.

"Go in through the wine cellar. She didn't even know where it was earlier. I doubt she remembers how to get back down there," I offer.

Bones snorts into his whiskey. "You've really thought this out." He shakes his head, laughing, as if that's the most ridiculous thing I've ever said.

I shrug. Emma Harker used to throw the best fucking parties. I've passed out many times in that wine cellar. It was also the easiest way to sneak out when I didn't want my parents parading me around like fresh, eligible meat. My stomach turns at the thought. They always gave me a choice. My twin sister, Libra, wasn't so lucky.

Truth be told, I want nothing to do with this fucking poison business anymore. It's tainted by the sins of my father.

"Hey, Ries, I'm just joking. *Relax*. That's good advice. I was planning to go in the side entrance but the wine cellar is better. I forgot how we used to party down there." He squeezes my shoulder.

"It's cool. I'm on edge. Draven is up my ass every five seconds about this fucking baneberry. It wasn't enough that I got Libra to sign away her shares over to me. Things were so much easier when we were kids. Before all this fucking nonsense."

He stares into space as he nods. "Yeah, you're right. When it was just the three of us. All we cared about was fucking and drinking. Everyone let us run fucking wild. It was awesome."

We were kings without a kingdom, ruling over ourselves and our carnal desires. Now we have to answer to lawyers and investors and everyone in between.

I finish up my beer and give him a light slap on the cheek. "Come find me later. I wanna know how it goes."

I hear Duff grumble from behind the bar when he orders another shot, and I can't help but chuckle on my way out. Booze and adrenaline are a deadly combination for Bones Crane. Poor Mia Harker is going to find that out real soon.

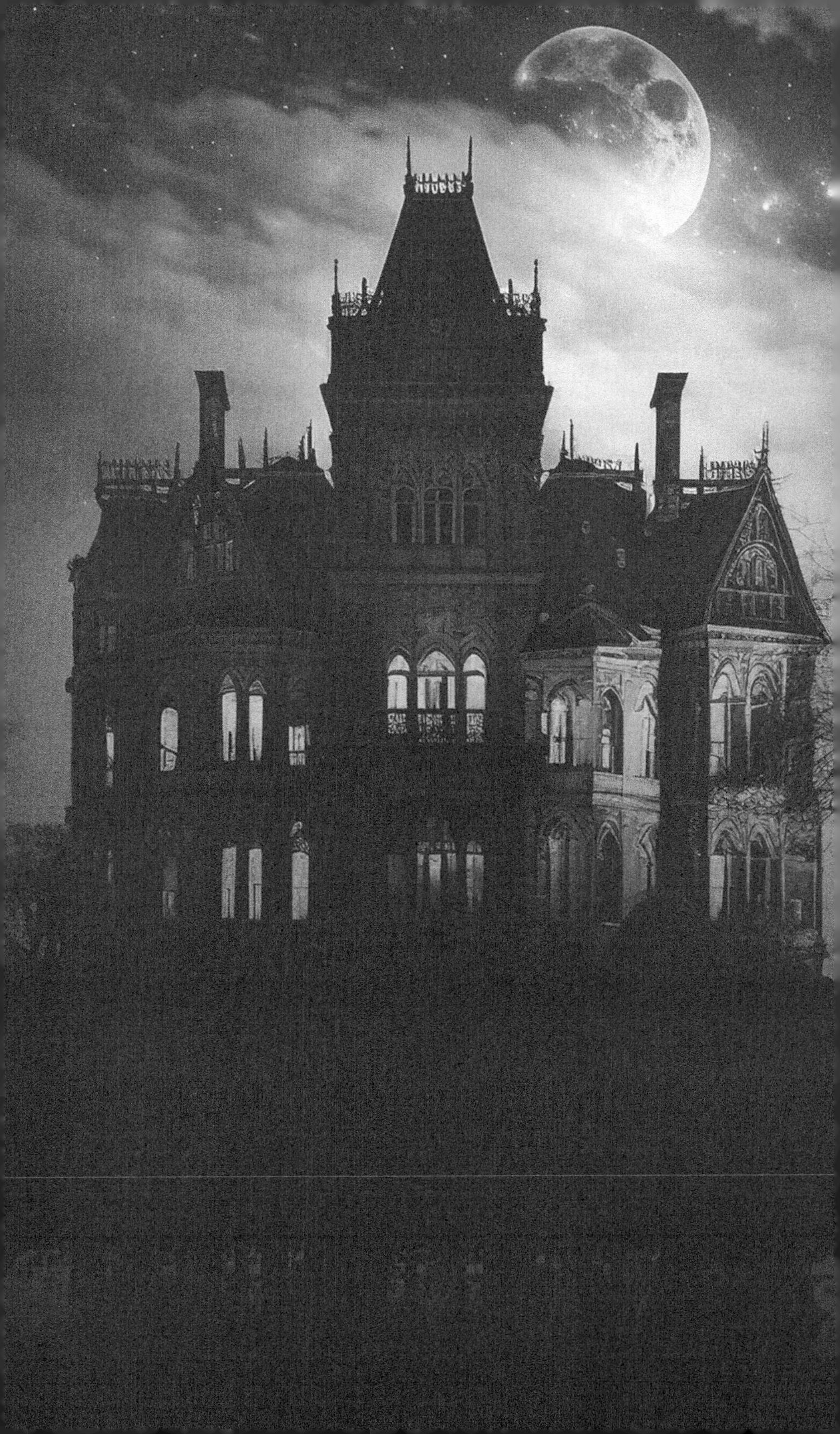

CHAPTER 5

Bones

Fucking Aries.

My cock swells as I catch a glimpse of Mia in the front window. He called her pretty, so I suspected she was hot, but fuck... This woman is gorgeous. I picture her down on her knees with my hands around her throat. I'd love to make her swallow every drop of my cum before I end her life.

She's closing the curtains as if that's going to keep the monsters out. *Nothing and no one can stop me.*

I pull down my black ski mask and creep to the back of the mansion. Lucky for me, I've partied here so many times, I know this stone fortress better than Mia herself. She's an outsider in our town *and* in her own house.

The door to the wine cellar is easy to open with my lock pick. I hold my breath and wait a few minutes after the wooden door creaks open. When I don't hear any footsteps stomping overhead, I keep going.

I lock the door behind me before I head up the stairs to the foyer. But not before snatching a bottle of bourbon from the single-barrel spirits shelf and setting it by the door. Mia's grandmother always kept a stash for me. She had a soft spot for me. Ever since that night, I kept her bastard of a husband from smashing her face in.

I smashed in his instead.

It's a shame I have to torment her granddaughter. But Emma is long gone. What she doesn't know won't hurt her. At least that's what I'll tell myself when Draven orders me to send Mia to the shallow grave next to hers.

I keep to the shadows, watching Mia move around the house. She walks through each room, turning on lights, unaware of the predator who lurks behind her. I smile underneath my mask. The thrill of the chase is what I live for. The adrenaline, the heat in my chest, my cock rock hard as I fantasize about the fear and horror in her eyes when I finally reveal myself.

The whistle of a tea kettle has her heading toward the kitchen. I hang back, hiding behind the wall, and wait for her to turn it off. My pulse races as I hear the boiling water slosh into the teacup. She breathes a heavy sigh, whimpering. *Her safety is an illusion.* The hot water comforts her. Which makes this so much more thrilling.

I turn off the foyer light and drag the tip of my blade down the kitchen door, digging it into the wood. The teacup rattles on the counter. I can almost hear her erratic heartbeat from the other side of the wall.

The door bursts open. "Who's there?"

I flatten myself against the wall.

She spins around, looking for the light switch. "Fuck."

I follow her in the dark, my need to touch her growing. She runs her hand along the wall in search of the light, which she won't find in that direction.

I inch closer and blow out a cold breath.

She trembles when it reaches her, folding her arms over her chest. *"Who's there?"*

In two short strides, I'm at her back. "Your worst fucking nightmare," I growl in her ear.

Without warning, she spins around, fists flying. One lands on the side of my jaw. Fuck. It staggers me for a second.

"Try again, asshole," she hisses. "I already have a nightmare."

I charge toward her, grab her shoulders, and slam her up against the wall. "Not one like me."

With my body pressed against hers, my cock swells. She lets out a quivering breath. "Is that all you got?"

I chuckle and wrap my hand around her throat. "Feisty, aren't you? I bet you're fucking crazy in bed. Should we find out?"

She swings again, but I duck out of it this time. I pin her arms above her head and nuzzle her neck. "Fight me as hard as you want; it only makes me want your pussy around my cock more."

"You're sick. Get out of my house." Her chest heaves with something other than fear. Dare I say our little lamb is turned on? Perfect. There's nothing better than the moment when fear turns to lust.

I press the full weight of my body against hers, smashing her limbs against the wall. "Not until you agree to pack up and leave. You're not welcome here, little nightmare girl."

Her eyes widen. "This is about the poison? I already told your boss I'm not selling. Now get the fuck out of my house."

Beautiful and defiant. I might become obsessed. "I don't have a boss, pretty thing. Just a disdain for the devil. And you brought him back to our town."

Confusion mixed with shock flashes in her eyes. "How do you…"

"This is Ever Graves, darlin'. I know everything that goes on here."

Her upper lip curls in disgust. Without warning, she jerks her knee up into my groin. "Fuck off!"

Fuck. A searing pain shoots through my balls. I lose my grip on her as I double over. "You're going to pay for that," I choke out.

She makes a run for the kitchen.

I take a deep breath and stagger forward. "You can run, but you can't hide, little lamb."

I regain my composure halfway there and charge the rest of the way. Now I'm pissed all the way off.

I practically knock the kitchen door off its hinges when I throw it open. Mia is up against the counter, a butcher knife in her hand.

"Now, what are you going to do with that, baby?" I creep toward her.

She backs up, her hands shaking. "Don't come any closer, or I'll gut you."

I laugh and keep moving toward her. "You'll have to be quicker than me then. *No one is quicker than me.*"

She whimpers when I reach her. "Time's up."

I dart to the side as she swings the knife wide. When I come back around, I seize her wrist, squeezing it between my fingers until the knife clatters to the ground.

"No," she cries.

I hoist her up and slam her down on the breakfast table. "Didn't your parents teach you not to play with knives?"

Her cheeks are flushed. I can't tell if it's from anger, fear, or desire. "My parents died when I was a baby, asshole."

I almost lose my edge at her words. The pain flashes through her eyes, and she goes limp. "You're better off," I grumble. Fuck. I forget she's a Harker for a second. Forget she's an orphan.

She stops struggling and gazes up at me. "Well, I know you're not Aries. He's *much* taller. So who the fuck are you?"

I can't help but laugh. If she thinks calling me shorter than my blond Adonis friend is going to annoy me, she's very wrong. "I'm bigger where it counts."

Her cheeks flush bright red. "Whatever."

I look down the length of her body to see that her oversize T-shirt is barely covering her ass now. It must've gotten hiked up in the tussle. Her panties are white cotton. I lick my lips, unable to control my cock from twitching. Most men salivate over black lace thongs or red G-strings, but I'm a sucker for the purity of white fucking cotton.

My breath hitches when I notice the wet spot in the middle of her slit. "You're not a good girl, are you, little lamb?"

She tries to sit up, but I push her back down and pin her hands against the table. "*Answer me,*" I growl.

She wiggles her hips. "If you don't get off me, I'm going to be *your* worst fucking nightmare."

I haven't felt this fucking alive in a long time. There's something about this girl. Something broken and feral and hungry. A streak of chaos that hides beneath her innocence and naivety.

I drag my fingertips down her arms, sending goose pebbles across her flesh. Her nipples poke through her shirt. I want to twirl my tongue around each one.

She stills, her pulse racing, as I make my way down to her bare legs. I stroke the insides of her thighs, inching closer to that sweet wet spot on her panties. I wait for her to kick or scream or make a run for it, but the only part of her that moves is her chest. It rises and falls erratically.

She's so fucking hot.

I tease at the edge of her panties, tracing the outline of them with my finger. I can easily slip inside…

Fuck, I'm supposed to scare her, not turn her on. I pull back and wrap my hand around her throat again. Her eyes widen, and she gasps as I squeeze so hard that she starts to flail. I need to remind her that I'm a fucking monster. "Sign the papers, Mia. If I have to come back, you will regret it."

I let go and make a run for it while she tries to catch her breath. I grab the bottle of bourbon on my way out and lock the cellar door behind me. I don't want any other monsters getting in here tonight. *She's my little lamb.*

The machine between my legs does nothing to soothe the ache tonight. When I pull into Aries's driveway, I can't remember how I got here. The entire drive was a blur. As I kill the engine, the house lights up.

I let myself in with my spare key and make a dash for the liquor cabinet. Aries's house is spotless as usual, all modern with state-of-the-art appliances, abstract paintings, marble floors, and white furniture. I feel like a bull in a glass house every time I'm here.

"How did it go?" Aries steps into the living room, barefoot and shirtless, wearing only a pair of gray sweatpants. His blond hair is wet and messy.

"Terrible. You downplayed how hot she is. I told you I'd find out." I can't keep the scowl off my face as I shoot a finger of whiskey down my throat.

He smiles and leans up against the wall, folding his arms over his chiseled chest. "I take it you didn't get her to sign the papers either then?"

I roll my eyes and give him a look that says don't fucking test me right now. "Draven has no idea what he's up against. She is stubborn as fuck. We might have to kill her. But I want to fuck her first."

"You're sexy when you're frustrated, you know that?" He tilts his head to the side, sending a quiver straight to my cock.

"I've been hard for the past three hours. All I can think about is bending that brat over her counter and fucking her pussy raw." I take off my leather jacket and toss it onto the nearest chair.

His eyes darken. "You know I don't like it when you get like this."

I can feel the darkness clawing at me. It runs in the Crane blood like a disease. Well, at least in the male blood. My little sister, Lettie, is the only one who seems to have dodged it. She's the sweetest, most goddamn cheerful person I know. I'm suddenly grateful that she's not in Ever Graves right now. Mia Harker brought the fucking devil back to town, and it's affecting us all.

I crack my neck. "I'm fine, Aries. It's not like before. I'm not going to hurt myself again."

He breaches the gap between us and cups my face in his hands. "I think you need a session in my *office*."

The heat in my body climbs. Fuck. I really need to release this fucking hard-on before I explode. But I always get carried away…

"I don't know."

"It will make you feel better, Bones. You know it will."

I nod and knock back another shot. "Yeah, you're right." If anyone can pull me back from the edge, it's Aries and his wicked fucking ways.

I follow him down to the basement. When he flips on the lights, my adrenaline spikes. It's been a while since I've been down here. As I glance around the red-lit room, my cock throbs. Different sizes of whips and paddles hang along the walls. There's a contraption in the center of the room that looks like a guillotine. And in another corner is a gurney with restraints hanging down.

I swallow hard as I remember the last time he tried to *fix* me. It was agonizing, brutal, and so fucking beautiful.

"Take off your clothes and lay on the bed over there for me." Aries's voice is soothing, coaxing, and laced with hunger. His sexual appetite is never satisfied—his tastes unusual to the average person. But there's nothing average about us.

I strip down to my bare feet and lay back on the bed—a mattress without sheets or pillows. I spread out and wait for him. This is the only time in my life when I give up control. And only to him.

"Good boy." Aries takes his time securing my wrists to the bedposts. He licks his lips as he stares at my engorged cock. "We're going to get that taken care of for you."

I nod, already euphoric. I love it when he plays with me. It's like a drug.

"Open your mouth for me."

As soon as I obey, he thrusts a ball gag into it, fastening it tight behind my head. It threatens to suffocate me, but I breathe into it, surrendering to the discomfort. The more I do, the more it turns me on.

Aries picks a thick wooden paddle from the wall. I feel a little pre cum leak out as he stalks toward me. "Spread your legs nice and wide for me, Bones."

Fuck. I feel all the blood rush to my balls as I open up for him. A growl escapes my throat. A fucking cry for mercy even though mercy is the last thing I want or need.

Aries towers over me. A sadistic smile creeps across his lips as he raises the paddle and brings it down against my inner thigh— not hard, just enough to wake me up.

I jerk my hips as if electric currents sear through me. But then a deep spasm grips me soon after. I moan and try to beg, but my words are jumbled with the ball gag weighing on my tongue.

He does the same to my other thigh, bringing the paddle down with a light smack. My skin tingles. It sends shivers to my cock, to my ass, the pleasure snaking around every inch of me.

Aries climbs onto the bed and settles between my legs. He sucks on his index finger before sliding it inside my anus. "You're so tight."

I clench and tremble around him as he thrusts in and out.

"Yeah, that's it. Relax for me."

My entire body contorts when he shoves his finger in past the second knuckle. I let out another moan. Sweat drips down his torso, casting a glowing sheen across his rock-hard abs. I watch the way his muscles flex as he grips me. He's a fucking work of art. Like a statue carved out of stone.

I lift my hips, moving to the rhythm of his finger as he fucks me with it. The tension in my shoulders starts to melt away.

"Such a good fucking boy. Letting me get so deep."

Fuck I'm about to break, and he's only just begun.

Without warning, he pulls his finger out and hops off the bed. He laughs as I whine through the gag.

When he comes back over, his pants are off, and he's holding a box of his *toys*. A pocket pussy is strapped to his waist. "I'm going to need you to take slow, deep breaths for me, Bones. You're going to cum so hard you might black out."

Oh, fuck. This is a new one.

My body aches with need as he straddles me. He wedges a pillow under my ass before squeezing half a tube of lube inside it. "Deep breaths," he coaxes.

I gasp as he lifts my balls and slowly inches his cock inside my ass. I shake and shiver at the feel of him stretching me. The pain and pleasure are indiscernible. I yank on my restraints, but they only get tighter, threatening to cut off my circulation.

"Shhh, relax. Breathe. Fuck, you feel so good." Aries rocks his hips, pushing in deeper with each thrust. "Now I'm about to really fucking get you going."

I gasp again as he grabs my cock and guides it inside the fake pussy he's got strapped to his waist. It's warm and squishy but so fucking tight. So fucking good. I let out a deep moan as he thrusts his cock deeper inside my ass while my cock burrows all the way inside the toy pussy.

"Mmm, now we can cum together." The way he moves his hips is dangerous. The way they roll up and down in slow circles threatens to shatter me with each thrust. I use my restraints as leverage and raise my hips to meet his, losing myself to the chaos of Aries Thorn.

Spasms flicker down my shaft, tormenting me in the best possible way from the tip of my cock all the way down to the deepest part of my anus. I twist and convulse around him, guiding my orgasm out for release.

"There we go. Cum for me, Bones. Cum inside my *pussy*."

Oh, fuck. I can't hold back any longer. A cry dislodges from my throat as I arch back. His hot fluid bursts into my ass just as I erupt. I grind into the toy pussy while Aries fucks me like an animal. He unleashes a demonic growl, digging his fingers into my thighs.

"Mmm, now you're my dirty boy, aren't you? Letting me fill you so fucking full."

I feel tears stream down my cheeks. I'm so fucking overcome with pleasure that I can't contain it in my body. My cum drips down my cock and underneath, soaking the both of us. I can't breathe, but I don't care.

Aries grabs my chin, pinching it hard between his fingers. "Who fucks you the best?"

My chest heaves as he rips the ball gag off my face. "Only you, Ries. It's always you."

He smirks and slaps my face. "Good boy."

With his cock still inside my ass, he kisses me deeply. Our tongues swirl together like two fireflies caught in a mating ritual. I moan as I taste the poison on his lips. The sweet fucking poison mixed with a dark desire that we reserve only for each other.

"You always know how to make me feel better."

He leans forward to release my wrists from the restraints. "That's because I know what's best for you, Bones." He sits back on his heels and slowly pulls the toy pussy off my cock. "We'll get through this Harker situation just like we've gotten through everything else."

I nod and rub my wrists, sad that they're free even though they hurt. "I'll check in with Draven later. I'm going to head down to Duffs again to unwind."

Aries smirks. "You mean you're going to go find someone to beat the shit out of."

I shrug but then give him a wink. *He knows me well.*

Fucking and fighting are my two most favorite things. If I can do both on the same night, then I'll take it.

Plus, I don't have the heart to tell Aries that a tiny sliver of me is still reeling over my encounter with Mia Harker. Cracking a few faces open should at least help me get some sleep tonight.

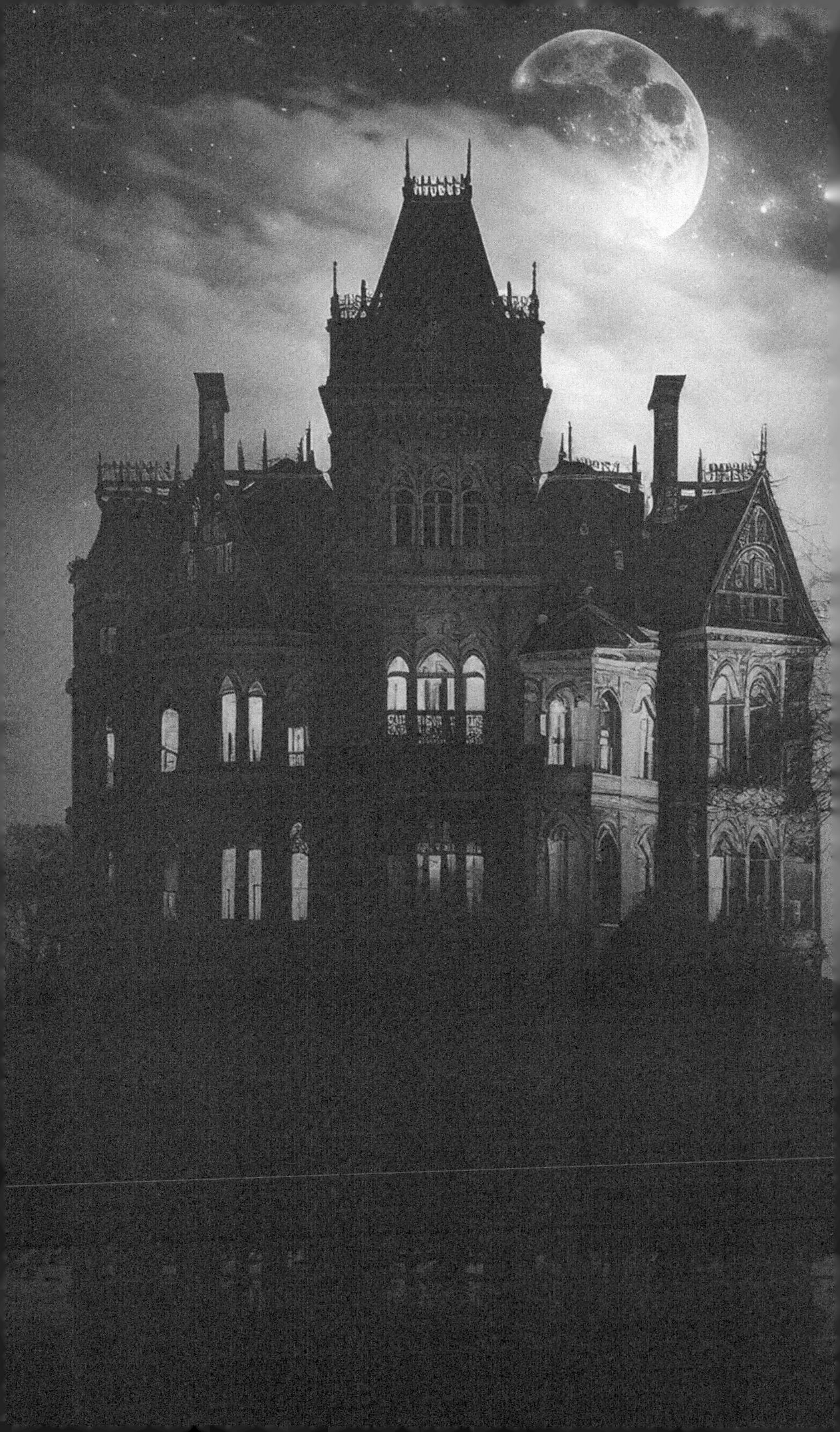

CHAPTER 6

Mia

I LAY ON THE BREAKFAST TABLE—MY LEGS STILL SPREAD—AND TAKE deep breaths. With wet panties and flushed skin, my heart races. *What the fuck is wrong with me?*

I resist the urge to touch myself as I think of his brown eyes, his masked face, the way he pinned me down… I refuse to let myself get off to that image. Maybe the priests were right. *There is a sickness in me.*

By the time I regain my composure, I'm pissed the fuck off. I really need to learn the layout of this house. There are too many doors. Too many ways in.

I storm upstairs to the second floor, to the room I've claimed as my own, and throw on a pair of pants and boots. I grab a flashlight out of the utility closet and stomp down the hall. One by one, I open each door, flinging it open and flipping on the light.

My heart pounds as I wait for each room to illuminate, bracing myself for the possibility of another predator lurking in the dark. I'd actually prefer the company of ghosts right now. But another masked man sent to scare me into selling *my* fucking house is not an option.

It's a good thing I have enough money to pay the monstrous electricity bill I'm about to rack up.

After securing the second floor, I make my way up to the third. This set of stairs is narrower and steeper, like the ones you'd find in a lighthouse. My adrenaline starts to wear off by the time I reach the top, and a prickle of fear returns. What if I actually find another psycho up here? I should've grabbed the butcher knife too. *A lot of good it did me earlier though.*

As I creep down the hall, I notice the air change. It's mustier up here; the scent of old wood is thicker. The halls are carpeted, unlike the second floor, making it impossible to hear if anyone's moving around up here. I take a deep breath outside the first room. *Put on your big girl pants now, Mia.*

I push the door open and shine the flashlight until I can flip the switch on the wall. I breathe a sigh of relief when I see it's just another bedroom. Although, all the furniture is covered in plastic. *That's fucking weird.*

Rinse and repeat. I light up every fucking room, leaving the door wide open before I move on to the next one. Each one is either a bedroom or a bathroom. My fear turns to annoyance at the indulgence of it all. While I slept on the streets, these people sat pretty in a mansion with over twenty guest rooms. What the actual fuck?

The last door on the left opens up to a study. There's a desk against the wall. Next to it is a bookcase, the black paint chipped, filled with the kind of books you'd find in an antique store. *I bet there's some first editions in here.* There's also a comfy-looking couch. It's so worn that the brown leather is cracked and faded like it did its job in comforting those who sat in it.

I linger in the doorway for a few minutes before my curiosity gets the better of me. I need to stay up, anyway. I walk over to a desk, dusty and cluttered with papers, and I pull out a few drawers to find nothing but bank account statements, some old article clippings from the Ever Graves Gazelle, and random shopping receipts.

I let out a sigh and sift through the papers on the top for now. Pouring through the stack, I find nothing too interesting. It's just a pile of paid invoices—water, electricity, landscaping. These must be the most recent ones. Like the last fucking ones that Emma paid before she died.

After flipping through the entire stack, the payee's name catches my eye on the last invoice. My stomach flips. *Absentia Asylum.* What the fuck? I go back through the stack and find three more payments to that dreadful place.

Were they the ones who had me committed, or was another Harker sent there?

Now I have more questions and still no answers. I huff out a sigh and turn off the light before shutting the door behind me.

On the way back down to the main floor, I rack my brain trying to figure out how my masked intruder got inside tonight. There was no crash, no sound of breaking glass. No sign of forced entry that I can see.

When you spend months at a time on the streets, you learn how to sneak into abandoned buildings. I can pick a lock easily now, but the doors here at Harker Mansion are old and heavy. This place is like a fortress.

My stomach sinks when I remember how Aries knew his way around my kitchen and the layout of my house. He probably knows all its secrets too. Fuck. *The wine cellar.*

I retrace my steps over to the door Aries led me to. I shine the flashlight down first, dreading going below into the dark. *Who puts a light switch at the bottom of a creepy stairwell?*

I grip the railing tight as I make my descent while praying I don't fall. No one would even bother to look for me if I broke my neck down here.

It takes me a few minutes to remember where the light switch is. When I finally flip it on, I take a moment to make sure I'm alone. For all I know that man could still be down here.

Satisfied that it's just me and a lifetime supply of overpriced booze, I jiggle the knob on the side door. Locked. But when I kneel down to get a closer look, I see the scratches in the keyhole, marks that only metal scraping against metal could make.

"Ow," I yelp as something hard digs into my knee. What the fuck? I pick up the culprit and snicker. That fucker was so excited to torment me, he dropped one of his lock picks. I stuff it in my jacket pocket.

A spark of rage flares in my chest. I need to find a way to bar this door. Although, I'm sure if he wants to get in again, he'll find another way.

I feel like I'm losing my sanity tonight. Between fighting off sleep so I don't slip into one of Nox's comas, and scouring my own house like a crazy person, I'm starting to regret my decision to move here.

I lock up the wine cellar, but not before snatching a bottle of whiskey. I return to the kitchen to make a pot of coffee. Tea isn't going to cut it tonight. And I can't resist pouring a little splash of whiskey into my cup.

These assholes are not going to give up. I need to face Draven Blackwell in person so I can tell him that I have no intention of selling. And that if he doesn't back off, I will have to resort to my own shady tactics.

Who the fuck is here now? The sound of tires on my front drive pulls me to the window. I peek out to see a shiny black Benz pulling up. Ugh. More fucking annoying rich people. I know I'm rich too now, but I'll never be one of *them*.

I yank open my front door and take a wide stance on the front porch, arms crossed. I won't be foolish and let another one of Draven's guns-for-hire into my house again.

My curiosity piques when a beautiful girl with long black hair exits the driver's side. She tosses me a warm smile and waves as she approaches. When she's almost to the porch I notice how flawless her brown skin is. It's literally glowing without the help of any makeup. I'm suddenly insecure, knowing that I'm pale as fuck and the lack of sleep has left permanent dark circles underneath my eyes.

"Hi, I hope it's okay that I dropped by? I heard you just moved in, and I wanted to welcome you to the neighborhood." Her voice is sweet and genuine; her face warm and inviting. There's nothing disingenuous about this girl, as far as I can tell. But then again, I thought the same thing about Aries at first.

I keep my arms crossed and my guard up. "And you are?"

Her eyes widen. "Oh shit, sorry! I should've led with that." She offers me her hand. "I'm Villette Crane. My friends call me Lettie. My family just lives up the road. I'm taking a break from school to spend some time with them. You know, self-care and all that. I go to Tenebrose in Raven's Gate. There's been a whole lotta drama there though. I'm happy to get away. Shit. Sorry, I'm rambling."

After this angelic beauty finally takes a breath, I burst out laughing. "That was entertaining actually. I'm Mia Harker. I must be the talk of the town, considering no one knew I existed until about a week ago."

Villette's handshake is firm but gentle. "You've definitely been in a lot of people's mouths. Shit. I mean your name, not you. It's none of my business whose mouth you've been in. Fuck. Sorry. I don't get out much." Her cheeks tinge with pink, and she lowers her dark eyes to the ground.

I laugh again. "I like you. You don't bullshit. It's refreshing. You remind me of a girl I knew back at the orphanage in Wickford Hollow. She always said what was on her mind too."

Her smile returns as she shyly gazes back up at me. "Thank the raven. Not everyone agrees with you. My brother Bones says I need to think before I speak sometimes."

I shake my head. "Nah, keep doing you. It's endearing."

She shrugs and twirls a strand of her black hair around her manicured finger. "Thanks. So how are you finding Ever Graves so far?"

My stomach turns. "Um… I haven't seen much of the town yet. Still unpacking." I gesture toward the house as if she can see my boxes from out here.

She nods. "Well, if you want a break from all that, my brother Bones is throwing a party tonight at his garage. You should come."

The thought of meeting new people makes me queasy, but I like this girl's vibe a lot. I'm guessing she wouldn't hang out with jerks. She seems to have a good sense about her.

"Yeah, sure. Why not? Text me the address later." She hands me her phone, and I add my number to her contacts.

"Great! And if you need anything, just let me know. I have a little bit of pull in this town." She winks.

I contemplate asking her about Draven Blackwell but think better of it. He sounds like a fucking asshole. I don't want to scare off my potential new friend with the fact that I've been here a little over a week, and I'm already in a soap-opera-style feud with him.

"Thanks, Lettie. Um, who all is going to be there? I'm not great in big crowds."

She twirls her hair again while she counts the guest list in her head. "Not too many people. Some of my brother's friends and a few people we went to high school with. Don't worry. It'll be chill."

I breathe a little easier, but small talk is not one of my strengths. "Sounds good. See you tonight. Thanks for stopping by to welcome me. It means a lot."

"You got it, girl." She waves again, warm and sweet and with her whole body, before hopping back into her luxury car.

My phone pings with a text from her before she even drives away. I save her contact info and rush back inside so I can stress out for the next six hours over what I'm going to wear tonight.

The only parties I've ever been to were with my ex-fiancé. And those were all stuffy gallery parties in the art district of Raven's Gate. He loved parading me around to his colleagues, hoping that if he gave me enough champagne and compliments, I'd forget about Nox. That, for once, I could act like a normal girlfriend. After we broke up, I retreated even further into the recesses of my own self-loathing.

I wring my hands in front of the mirror. I'm nervous as fuck. But I know it will be good for me. That's what my therapist used to tell me, anyway.

I let out a deep, dramatic sigh and turn on the shower. As the hot steam fills the bathroom, a little smile plays on my lips. Maybe that hot guy from Duff's Bar will be there. I wouldn't be mad if he wanted to fuck me again.

My mood lightens at the idea of him bending me over a stranger's bathroom counter. I lean back against the shower wall and shudder. The water rushes down my back, heating my skin. I slide my finger down the center of my pussy while I picture my mystery man. I remember his golden eyes staring back at me in the mirror as I thrust my finger inside.

Fuck. I arch my back and close my eyes as I imagine his hands on me again. "*Uhhh.*" It doesn't take long for my nub to spasm. I add another finger as I pump faster, fucking myself hard at the thought of him.

I'm so close, so sensitive. I shudder and moan as a sharp

orgasm rips through me. My legs shake as I cum all over my fingers. I smear it in circles around my swollen clit, drawing out a second wave of spasms in seconds. *"Fuck..."*

My chest heaves, and my heart beats out of control. I huff against the shower wall, my pussy raw and tingling. Fuck. I'm so horny right now I'd probably let that masked intruder fuck me. I'm a hot, sticky mess, and I need more than just my own hand.

Suddenly I'm looking forward to this party tonight.

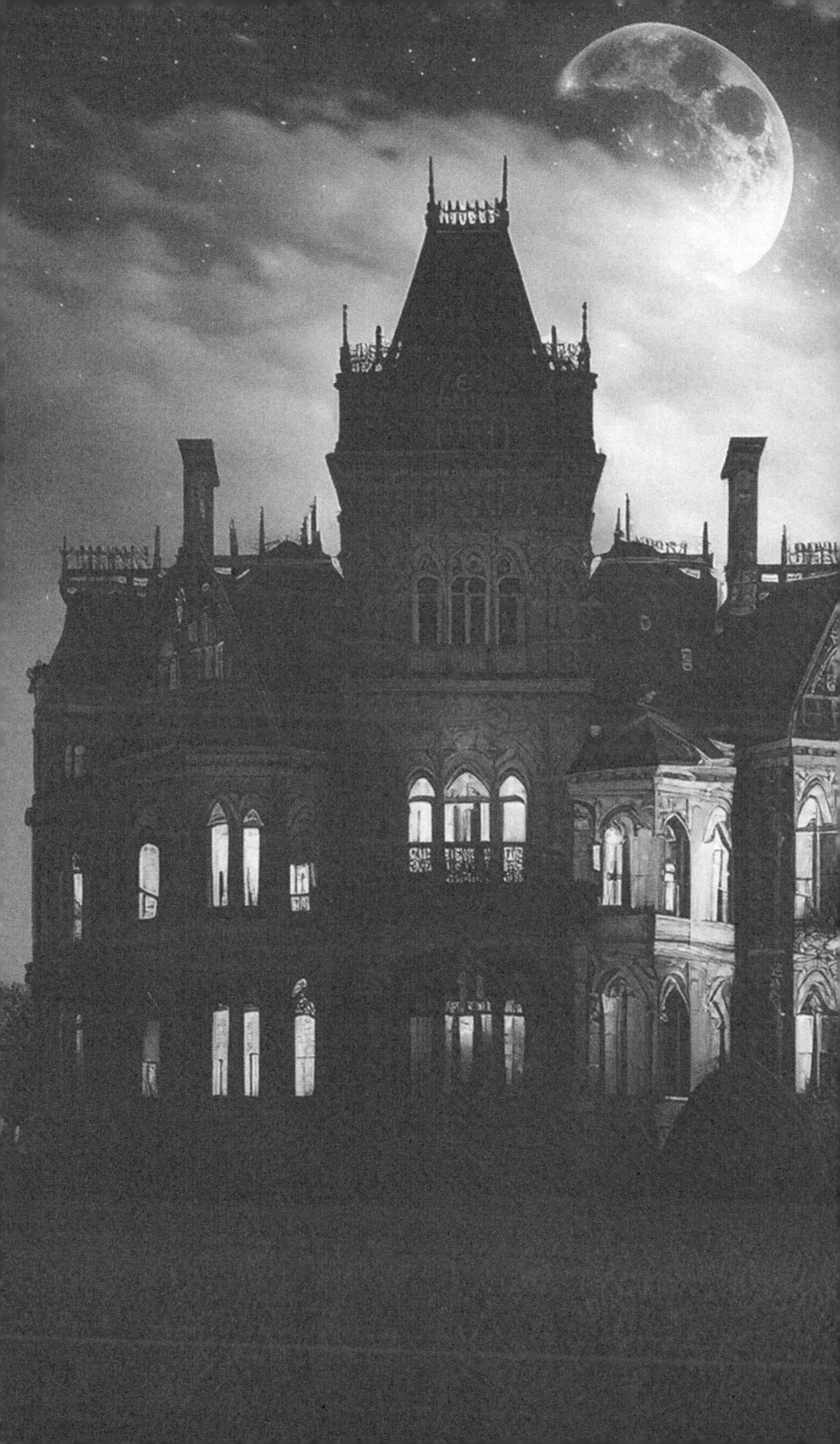

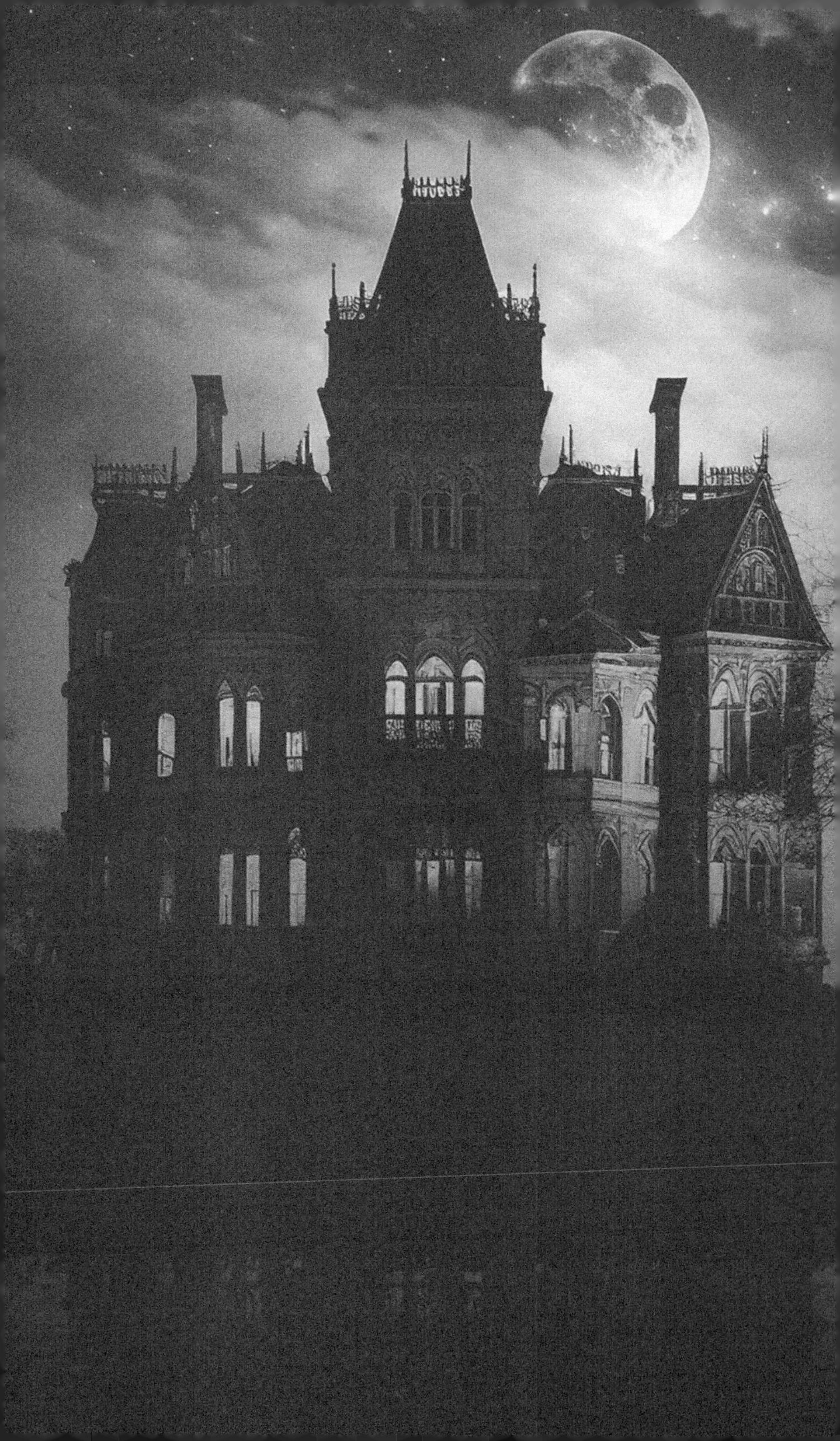

CHAPTER 7

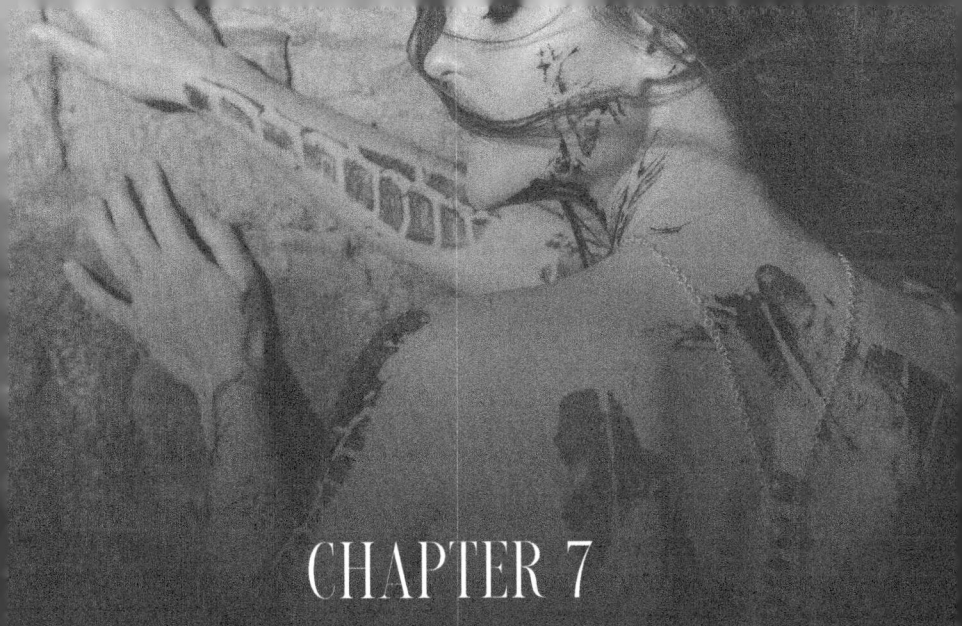

Mia

The building literally says *Bones's Garage* on the side. I stand out front, feeling awkward and overdressed in my tight black dress and heels. In the middle of nowhere, the garage lights up the woods like a beacon. Loud music pours out, adding to the eeriness. There's something off about this town. I can feel it.

I almost chicken out until I see Villette. She waves at me from the doorway, beckoning me forward.

"Fuck," I mutter under my breath as I plaster on a fake smile and amble forward.

I almost break my ankle when my pointy heel gets stuck in the mud for a second. I recover quickly, though, and I don't think anyone notices.

"You made it!" Villette grabs my hand and pulls me inside.

She looks gorgeous in tight black jeans, black boots, and a purple cropped sweater that shows off her diamond belly button piercing.

I try to pull back. "I should go change."

Her eyes widen. "No fucking way. You look hot."

"Um, are you sure? I feel like people are staring at me." I look around the garage and find more casually dressed people sandwiched in between the muscle cars, motorcycles, and mechanical equipment.

She giggles. "Only because you're gorgeous. Relax, Mia. Let's get you a drink, then I'll show you around."

I nod even though I want to run deep into the woods and offer myself up as a sacrifice to the fashion gods. I couldn't be any less cool if I tried.

A twinge of envy sparks up when I see how effortless it is for Villette to mingle. She's beautiful and nice, which is a rare combination. People genuinely like her. I can see it in the way they look at her.

Having grown up in an orphanage, I'm not used to social situations. Even the art gallery parties were awkward for me because I didn't have the experiences normal teenagers usually have. When I wasn't spiraling into a sleep coma with Nox, I had my nose in a book in the orphanage's library. There were no spring break trips, no weekends at the mall, and no boys to gush over. I'm basically a weirdo with zero social skills.

But Villette makes it look easy. I bet she had a great fucking upbringing. And not because her family's rich, although I'm sure that helped, but she has the aura of someone whose parents love her.

I smile and nod when Villette hands me a glass of white wine. As I curl my fingers around the stem, I notice my chipped black nail polish. Ugh. I should've touched them up before tonight. That's just another example of how ill-equipped I am for polite society.

After meeting several more groups of people equally as nice as her—rich and beautiful and also very polite—we take up a spot against the far wall next to a sleek black Mustang. It's custom-painted with shiny chrome rims and windows that are tinted so dark you can't see inside at all.

The hood is propped open to show off the car's brand-new engine. "Wow. Your brother did all this?"

Villette nods. "Yup. He's been working on cars since we were kids. Much to my father's disappointment."

The first crack in her perfect façade. Interesting. "Why? He's really talented."

She arches an eyebrow at me. "You know about cars?"

I shrug. "A little. One of the nuns at the orphanage was also a mechanic. She let me watch her work in the yard a few times." *I helped her restore an old Chevy Impala one summer, but Lettie doesn't need to know all that.*

Her eyes widen. "You are full of surprises." She waves to someone behind me. "Bones, come meet my new friend. She knows more about cars than you do." She winks at me.

My cheeks burn. "Oh, no. I don't know anything, really. Please don't tell him that."

She laughs as I feel a draft blow past me, carrying scents of cedar, motor oil, and tobacco. The man, who I assume is her brother, throws an arm around her neck and gives her a peck on the forehead. "What are you yapping on about, Lettie?"

Holy hell, he is fucking ripped. Wearing a tight white cashmere sweater with the sleeves rolled up and low-slung jeans, his knuckles bandaged with blood stains seeping through, he's a combination of sexy and dangerous. His chiseled forearms are covered in tattoos, and they don't stop there. Black and gray ink peeks out from his collarbone, traveling all the way up to his jaw. He's fucking gorgeous in a raw, unkempt way.

"Bones meet Mia. Mia, Bones. She just moved into Harker mansion. So be nice, big brother."

My breath hitches when he turns to face me. His eyes... there's something about them. His gaze is intense—alluring and haunting. I feel like my insides curdle, melting, as he stares back at me.

"Nice to meet you." His tone is flat and cold. He gives Villette another quick peck on the forehead. "I gotta go take care of something. Enjoy the party, little sister. And stay out of trouble. You tell me if anyone here fucks with you."

She rolls her eyes. "Everyone knows I'm your sister. They'll only fuck with me if they have a death wish."

He looks away, avoiding looking at both of us. "That's because they're smart."

She playfully punches him in the arm. "*No*. It's because you're *you*."

Bones flashes her a wicked grin before ambling off without another word or glance back. Fuck. He has zero warmth toward me. *Maybe that Draven guy has already told everyone not to be friends with me. Could one person really hold that much power over a town?*

"Don't worry about Bones. He warms up once you get to know him better. Sorry if he seems rude. That's just his schtick." Her eyes sparkle with obvious love and admiration for her brother.

I shake my head. "No worries. I'm the newbie here. He probably just doesn't want to make his girlfriend jealous." *Okay, so now I'm fishing? I'm such a hot mess.*

Villette almost spits out her drink. She chokes back a sip of chardonnay, wiping her mouth with her sleeve as some of it drips out. "Bones has *never* had a girlfriend. All he cares about are his friends and this shop." She laughs. "Fuck, that was funny. My parents would sell their souls to see him settle down, but they gave up on that years ago. My oldest brother, Felix, finally met someone, so that is keeping them occupied."

I nod, even more embarrassed than I was to begin with. "Gotcha. So he's just a dick then?" I tease.

"Pretty much."

We both laugh at that, but I can't shake the feeling that I know him from somewhere. His brown eyes and long black lashes... I've seen them before. He was probably at Duff's the other night. That's the only other place I've been since I arrived in this strange town.

Villette excuses herself to go to the restroom after profusely promising to be right back. She's too sweet for her own good. I assure her that I'm a big girl and can handle a few minutes of being by myself.

I'm admiring the Mustang's engine when another beautiful man catches my eye. Fuck. Now this one, I know for sure. *Aries fucking Thorn.* Of course, he'd be at this party. With his designer suit and million-dollar smile, he's the type of guy who parties were designed for.

I'm a little tipsy and sleep-deprived. But I don't have time to talk myself out of it because I'm already charging toward him before I can think any other rational thoughts.

"Taking a little break from harassing helpless women? Or are you trying to get her to sell her house to you too?" I snarl.

The pretty blonde girl he's talking to snorts into her drink before scampering off.

Aries widens his stance, a show of dominance, as he flashes me a wicked grin. "You're far from helpless. Or so I'm told."

I know it was him who sent the masked intruder, but hearing him allude to it, pretty much admitting guilt, fires me up. "You assholes are out of control. You can't just break into someone's house in the middle of the night and expect to get away with it."

Aries licks his lips and bridges the short gap between us. He towers over me, his blue-green eyes sparkling with charm and malice. "Be careful, Mia. I don't like threats."

I take a step toward him, forcing him to inch back. "Neither do I."

We glare at each other in a way where I don't know if I want to slap him or fuck him. He's beautiful and hot as fuck. But the way he looks at me… he's more dangerous than the one he sent to scare me. He's too controlled. Too fucking cold for my blood.

He hovers his mouth over my ear. "Just sign the papers, Mia. Then maybe we can be friends. I'd love to share another bottle of expensive wine with you."

I'm fucking fuming. "You can't threaten me and flirt with me at the same time, asshole. That's like... like not okay." My cheeks are burning.

He chuckles. "You're flustered. Your pussy must be so confused right now. I bet my cock can get her to relax," he whispers in my ear.

I gasp. *The fucking arrogance of this man.* Without thinking, I step back and throw the last few sips of chardonnay at his face.

His eyes darken like he wants to murder me. He grabs my wrist, and the empty glass goes crashing to the ground. Luckily, the music is so loud only a few people hear it break on the cement. I look around to see the few witnesses turn away. No one fucks with Aries Thorn, apparently. Even if he's manhandling a woman half his size. Good to know. Fuck.

"You wanna play rough with me behind closed doors? Well, I'm game, little lamb. But don't you ever embarrass me in public like that again." The tone of his voice sends a chill up my spine.

"Get your hand off me, and stay the fuck away from my house," I bite back. I cannot let this man start to think he has any power over me.

"What is going on here?" Villette cries. "Aries, let my friend go, please."

He drops my wrist immediately and steps away, slipping his mask back into place with a charming, albeit fake, smile for my beautiful host. "She stumbled, and her drink spilled. I was just holding her up. Isn't that right?"

I shoot daggers at him before turning to Villette. "I didn't fall. I threw a drink in his face because he's an asshole who's been harassing me for a week to sell my property."

Aries rolls his eyes and lets out a deep, dramatic sigh. "It's not harassment, it's business. Your new friend here is confused."

Villette's mouth drops open. "Are you fucking for real, Ries? Is this what you all have been whispering about since I got back?"

"Lower your voice, Lettie," Aries cautions.

"Don't tell her what to do," I snap a little too loudly.

He steps toward me again, his eyes murderous. "This is not your town, little lamb. And we are not your people. So sign the papers, take the money, and get the fuck out."

"Aries Thorn, how dare you?" Villette yells. "I know your mother did not raise you to be a heathen. Apologize right now."

From behind him, I see Bones charging toward us, his jaw clenched. "Que chingados esta pasando?"

"What the fuck is going on is that Aries is harassing my new friend," Villette huffs out.

He sighs and gives Aries a death stare. "Lettie, you don't understand the whole situation. It's complicated."

Her eyes widen. "Are you fucking kidding me? You're a part of this too? I should've known."

While I'm grateful to Lettie for sticking up to her brother and his friend for me, the realization of why he looks so familiar hits me like a ton of bricks. *Oh, fuck.* My palms sweat, and my stomach knots.

"It was you." I jab my finger into his chest, cutting Lettie off.

"I don't know what you're talking about."

Oh, he knows exactly what I'm talking about. That's why he can't look at me. I reach into my purse, pull out the lock pick, and chuck it at him.

"Bones, what did you do?" Villette is shaking now.

Aries steps in between us. "Calm down, Lettie. None of this concerns you."

"I knew I'd seen your eyes before, but I couldn't place you because you were wearing a fucking ski mask," I grit out as I step back, shaking. "You-you broke into my house and…" I can't finish my sentence because I catch another familiar set of eyes on me from across the room.

I tune out the screaming match that Villette, Aries, and Bones are having to drown in my mystery man's eyes. My breath hitches as a flashback from the bathroom at Duff's resurfaces again. That night that I can't get out of my mind.

He walks toward us, and I can't breathe. He's more beautiful than I remember—tall, muscular, with black hair and golden honey-flecked eyes. His lips are thick. I never got to kiss him that night. We were too busy trying to get off as quickly as possible, determined not to know anything about each other. Convinced we'd never see one another again.

I want to run to him. To tell him what these people are doing to me. Would he help? Would he even care?

"*Mia*," Villette says in a way that sounds like she's called my name more than once.

I look back at her, breaking out of my reverie. Bones and Aries are still arguing behind her. "Who is that?" I jerk my head toward my bathroom man.

Her neck is flushed, her brow furrowed. I can tell how fast her heart is racing by the way her chest heaves between each breath. She's just as furious as I am. But I need one sliver of joy tonight. "Please, Lettie. Tell me who that guy is."

She shakes her head in frustration. "That's Draven. Draven Blackwell. If my brother and Aries are tormenting you, then the odds are that *he's* the one who put them up to it."

No.

Please, for fuck's sake, no.

The room starts to spin. My knees wobble. I take a shaky step back as my fight or flight response kicks into overdrive. How in the fuck is this happening? "I-I need to get the fuck out of here, Lettie. Like out of this fucking town."

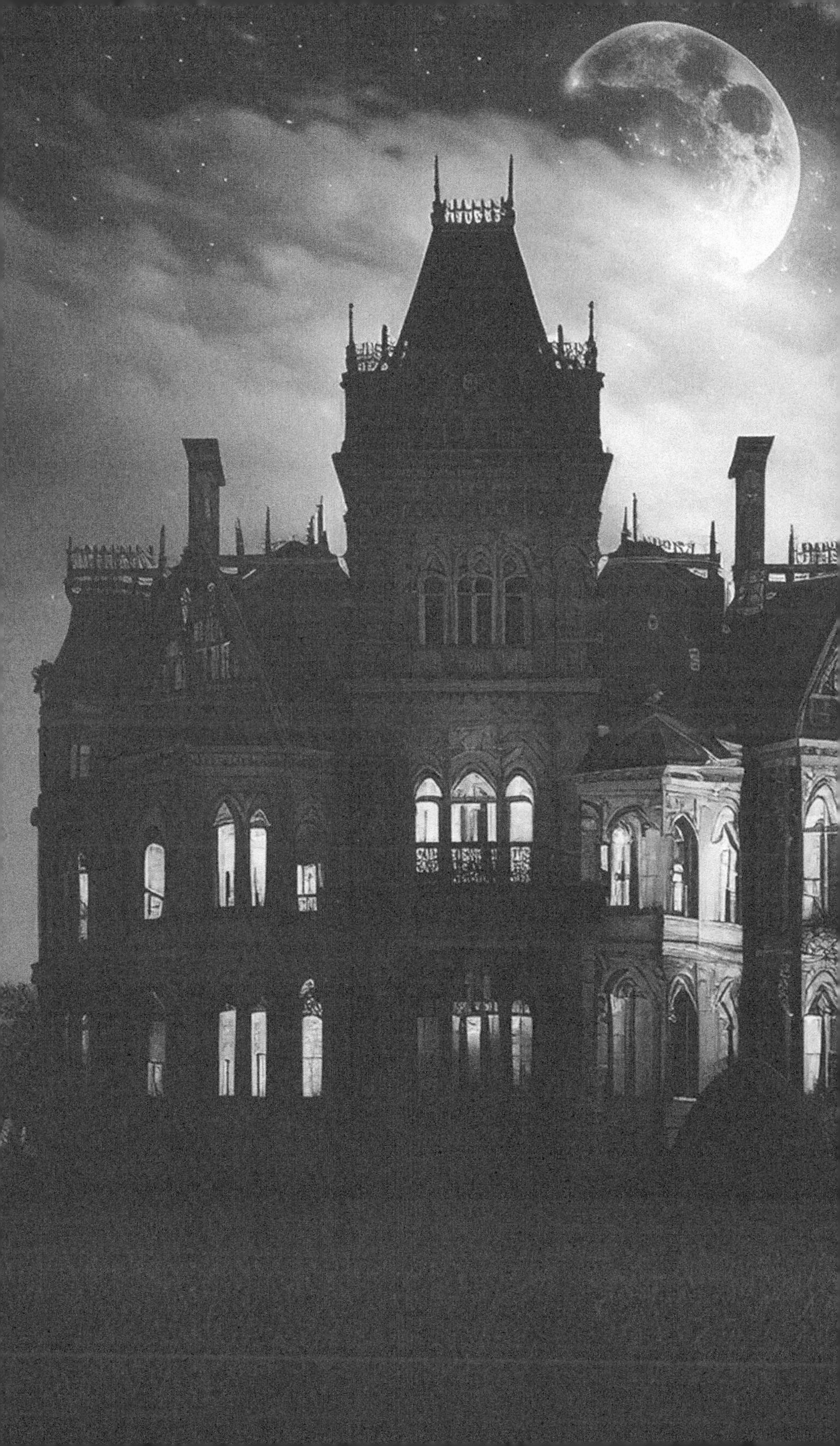

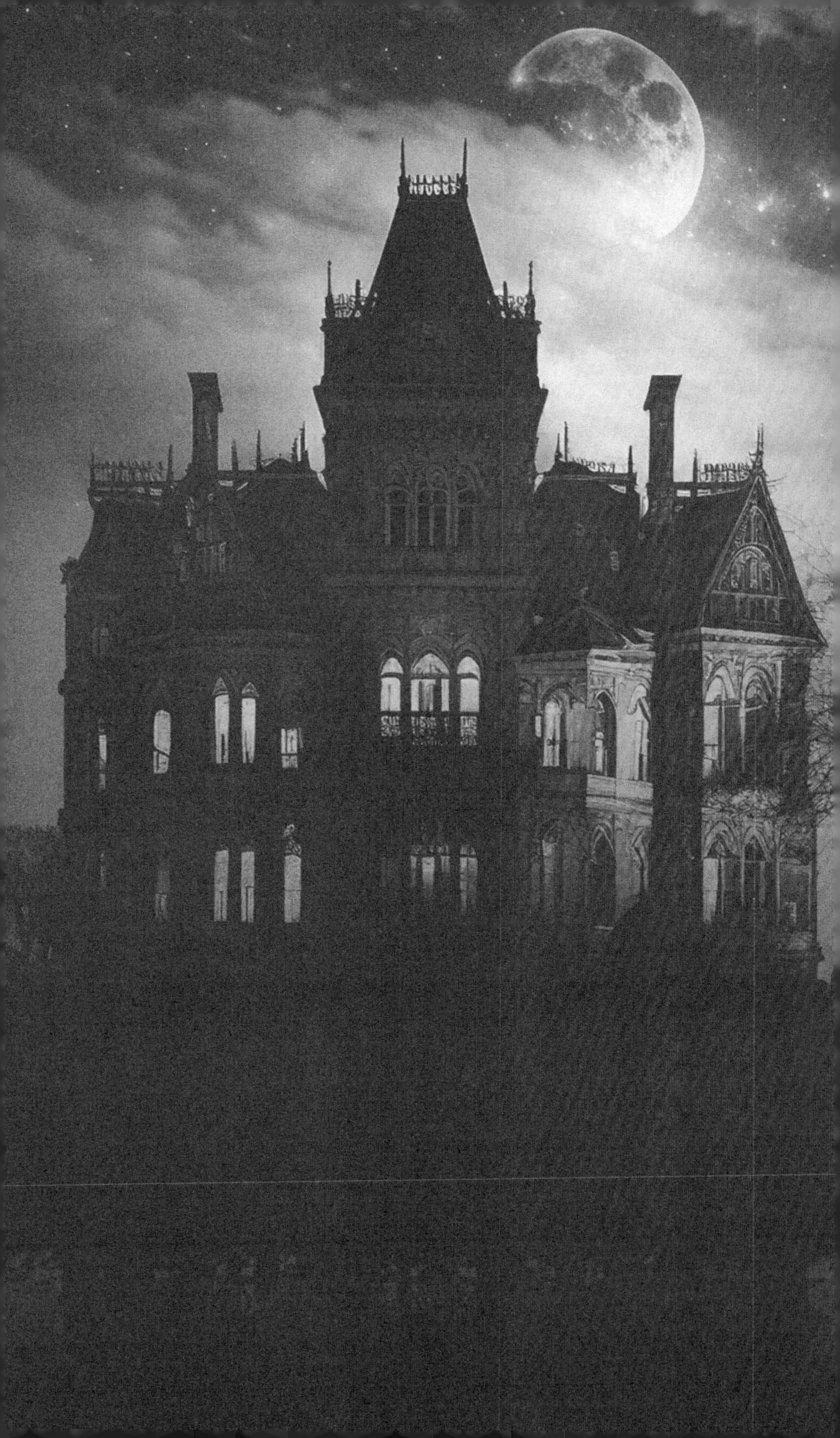

CHAPTER 8

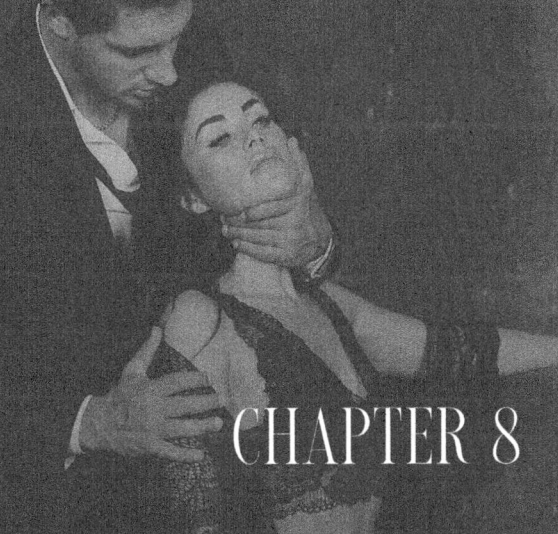

Draven

Black hair. One blue eye, one brown. It's *her*.
Fuck.
I can smell the jasmine from across the room. But why the fuck is she sandwiched between Bones and Aries in what looks like a heated debate?

I make a direct line for them, walking as fast as I can without looking desperate. *That fucking dress she has on.* Black and skintight. I'm guessing she's not wearing any panties. Just like the last time we met.

Why the fuck is she still in town? I figured she'd be long gone by now. Off to wherever she came from to recover from our autumn equinox festivities. I can't have this girl here right now. Not with all the fucking shit I have to deal with.

A storm brews inside me as we lock eyes. A tug of war between my dick and my head. The anger and rage I felt after that night sparks in my veins again. The fury of knowing that the brief time I spent inside her pussy were the only minutes of peace I've felt in years. So long that I can't even remember when the last time was.

But the closer I get to them, the more the knots in my belly twist. Something isn't right. Lettie is visibly upset. My mystery girl is, as well. Aries's shirt is wet, and Bones looks like he's about to brawl. Fucking hell.

I stop in my tracks. *No. Fucking. Way.* It can't be her. If I get any closer, then it will be. And my fantasy will be destroyed. Decimated.

It's the body language. The way she backs away from them, her eyes full of rage. A picture says a thousand words. Judging by the look that Aries tosses me, this picturesque moment has only two words that matter…

Mia Harker.

Sweet fucking hell.

I take a deep breath and flip the switch, instantly burying any lingering feelings I had for the girl who brought me peace in the bathroom at Duff's. I don't owe her anything. And I will be damned if I give up an entire legacy of poison for pussy. Even one as fucking perfect as hers.

Her mouth drops open when I approach. It looks like she's figured out who I am too.

"Well, I didn't expect to see you ever again. It seems like you really are trouble, after all, *Mia*." I can't rid the sour taste of her name from my mouth. She's been causing me nothing but grief since she moved here.

Her lips quiver as she looks up at me. "You… This was your plan all along. You think your dick is so magical that I'd just sign over everything I own to you after one night of riding it?"

Now it was my friends' turns to look shocked, their mouths agape. Aries snickers while Bones shakes his head.

I unbutton my cuffs and roll up my sleeves. I smirk as her eyes light up when she sees my ink. If my body is her weakness, then I'll fucking play that angle. "I could say the same thing about you,

Trouble. Maybe you think your pussy is so sweet that I'd just forget all about the fact that you're sitting on fifty acres of baneberry."

Her face turns bright red. "I just moved here. How the fuck was I supposed to know that *you* were the asshole sending his lackeys to harass me? You orchestrated the whole thing."

The tension between us is carnal—unnatural. I have to fight the urge to shove my fingers down her throat. "You bumped into me at the bar, remember? Pretty fucking convenient."

We both know that neither one of us knew who the other was, but I'm enjoying the fuck out of getting her riled up.

She huffs as she turns toward Lettie. "Thank you for the invite, but I'm leaving now. Please lose my number. I'm sorry, but I can't be friends with you if *they* are who you hang out with."

Oh, hell, no. Lettie is a fucking angel. I grab Mia's arm and spin her back around. "You don't get to unfriend her because *we* are forbidding *her* from hanging out with *you*."

"Dray, stop," Lettie orders. She pries my hand off Mia. "She's right. This is why I have zero female friends in this town. They're either afraid of the three of you or pissed off because you fucked them and never called them back. Let her go."

Lettie is like all of our little sister, not just Bones's. She's sweet and kind, but when she gets that tone, you don't argue. I give her a nod. "Sorry, Lettie."

I look back at Mia while I will my cock to forget what she feels like. "This conversation isn't over, Trouble."

She glares back at me with the disdain of a hundred angry demons. "It actually is. You can talk to my lawyer from now on. Have a nice life, *Slick*. Or don't, actually. I hope you have a miserable fucking life."

I watch her walk away, my stomach twisting with each shake of her hips as she stomps out of the garage. But I can still smell that fucking scent of jasmine in the place where she just stood. My lungs burn from it.

"Everyone upstairs. Now. Except you, Lettie," I rasp. Now that I know who Mia Harker truly is, the rules are about to change.

Bones could live anywhere he wants—the country estate his parents gave him on his twenty-first birthday five years ago, Aries's house, my house—but he loves this fucking garage. So much so that he built himself a loft above it. I personally don't know how he can sleep with the smell of gasoline and tar constantly hanging in the air. But then again, Bones has a lot going on in his head.

Sometimes I think the smells and the sounds of bikes and old cars keep him grounded. Focused. Otherwise, he'll slip back into old habits. Bad fucking habits that almost cost him his life once. I can't watch his family go through that again. *I* can't go through that again.

We gather around Bones's poker table, the only actual table in here. His loft is a true bachelor pad, complete with a wet bar, weight set, and a flat-screen TV that takes up an entire wall. My tastes are more refined or, as Bones would say, *uptight*. But nothing compares to the pristine, so-clean-you-can-eat-off-the-floors house that Aries resides in.

"You fucked her?" Bones growls.

I pinch the spot between my brows in an attempt to stifle the migraine that's forming. "I didn't know who she was that night. We agreed on no names. She was just some slut I fucked in the bathroom."

Aries snorts. "Apparently not. I think it's only fair that Bones and I get to fuck her too."

The absurdity that comes out of his mouth sometimes. "Yeah, she looked really interested in both of you tonight," I quip.

Bones lights a cigarette and takes a deep drag as he glares at me. "When I had her pinned on the table… her panties were soaking wet. Like she was enjoying it."

Aries leans back and unbuttons the top two of his shirt. "You didn't tell me that part. You broke in wearing a ski mask... *Fuck.* Sounds like our little lamb has a dark side."

"She's had the devil attached to her since she was born," I snap. "Dark side doesn't even begin to cover it."

Bones huffs. "I don't give a fuck. The darker, the fucking better."

My head is about to explode. "Calm your fucking dicks. Both of you. No cute pet names and no deviant fantasies. We just need her to sign the papers and move out."

Bones arches an eyebrow at me. "That's it. That's what we're doing wrong. Instead of trying to scare her into signing—"

"We make her cum so hard she'll do just about anything for us," Aries interjects.

Fuck me. I cannot be around Mia Harker without feeling anything but pure fucking rage. But maybe they have a point. "Do whatever you have to do to get this done. But don't kid yourself into thinking she's going to spread her legs for you now."

Bones and Aries exchange a devious grin. "We'll see about that."

"Why is your shirt wet?" I ask.

Aries rolls his eyes. "She threw a drink in my face."

Bones chuckles. "She's not as timid as she looks. She might be more of a wolf than a lamb."

I pound my fists on the table, sending a stack of poker chips crashing to the floor. "I don't give a fuck if she's little red fucking riding hood. If she doesn't sign by the end of next week, I'm going to kill her."

Bones gives me a nod. "I'm on it."

"We'll get her to sign, Dray. If not, we'll be right there next to you when she takes her last breath," Aries adds.

I fly out of the chair and storm from the room without another word. I rip off my tie on the way to my SUV, wishing I hadn't given Rodrick the night off. But as pretentious as I can be, pulling up to a party in a limousine isn't my style.

I stuff the tie in my jacket pocket and blast the AC. Sweat clings to my body like a disease. The migraine has now taken a full assault on my brain, and I'm close to vomiting. Fuck. I close my eyes and listen to the hum of the engine, knowing full well that there's only one cure for this panic attack. I hate that it's her.

"Fuck," I yell as I slam my palms against the steering wheel. "Fuck this," I mutter to myself.

I throw the car in reverse and peel out of Bones's driveway. As soon as I hit the main road, I put it in drive and floor it. With all the windows down, the cold wind whips through the SUV. But it does nothing to calm the inferno in my chest.

I run my hand through my hair, pushing it back from my forehead as the filth rotting in my gut twists tighter, making it harder to breathe. I hate that her house is on the way to mine. Fuck.

I can't fucking take this anymore. I slam on the brakes as I pass Harker Mansion and shift back into reverse at full speed. I fly all the way past it and then shift forward and punch on the gas. This stubborn fucking girl is making me lose my goddamn mind.

I don't let up on the gas but, instead, push the pedal down farther. I'm crazed, wild, the most unhinged I've been in a long time as I crash through her iron gates going thirty miles per hour.

BOOM.

My entire body jolts forward on impact, nearly throwing me through the windshield. "Oh, fuck!" My head bounces back against the seat, making my migraine from earlier seem like a wet dream. I glimpse pieces of iron flying through the air as my tires spin, pulling the entire vehicle into donut circles around the front yard.

It only makes my anger grow hotter, deadlier, as I scramble to right the SUV. The side of my head meets the inside of the car door with a whack, and stars blur my vision. But I don't stop.

I grunt and finally get the tires straight and under my control, but I'm still plowing down her front drive at about twenty miles an hour.

I see her now, watching my destruction from the safety of her porch. *Safe.* I snicker. I'm going to give her back the hell she's given me. My heart caves in on itself. The darkness pulsing through my veins sparks like a fucking meteor shower. *I can drive up the steps and keep going if I want to. Plow right into her. Who will fucking stop me?*

Our eyes lock through the glare of the headlights. She doesn't flinch, steadfast in her position on the porch. Her brown eye darkens while the blue one glows like a firefly caught in a mason jar.

She's barefoot and barely clad in a thin white cotton dress. I slam on the brakes just inches away from her. And she still doesn't move a fucking muscle. But the rage in her eyes… well, she looks how I fucking feel. *Murderous.*

As she takes a step toward my wrecked SUV, the sky cracks with lightning, like the devil himself is shaking his fist at me. Rain pours down in buckets, soaking her and everything around us. She glares at me, her chest heaving from the cold and her rage.

I have to jam my shoulder hard against the driver's door to get it open. I stumble out and almost slip in the mud. The rain drips down my face and through my lips. The acrid taste of metal mixes with the rainwater and fills my mouth. *Blood.* Fuck. I hit my head so many times, now I'm pissed and deranged.

She's shaking, her fists clenched at her sides. "What the actual fuck is wrong with you?" she screams.

I take another fumbling step, not sure what I'm going to do or say when I actually reach her. But I've come too far now.

"You're crazy. Look at what you did to my gates. Look at your car, for fuck's sake. Don't take another step closer, asshole." Her bottom lip quivers, but she makes no attempt to retreat.

I keep going, stalking toward her, hell-bent on unleashing every evil thing inside me. I picture my hands around her throat, squeezing the life out of her. But the closer I get, the more the ache in my chest burns. Her dress is soaked through, revealing the shape of her body, her hard nipples, and the sweet fucking slit of her pussy.

"*You* are what's wrong with me." I slide my hand around her throat, but I don't squeeze.

She gazes up at me, her long lashes wet. "Why are you here, Draven?"

"You pissed me off. So I wanted to return the favor." My heart races at the feel of her pulse throbbing against my fingers, beating as fast as mine.

"You can't just show up here whenever you want and destroy my property. We're a bit old for temper tantrums," she snaps.

Who does this woman think she is? Insulting me, driving me mad with lust and rage. "Like the one you just had at Bones's party?" I tighten my grip on her neck and almost lose it over the way her throat bobs.

She latches her hand onto my wrist. "Seriously? I threw a drink. You drove through my front fucking gates."

My breath hitches as she strikes another nerve inside my chest. We shouldn't be allowed to touch each other. Not like this. "Because you infuriate me, Mia," I scream in her face.

A devious smirk pulls at the corners of her lips. "Good," she yells back. "Because ever since I heard the name *Draven Blackwell*, all I want to do is bang my head against a wall. I wish I'd never come here."

I don't like my name in her mouth. It sounds too familiar, too comfortable. Like she isn't a stranger I fucked in a bathroom but a piece of something holy that I don't have the right to touch.

The rain is coming down harder, numbing my fingers and lips. But all I can think about is this villainous creature in front of me driving me mad. "And ever since you came to town, my life has been hell. You have no idea the evil that lives inside me, Mia. The things I want to do…"

She sucks in a sharp breath. "I think you're a coward."

"Mia," I warn her. I'm so close to the edge.

She arches her back, tilting her head up to look deeper into my eyes. "You sent Aries to try to get me drunk. When that didn't work, you sent Bones to scare me. But all it did was make me wet."

The thick rot that lives in my veins is churning, tempting me to lose control with every torturous word out of her mouth. I squeeze her throat harder. "Watch your fucking tongue."

She grins like the devil. "And now *you* show up, acting like a child who wants to break all his toys. You're pathetic."

"Shut. Your. Fucking. Mouth," I grit out.

"Or what? You gonna kill me, Draven?" Her chest is heaving out of control. We're both trembling, freezing in this storm that seems to rage only for us.

I look down at her body. Her dress is useless, plastered to her skin like wet paper. And mine wants hers so fucking bad. My soul wants to relive that sliver of peace again. Even as her very existence is the catalyst for my madness.

I don't want to kill her. Not tonight. Not yet. Fuck. I let go of her throat and inch my hand down her chest. "You're going to freeze to death, and that's not how I want you to die."

"You're a psycho," she fires back.

It's the ache in her voice that breaks me. I swoop her up and carry her inside.

"Wait, what are you doing?" She pushes against me, trying to wrangle free.

I set her down in front of the fireplace and start taking off my clothes. "I'm going to hate fuck you until I get you out of my system. Because I swear to the ravens if I have to hold my breath every time I get a whiff of jasmine, I'm going to check *myself* into an asylum."

Her eyes darken, even the blue one this time. "Charming as ever."

I notice how her pupils dilate when I slide off my pants and boxers. She can't take her eyes off my cock. "Don't fucking act like you don't want the same thing."

She licks her lips before finally lifting her gaze back up to mine. "But I hate you, Slick."

I nod as I step toward her and rip her dress off in one swift move. "Yeah, I fucking hate you too, Trouble. I hate that we're going to make each other cum so hard that we forget that part."

Before she can utter another traitorous word, I thrust my tongue into her mouth.

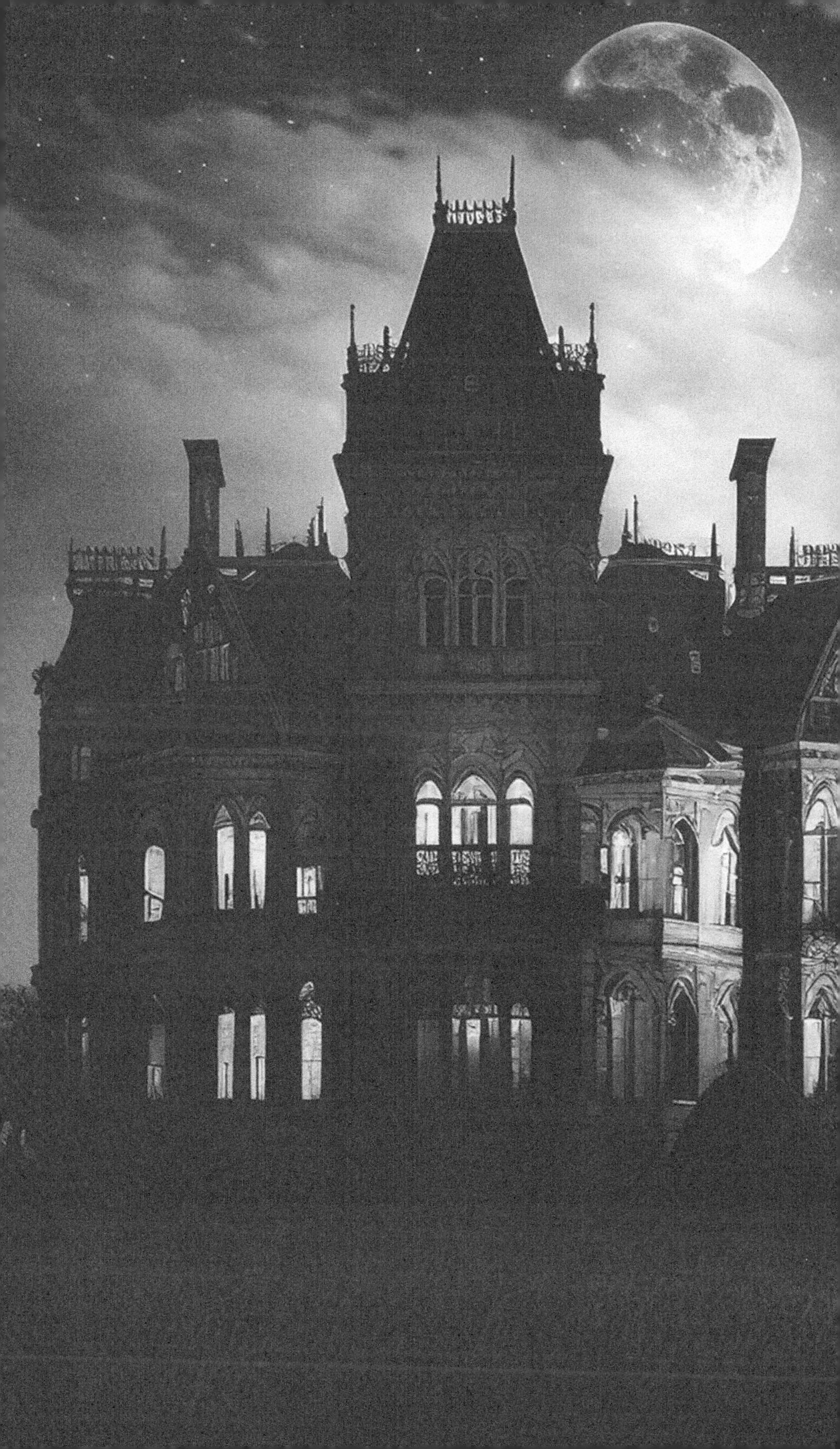

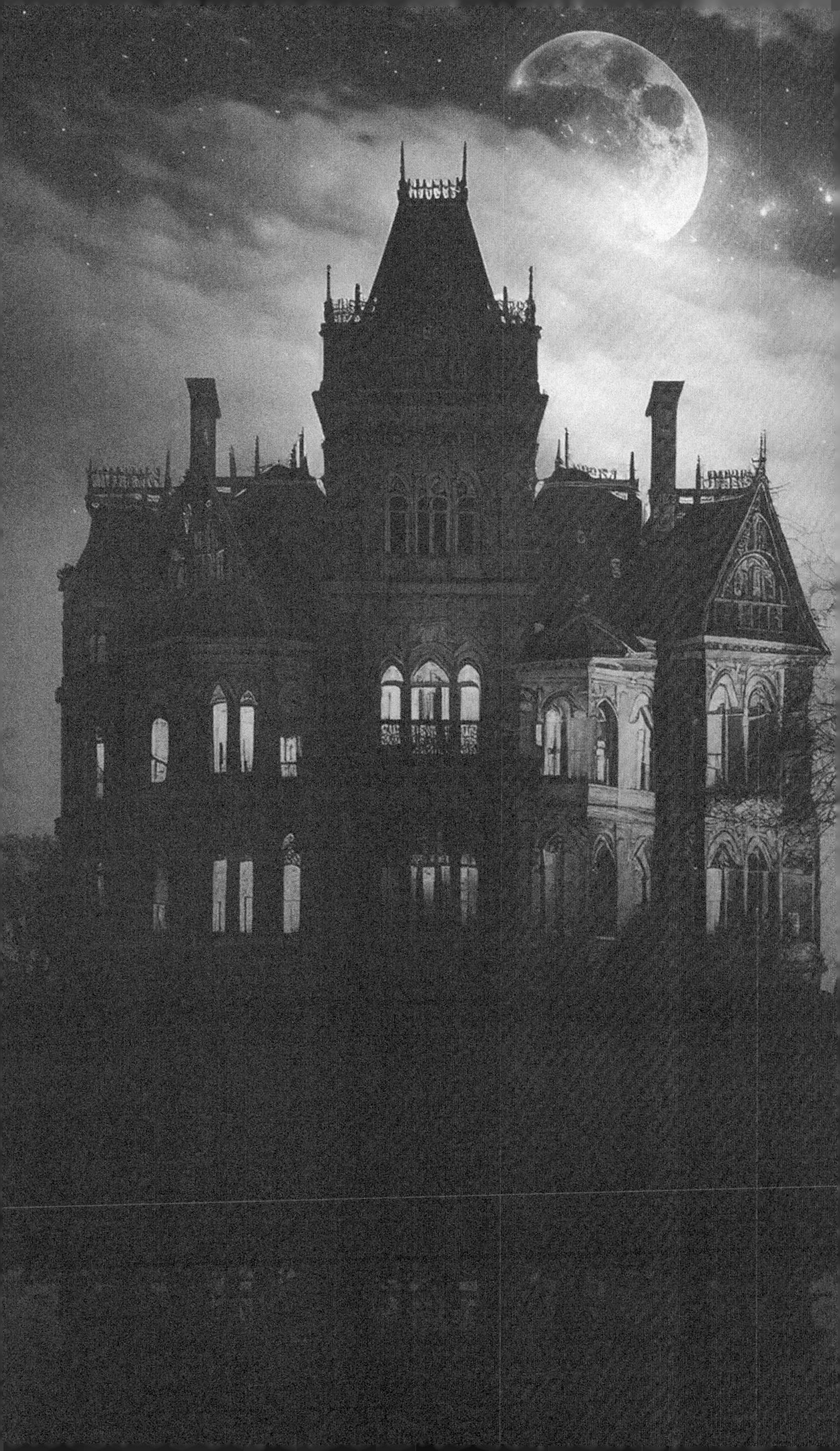

CHAPTER 9

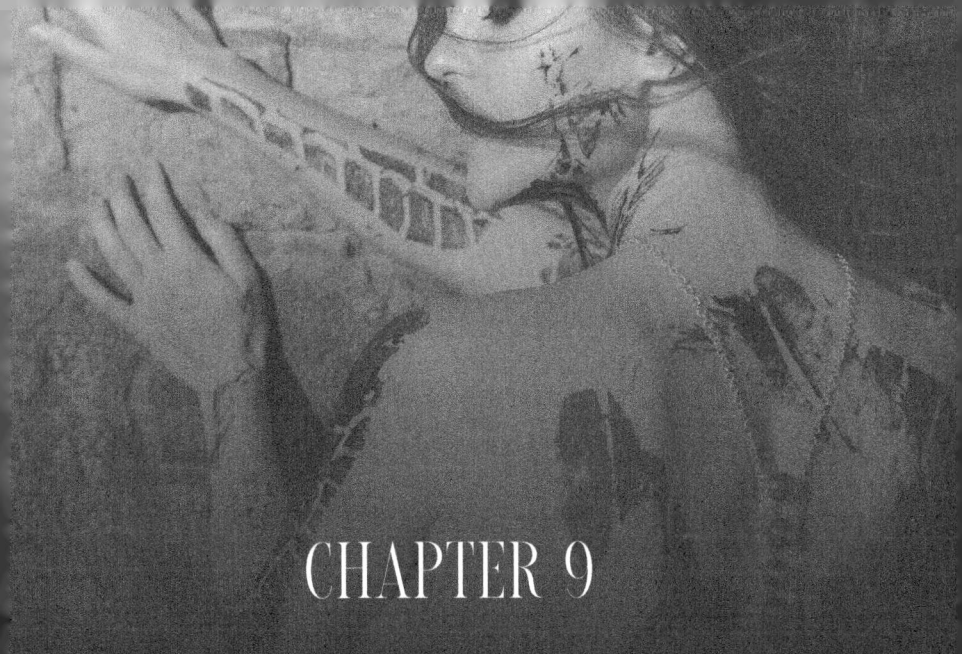

Mia

I'M CRASHING, SPIRALING, BREAKING APART LIKE TWISTED METAL. Destroyed like the iron gates Draven plowed through. His tongue is violent and bitter in my mouth. His hands are all over me, his cold fingers sending sparks across my frozen flesh. The heat sets fire to the numbness. Everything hurts. Everything is ecstasy. And the only air I can suck down into my lungs is his breath.

He yanks my head back and snarls as he rakes his teeth down my neck. "Get on your knees. I want you to fucking bow to me."

The way this man thinks he can order me around is disturbing. I pull back and hiss. "Go fuck yourself, Draven."

He growls, his eyes glowing, as he comes for me again. In one quick swoop he flips me around so that my back is at his chest. "You are going to do at least one fucking thing I tell you to do."

Before I can utter another hateful word, he slips two fingers inside my pussy. My breath lodges in my throat, and I have to bite back a moan. Fuck, he's too good at touching me. It's not fair. It's not fucking right.

"Yeah." He breathes heavily in my ear. "I hate you so fucking much. I loathe what you have done to me. Now get on your fucking knees."

With trembling legs, and his fingers still inside me, guiding me forward, I lower myself to the fur rug that's splayed out in front of the fireplace. Every inch of my body is revolting against my mind. It's like I no longer have control over it. He does.

He walks around and stands in front of me, his swollen cock just inches away from my face. *From my lips.*

He shoves those same two fingers in my mouth. I release a deep moan when I taste myself on his skin. But I have to stop this. I'm losing myself to his melancholy.

I stand up and back away. Even though my pussy is aching. Even though my nipples are stiff and hard and begging for a lashing from his tongue. "I will *not* bow to you. Not tonight. Not ever."

His nostrils flare as he charges toward me. Before I can react, he pushes me against the wall, pinning me to it. "Fine… then I'll bow to you."

Wait. What?

He kneels in front of me and tosses my leg over his shoulder. "Draven, what are you—oh, fuck."

I jerk back as he thrusts his tongue inside my pussy. I thread my fingers through his black hair as he explores the deepest parts of my core. It's agonizing and brutal and so fucking hot. The way he rolls his tongue over my clit then darts back inside. Up and down. In and out. Like a fucking melody that I can't hear but feel the vibrations.

I cry out and clench around him as he digs his fingers into my thighs. As he lashes his tongue harder with the fury of a man who wants to consume me and destroy me at the same time. To annihilate me until there's nothing left.

I shriek as a surge of flutters spread from my center to deep down inside my cunt. "Draven… fuck." I close my eyes and surrender to it. It's an explosion in my body. A storm that takes out everything in its path. My throat burns as I scream from a place in my belly so deep and guttural I scare myself.

He growls inside my pussy, tormenting me over and over again with his tongue, scraping my tender flesh with his sharp teeth as he sucks and bites and laps up my juices. We are rocking against each other, my back slamming against the wall with every brutal lick. I ride his face until I am spent, my limbs turning to mush.

"You even taste like jasmine," he rasps as he picks me up and lays me down in front of the fire.

I am weak with him. Too weak to shut him out. I spread my legs for him as he glares down at me. "Come, get your peace. I know that's what you want."

His eyes are so dark, I can't see the gold flecks. I can't discern the size of his pupils. He's lust-drunk, desperate with need, and hungry for his release.

He presses my thighs back, pinning them to the floor as he edges my entrance with the tip of his cock. "This troublesome fucking pussy... Fuck. Mmm." He closes his eyes, his breath hitching as he enters me.

We both gasp when he's halfway inside. "Oh my god," I say on a deep breath. The night at Duff's flashes in my mind, reminding me how good he felt inside me. But somehow, tonight it's hotter than I remember. *How the fuck does this man's cock keep getting better?*

"This is the last time, Mia. After tonight, we're done." *Thrust.* "I want... nothing"—*thrust*—"to do with... you." *Thrust.* "Fuck."

I whimper as he slides so fucking deep inside me. "I don't want to know you either," I whine.

He fucks me slowly. Our eyes dart back and forth between each other's gazes and the sight of his engorged cock sloshing in and out of my sopping wet pussy. This is blasphemy. Sick and beautiful blasphemy.

I cry out as he hits my sensitive G-Spot. He grunts as he presses on it, pleased with the way it unravels me. "I hate how good that fucking feels."

He snickers as he continues to swivel his hips, taunting me with another orgasm. "And I hate how I don't want to fuck anyone else like *this*. I hate you the most for that."

There are no more kisses, no touching, just pure penetration. And it's orgasmic in itself. Every nerve ending from my clit to deep inside my pussy's core is tingling with enough sparks to start an electrical fire.

It's a quiet rage. A slow and brutal loathing that roots itself deeper with every thrust. An unearthly tremor jolts me. I pump my hips. "Oh, fuck, I'm…" I can't finish my sentence. I can't even think. I clutch my throat as a gurgled cry escapes from it.

He growls and bares his teeth as he plays my body like a violin, strumming his cock in and out while I cum all over it.

"This is the debt we're owed. *Fuck*. Yeah, just like that, Trouble. Cum hard for me. Cum like you will never cum again." He rides me harder, faster, as I scream and claw at his arms. And it feels like an exquisite death.

"*Ahhh*," he moans into the space between us. He grinds down hard just as his hot, thick cream bursts out. I'm stuffed to the hilt, full of his essence and throbbing cock. We scream like animals. Like two psychos casting demonic shadows in between the reflections of the flames.

He fills me with darkness and fire and death. The space around us becomes a sea of crackling flames, hysterical breath, and the smack of skin against skin. And I don't want it to stop. When it ends, all we'll be left with is the violence. When the pleasure is over, the pain of who we are to each other is all that will remain.

We lock eyes as the last of our explosion sputters out. He stills himself inside me. "No more."

His bitterness consumes me like a drug. "Did it work? Did you hate fuck me out of your system?" *If his answer is yes, then maybe that means he's out of my system too.*

He slowly pulls his cock from my pussy but doesn't move to get up. "I will double my offer again. The next time I come back here, it will be to collect that signature from you."

A cold fury snakes its way back into my veins. I feel like his whore right now. "Well, you know what they say. The pen *is* mightier than the sword." I look down at his dick as I say it.

He springs forward and pins my arms over my head. "Maybe I'll fuck you with that pen, Mia. Over and over again until you're so broken, you beg me to sign the papers for you as a proxy. Do not underestimate my crazy. You have no fucking idea who I really am."

And I'm fucking wet again. Fucking bastard. It's the devil in me… "How did you know I was in an asylum? That's confidential."

He snickers and sits back up. "I know everything about you, Mia. Even what you dream about. *Everything.*"

I lie there dumbfounded as he quickly dresses and slicks his hair back off his face. "You have until the end of the week to sell me this property, or I will bury you underneath it."

Fuck.

He just threatened my life. Right after fucking me. But all I can focus on is…

He knows about Nox.

I let myself fall. Two days awake and look at all the destruction I've caused… I deserve sleep. And Nox deserves an answer…

When I open my eyes, I'm stretched out on the bed, naked, my wrists bound to its posts. Nox's long black tail slithers around my thighs. It's rough with deep ridges and skin like cracked leather that only add to its thickness.

"You have been a naughty little girl, haven't you?" His voice rumbles low, prickling the hairs on my arms.

"I have." Tears stream down my cheeks.

He licks them off, the two sides of his tongue splitting down the middle. "Shh, relax, dark one. You know what has to happen now."

I nod and spread my legs apart for him. Shame fills me because the filthy things he does to me turn me on.

"Yes, you know I'm going to defile you. I'm going to remind you of our promises. Just like before when that idiot you almost married played with your pussy." He slinks his tail higher up my leg. "You fucked someone up there, so now I'm owed penance."

I nod, my body shaking as the tip of his tail nips at my entrance. "I will give you whatever you want."

He circles my nipples with his pointy claws. "Mmm." He slides his hands down my breasts, across my belly, and stops at the apex of my thighs. "Do you know what's going to happen?"

I can't stop shaking. It's wrong and dirty. *Unholy.* "You're going to fuck me with… *him.*" My juices drip down my thighs.

He licks those too. "You're going to lay with him inside you all night."

I gasp as he pulls back the lips of my pussy and watch as the tip of his tail slithers inside my pussy. I cry out as its girth stretches me. It scratches at my walls, rubbing me raw as it burrows itself deep.

Nox moans. "Oh yeah, that feels naughty. Mmm."

He confessed to me once that his tail is even more sensitive than his cock. That he would rather fuck me that way.

I breathe deeply as I try to adjust to its thickness. "Nox…"

He leans over me, his hands on my belly. "Yes, call out my name." His eyes are bright red, glazing with a carnal lust so demonic he personifies sin itself.

I try to fight the sensations, afraid of what it means if I take pleasure from this. But I can only resist it for so long. He winds in deeper, filling me so full I can barely breathe. It feels like it may explode out my back.

He spreads my pussy open wider with his clawed fingers. "Only your juices can quench my thirst."

I can't bite back the moan any longer. I set it free from my throat. It pleases him so much that he spins the length of his tail in circles. I lose possession of my body, my back arching from the pressure, my hips grinding, rolling from the stretch.

"That's my beautiful dark one. Swallow me whole. Take every part of me like a good girl." He tickles my clit with the tip of his claw. "This is how you repent."

I think my soul may leave my body this time.

With one more rough thrust, he shatters me, and I fall apart. I break, soaking his thick tail with my cream as I cum so hard my vision blurs. I scream as he rips me apart. It hurts so fucking good. It shouldn't, but it does.

He fists his two-headed cock as I climax, stroking it furiously as he watches what his tail has done to me. *What he has done to me.*

"You're almost redeemed, dark one… *almost.*"

His tail retreats, whipping back without warning.

The nerves in my tender flesh burn and sting. I pull at my restraints, desperate to get free, but it only makes them tighter.

He mounts me and spreads my thighs farther apart. My chest heaves with ache and need. A tug of war between my rational mind and my corrupted soul. I let out another deep moan as he thrusts one head of his cock inside my pussy. The other head suctions itself over my swollen clit.

Nox's eyes roll back in his head, his red pupils gone, leaving only a sea of black in their stead. "Ohhh, my little dark one," he rasps, his lips trembling. "*I am yours.*"

I'm stuffed full, cumming hard again as he penetrates me. He commands every inch of me, every spasm, every fucking sensation that stimulates and assaults me.

Our screams become one, morphing into one another as he unleashes his thick cum inside me. I grind against him, inviting him in deeper. It's toxic and unhealthy and masochistic, like a drug. Like a disease I've convinced myself I deserve. But it feels so fucking good.

When he finishes, it feels like a hangover. I whine as he leaves my body. And that satisfies him even more. He gazes down at me, his eyes glowing red. "You can fuck whoever you choose to, Mia. But you still belong to me."

I don't know what it's like to not belong to him. Our existence is tied. "I know, Nox. Don't be angry with me."

"It's agony to be away from you. It's infuriating. I want to be free from here. I want to lie with you in your bed. The power is in your hands. Why won't you use it?"

My stomach knots. I've driven myself crazy trying to justify his request. If I bring him to life, he'll consume me twenty-four-seven. If I leave him here, he'll torment me every time I go to sleep up there.

And I know nothing of where he comes from, why he's attached himself to me, or what he'll do to me if I let him out of this cage. He won't tell me anything.

"You know I can't do that until you tell me who you really are," I murmur quietly, not wanting to upset him again. Although, I wouldn't be entirely upset if that tail of his was back inside me. I'm a glutton for punishment.

He curses and leaps off the bed. "I am darkness, Mia. That is all I know. I've told you this." It doesn't take long for him to release me from my restraints. With just a quick slice of his claws, my ropes fall away.

I sit up and rub my wrists. "You don't belong in my world. Fuck, I don't belong in here."

He smooths his black hair up into a topknot in between his horns. "Do you wish to never see me again then? Am I really such a thorn in your side?"

That familiar guilt sloshes through my veins. "No, that's not what I meant. It's just that… if I do what you ask, it could cause chaos. I need more time to figure it out."

His face softens as he lies down next to me on the bed. He caresses my face, his claws retracted now. I love both his sharp points and his gentle fingers. "I need you, Mia. My heart breaks every time you leave."

I curl up next to him and sigh as he drapes a possessive arm around me. Nox is a nightmare. My nightmare. He's a part of my shadow self. I need to know more before I do something I can't take back. "I'm tired, Nox."

He leaves a trail of kisses across my back and shoulders. "Shh, rest. We will figure this out next time."

His words coax me to sleep, pushing me into a dreamless abyss. He wraps himself around me like a cocoon as I try to let my mind drift into nothingness. It's the only peace I get in between worlds.

But tonight is different. Because I know when I wake up on the other side, I have to deal with three more nightmares. Monsters who get to walk around as free as ravens. My heart races as I try to prolong my sleep, willing it to stretch out for as long as possible.

But when I finally give up the fight and surrender, it's not Nox that's on my mind. It's Bones Crane, Aries Thorn, and Draven Blackwell. Their faces are the last ones I see before I pass out.

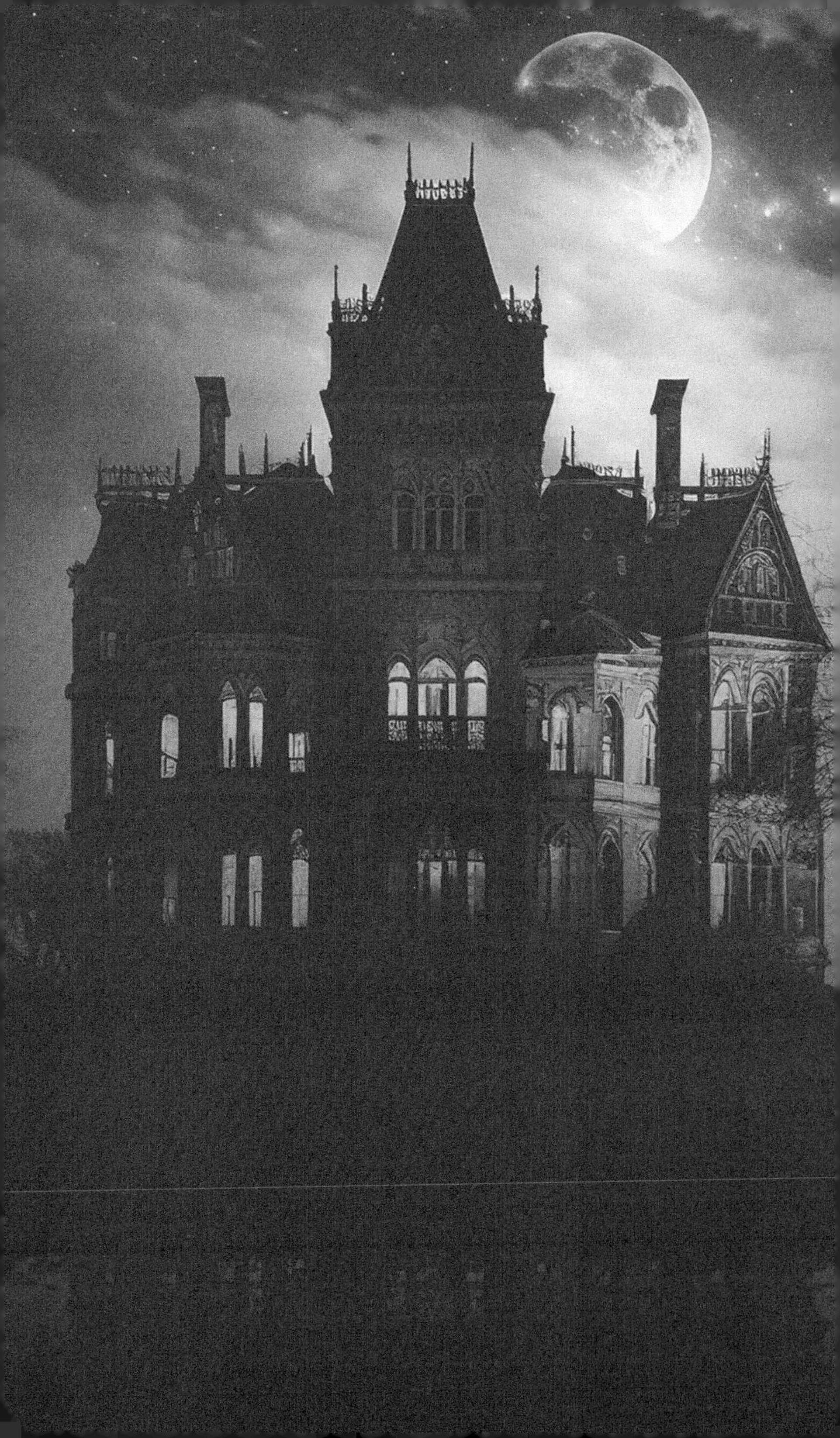

CHAPTER 10

Bones

"Why are you getting involved in Draven's mess again?" Lettie has always been the best of our family. With Felix and I for brothers, it's a miracle that she's as pure and sweet as she is. But that also makes it very difficult for her to understand how I live my life.

Of course, she'd corner me when I'm lying flat on my back underneath a lifted car. "This coming from the girl who just watched her other brother join a cult. That's really rich, Lettie. Were you this annoying with Felix too?"

All I can see are her ballet flats pacing around the car. "Oh, I gave him hell too. Don't worry about that. But at least he's doing it for love. You, on the other hand, are being destructive for no reason as usual."

You have one weak moment, and now every time you have a bad day, everyone thinks you're going to off yourself.

"I'm doing it for friendship. Which is stronger than love. Plus, it's business. It's nothing for you to worry about."

Suddenly, her face is in mine as she drops down to her knees. "*Van Bones Crane*, you broke into that girl's house wearing a ski mask like a criminal. That is not how Papa taught us to do business. Those friends of yours are going to get you into more trouble than we can get you out of this time."

I hate when she calls me by my full name. It reminds me of my mother scolding me as a child. I'm a grown man, and those three words reduce me back to pre-pubescence. Especially coming from my baby sister.

I sigh and roll out from underneath the car. "When you put it like that, you make me sound like an asshole."

She stiffens her upper lip and folds her arms over her chest, her brows scrunching together. "Well, quit acting like one."

"I wasn't going to hurt her, Lettie. Draven really needs that baneberry so they can push Aries's father out for good. You know what that monster did to Libra."

She drops her arms, her eyes softening. "It's awful. But tormenting Mia doesn't make you any better than Gemini Thorn. Just think about it, okay? For me. Please?"

I nod and wait for Lettie to leave the garage before I roll back to finish working.

I have thought about it. I've thought about *her*. Mia Harker is so sexy it hurts to look at her. I think about her every night now and wonder how far she'd let me go next time. *And there will be a next time.*

I want to see that look in her eyes again. The way she trembled with something much darker than fear. I want to see that wet spot on her white cotton panties again. Only next time, I'm not going to stop at the seam. Next time I'm going to slip inside her wet cunt and fingerbang the life out of her. I want to see her cum so hard her soul leaves her fucking body.

Fuck. Now *I'm* hard. Great.

I can't even focus on my work today. I'm so riled up. Draven wants the baneberry, Aries wants to screw over his father, and I just want things to stay the same. I need routine. Along with a healthy dose of drinking, fighting, and fucking to keep me sane. But ever since this chick got to town, it's thrown everyone into chaos.

Draven is obsessed with getting her land, but after seeing the way he reacted at my party the other night, I'm guessing he's obsessed with her pussy too. Especially since he's already gotten a taste of it.

This girl could be our ruin if we're not careful.

My phone buzzes with an incoming text from Aries.

You ready for the fight tonight?

Am I fucking ready? I snicker. I love how he still checks in on me like it's my first time stepping into the *Circle*.

Always. Now fuck off.

I grin as I hit send. He's never missed a single one of my fights in all these years. But I love to give him shit for acting like an overprotective boyfriend. The truth is, he's the closest thing I've ever had to one. But our friendship comes first. Those are the relationships that last longer.

I finish up my repairs and hop in the shower, scrubbing hard to get the grease off my arms and hands. I actually like being dirty, but I've been working on presenting myself more respectably. It makes my sister and my parents happy. And it gets me into less trouble.

I throw on a white muscle tee and a pair of gray sweatpants, still sporting the blood stains I couldn't get out from last time. I take a look in the mirror before I leave, admiring my own shredded physique. I've never been a vain man, but I am prideful. I work hard on my body, sculpting it like a fucking piece of art. Like a machine.

Where Draven and Aries are attractive in the universal sense, pretty boys who dress to kill, my appeal is edgier. I'm the bad boy parents warn their daughters about. From my back alley tattoos and knuckles that are constantly bruised and bloodied, veins that are always bulging from adrenaline, *I'm* the guy they want to fuck in the bathroom at Duff's. Not Draven. If I had crossed paths with Mia first...

Fuck. We've shared women before, but this chick has got us acting feral. Possessive. The most fucked up part is the fact that neither of us has any business being inside her panties when we are literally trying to force her to sell her home to us. Every time I see her, the lines blur a little more. I know Draven and Aries feel the same. I can see it in their eyes. The energy has shifted. And I'm not sure if this will end well for any of us.

I dab a tiny bit of cologne on my wrists before grabbing my leather jacket and hopping on my bike. I need to ride for a bit so I don't get into a fight before my actual planned fight tonight.

These woods used to terrify us as kids. We grew up hearing stories about the monsters that lurk in the trees. In the shadows. But Draven, Aries, and I weren't like other kids. It wasn't the threat of evil outside that scared us. It was what lurked inside. I used to wonder what our families would think if they found out that we were more monstrous than their urban legends.

We were terrified of the woods because we thought that the monsters would recognize us as their own, claim us, and turn us into a fucking tree or something. As I ride my bike through rocky paths in between the skeleton branches and dark spots where even the sun is afraid to shine, I dare a bitch to fuck with me.

Maybe that's what I need. What I crave to quell the demons in my mind. A fucking worthy opponent for once.

I hit the throttle until I'm flying so fast that my heart is practically in my nuts. The bitter wind whips at me like venomous snakes, attempting to peel the skin from my bones. I fucking love it. The pain, the rush, the struggle to catch my breath at every turn. It's my little slice of peace. The only thing that calms the anger in my veins and the self-deprecating voices in my head.

It's even better when I crash. On the days when I feel like I have an extra death wish, I push it to about two hundred and fifty. I know these dirt roads like the back of my hand, but even then, sometimes I get lost in the hum of the engine when the scenery whips by so fast I can't see anything around me. I just hold on and let my instincts take over.

The last time I wrecked, I was in a coma for weeks while they sewed me back together. But I always bounce back. I have poison running through my veins. There's not much that can kill me.

But I promised my family that I wouldn't scare them like that again. I still hear the sadness in my mother's voice. *You are strong but not invincible, mijo. Don't break my heart like that again.*

My brother, Felix, has made her cry enough tears over the years. There is something wrong with the Crane men. A wild abandon that shatters our need for safety and comfort. That fear that most people have, the healthy fear that keeps them from doing dangerous things... Yeah, we don't have that.

I still throw some caution to the wind, but I don't want to send my mother into an early grave. *She's already lost so much...* So, I have to focus on staying in control. Felix became a professor, soaking up his pain with poetry and college pussy. And I work on my bikes. I ride, I fight, and I drink.

Then there's Lettie, who is perfect. She's a good student, dutiful daughter, and has never brought a piece of shit boyfriend home. She's our angel, the only good that came from my mother's womb.

Sweat drips down my back despite the cold. My energy is chaotic, erratic, as I think about tonight. A ride before a fight is the best kind. It gets me out of my head and in sync with my body. Week after week, it still surprises me that dudes are willing to go up against me. I keep the Ever Graves ER extremely busy. I even heard that they add extra staff on Friday nights just because of me.

This puts a shit eating grin on my face as I spin around and head back to the garage.

But as I pass the cemetery, a chill snakes up my back, hampering my mood like it always does. I purse my lips and hit the throttle, speeding up so I'm not tempted to look. It was a long time ago, but it still feels fresh. Luckily, it happened before Lettie was born, so she doesn't have to bear the burden that Felix and I do.

Fuck.

I grip the handlebars so tightly that I pop open the cuts on my knuckles. My stomach knots in remembrance. *It's my fault.*

When I'm finally out of the woods and back on the main road, my chest loosens again. I slow my bike and take a deep breath. I shake it off, leaving the pain back there in my baby brother's grave. I have to. If I take it with me, then I'll for sure find myself lying in the dirt next to him. No one wants to talk about it, but that's why Felix left this town. The darkness was suffocating him. *The guilt.*

But I don't have anywhere else to go. This is my home, my heart, even as it breaks all over again every day. For that moment when I first wake up, that split second, I forget that I only have one brother now instead of two—it's almost euphoric. Then reality sinks in, and I remember it all over again. Like it just happened.

When I get to the garage, Aries is already inside, waiting to help me warm up. Dressed in a black tracksuit, he looks like a rich white guy who's watched *The Godfather* too many times.

"You're missing a couple of gold chains," I taunt.

He snickers and slaps the focus mitts together. "I left them in your mom's car, asshole."

Oh, hell no. This fucker. I don't even bother with gloves or wrist wraps. I take a swing for one of his mitted hands, knowing he's not ready. His wrist snaps back, and the mitt hits his cheek. "Never talk about my mother like that, pendejo."

Aries laughs as we square up. "Yeah, get fired up. Give me all that aggression."

I shake my head and throw a combination so fast that he almost trips over his own feet keeping up. "You're getting soft on me, Ries. My abuela moves faster than you."

He cocks his head to the side, his ego bruised. "All right, let's make it interesting then." He grabs a vial of nightshade from his pocket and drinks all three ounces of it. My adrenaline spikes as his blue-green eyes glow, a ring of gold light circling his pupils.

I bounce on the balls of my feet, shifting from left to right as I ready myself. He shoots toward me at full speed. His right arm swings at my head, and I duck, bending down then popping back up to land a hook into his waiting mitt. His left hand jerks toward my ribs, and I drop my right arm, hugging it to my side to block him. I dive toward him, getting into his space, and throw an uppercut into his other mitt.

Sweat drips down my back as we dance around the garage in a rhythm of punch, block, duck. I grunt through shallow breaths, fixated on Aries's every move. It's a rush, a high like no other. But nothing compares to the feeling of connecting with bone and teeth and soft flesh. To watch blood spurt out of your opponent's mouth, their eyes glazing, knowing they're about to tap out. *Or get their ass knocked out.*

We go until the poison wears off, and Aries throws in the towel.

"Thanks, bro. I needed that." I peel off my shirt and use it to wipe my face.

The vein in his neck throbs as he struggles to steady his breath. "You know I got you."

"I'm gonna jump in the shower. Stay as long as you want." I snatch a bottle of water out of the mini fridge and offer it to him.

That devious smirk of his takes over his whole face. "Want some company?"

"You know I don't like to cum before a fight. I gotta save up all that energy." My cock tents my pants, contradicting my words.

He shrugs. "After then. A celebratory fuck."

I nod as I readjust myself. "See you tonight, Ries."

We've been playing this game with each other since we were fifteen years old. But it's always surface level. Nothing deeper than exploring our carnal desires. Our attraction for each other is chaotic. In between the girls and the booze, we always find our way to each other's beds. If Draven knows, he doesn't let on. It's just something we don't talk about when he's around. I don't think he'd give a fuck. It's just something that we keep between us.

The only person I want to defile as much as Aries is Mia. And the thought of her positioned between us makes my dick so hard that I almost break my rule and jerk myself off in the shower.

Fuck. I need to get my shit together.

But I can't help myself. Before I hit the shower again, I send off a text to Lettie.

Convince Mia to come to the fight tonight, and I promise I'll talk to Draven about backing off from her.

I'll beg for her forgiveness later.

The return typing bubbles come in hot. I chuckle as I can imagine the confusion on my sister's face.

Deal. But don't fuck it up.

And so it begins…

Lettie is going to fucking kill me.

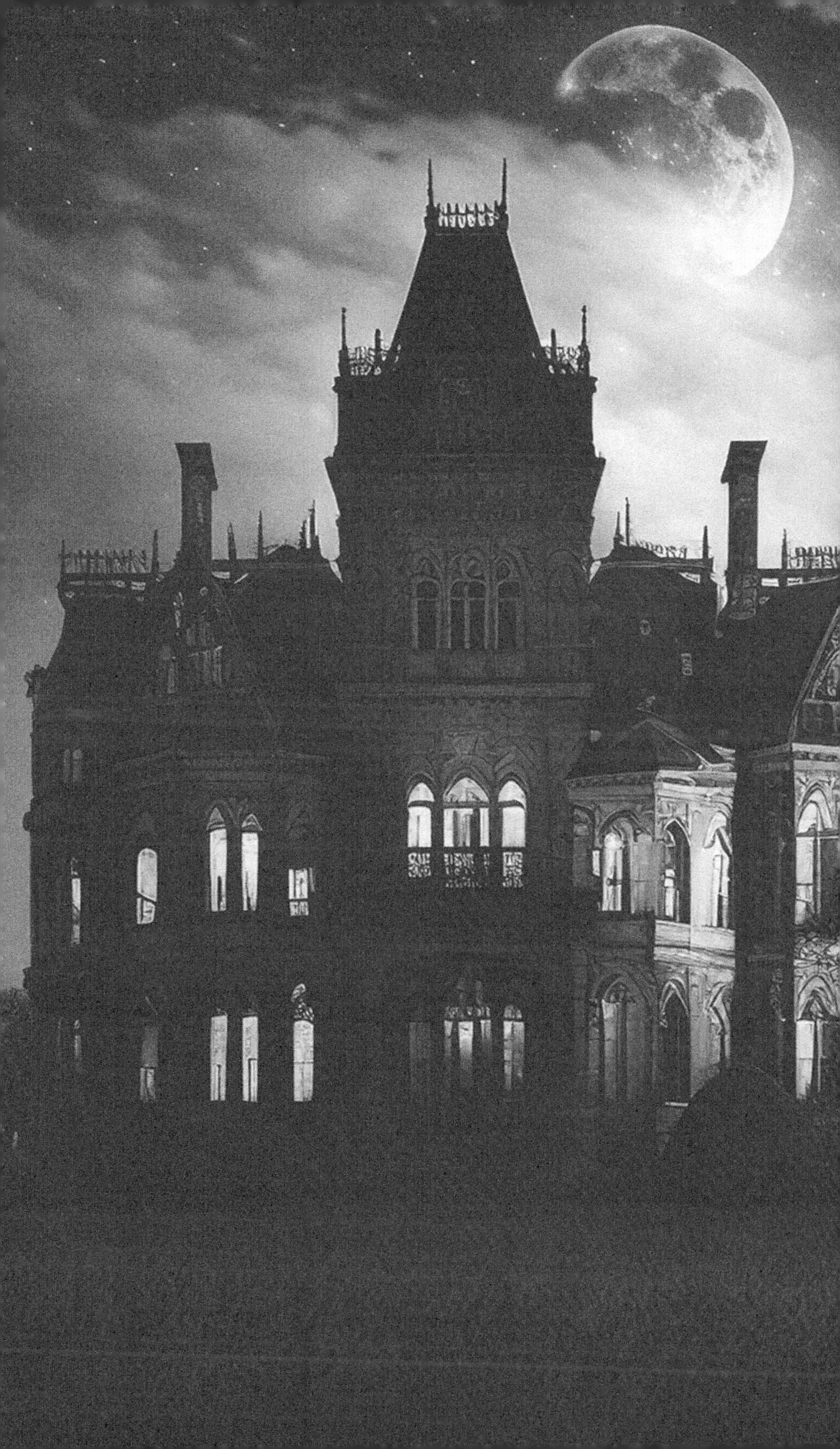

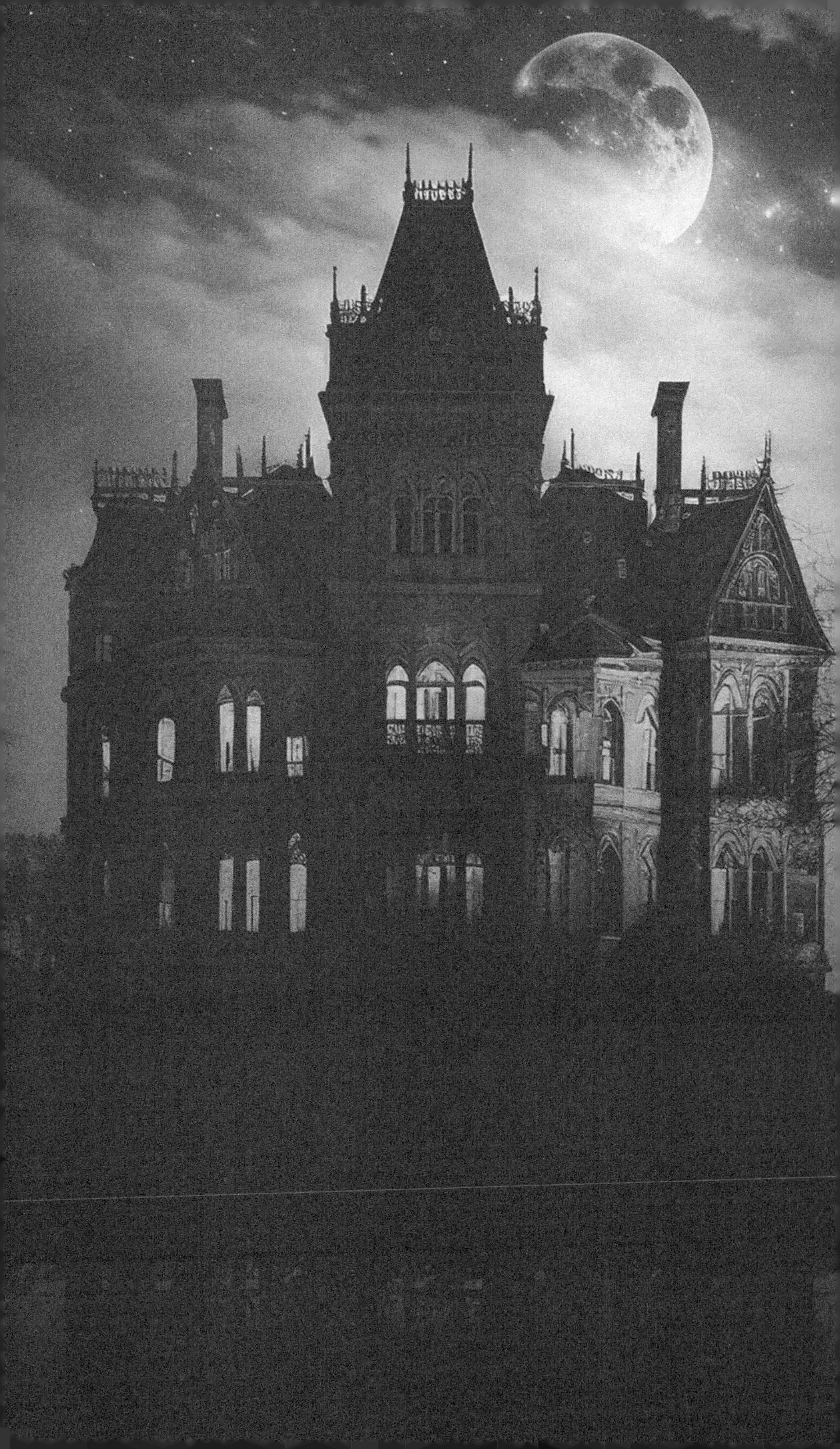

CHAPTER 11

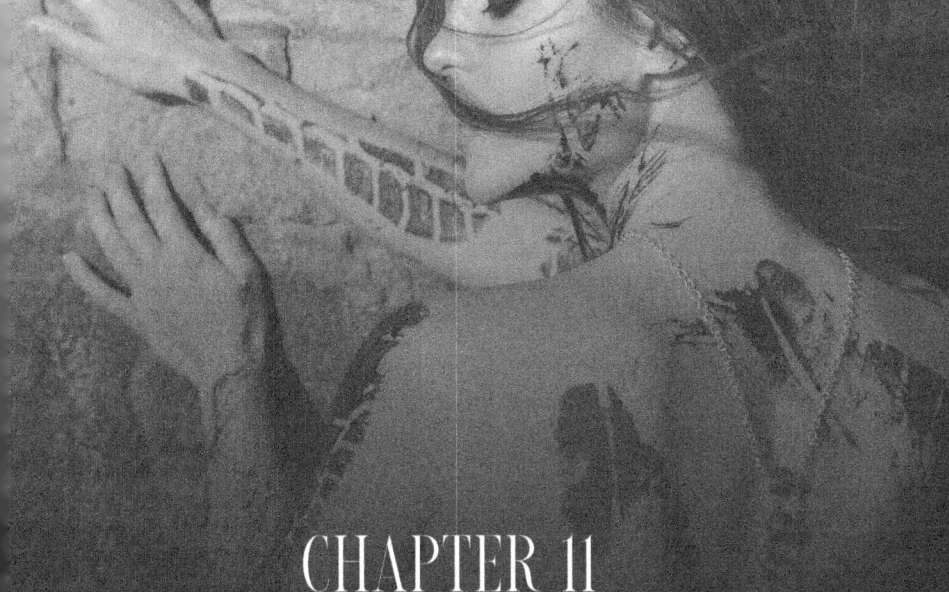

Mia

One of the things I learned from the orphanage is self-preservation. How to survive even when it seems impossible. But what terrifies me more than anything is being vulnerable. When I sleep, I'm in my weakest state. So I fight for control of everything when I'm awake. Last night reminded me of that.

Are there others like me? Do they know? After all these years, Nox still has so many secrets. He's told me nothing of where he comes from or why he's with me. It took me so long to come to terms with the fact that he's real. That I didn't just make him up in a fever dream. Even when the doctors and priests called me crazy, I knew Nox had to be real. There's no other explanation for the marks that I wake up with. Yet sometimes, I question my own sanity. I question everything...

If there are others who know he exists, then maybe I can get some answers as to why he's attached himself to me. Maybe I can finally accept that I might be cursed, but not insane.

But that's not the only thing weighing on me this morning. I need to apologize to Villette. It's not her fault that her brother and his friends are psychos. She's the first person who's been genuinely nice to me in a long time. Plus, she was born and raised here. She might be able to shed some light on my affliction. Or, at the very least, maybe be someone I can talk to about it. It's hard keeping this pent-up inside me. For years, I've lived with this secret. This shame.

I shoot off a text to her and try not to hold my breath while I wait for a response. I clean up the kitchen, make a pot of coffee, and do my best to distract myself. There's still so much work to be done around here. I have to finish exploring the house, put away my things, and call someone about fixing my front gates.

I sip on my coffee while staring hard out the front window. Seeing all that twisted metal scattered all over the yard makes my blood boil. But thinking about what happened right after sends a flush across my skin. *I have to stop having sex with Draven Blackwell.* He's the enemy. The asshole who is trying to run me out of town.

I think a small part of me is afraid to fully unpack. I've spent my whole life feeling unsettled. Even at the orphanage. It was the only place I ever knew as a child. And yet, I still kept a bag packed, thinking my parents were going to show up one day and take me back home.

That day, of course, never came, and it never will. But I'm still waiting for something. A sense of home. Of belonging. And until that clicks into place, I think I'll always have one foot out the door.

My phone buzzes, breaking my trance. I look down to see it's a text from an unknown number.

A couple of men will be by later today to start work on your gate. Don't give them any trouble... Trouble.

Well, fuck.

This man never ceases to amaze me.

I respond back with: *Great. It's the least you can do.*

He texts back: *I'm not doing it for you. Once you sign the papers, I'll have to fix them anyway.*

I grit my teeth as a spark of anger returns. This fucking guy. He can't do or say anything nice. Even when he's fucking me, he's a complete prick.

My phone buzzes again, and I'm about to tell him off when I see this one's from Villette.

Thanks for reaching out, girl! I'd love to hang out. Meet me at the Headless Horseman in an hour. My treat!

I reply back with a thumbs-up emoji and finish my cup of coffee in the front window. My broken gates look even more insulting to me now that Draven is determined to fix them out of the *unkindness* of his heart.

I'm not sure what to expect when I pull into town. I've only been to Duff's, and that was at night. *And I was pretty drunk.* But in the light of day, this place is charming. It's old world with its Victorian-style lampposts and cobblestone sidewalks—quaint and cute despite the creepy, dark forests that surround it. The fog is thick, and the air is crisp. Like something out of a Gothic novel.

I park my truck in one of the many empty slots in front of the Headless Horseman, wondering if I'm about to have my third cup of coffee or a mimosa brunch. I don't know what type of girl Villette is—a caffeine freak like me or a day drinker.

All my questions are answered the second I waltz through the door, and the sharp, pungent scent of freshly roasted beans hits my nostrils. A wave of euphoria seizes my senses. My shoulders drop, all tension flitting away as I spot her at a corner table. As much as I love a stiff drink, coffee truly is my preferred poison.

She waves me over, her face bright, skin glowing with hardly a stitch of makeup. Her black hair is piled high on her head in one of those perfect messy buns that really isn't messy at all.

When she stands to greet me, I can't help but drool over her outfit—skinny jeans, brown leather knee-high boots, a lace camisole, and an ankle-length patchwork cardigan that looks as expensive as it is soft and fuzzy. She looks like she just stepped out of a fall fashion catalog.

"You look amazing," I sputter as she hugs me. Fuck. She even smells divine. Like freshly baked cookies.

"So do you," she replies, her tone matching the warmth of her smile.

I look down at my ripped jeans, motorcycle boots, and black zip-up hoodie, and I cringe. "You don't have to lie to be my friend," I tease.

She giggles in that infectious way that you see pretty girls do on television. "I'm not. You have a unique style. I like it."

I order a black coffee while Villette sips on her pumpkin-spice latte. It literally goes with her outfit, so I refrain from making a smart-ass comment about having a little coffee with her sugar.

"So, I want to apologize for the other night. I was not my best self, and I shouldn't have taken it out on you," I ramble out without taking a beat.

She shakes her head. "No need. You didn't offend me. I grew up with those guys. I know better than anyone how infuriating they can be. *I'm* sorry that my brother is acting like such a creep. I can't believe he broke into your house."

I'm dumbfounded. I threw a drink at one of her friends, insulted her brother, and told her to fuck off, and she's apologizing to me? This girl is an angel.

"Well, I appreciate that, but still... I had no right to snap at you. It's not your fault. Friends again?"

"We never stopped." She grins over her sugary drink. It lights up this entire room.

It's nice to have her to talk to. I've been around girls my whole life, but as soon as I left Wickford Hollow, it was just me. Then my ex for a bit. But I never made any girlfriends outside of the orphanage.

Most people think I'm weird and unapproachable. I guess I am. But Lettie is different. I don't think she has a judgmental bone in her entire body.

"So what's the deal with the three of them? Why do they want that poison so badly?"

She rolls her eyes and huffs. "They are relentless. I'll try to bring you up to speed. Are you familiar with the poison trade?"

I've never been one to partake in it. It's like the crème de la crème of drugs. Better than all of them put together. But it's lethal to most unless taken in small incremental doses. "I've heard that some people are immune to it. That they can drink it like it's a glass of wine or a shot of whiskey. But I don't know much else."

She nods. "It's true. There are families who have built up an immunity to it—the Thorns, of course. They make and supply the poison. Then there's the other four, Blackwell, Erebus, Graves, and Crane. Our history runs deep in this town and in Raven's Gate."

Somehow she looks even more badass to me now. "Crane? That's your last name, right? You can drink poison?"

She sighs. "I can. I don't though. Not in a long time. So, Aries's father is a monster. He did horrific things to Aries's twin sister, Libra. He didn't even bother to look for her when she went missing last year. Anyhow, she finally resurfaced about a month ago, and we learned that she'd been held captive in Absentia Asylum. And it had been arranged by Draven's grandmother, Penny Blackwell."

What the fuck? These people are nuttier than I thought. I order a refill and lean back in the booth, wishing I had popcorn for this story. "Wait, aren't Draven and Aries best friends? I can't believe his grandmother would do that."

Villette snickers. "Oh, you didn't know Penny Blackwell. Up until recently, she was the most formidable person in this town."

"What happened to her?" This just keeps getting more unhinged.

She nods. "I can't say it out loud, but... let's just say she got what was coming to her." She mouths *Libra*, her hand cupping the side of her mouth, blocking the view of the other customers.

"Holy shit."

"Libra signed over her shares of the poison fields to Aries so he can have a bigger stake than their father. They are working on ousting him from the business altogether. In order to do that, they need more buyers, more money, and more poison. That's where Harker Mansion comes in."

I gasp. "The baneberry. Fuck. I thought Draven was just being a self-entitled rich asshole. I had no idea that I was sitting in the middle of a fucking poison war."

She looks at me with pity, like I'm a wounded puppy. "I'm sorry you got mixed up in all of this."

Fuck. This changes everything. "What will they do if I don't sell?"

She looks out the window and bites her lip. "I don't know."

But something in her expression tells me that she does and can't bring herself to say it out loud.

"Lettie. Be honest with me. Please."

She sighs, and when our eyes meet again, she shivers. "Our world isn't meant for everyone, Mia. Maybe consider taking the offer."

No one put her up to this. She's actually terrified for me. I fold my hands in my lap to keep them from shaking. "I… I've never had a home before. Or a family. Harker Mansion is the closest I've ever had to having one. It's not about the money."

Lettie's eyes water as she reaches for my hand from across the table. "I'm sorry, Mia. Whatever you need, I'm here for you. Maybe there's another way."

Ahhh, fuck. I dab at my eyes with my crumpled napkin. "Why would my grandmother leave me this mess? She had to have known this was coming."

Lettie shrugs. "Emma Harker was kind but also cunning. I'm

sure she had her reasons. Maybe there's something in that house that can give you the answers you're looking for."

That's the one thing I've been avoiding—searching through things that belonged to people who never wanted me. "All I have is a letter, but it doesn't make sense. It's like a riddle."

Her eyes widen. "Then it means something. That's how the founding families communicate when it's important and top secret. Can I see it sometime? Maybe I can help you decipher it."

Finally, I catch a break. She's so sweet and genuine. It's baffling that her brother is such a psycho. "I'd like that. Thank you."

Her warm smile returns to match the sparkle in her eyes. "You can bring it tonight. To the *Circle*. That is if you don't have other plans."

I snort. "Lettie, you're the only friend I have in this town. What plans?"

She giggles and blushes. "Perfect. I'll text you the directions later. Um, but… full disclosure. The three of them will be there. But I promise they won't harass you if you're with me."

My stomach knots. I can't avoid them. This town is too small. And I refuse to hide out in my house every night. "It's fine. What is the *Circle* anyway? Is that like a club or something?"

She shakes her head and snatches the bill before I can reach for it. "It's a fight club in the woods. Bones is the main event every Friday night. I hope you aren't squeamish. It's pretty brutal. But it's tradition."

Well, fucking hell. This town is psychotic. Even this sweet innocent beauty across from me might be a little cuckoo. But the longer I'm here, the deeper I get drawn in. Fuck it. "Well, then I can look forward to watching your brother get pummeled. No offense."

She smirks. "Don't get your hopes up too high. Bones never loses."

My heart sinks. I have a feeling that none of them do. When it comes to anything.

Ever.

    I shrug off this feeling of dread. Part of me wants to cancel on her later to avoid any drama. But if I stay home, they'll only think they have more power over me. I still haven't even processed the fact that my property is the key to them winning a poison war. If I don't sell... they might actually kill me.

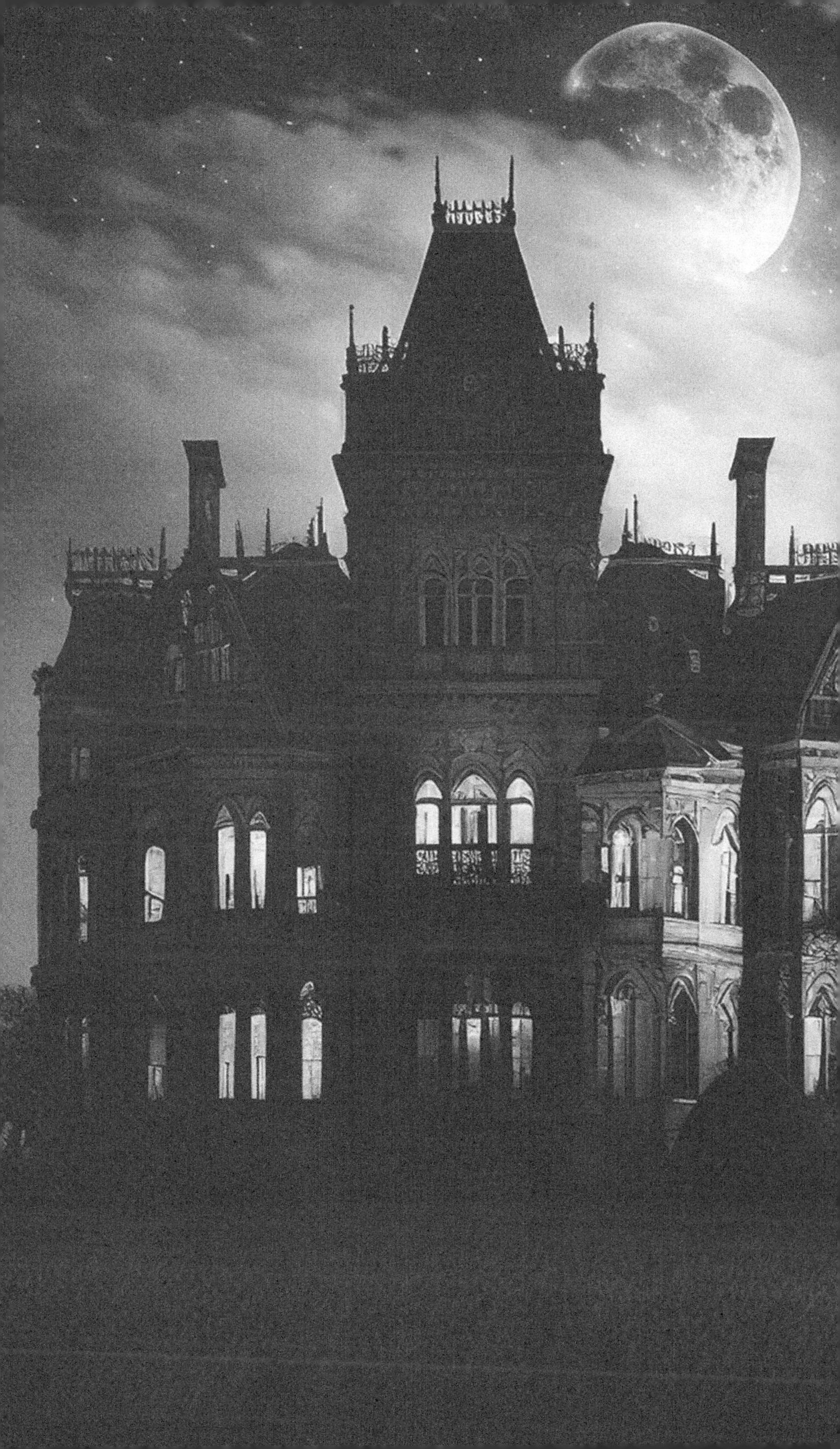

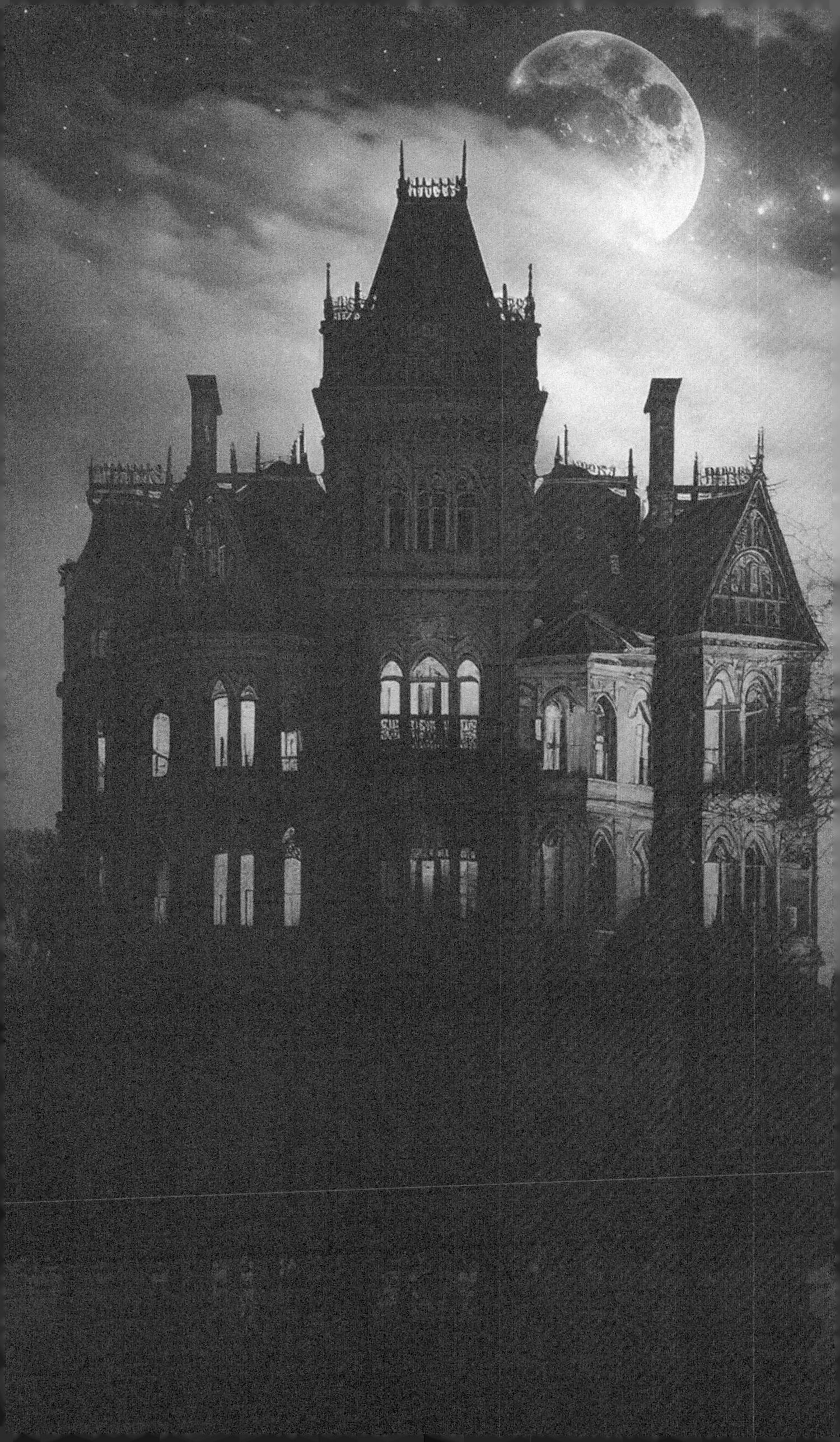

CHAPTER 12

Aries

HEADLIGHTS AND TORCHES LINE THE PATH THROUGH THE WOODS. But I could find my way to the *Circle* in the dark if I had to. I pull up my hoodie before downing a vial of nightshade. The poison warms my blood and my skin as it snakes its way through my veins. It's the closest thing to matching the adrenaline that courses through Bones on fight night.

He doesn't need anyone to have his back, but I'm always ready. So, every Friday, I trade in my suit for sweats, sneakers, and brass knuckles, just in case. I don't like blood on my good shit.

I chuckle when I spot Draven leaning against the hood of his SUV, seeing that his idea of casual attire is a black cashmere sweater, gray dress slacks, and Italian leather loafers. With his black hair slicked back off his forehead, he looks very much the part of a small-town gangster.

At six-foot-four, I tower over him. But what he lacks in height, he makes up for in pure fucking psychotic tendencies. He doesn't get in many fights because one glare from his glowing eyes usually sends most dudes backing off within seconds. And they're smart to. If pushed too far, this motherfucker goes into a blackout rage. It took all of my strength to pry him off the last guy who crossed him. And he holds grudges. He went back later that night and finished the guy off. Unhinged as fuck.

"You good?" I fist-bump him.

He nods but doesn't look at me, his gaze scanning the woods. "Bones better knock this fucker out quick. I don't wanna be here tonight."

"He always does and you never want to be here. What else is fucking new?" If Draven never had to leave Blackwell Manor he'd be as happy as a groom-to-be getting his dick sucked by a stripper in the champagne room for the first time.

"My grandmother's estate is stressing me the fuck out." He lights up a cigarette and takes a long drag.

I squeeze his shoulders before clapping him on the back. "Why don't *you* get in the *Circle*? There's nothing like beating the fuck out of someone to take the edge off."

Draven finally looks at me, his face deadpan. "Because I'm not trying to commit murder tonight."

Fuck, he is in a fucking mood. I start to shrug it off when the sight of his biggest trigger makes her way through the crowd. The muscles in my back tense. She tests every one of my nerves too.

"Mia is here," I mutter.

He sucks in a sharp breath and follows my gaze. "This fucking cunt, strutting around here like she's one of us."

I place my hand on his chest as he starts to charge toward her. "Not yet. Relax. Let her squirm for a bit."

He grits his teeth but settles back against the hood again. "How the fuck does she even know about fight night?"

I nod in her direction. "Look who's standing next to her."

Draven lets out a low growl. "Lettie. Dammit. I told her to stay away from Mia."

It seems like we are all having issues staying away from Mia Harker. There's something about that girl. We're acting like a bunch of moths, and she's the flame.

Through the flickering torchlights, her eyes seem to glow—the sparkling blue offsetting the haunting darkness of the brown one. Like shadow and light. I lick my lips, my cock stiffening at the sight of her tight shredded jeans hugging the curves of her hips. Fuck. Her black hoodie is unzipped, revealing two erect buds pressing against her thin white tank top. It's fucking cold out here. She knows exactly what she's doing. And that makes me want her even more. *I bet she's a naughty little thing.*

I blow out a deep breath. "She's not wearing a fucking bra."

"I doubt she's wearing panties either," Draven rasps as he exhales another puff of smoke.

"We shouldn't mix business and pleasure, Dray." *I need to remind myself of this every time I see her.*

He stomps his cigarette out on the ground with a huff. "There's nothing pleasurable about that wretched creature."

I lift an eyebrow at him. "Is that what you told yourself the other night after you fucked her again?"

He shoots me a glare. "That was a mistake. A stupid, reckless mistake. It won't happen again. But I'm down to watch you do whatever the fuck you want to her."

A plan forms in my mind. Every inch of that woman calls to me. It's a feral need to stalk her through the woods and corner her like a predator. I want to strip her of all her comforts and securities.

My pulse races as I fantasize about catching her. "I want that tight little cunt sliding down my dick."

Draven's eyes darken, filling with lust. An ache that he no doubt recalls what that felt like. "She has demons, Ries. Darker than all three of ours put together. That thing is attached to her. I can see it in her eyes."

I nod. "I know. And I don't care. That's between her and the devil. But as long as she's in Ever Graves, we should get to play with her too, right?"

He nods toward a clearing in the trees just as Bones emerges from the shadows. His hands are wrapped and ready to pummel tonight's victim. I can feel the adrenaline pulsing from him, even ten feet away. As he bounces on the balls of his feet, sweat stains his white muscle tank top. It streaks his chest and arms, his skin glistening under the torchlight.

I spot Mia ogling him too. She licks her lips and crosses her legs, clenching her thighs together. "I think our little lamb likes a big bad wolf."

Draven snickers as he grits his teeth. "Good. We can all take turns breaking her."

A tingle shoots down my shaft. I palm my cock, adjusting it in my pants. "That might take a while."

Draven finally turns to face me, the look in his eyes murderous. "I want that baneberry, Ries. I don't care if we have to tie her down and force her signature. We have just as much right to that land as she does. Probably more. We've lived here our whole lives. She's been here for five seconds."

Fuck. He's more obsessed than I am, and it's *my* father we're trying to push out. "She is a Harker though. That still means something in this town."

He shakes his head as he glares over in her direction. "It means nothing. *She* means nothing… I'll see you after the fight." He lights up another cigarette and stalks off.

I blow out a deep breath as I watch him cross to the other side of the *Circle* and retreat to the shadows. Ever since we were kids, I've worried about him getting lost in the dark places of his mind. If it weren't for me and Bones, he'd never socialize with anyone. And now Mia's pushing his buttons, triggering him into old patterns and behaviors. It's only a matter of time before he snaps.

I wouldn't want to be her when that happens. She just needs to sign the fucking papers before Draven explodes like an atomic bomb.

The crowd cheers, snapping me out of my daze. Bones is spinning around a much bigger opponent, like a ballerina on his tippy toes. He moves with swiftness and precision, alternating between punches to the face and jabs to the ribs.

I can't help but chuckle to myself. Every weekend, some local asshole thinks he will be the one to defeat my best friend. As much as I'm enjoying the show, my gaze is pulled back to Mia.

There's something so intoxicating about watching her watch him. Her eyes are wide, her throat bobbing in anticipation of his next move. She feels the adrenaline just as much as the rest of us, and that turns me on so fucking much. It's all I can do to stop myself from stalking over to her and fingering that tight pussy of hers while she salivates over Bones beating the shit out of this dude.

Fuck me. My cock is so hard I can barely stand upright, let alone walk. Her gaze flits to mine as if she senses me staring. When our eyes lock, a tiny spurt of pre cum trickles out. It's a good thing I'm wearing baggy sweats and not my usual tight slacks. I'm not trying to amble around with a wet spot on my fucking crotch.

I give her a nod and a wink. I came to fucking play tonight.

The crowd cheers again. I jerk my head toward the fight just in time to see his opponent's jaw crack. Blood spurts out his mouth right before his eyes roll back, and he crumples to the ground. That's a mother fucking wrap. *Goodnight.*

Bones grunts and holds up his fists, his eyes wild with bloodlust and mayhem. Sweat glistens over his skin, highlighting the beautiful indentions of his taut muscles. Fuck, this isn't helping my erection one bit.

Draven slinks up behind him and pats him on the back. He smiles as he whispers something in his ear. As I make my way toward them, my plan fully forms. I want to break our little lamb tonight. Piece by piece, until we destroy every bit of her.

I throw my arm around his shoulders and yank him to my chest. "Thatta boy. Fucking unstoppable."

"Yeah, and don't you fucking forget it," he pants out.

I relish the energy between the three of us standing there in the dirt while the crowd continues to cheer for our champion. The women devour us with their eyes while the men envy our every breath. Draven, with his dark, striking features, resembling a mafia boss, me as their token Greek god, and Bones, our fucking ferocious warrior. *The Kings of Ever Graves.*

As we make our way back toward the cars, I pull Bones in close again. "Feel like having some fun with our little lamb tonight?"

His grin lights up his eyes. "Yeah," he mutters. "What do you have in mind?"

Draven grits his teeth. "Tell me it involves tying her to a tree until she fucking submits."

A rush of adrenaline sends a tingle down my spine and straight to my dick. "All we have to do is find a way to lure her into the woods."

Bones licks his lips as his gaze lands on Mia. "Let me handle that. You just set the trap."

If I'm not careful, I'm gonna cum before I even get inside her pants. The exhilaration of what's about to unfold has me so wound up that I can barely breathe.

Draven rolls up his sleeves, takes off his tie, and stuffs it in his pocket. "Just so you know, her pussy is addictive."

I palm my crotch as my cock pulses against the soft fabric of my sweats. "I bet it fucking is."

If Bones can somehow get Mia away from Lettie and alone in the woods, I'll be finding out real soon just how fucking addictive that tight little cunt is.

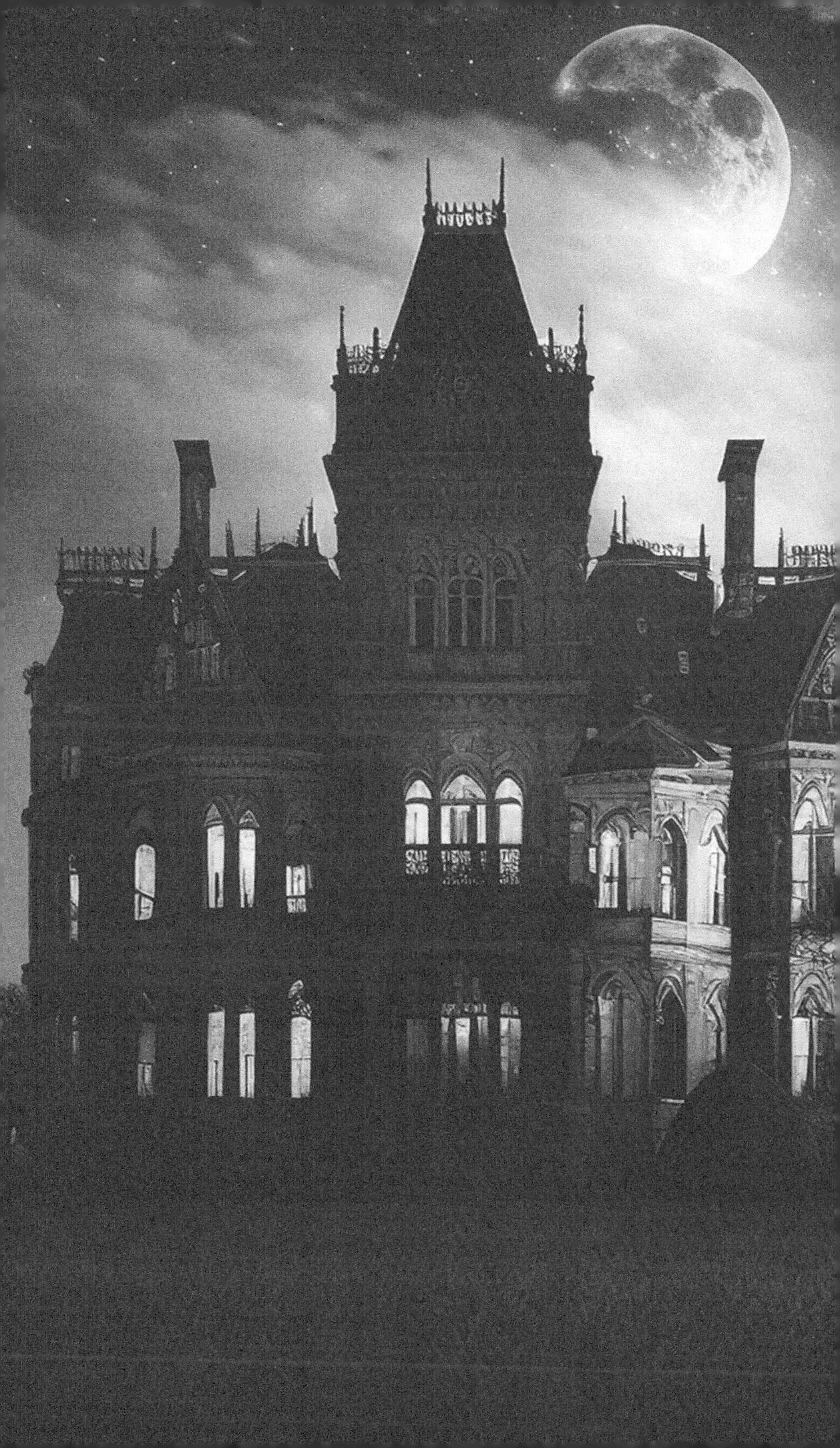

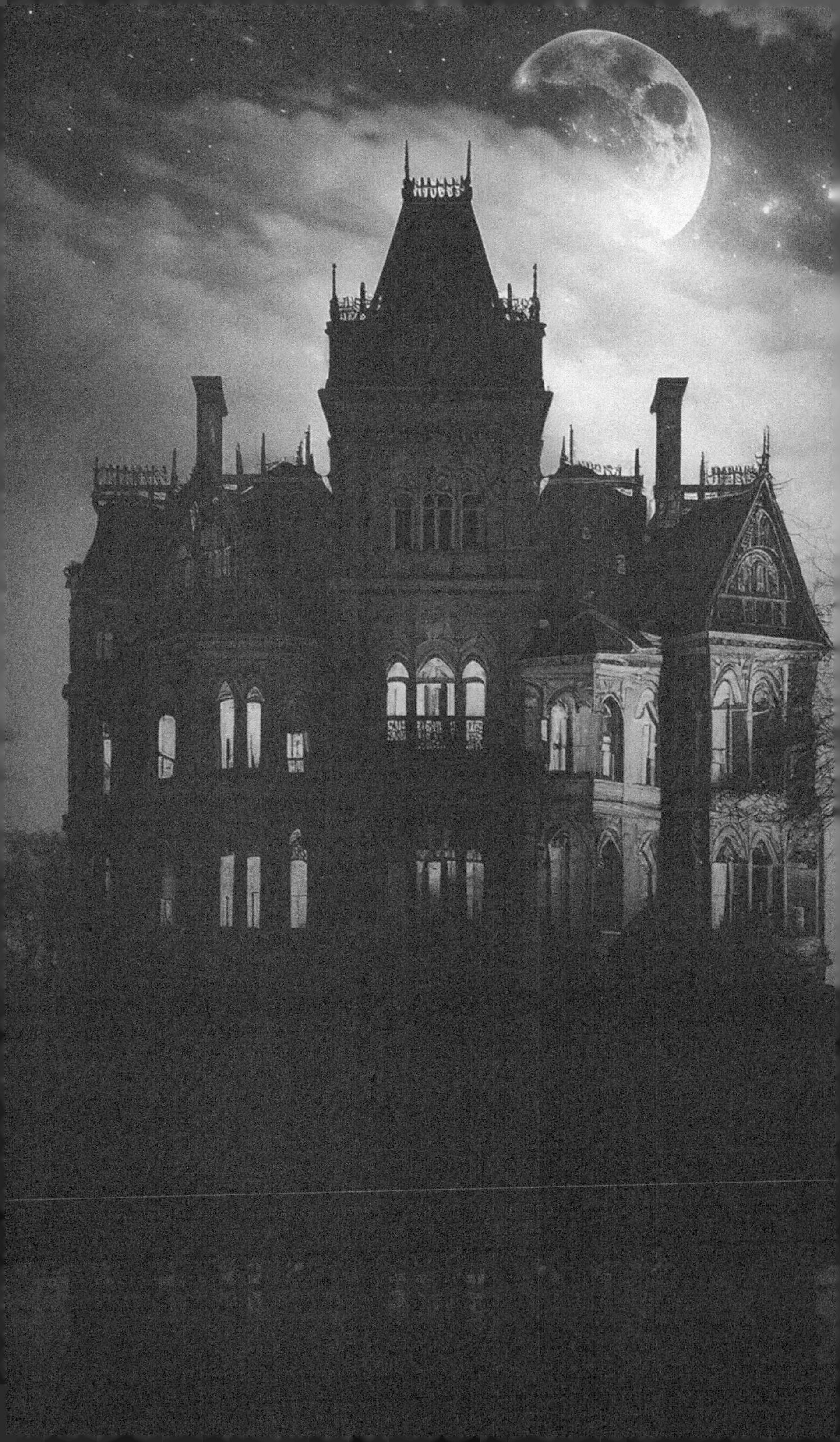

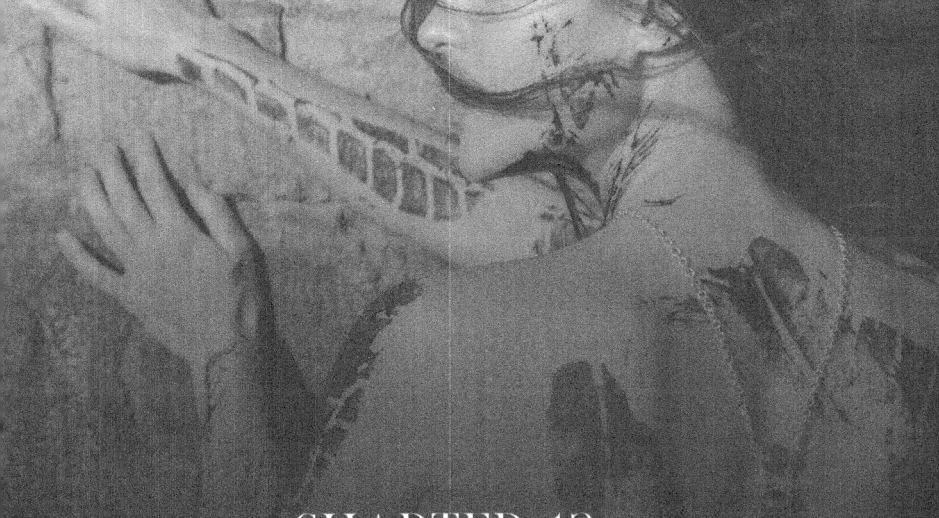

CHAPTER 13

Mia

Holy shit that was hot. The brutality of it all stirred something in me I wasn't expecting. I'd never seen a man fight for sport like that before. It was primal and depraved and so fucking exciting to watch. I just hope Lettie didn't notice me salivating over her brother.

I could feel all three of their hardened stares on me at various times during the fight. I should be worried, afraid, and pissed off. But all I feel is lust and a dangerous curiosity that's sure to get me killed.

It's unlike anything I've ever experienced. My whole life, it's only been Nox. Other than my ex, I've never allowed myself to get close to anything real or tangible. *And look where that got me.*

Even though Bones, Draven, and Aries are crude, depraved, and borderline psycho—*as I remember Draven plowing his SUV through my gates*—they give me an adrenaline rush every time they challenge me. And I can't decide if I want to run away from them or toward them. It's exhilarating.

"So, what did you think?" Lettie asks.

"Huh?" I'm lost in my dark, twisted fantasy, consumed with want and need for three deviants who make my blood boil and my pussy wet.

"About the fight," she says over a chuckle. "You haven't said a word since Bones knocked that guy out."

I draw in a deep breath, remembering I have to actually be social if I want to keep friends. "It was… brutal. And weirdly beautiful to watch." I bite my lip, afraid that she's going to think *I'm* the weirdo even though her brother is the one who fights for fun.

Lettie nods and flashes me a warm smile. "Yeah, Bones somehow manages to make bloodsport poetic. I think the melodrama runs in our family."

"Yeah, it's romantic in the most fucked up way. He tells a story when he fights. I can't explain it. Isn't your other brother a poetry professor?"

She slings her arm through mine as we head back to our cars. "Yes, Felix is a bleeding heart, obsessed with Edgar Allan Poe, poison, and his woman. We Cranes love hard, and we hate harder…" Her voice trails off, and her eyes darken for the first time. I didn't think this bubbly creature was even capable of having a bad day.

"And what about you? What or who do you love? What are you passionate about?" I rapidly fire at her, desperate to forge a stronger connection with my new friend. Desperate to confide in her all my darkest secrets. But afraid to confess until our bond runs deeper than superficial banter.

"I love my family and my friends. As far as passion? I'm still trying to figure that out." She almost seems shy for a second. But the girl who showed up on my doorstep to welcome me to town is anything but.

When we reach her car, I cradle her hands in mine. "Whatever it is, you can tell me. I know we are new friends, but I promise you're safe with me."

Her eyes glass over, and her throat bobs. "You're sweet, Mia.

But there's nothing to tell. My major at Tenebrose Academy is undecided, and my love life is nonexistent." She forces a smile to try to hide her sadness, but I see right through it. I'm an orphan. We are kind of the experts at facades.

But if she's not ready to open up, then I'll wait. "Well, I'm here if you ever want to talk it out."

This time she flashes me a genuine smile. "I knew I liked you from the second we met. You're good people, Mia. My abuela has a saying, amigos nacen, no se hacen. Friends are born, not made. I think you and I were born to be friends."

"I love that, Lettie. I've not had many friends…" Now it's my turn to act shy. The bonds that the other girls had in the orphanage didn't extend to me. I was the weirdo. The freak who would slip into a coma for days at a time.

My roommate was sweet, but she had one foot out the door. While I was afraid to leave and be on my own, Bailey Bishop had friends on the outside who she couldn't wait to get back to.

"Well, you've got one now for life." Lettie gives me a hug before sliding into the leather seat of her Benz. "Let's grab dinner this week."

I need to get more familiar with this town and the locals. "Sure. Take me to your favorite restaurant."

"I know the perfect spot. Café Thai has the best yellow curry in Melancholia." She rolls down the window before closing her door. She leans out, resting her delicate hand on its frame. "You okay to drive out of here? It's a lot darker than when we first came in."

I ignore the chill on my back, the tingles spreading across my flesh as I still feel like I'm being watched. Just the mere mention of the dark sends off alarms in my head. It's super creepy out here. And that's saying a lot coming from the girl who grew up in Wickford Hollow. That town is literally haunted by ghosts.

"I'll be fine. I have a good sense of direction."

She waits until I'm safely in my truck, the engine running, before she waves and drives off.

I lock the doors and wait for the heater to warm up. This old clunker is reliable but takes a while to get going. It blows cold air for about five minutes, but once the heat kicks in, it's like an inferno.

When the vents finally blast out the hottest air imaginable, I latch onto the gear stick. In these old trucks, the shift stick is actually up top and behind the steering wheel. As I pull it in and down, something cracks.

My stomach knots. What the fuck? The stick jams in between park and drive. Oh no. Fuck. I try to push it back up into park, but it won't budge.

Fuck.

I fish my phone out of my purse and click on Lettie's icon. "Come on," I mutter. The line is silent. I look and see that I have zero bars; the display at the top of the screen shows *SOS*.

No cell service.

"Fuck!"

My heart races as I try to unjam the gear stick, but it's no use. I look out the window into the darkness that exists past my headlights. I spot a few cars still remaining. Maybe I can find someone to give me a lift into town…

A tiny voice in my head says, *don't get out of the car, Mia.*

But I can't stay out here all night. I can't turn off the engine with the gear shift stuck. I only have a half a tank of gas, and there are at least six hours left until sunrise. And if I accidentally fall asleep… If Nox gets me… I'm so fucked.

I open my glove compartment and snatch the can of pepper spray I have stashed. With that in one hand and my phone in the other, I hop out of the truck and pray I can find help before my car dies. *Or I do.*

The wind whips through the makeshift holes in my jeans, sending goose pimples across my thighs. I take careful steps as I shine my cell phone light on the ground in front of me. *Thank god I wore sneakers tonight.*

As I approach the first car, the windows are fogged, and the whole car is bouncing. Yeah, I'm not interrupting that. Fuck.

I sigh and keep going, determined to find someone still partying out here. I pass another two vehicles—a black luxury SUV and a yellow Ferrari. *A fucking Ferrari?* I shake my head as I peer inside each of them, only to find them empty. I knew there was a lot of old money here in Ever Graves, but I wasn't expecting to see a sports car in the woods.

There's only one car left up ahead. My stomach drops when I see what it is. Or rather, who it belongs to. It's that rebuilt Mustang from the garage. *Bones's Garage.* I draw in a deep breath and curse under it on the exhale.

Three cars. Three psychos. Suddenly, disturbing the random couple fucking back there looks more appealing. And like a bad omen, as soon as I take a step back, the bouncing car with fogged-up windows peels out.

Fuck.

Now I'm alone in the woods with monsters.

I pull up my hood and hold my phone out, shining the light in a circle around me. My pulse races as I imagine all the worst-case scenarios for a woman. If this isn't a *choose-the-bear* type of situation, I don't know what is.

Except that I'm a sick fuck. A woman who enjoys being food for monsters. *Nox can attest to that.* Nope, no damsel in distress here. I'm more of the trip-and-fall-on-purpose kind of girl because catching me is the quickest way to get me wet.

No. I shouldn't do this. Fuck it. I'll go back to the truck and wait. I spin around and can't see my headlights anymore. *I can't see my truck.* My stomach drops. What the actual fuck?

It's pitch dark except for the light from my phone. Which won't last long. I'm at thirty percent battery. Fucking hell.

I hold the can of pepper spray in front of me and keep walking. "Bones?" I call out. I know he's here. That they're all here. I wish they would stop acting like creeps and just come out. I don't think Lettie would be too happy with them if they let me die out here. She seems to be the only person they care about pissing off.

Every leaf that rustles, every branch that snaps in the wind sends my heart racing and my adrenaline into overdrive. It's times like these when I start to entertain the idea of bringing Nox to the surface. If he wasn't trapped in my dream world, he'd be here in seconds, scooping me up and taking me home. He'd kill anyone who tried to harm me with his bare hands.

But the thought of unleashing him on Ever Graves… the thought of him in a power struggle with Bones, Aries, and Draven… it would be a disaster.

Even now, his voice echoes in my head, taunting me. *Let me out, dark one.*

I shake it off. *Focus, Mia. Stay alert.*

Crunch.

My heart almost leaps from my chest. I spin around, convinced something is behind me. But it's nothing but darkness. Fuck me.

"Guys? This isn't funny. Please come out," I plead. Now I'm getting scared for real. Maybe I'm wrong, and it's not them. There could be a serial killer out here. A sicko who preys on all the adrenaline-fueled women who come out here every weekend to watch hot, sweaty men fight like animals.

With all that sweat and pre cum… *I bet our pussies taste the sweetest.* Or am I the only one who gets aroused by violence?

Every step I take leads me farther away from my truck and deeper into the woods. I'm so turned around now that it's too late to go back.

A woosh of air blows past me, tickling my neck. I scream and break out into a run. Fuck. Something is hunting me. I can feel it. I'm not just being paranoid.

My chest hurts as I struggle for breath while I zig-zag through the trees. I don't have time to be careful. I just need to get as far away from whoever that is as possible.

I'm sprinting, leaping, twisting and turning through rocks, branches, and overgrown foliage. The scenery is becoming a blur as I let my instincts and adrenaline carry me.

My heart sinks when I spot the fallen tree up ahead. Fuck it. I have to get over it. I jump up and leap across, praying I don't break my neck. When I come down, I hit the ground hard and lose my footing. "Ahhh!" I throw my hands out in front of me to break my fall. My knees hit the cold ground with a thud. I yelp as the pain shoots up my legs.

I should've stayed in the truck.

My stomach knots when I realize I've dropped the pepper spray and my phone. "Oh, no," I whine as I crawl toward the little trickle of light peeking out of the grass. My screen light is fading with the fucking battery life. If I can just get to safety before it dies…

I claw at the grass, using it to pull me forward. Only a few more feet. Fuck. My knees and shins are throbbing. I'm scared to even try to stand up.

As I cross the last bit of ground that separates me and my only connection to the modern world, heavy footsteps sound in the darkness. My blood runs cold. Everything in my body freezes as a shadow reaches out and yanks me up by my hair.

I'm lifted off the ground and pulled backward. I scream as I'm thrust back against a tree. A shudder so deep and dark ripples through me when we lock eyes.

"Gotcha." Draven grins, baring his teeth.

I'm hyperventilating, but my fear turns to anger. "Fuck you!"

A sinister laugh erupts from behind him just as another figure steps out of the shadows. "Fuck is my favorite word, little lamb."

Oh, shit. Aries towers over both of us, his hood up over his ice-blond hair.

"*You* screwed with my truck. Both of you." I'm livid now. They lured me out here so I could freeze or starve to death just for their own amusement.

Draven digs his fingers into my scalp as his grip around my strands tightens. "Your defiance sends a message that I can't allow. The people of Ever Graves need to see what happens to those who go against me."

His lips are inches from mine. His breath is hot, just like it was that night when he sucked on my pussy. Fucking hell. *Why am I like this?* "If refusing to sell *my* home to bullies is an act of defiance, then I will do it a thousand times. Maybe the *people* of Ever Graves will learn to start sticking up for themselves too."

Aries rests his arm against the tree, boxing me in. "Yeah, look where that got you, little lamb." He leans in closer, his lips grazing my ear. "Look how pathetic you are. So weak and fragile."

Another shudder races up my spine. They both loom over me, larger than most men, their gazes ravenous, *murderous*. They won't let me get away. They will overpower me. I have no choice but to submit to whatever this is. "Don't you think the woods is a strange place to do business? What is it that you really want right now?"

They exchange a devious look. "That sweet, sweet pussy of yours," Aries whispers in my ear. "I want it locked tight around my cock like the darkest sin. Because my cum is your holy water."

I glare at Draven. "I thought you said *never again*."

He caresses my cheek with the back of his hand. "Oh, I'm not fucking you tonight, Mia. Aries is. I'm here to make sure you don't get away. And I'm going to enjoy watching you unravel. Every tormented second."

I never fully understood the word fury until now. I ball my fist and swing at him, landing a punch in his shoulder. "Let me go right now. I want nothing to do with either of you."

Draven pushes me back against the tree. "*Liar.* When you don't wear panties, we can see your arousal, Mia. Your cunt is so wet it's soaking through your jeans. And these…" He unzips my hoodie and pulls it back. His gaze rests on my swollen nipples. "Look how hard they press against your shirt. I don't even know why you bothered to wear one tonight. We're just going to take it off you."

A flush falls across my skin. My cheeks burn, and my chest heaves as I struggle to control my breath. "No. You're wrong."

"Is he?" Aries brushes my hair back off my shoulders. He grazes his fingers over my collarbone, eliciting a whimper from my throat. "Then why are you looking at me that way?"

"Like what?"

He slides his fingers underneath one of my spaghetti straps. "Like you're more afraid to say no than yes." Using both hands, he tears the strap off. With a smirk, he does the same to the other one. "Because you want this more than you don't."

Draven pins my wrists over my head. "Stop trying to pretend you're some innocent little girl when we all know you're a filthy fucking slut."

Is he right? Would I be this turned on if I wasn't? My brief hesitation gives Aries the green light.

He unbuttons my jeans and slips his hand inside. I gasp as his cold fingers slide down my slit.

"Mmm, little lamb… Fucking hell…"

Draven snickers. "Now you get to feel the way I do, Ries." He sucks on my earlobe. "This perfect fucking pussy. A beautiful fucking disaster for my cock."

I bite back a moan as Aries thrusts his middle finger deep inside. He wraps his free hand around my throat. "Move your hips back and forth for me," he murmurs.

I clench around him. "Go to hell."

He presses the heel of his palm against my clit. "Stop fighting and give in. You know you want to cum for us."

I fucking hate both of them because he's right. I want to cum so fucking bad I can barely breathe.

I whine and look away as I rock toward him, then back.

"Yeah, just like that, little lamb." He adds his index finger, sliding it in slowly as I grind against his hand.

"*Filthy fucking whore.*" Draven presses my wrists harder into the bark of the tree, splintering my skin. "Spread your legs more. I know you want him in deeper."

Fuck, what is happening? Why do I keep letting them do this to me? I'm furious, but I can't fucking help it.

"Not yet. Let's get these off first." Aries's blue-green eyes sparkle with sadistic lust as he bends down and takes off my sneakers.

"Someone is going to see us," I whisper.

Draven bites down on my ear. "I hope someone does. This town has gotten too fucking soft for its own good."

My body trembles as Aries slides my jeans down my legs, pulling them off. He throws them to the ground. "Your turn." He presses his hand against my abdomen and looks down, waiting for me to obey.

My heart races out of control. Fuck. I don't have a choice. But that's not why I do it. For fuck's sake, I am their fucking slut right now.

He raises an eyebrow, not satisfied with my stance. "Come on, little lamb. I know you can do better than that."

I blow out a shaky breath as I step out until my feet are past shoulder width. The bark of the tree scratches against my bare ass, digging into it like shards of glass.

Aries slides his hand down my abdomen and cups my pussy. "I have your pulse in the palm of my hand now, Mia. It beats so fucking fast for me."

A whimper escapes my throat. "Please…"

Draven looks down and licks his lips. "You thought she was wet before…"

I gasp as Aries slides his fingers down my slit. He pulls my tender flesh apart, pressing each side back as wide as he can stretch me. "Fuuck…pink is my new favorite color."

I don't know why the anticipation turns me on just as much as the act, but it does. "Oh, fuck," I whine.

He slides his thumbs up and down my exposed folds. "You sure you don't want to join in, Dray? I don't want to be greedy."

Draven snickers. "I told you, she's all yours. I just want to watch you violate the fuck out of her."

He growls in my ear, "And when I'm lying in bed tonight, I'll make *myself* cum to the image of Aries's swollen cock fucking you raw."

His words both piss me off and turn me on. I want to be a fly on the wall when he jerks himself off to the memory of me later. Fuck. "You're both the biggest assholes I've ever met," I grunt out.

Aries chuckles as he continues to make my pussy twitch and tremble with his fingers. "Lay down."

I gasp. "Down where? The ground is dirty and freezing."

Before I can protest anymore, they are both pulling me down to the ground. Draven is above me, pinning my arms over my head again.

Fuck. My anger turns to rabid desire. I arch my back as Aries pulls what's left of my tank top down to my waist.

I shiver at the cold air hitting my nipples.

"I can't wait to suck on those." He stands back up, hovering over us as he pulls his sweatpants down, yanking them off with his sneakers in one fell swoop.

Oh fuck. His cock. It's at least eight inches long. And the fucking girth. I'd have to use both hands to jerk him off. Fucking hell. *Now I'm scared*. But in the best fucking way.

He kneels down in between my legs, pushing them wider apart. "Isn't this why you left your panties at home tonight, little lamb?"

My breath is sporadic. I think I might have a fucking heart attack. "Don't flatter yourself."

Draven presses harder on my wrists. "Have you ever been fucked like this, Mia?" He nuzzles the side of my face. "Ever been fucked by one man while another one holds you down? Like a fucking whore."

The more he degrades me, the wetter I get. The needier I am to cum. To be dominated and defiled in the woods. I shake my head. "No."

Aries drags the tip of his cock down my entrance. "No, what? Use all your words, Mia."

I swallow hard, my throat dry. "No, I've never been fucked like this."

"Tell us… Do you want to be?" Draven coaxes.

I bite my lip. If I admit it out loud, then it does make me their whore. So I look away as I nod.

Draven hisses. "*Use your words*, Mia. Do you want this?"

I bite down harder on my lip to hide my gasp. Everything is still. Everyone is waiting on me. It hits me like the cold wind that swirls my flesh. I hold the power. Not them. This is a game. A sick and twisted game. But they won't make another move unless I do.

I take one more deep breath, and my teetering morality switch flips completely off. "Yes." Without any more hesitation, I arch my hips, raising my pussy up to meet the tip of Aries's cock.

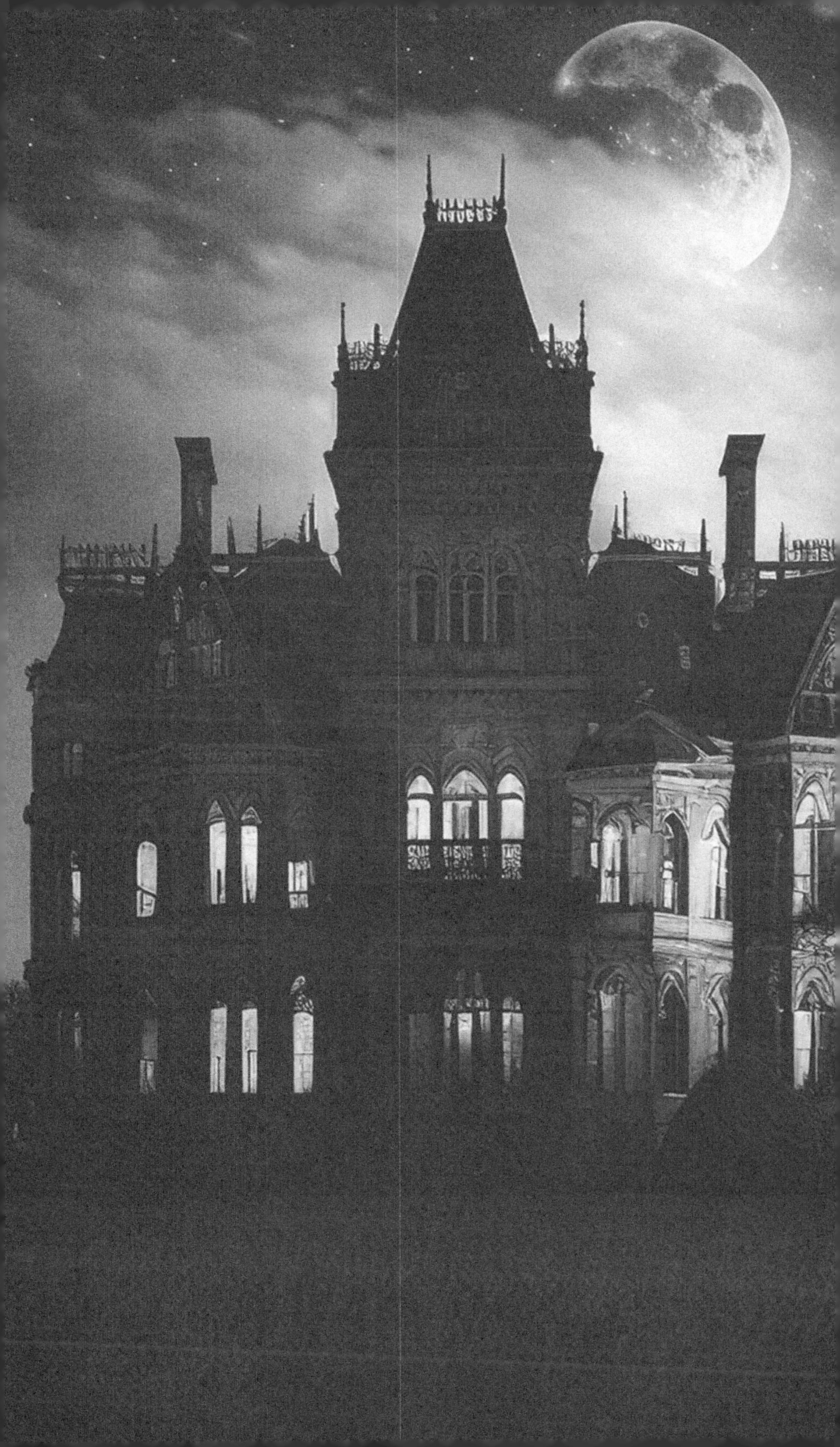

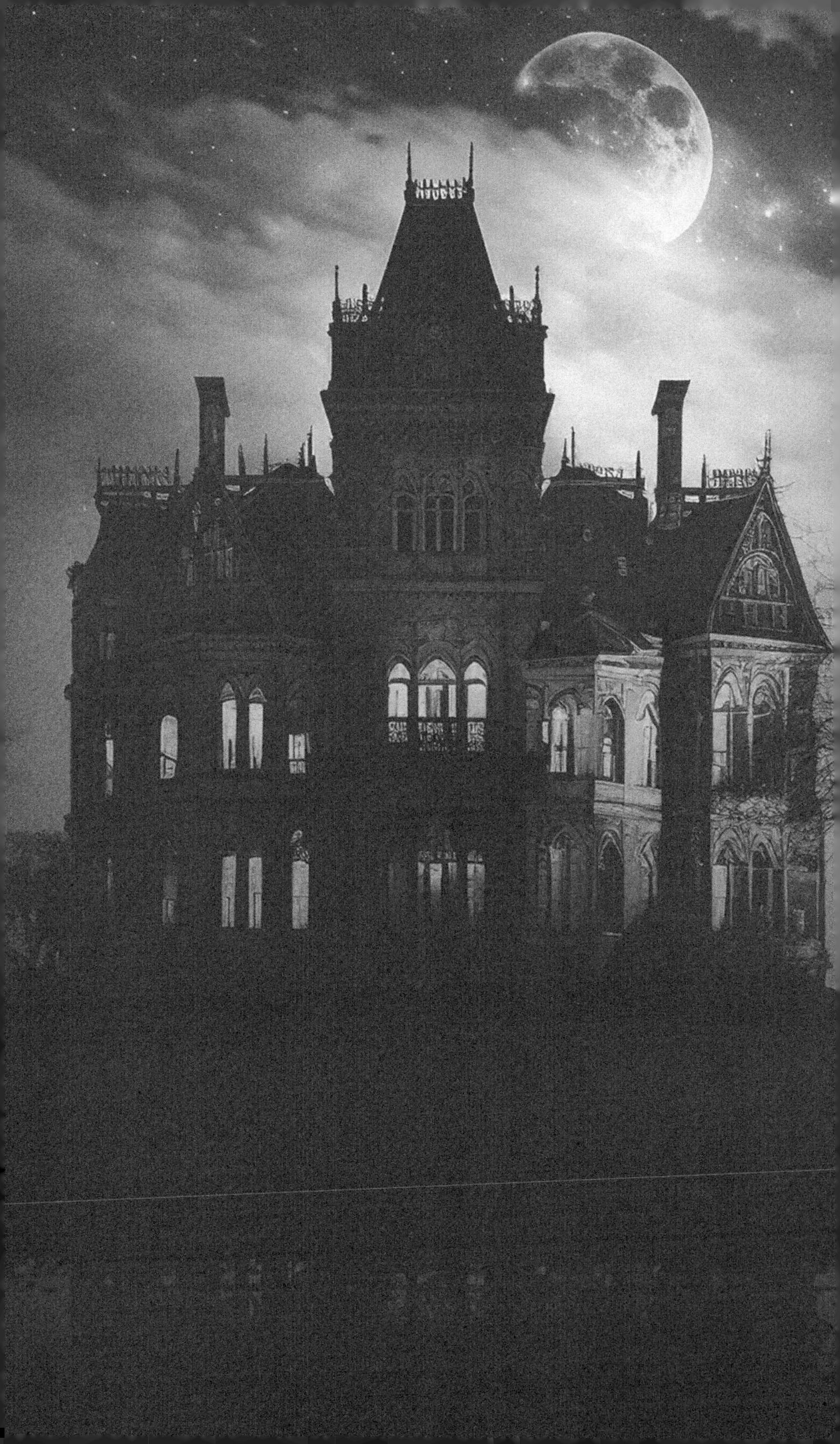

Chapter 14

Bones

"Got room for one more?" I rasp.

I've been stalking them for what seems like fucking forever. It only took me five minutes to jam her steering wheel, but the hunt was agonizing. Every step she took, I was right behind her, herding her toward them, pushing her deeper into the woods.

I like to watch. I waited until my cock was about to burst in my pants. And now I want what's owed to me.

She looks up at me, her eyes glazed with lust. I take my time looking her over, admiring the flush across her cheeks, the tautness of her pink nipples. I follow the trail of glistening sweat that leads to her thick patch of dark pubic hair. I fucking love it when they don't shave it all off. Fuck. I just want to thread my fingers through it while I suck on her clit.

"Mmm, not yet. She has to earn that," Aries drawls.

I kneel down next to them and slide my hand up her thigh. "Relax, baby girl. He's thick."

She lets out a whimper. "How dare you... I know it was you, Bones. You fucked with my truck."

I chuckle as her words don't match her body language in the slightest. "That's right, little lamb. I can get to you anywhere. Remember that."

"We all can," Draven growls. He looks and sounds angrier than usual. Mia does this to him. I've never seen a woman make him this unhinged. I can feel him fighting with himself as he salivates over her naked body.

I raise her leg and slide a finger down her ass crack. She squeals and flinches. "Shhh, relax. Go ahead, Ries. I've kept you from it long enough."

Aries licks his lips and gives me a look that I'm very familiar with. He has very dark tastes. Ones that extend way beyond fucking in a forest. Mia will learn soon. This is just the beginning.

Aries gives her a wink as he drops a massive wad of spit on her pussy. I reach over and rub it in.

"Oh, fuck," she cries out. "What... what the fuck are you doing to me?"

I take my time smearing his saliva up and down her entrance, from her clit to her taint. "More." This time I press the lips of her pussy back.

He fists his throbbing cock as he grunts and launches another gob of spit in the center of her entrance.

"Good boy, Ries. Good fucking boy." I take two fingers and push his saliva all the way inside her. Fuck she's like an oven. I push back as far as I can go and flick my fingers up and down.

She arches her back and moans. "Holy fuck... I can't breathe. Fuck."

Even Draven releases a quivering breath.

I pull out and push my fingers into Aries's mouth.

He lets out a growl, his nostrils flaring as he thrusts his cock inside her pussy. "Ahhh, fuck, that's good." He looks up at Draven. "Starting now, no one in Ever Graves is allowed to touch Mia but us."

Draven looks down at her and sighs. "This is a fucking disaster."

I know.

We're not supposed to want her like this. But it's too late now. We've crossed so many lines. And for different reasons. Mine are not the same as theirs.

Her eyes widen, and her mouth forms a perfect O shape when Aries thrusts his thick cock inside her. She gasps and arches her back.

"Oh my fucking god," Aries curses. He anchors her hips to the ground, inching himself farther inside her. "I'm gonna cum so fast."

"Deeper," she begs as she writhes underneath him. She bites her lip as she whines like a cat in heat.

I keep stroking her thigh, kneading my knuckles into her creamy flesh. Aries grunts as he thrusts violently, bucking and grinding into her so hard all she can do is hold onto Draven's hands for dear life.

"Fucking hell, Mia… I'm gonna fill you so fucking full." Aries strokes her clit as he slows down into a rhythm that makes her eyes roll back into her head. She moans softly as he rocks against her. No doubt hitting her sensitive little G-spot. *Aries knows how to find all the sweet spots.*

It's beautiful to watch. And I'm content with watching for now. I reach up and pinch one of her nipples, rubbing it back and forth between my thumb and forefinger. Fuck I love how her face flushes bright pink. How she sucks in a deep breath at the friction.

But it's only making Draven more pissed off. He wants her so badly but still wants to deny it. The sight of him in his designer pants, kneeling in the dirt, while he has a tug of war in his head is amusing to watch as well. But his dark side always comes at a price.

This fucker is going to lose it soon. He's going to break.

He looks down at her face for the first time. "Look at me, Mia," he growls.

She whimpers, her lips trembling, her body shivering as Aries destroys her. I don't know who I want to watch more. It's more beautiful than any holy sacrament.

"*Mia*," Draven demands, the edge in his voice making him sound demonic.

"Never again, Draven," she says on an erratic breath. "That's what you said."

"Look at me right fucking now."

She gazes up, her eyes glazed. "I hate you."

A flicker of madness takes over his expression. "Good. Cum. Now. And don't you dare look away."

Fuck. I'm so fucking aroused just watching their exchange. I give Aries a nod, and he lets out a moan. He digs his fingers into her hips as he angles them up and drives his cock in deeper. Her mouth drops open, and she lets out a deep guttural moan.

I'm so fucking hot for this woman right now. I need to taste her. Need to feel her against my lips. We've shared women before but not like this. Not with this level of brutality and depravity.

"Ohhh, I can't… please. Fuuck," she cries out.

Aries roars as he pumps faster. "Yeah. Fuck. Little. Fucking. Lamb."

I move behind him and grab her ankles, pinning them down to the ground as he unravels inside her. "Good boy, Ries." I press my chest against his back and rock against him, pushing him into her. "Fill her up."

He sounds like an animal. A rabid fucking animal. But what I'm not expecting are the noises that come out of her mouth as her juices soak his cock.

I peer over his shoulder to see Draven practically hyperventilating as they hold each other's gaze. She hate fucks him with her eyes while she cums all over Aries's cock.

I've known these guys my whole life. Neither of them has ever looked at a woman as they look at Mia. None of us have ever felt this strange and toxic pull to another outside our group.

She's going to be the fucking death of us all.
Her and that fucking baneberry.

Draven stands over her quivering body. "Think long and hard about what you've done, Mia. The utter fucking fury you've unleashed in me. I will destroy your fucking soul if you don't give me what I want."

She glares back at him. "Over my cold dead body."

He snakes a hand around her throat. "That can be arranged."

I drop her phone, keys, and pepper spray on the ground next to her head. "Get dressed and go home, Mia. Or he really will kill you tonight."

Aries chuckles. "You know you're fucked when the man who likes to fight for fun is the diplomatic one."

She curses as she tears away from him and scrambles for her clothes. We don't bother to help. I'm still hard as I notice the bruises on her thighs in the shape of my fingers. The sweat on her skin makes the dirt stick to her. And it only adds to her appeal. Our slutty little forest witch who took every inch of our brutality and is now drumming up incantations in her head.

We watch in disturbing silence as she shimmies back into her jeans. No one tries to offer her a hand as she hops on one foot, looking for her other shoe.

"Unfuckingbelievable," she mutters. "I'm going to need three showers and five years of therapy after this."

Aries uses the shirt we tore off her to clean his dick off. "You say that like it's a bad thing, little lamb. When we know you enjoyed every fucking second of it."

Draven huffs. "This is boring me now. I'm out of here."

Mia zips up her hoodie and stomps over to him. "You're bored? I forgot you were even here."

Oh, shit. Here we go.

His jaw flexes. "Let me give you something to remember me by then."

She squeals as he sweeps her legs out from under her, slams her to the ground, and rolls her over onto her stomach.

"Fuck, where's the popcorn?" Aries quips.

I let out a sigh and lean against the tree.

Draven pulls out a tie from his pocket and uses it to bind her wrists behind her back. "This is what happens when you fucking provoke me."

"Get off me!" Mia squirms underneath him.

He yanks her jeans down to her ankles, not bothering to take her shoes off this time. "I said I wouldn't fuck you again, and I meant it. But that doesn't mean I won't use something else to penetrate you with."

She lifts her head and gasps. "Draven, what are you fucking doing?"

He retrieves a vial of nightshade from his jacket. "Punishing you with the very poison you deprive me of."

The hairs on the back of my neck stiffen. Aries takes a deep breath as he ambles closer to me. Just one whiff of it has us both salivating.

Draven's lips quiver as he pours half of it down his throat. "Mmm. Fuck... Now it's your turn."

Mia shrieks. "Are you crazy? I'm not drinking poison!"

He snickers. "No. You're not drinking it." He rolls her onto her back, crushing her wrists underneath her. His eyes darken as he tips the vial over and lets the last of it trickle down in between her pussy lips.

Fuck. She's a Harker, so she probably won't die. But we don't know that for sure. I'm oddly aroused as I am alarmed. His hatred of her is his alone.

Aries arches an eyebrow at me. "It's a small dose. She'll be fine."

I shake my head. "I guess we're about to find out."

"Bones, she's been sitting on thousands of baneberry plants, breathing in tiny traces of the fumes for weeks. She doesn't even know, but she's already starting to build an immunity." Aries licks his lips as he turns his attention back onto Draven and Mia.

She screams. "Fuck, it burns. I feel weird. I can't breathe. Please."

Draven drags the empty bottle down her slit, brushing it past her taint and back up. "Shhh, the pain will pass." He coaxes her like the devil, tricking her into selling her soul.

The first sip of poison is always the hardest. But he's right. When the pain passes, a wave of euphoria like you've never felt bubbles up. The high is unlike any other. It amplifies every touch. Stimulates every nerve.

Her voice is gurgled as she whines. Her legs shake. "Make it hurt less, Draven. Please."

"I have no intention of showing you any mercy." He inserts the vial inside her pussy.

"*Fuuck*," she moans.

He jerks his hand back and forth as he thrusts the vial in and out like he's out for blood. Like he wants her to cum just as bad as he wants her to suffer.

Fuck.

"Mia," I call out. "Relax. If you clench, the glass will break."

Draven's eyes light up, wild with lust as he slides the long, slender vial out slowly. He rubs the rim in circles around her clit. "Does it still hurt, Mia?" The rasp in his voice is pure smoke.

She bites her lip. "No."

"No, what? Use your words."

She sucks in a deep breath and whimpers as he drags the vial back down her slit. "No, it doesn't hurt."

"That's unfortunate." He thrusts it back inside her, fucking her hard, neither one of them caring about the possibility of broken glass at this point.

She twists her hips, bucking up and down as he sends her body convulsing into another orgasm.

Aries grabs my shoulder and squeezes. "The devil must fucking love us. And all the things we're going to do to our little lamb…"

I blow out a shaky breath, my cock pressing against my pants so hard it might tear a hole through them. "Nothing holy lives in these woods. Or in us."

"Uhhh," Mia moans out. Her belly spasms as Draven forces her to climax.

And when he pulls the vial out of her pussy, it's filled with her cum.

"I'm saving this for later." He twists the lid back on and stuffs the vial back into his pocket. "My celebratory drink when I'm sitting in Harker Mansion with the deed to it in my hand."

He stands up and over her. "Now I'm actually leaving."

We watch him disappear into the shadows.

I blow out a deep breath and roll her over so I can untie her wrists. Once she's on her feet and pulling her jeans back up, I point to the trees behind her. "Walk in a straight line for about a half mile, and you'll find your truck. I fixed your steering wheel."

She snorts. "You say that like you weren't the one who fucked it up to begin with."

I shrug. "Same difference."

Aries gives her a wink. "Don't get lost in the woods again, little lamb. We're not the only wolves out here tonight."

A darkness seems to encircle us at his words. An ominous energy, reminding us that Ever Graves is a cursed town. Yet something tells me that the devil favors Mia more than anyone. The murderous look in her eyes tells me she just might be the devil herself.

In one night, we may have unleashed a new hellscape. A furious inferno of black hair and eyes that glow blue and brown.

"I guess there's no point to this." She tosses the pepper spray onto the ground.

I chuckle. "Nah. That's about as dangerous as candy. There's not much that will protect you from us, Mia."

She glares back before stomping off. "We'll see about that."

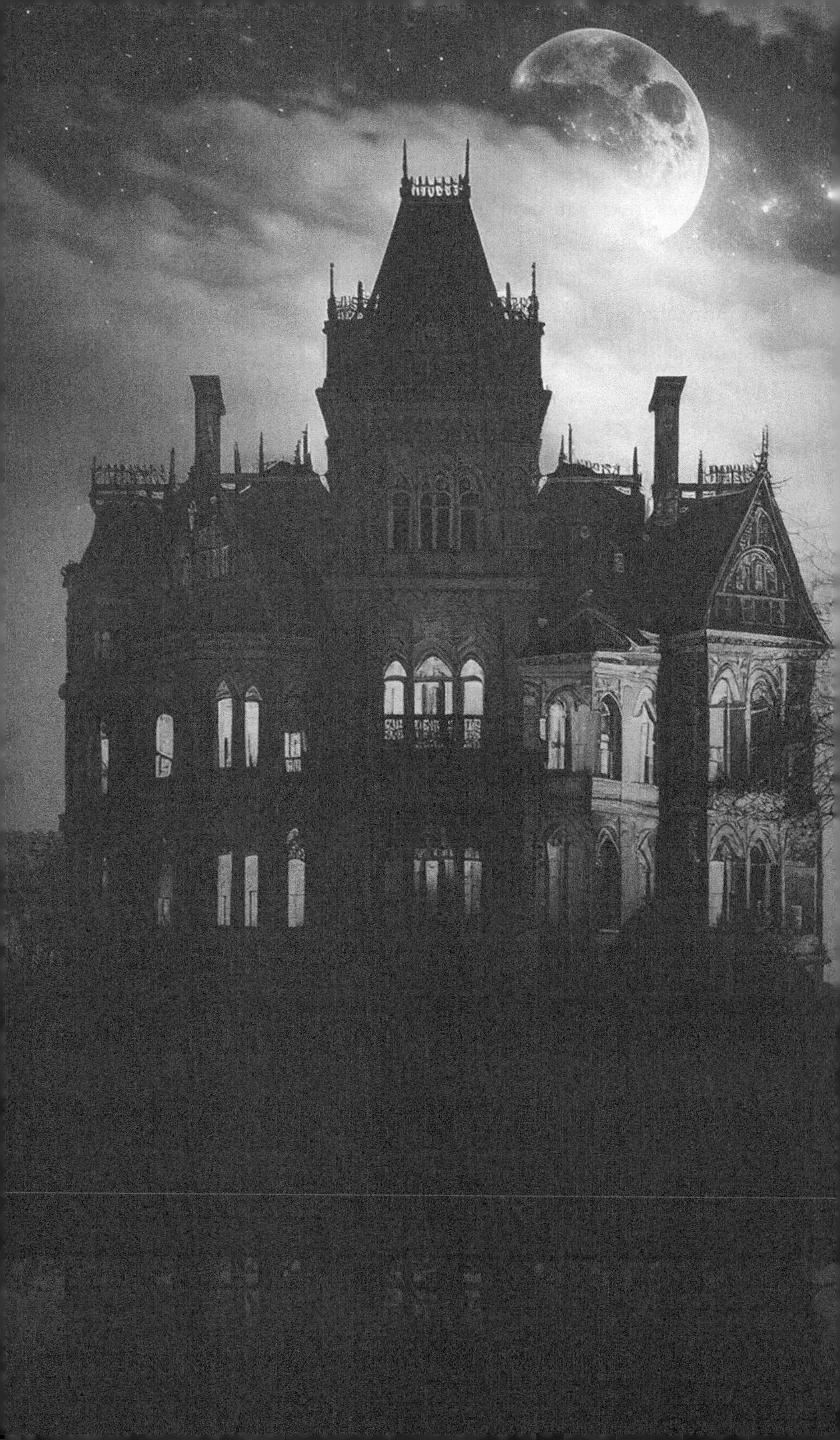

CHAPTER 15

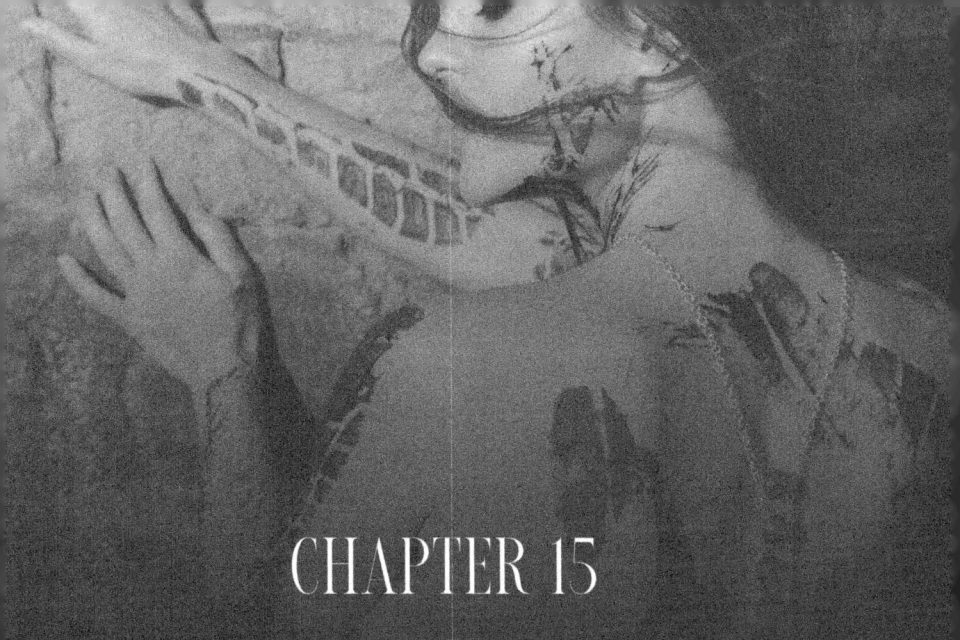

Mia

I press my forehead to the shower wall and close my eyes as the hot water runs down my back. I'm unholy. Disgraced. Broken. Cum and poison drip down my legs, taking my pride with them. *Right down the fucking drain.*

My wrists are bruised, marked by Draven's fingers. Red and swollen from his necktie. I wince as I lather shampoo into my scalp, sore from the grip he had on my hair. I shudder as I recall every second of it. My pussy is raw—aching.

I came so fucking hard.

What is wrong with me?

This is Nox's fault. He made me like this. He turned me into this fiend. A monster like him. What other reason could possibly exist that would make me crave what Draven, Aries, and Bones did to me tonight?

And I do crave it.

Aries was right. I loved every second. And I hate them for it.

I finish rinsing the filth out of my hair and look down at my body. The bruises extend to my thighs and hips. More fingerprint-size marks. My nipples are still hard and swollen from the edging Bones gave me. I'm angry that he didn't keep playing with them.

I need sleep and rest, but as soon as I close my eyes and drift off, I will wake again inside my nightmare prison. I wonder what normal people dream about. I envy them.

I don't bother to put on pajamas but slip into my four-poster bed naked. The silk sheets caress me, soothing my tender flesh. I lie back against the feather pillows and stare at the chandelier that hangs above me. It's vintage and decadent like this house. I'm pretty sure the beads are made of real diamonds instead of crystals, unlike the gaudier versions I've seen in thrift stores.

My eyelids are heavy. I fight to keep them open for as long as I can. Nox doesn't always come for me. There have been stretches of time when he's left me untouched. I don't know why or where he goes. He never tells me. And in *those* bouts of sleep, I don't dream of anything. It's exhilarating yet empty. I find myself missing him. I'm as attached to him as he is to me, cursed to love and hate the only one who has never abandoned me...

A deep yawn consumes me. I let myself drift. Falling, tumbling into sleep's abyss. Shadows envelop me. I'm transported, elevated, and thrown violently into my prison.

"Hello, dark one." Nox lays next to me, caressing my collarbone with his claws.

I blink a few times to orient myself. This room is dimly lit from a light source I've never been able to pinpoint. When I was a kid, he'd always meet me in the tunnel. I don't know if it's even real or a figment of my imagination. A construct I created to put in place of real-world physics.

But as soon as I was old enough for him to touch me, I'd wake up here in this dark and damp room with no furniture except a bed.

"What is this place?"

His eyes flicker with amusement. "This is your mind. I've told you many times."

"But how?" There are so many unanswered questions.

He stretches out next to me, his feet dangling off the edge of the king-size bed. "How does anything exist? All that matters is that *we* do."

I prop myself up on my side to look at him. He's strange and beautiful, simple yet complex. I devour him with my eyes. His muscles are pronounced—chiseled and carved—like a god. Tonight, he has his black hair swept up between his horns in a topknot. It shows off his deep-set eyes and high cheekbones.

His lips are thick and soft like pillows. I shiver as the memory of them suctioning my clit pops into my head.

The corners of his mouth turn up into a smirk. "You enjoying the view, dark one?"

I nod and continue my ogling. These quiet moments are rare. "Did you exist before me?"

His tail coils around his naked thighs. "I have no memory of anything before you."

The movement draws my gaze to his erection. For a long time, I thought every man had two cock heads. *Imagine my shock and disappointment.* "Would you look like this on the other side? If I brought you back with me?"

He wraps his tail around my waist and pulls me on top of him. "So many questions…"

My heart races as he skates his claws down my back. "And I'll keep asking them until you give me some answers."

His forked cock stirs between my legs, probing at my folds. "I can make myself look like anything. Like your human men. If you prefer."

A ripple of shame grips me. Guilt and fucking shame. I find a spot on his chest to fixate on. "They keep coming after me. I let them touch me, but I hate it."

He tips my chin up. "No, you don't. You can lie to them and to yourself when you're in their world, but you cannot lie to me in here."

I bite my lip. "I'm behaving like a greedy slut. It's not right."

He lifts my hips and sits me back down on one of his cockheads. I let out a gasp as he fills me so full the pressure builds in my belly. His other head probes at my anus. "Nox…" I whimper.

"No, my love. You are a beautiful dark angel. Embrace your desires. Claim them as I've claimed you." He burrows in deeper, and I almost black out.

Fuck, it feels so fucking good.

I let out a deep shuddering breath. "You're not angry?"

He thrusts hard. "I'm always angry." *Thrust.* "I want to be with you always," he growls.

Tingles rip through my core as he rubs his abdomen against my nub. I roll my hips in a circle and clench my pussy around his engorged shaft as I slide up and down it. "Mmm, fuck. I just might make that happen."

I'm playing a dangerous game with the devil now.

His red eyes widen as he slithers his tail up my back and wraps it around my neck. "Don't make promises you won't keep."

I jerk forward as a deep spasm shatters me. "I'm not. I just need more time."

He jolts up and pulls my legs around his waist. He shoves his forked tongue into my mouth as he fucks me harder. With one cockhead buried deep inside my pussy, the other one still teases the tip of my anus while his tail tightens around my throat. Every inch of me is possessed, constricted, and consumed by him.

He tastes like smoke and honey. Like hell and heaven wrapped into one. I explore his hot mouth hungrily, desperate to swallow every ounce of his essence. No one tastes like Nox. No one feels like him. I am fragile, wrapped inside his massive frame. *My delicious monster.*

"Hold on, dark one. I'm going deeper." He thrusts his second cockhead past the threshold of my anus, inching it farther in.

I gasp and grab onto his horns. "Oh, fuck... Nox. Fuck."

"*Relax*. Let me in." He reaches around and spreads my ass cheeks open wide. He slides deeper in, filling me so full in both holes.

An explosion erupts in my core, blurring my vision. I buck and ride him harder, grinding my hips against his like a wild animal.

"That's it. Cum hard for me. Drench me with every fucking drop." He grunts as his cockheads swell and pulse against my folds.

Tears stream down my cheeks as all the blood rushes to my center. The tingles spread to every inch of me, shattering my sanity, destroying every ounce of my soul.

"Nox," I cry out.

I feel his chest rumbling, vibrating against mine as he fills me with liquid. "You're not a greedy slut, Mia. You're the devil's whore. *My whore* who makes me cum so fucking hard."

His words push me over the edge again, and a second orgasm rips through me. "Fuck," I scream. I'm drowning in his thick cream. It oozes from my ass and my pussy, dripping down my thighs and soaking the mattress.

I stay sitting on him, not wanting to separate our bodies. My pussy trembles. I take shallow breaths as I ride out each spasm. "But what if I'm their whore too?" I say on a breath.

His tail constricts around my throat. "I hate it, but I will never deny you your desires."

I press my forehead to his, my hands still around his boned horns. "Then my sins will be the fucking death of me."

His cocks pulse inside me. "There is no life without sin. No human is free from it. Those who claim to be the most pious are the biggest sinners of all. The most dangerous. Steer clear of the self-proclaimed saints, dark one. They cause nothing but destruction in the name of their gods. And they will be the death of everything."

Nox is a mystery, a paradox of ancient DNA, myth, and urban legend. When he's not speaking in riddles, he makes more logical sense than any scholar I've ever read.

I kiss his cheek, relishing the way his soft skin feels against my lips. The ache in my chest is for him tonight. It overwhelms me. He's the closest thing to love that I've ever had. And it scares the fuck out of me. "Be patient with me. I'm close."

He brushes my hair back. "All I have is time and my love for you. Here or up there, it doesn't matter. In every world and every lifetime, *you are mine.*"

I nod and lie down next to him. He pulls me to his chest and caresses my back until I fall asleep.

I slurp curry off my spoon while Lettie reads my grandmother's letter from across the table. Maybe she can make more sense of it. I'm on edge, full of shame, and looking over my shoulder every five seconds. I haven't slept in days, and the only thing that's keeping me going is the hope that someone in this town can tell me who I really am.

She reads it a few times to herself, her lips moving as she skims the page.

Dearest Mia,

It pains me to write these words because if you are reading them, then I am gone from this world. I know you don't remember me. You were just a baby when you went away.

You must have many questions. Questions I will no longer be able to answer. Especially not in this letter. For, I fear this may fall into the wrong hands. But what you seek is in this town. In Ever Graves. In these very walls of Harker Mansion.

Between the living and the dead, secrets abound. I pray you have your father's cunning and your mother's heart. I will leave you with this, my final gift to you:

> Roses bring Thorns
> Night is ever Black
> When the shadow comes
> The Crane will attack
> Heads will roll
> When the nightmare roams
> Stick close to the well
> Of broken Bones

Your ever-loving grandmother,
Emma Harker

Her fingers tremble as she sets the letter on the table. "You were born here... Fuck."

I shrug. "Yeah, so? Weren't you?"

"No, Mia. Pregnant women are sent away because of the curse. I was born in Raven's Gate." She pushes her pad Thai noodles around on her plate.

My pulse thrums. I'm pretty fucking sure I know exactly what she's talking about. But I want to hear someone else say it out loud. I need to know I haven't been hallucinating Nox my whole life.

"What curse, Lettie?"

She tucks a strand of her dark hair behind her ear. The overhead lamp shines on her diamond earring, sending a ray of sparkles around her head like a halo. "I didn't believe it for a long time. It was just an old superstition that our families passed down to each generation. But it's true."

I swallow down the lump in my throat. "*What* is the curse?" I plead again.

She rubs her fingers together, a nervous tick I never noticed before. "The devil came to Ever Graves and fell in love. When his love wasn't requited, he put a curse on the whole town. Every girl born here would have a nightmare man attached to her soul. A depraved tormenter who would do everything in his power to seduce and manipulate."

A gasp slips past my lips. "How do you know for sure?"

"Because my best friend is a child of one of these unions. Her grandmother sent her mother away before she was born. To Wickford Hollow. Maureen Blackwell is half-nightmare. The only one of her kind that we know of. She's also Draven's cousin. And she is romantically involved with my brother Felix. Penny Blackwell was convinced that her presence would summon the devil back...." Lettie arches an eyebrow at me. "Maybe she was right."

Fuck.

It's a lot more fucked up than I thought. "What do you mean by that?"

She places her hand on my grandmother's letter. *"You were born here.* And now you're back. I'm guessing your nightmare man came with you."

A flush of relief mixed with fear washes over me. *I'm not crazy.* I knock back my sake and pour another one without skipping a beat. "Yes," I murmur.

We sit in silence and stare at our food for what feels like forever.

Lettie finally lets out a deep breath. "Emma must've thought she could spare you by sending you away. I can't imagine why your mother didn't leave before she had you. That's what all the women of Ever Graves do."

I shrug, more confused than ever. "All I know is that my mother spent some time in Absentia Asylum. Like me. I found some old invoices in the study. Maybe that's why."

She folds her hands in her lap to conceal her shakes. Panic disorder. I know the signs well. "What's it like?" she asks.

I've wanted someone to talk to about Nox my whole life, but

now, I don't know how to explain him. "It's like he's a part of me but also his own separate being. He's a monster, Lettie. And I have let him defile me since I was eighteen years old. The things I let him do... Anyway, it's a dream world, but it's as real and vivid as you and I sitting here in this restaurant. I don't know why or how. It's all I've ever known."

Lettie white-knuckles the table, her eyes wide. "Fuck."

I snicker. "No pun intended, right?"

She blushes. "I'm sorry. That's none of my business. But it might be my brother's if the rest of this letter means what I think it does."

I shake my head. "No need to apologize. You're the first person I've ever told who actually believes me. But... your brother? Please elaborate."

She holds up the letter and reads a section aloud. "*Roses bring Thorns. Night is ever Black. When the shadow comes. The Crane will attack. Heads will roll. When the nightmare roams. Stick close to the well. Of broken Bones.*"

"So, Emma Harker was a poet." I furrow my brow at her. I still don't get it.

She sighs and retrieves a pen from her purse. "May I?"

I nod, dumbfounded.

She circles six of the words. "Look, Mia. Thorns. Black. Crane. Well. Bones... It's cryptology. Emma embedded a code in this letter. Aries Thorn. Draven Blackwell. Bones Crane."

A wave of nausea hits me. "Fuck. It's been staring me right in the face. It's not even well hidden. I'm an idiot."

She clasps my hand. "No, it's out of context for you because you didn't grow up here. It would be confusing for anyone who isn't part of these fucked up founding families."

A dark energy slides through my veins like black sludge. I shudder. "Draven hates me. Aries thinks I'm a toy to play with. And your brother jammed my truck's gear shift the other night so they could lure me into the woods. And Emma wants me to trust them? What in the hell was my grandmother smoking?"

Lettie starts to take a sip of her sake but pauses mid-air. "Bones did what?" A few snickers come our way at the sound of her raised voice.

I motion for her to lower it. "It's fine. They've made it their life's mission to torment me."

She slams her cup down and fishes for her phone, all while cursing in Spanish under her breath. "I'm sorry, Mia. I should've waited for you to drive out before I left. Bones asked me to invite you. He promised me that it was with good intentions. I feel like the idiot now."

I stop her from dialing. "I'm a big girl, Lettie. And you aren't responsible for Bones."

She huffs. "Those boys and their stupid poison wars. I don't want you to get caught in the middle."

"I already am... The second I moved into Harker Mansion, I became a part of it. I just have to figure out what I want to do about it." I sigh into my sake.

Lettie motions to the server for the check. "Well, your grandmother is trying to tell you something about them. Maybe there are more clues in your house. I can help you look if you want."

I'd go through life without friends all over again if it meant it would lead me to this one. She's worth the wait. "Thanks, hon. But can we just get really fucking drunk tonight? I need to take my mind off everything."

She lights up. "Hell yeah, we can. Happy hour at Duff's is just about to kick off."

"Perfect." I smile back. Hopefully, Draven, Aries, and Bones are brooding in a dark hole somewhere. Although, a tiny little depraved part of me is hoping I run into them.

Fuck. I'm such a glutton for punishment.

To my disappointment, my new stalkers are not at Duff's when we arrive. They seem to be the only ones in the whole town who aren't here. We grab a couple of shots of whiskey, wade through the crowd, and find an open spot to stand by the pool tables.

The spicy liquid burns on the first sip, but it sends a warm flush through my veins that I welcome and breathe into. "Fuck, I needed this tonight."

Lettie surveys the crowd, her eyelids fluttering toward a group of pretty girls over by the bar. "Mmm, same." She takes a slow sip of her drink.

"You know them?" She can't take her eyes off the group.

She sucks in a deep breath. "I used to. I haven't seen them in a long time. Ever since I moved away for school."

"Do you wanna go say hi? I'll hold our spot here." There's a storm brewing in her gaze.

She shakes her head. "No. Some things are better left alone. You know?"

Oh, yes, how I know that all too well. But I don't have that luxury. My past is all around me. A history that I can't escape no matter where I go. I leave Lettie to get us two more shots at the bar. I side-eye the girls she was staring at, curious as to what the history is there. They whisper and giggle when they catch me looking. I snicker. *Catty bitches.*

Fuck it. "Can I get four shots of your house bourbon?"

The big, bald man from behind the bar nods as he lines up the shot glasses and pours them all in a row without spilling a drop.

"Nice."

He gives me a wink. "You want a tray to carry them?"

"That would be awesome. Thanks." He must be the owner. He has that air about him.

"No problem."

As I walk back through the crowded bar with the wobbly tray of shots, I pray I don't drop it on someone.

Halfway to our spot, an arm snakes around my waist. "Hey, darlin'. Come back over after you deliver those drinks. We want to order another round."

I snort and look up to see a handsome blond man with a sloppy grin plastered on his face. "Um, yeah. So the bar's over there, buddy. Go get them yourself."

He bursts out laughing. "Oh, shit. You don't work here. Sorry, beautiful. I'll bring back another round for you too."

I feel my cheeks flush. The whiskey is working. "Cool. Whatever."

By the time I get back to Lettie, there are two more frat-looking guys on either side of her. "Wow, you guys don't waste any time."

She tucks a strand of hair behind her ear. "Friends of yours?"

I laugh. "New friends, I guess."

As we make introductions, the first guy I bumped into races back with a tray of his own. It's filled to the edges with shots. "All right, ladies. What are your names, and what are we toasting to?"

I hold up one of my shots and raise it. "I'm Mia, and I'll be drinking to welcome distractions."

Lettie grabs one of my whiskey shots and wrinkles her brow at his tray. "I don't drink tequila."

"Well, we'll get you something else. What's your name, sweetheart?" he asks with that lazy grin still stuck on his face.

She crosses her arms over her chest. "Villette Crane."

"Pretty," one of the other ones says. I've already forgotten their names.

She leans over and whispers in my ear, "I'm not feeling them or this bar tonight."

I nod. "We can leave. Wanna go somewhere else?"

There's hesitation in her eyes as her gaze flits back to the group of girls by the bar. But I don't know her well enough to read her. "I think I just want to go home, Mia. Sorry."

My heart sinks. I'm not ready to go back to my big, old, empty mansion yet. But I don't want to guilt her into staying if she's uncomfortable.

I shake my head. "It's okay. I understand. I think I might hang here for a bit longer though."

She sighs. "I don't want to leave you here by yourself."

"Ladies, what are we whispering about?" the jock drawls.

I ignore him. "I'm a big girl, remember? I'll be fine. I'll just call a car service if I drink too much. You do have those in this town, right?"

She nods as she side-eyes the three dudes. "Are you sure? I can stick around for a little longer."

I pull her into an embrace. "Don't be silly. I'm having a good time, and you aren't. Go home and get some rest. I'll call you later."

She hugs me back. "Please be careful and text me the second you get home."

Her concern is new to me. It's nice to have a friend who gives a shit about my wellbeing. "I'll do one better. I'll text you when I leave the bar *and* when I get home."

She gives the guys a shaky wave before she stalks off. I watch her walk over to the bar, lean over it, and whisper something into the bald man's ear. He nods and looks over in my direction.

I can't help but smile. I assume she's asked him to keep an eye on me. It's sweet but not necessary. But it makes my heart melt all the same. Lettie is good people.

A hand slides across my lower back, his fingertips inch up underneath my shirt. "Her loss. More drinks for us now."

I don't like the feel of his skin against mine. He's good-looking, charming, and exactly the type of guy I would take home from a bar in Raven's Gate. So why am I annoyed by the gesture?

The three of them crowd in around me as my head starts to

spin from the booze. "One more, and then I'm heading home as well, boys."

"Come on. Don't be like that. Stay and party with us," jock number two pleads as he shoves one of his tequila shots toward me.

I down my last shot instead, wincing as the bourbon stings my throat. I'm not a big tequila fan either. "Thank you for the offer, but...."

My focus is pulled away when I spot *him* in my periphery. No, not just spot. When I *feel* his eyes on me. Fuck. My pulse ticks up, and my palms sweat under the dark and twisted heat of his gaze. *Draven fucking Blackwell.*

I'll be fucking damned if I let him think he's the reason I leave. He does not get to have that power over me. *I can't let him.*

I flash the jocks a seductive grin. "Sure, why not? Let's party."

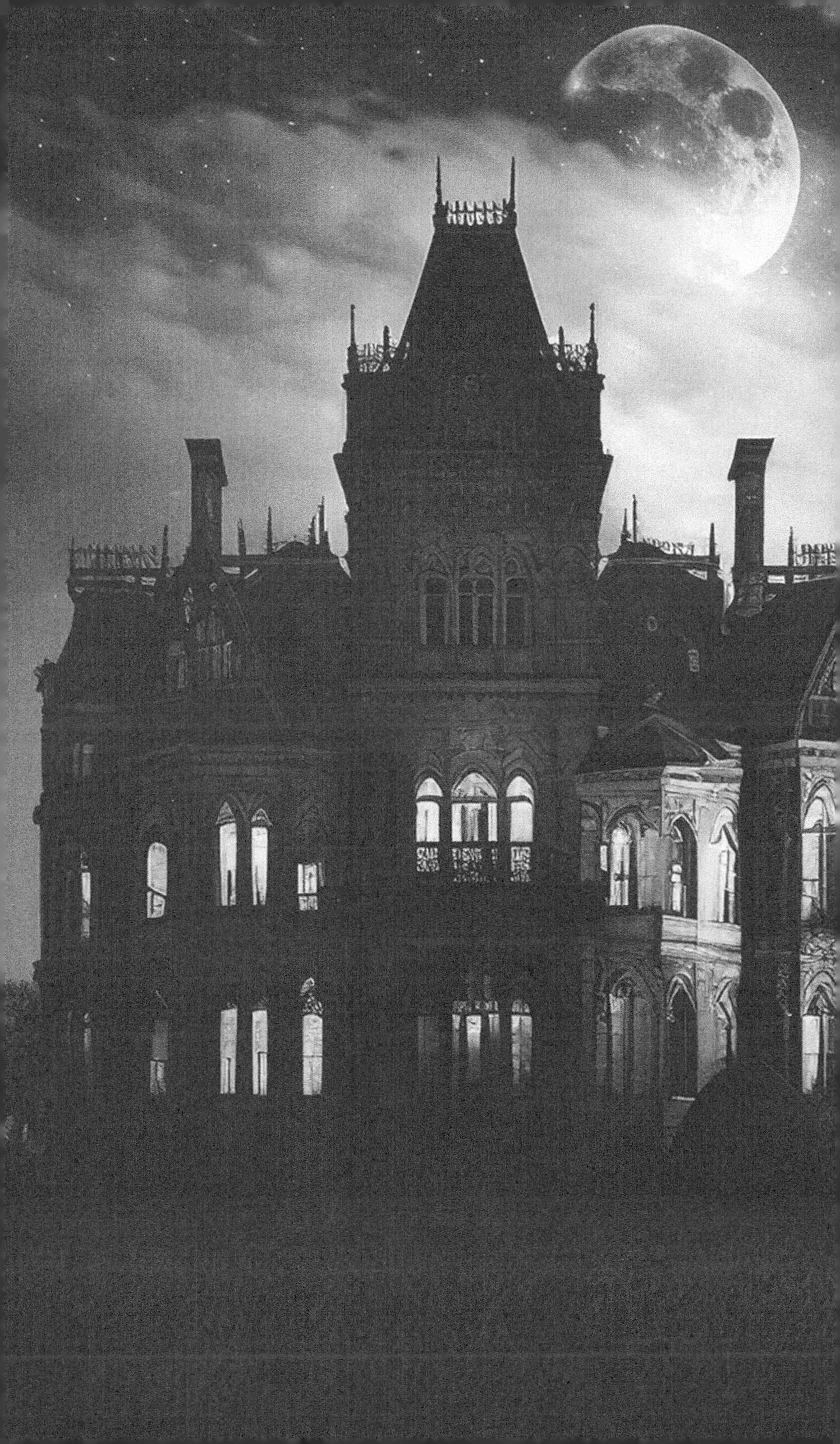

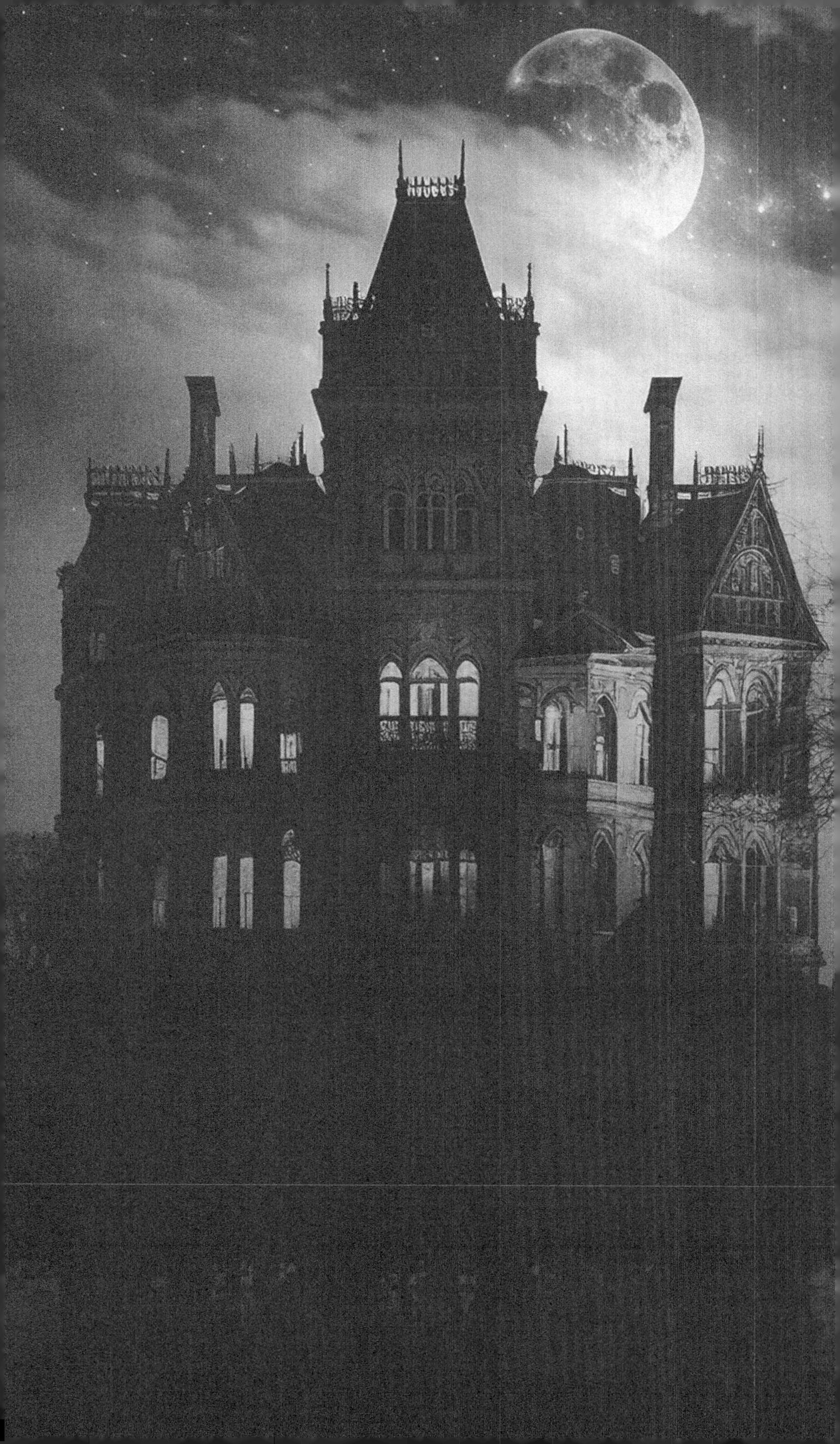

Chapter 16

Draven

His hand is on her back. Why the fuck is his fucking hand on her fucking back?

Murder moves to the top of my list tonight.

I shoot off a text to Bones and Aries while I wait for Duff to pour me a gin, my fingers are shaking as I type. If Mia thinks she can run around *my* town doing whatever she wants, she's sorely mistaken. As if our little party in the woods didn't make my message clear enough. It's time I remind her again.

I grab my glass and stalk toward my dark little temptress.

Her eyelids flutter when she stares up at me, her throat bobbing as she tries to swallow down her nerves.

I snatch the shot of tequila from her hand before she can take a sip and set it on the edge of the pool table. "You're really trying to earn your nickname, aren't you, Trouble?"

She edges away from the big dumb-looking oaf with his hand on her back. "What I do is none of your business, Draven."

Everything in this town is my business. *She'll learn.* "You should be home signing papers and packing, not prancing around like a whore."

"Whoa, watch your mouth. Where I come from, we don't talk to women like that," the blond idiot interjects.

If I could murder him with my mind, I would. But I'm going to enjoy doing it with my bare hands instead. "Well, maybe you should go back to where you're from. This is Ever Graves, and here we don't meddle in business that doesn't concern us."

The oaf side-eyes Mia. "Is this your boyfriend or something?"

She snort laughs out loud. "Um, no. He is whatever the opposite of a boyfriend is."

I grip the edge of the pool table. "I don't care what you call me, Mia. But as long as you live in that house, *in this town*, you will have me breathing down your neck. Keep pushing me, and you'll see the full extent of my wrath."

Her eyes darken, but she licks her lips. There's a slight twitch in her jaw, a telling tick that shows me how her glands salivate for me. "Go fuck yourself, Draven."

Okay, this is how we're playing it? I chuckle and reach for her arm. "You've had too much to drink. Time to go home."

Douchebag intercepts me.

"She says she's not with you, bro." He holds his pool stick up, waving it at me like he's declaring it a weapon.

"I'm not your bro. But because you're not from here, I'll let it slide. This has nothing to do with you, so I suggest you go back to your buddies over there and have another round on me." I can sometimes be rational when provoked. But my fuse is fucking short.

He puffs out his chest and laughs. He looks me up and down, sizing me up. This poor bastard assumes because he's bigger than me that it's going to be an unfair fight. And it will be. For him.

Mia rolls her eyes. "You can't throw money at everything you want to go away, Draven. Leave me alone and let me have some fun for once."

"No means no, *bro*," the douchebag drawls.

Fuck, diplomacy. I'm going to kill him.

"I'll wire you money for the damages," I call out to Duff.

He almost drops the glass he's buffing. "What damages?"

I turn back to the douchebag. "I know you think you're a big deal wherever it is you're from. Let me see if I guess right. You get free drinks at your local dive bar, even though it's out of pity because you injured yourself playing high school football and never made it to the big leagues. And I bet all the washed-up cheerleaders line up to suck your cock, but you secretly love how your *buddies* suck it the best—"

"Watch it." His smug smile fades into a sneer.

"Oh, am I hitting a nerve?"

Mia clutches her neck. "*Draven.*"

I inch closer and slide my fingers through the brass knuckles in my pocket. "But you see, this is Ever Graves. And *here*, I'm in charge. People buy *me* drinks to stay on my good side. And trust me, you don't want to be on my fucking bad side. Isn't that right, Duff?"

The exasperated bar owner shakes his head. "Can you at least kill them outside this time?" he calls back.

I grin but never break contact with the stupid fucking white boy in front of me. "You have two options: walk away and enjoy some free drinks on me *or* stay right here and see what happens. I doubt anyone will actually miss you."

His nostrils flare. "How about the option where I beat the shit out of you?"

I laugh in his face. "Yeah, that's not even remotely close to happening, *bro*."

Two of his buddies, who match him in size, move closer, flexing their arms behind him.

Mia grunts in frustration. "Enough, Draven. Let's just talk about this outside." She goes to move past him and his little posse, when he grabs her arm and shoves her behind him. His buddies hold her back.

"Okay, everyone, chill, please," she groans out.

I light up a cigarette and count to ten before I exhale. "So, option four, then?"

He crosses his arms over his chest and cocks his head to the side. "And what's that? Your girl fucking all three of us tonight while you cry yourself to sleep?"

"Yeah, not helping your cause." I take another long drag before putting my cigarette out in the palm of my hand.

He wavers slightly as he stares at the smoke singeing off my flesh.

I pull out a vial of nightshade and give him a wink before I shoot it down my throat. "I bet you think this is gonna go your way somehow."

The guy gasps when he looks back into my eyes. "Your pupils… they're fucking glowing. What the fuck?"

His two buddies back up with Mia still in their grasp when they hit two hard walls of solid muscle behind them, Aries and Bones.

The distraction breaks their grip, and Mia wrenches free. She charges forward, directing her anger at me instead. "You don't own me. I can have drinks with whomever I want."

"I disagree. It's time for you to leave now. I'll call Lettie to come back and get you." All I see is red right now, and she's only aggravating me more.

Her mouth falls open. "No, Draven. You don't get to tell me what to do. You're not my boyfriend or my father."

I wrap a hand around her throat, startling everyone around us. "Yeah, but I'm sure you'd love to call me both. Especially *Daddy*."

She jerks back, desperate to break free from me. "*Never*. Now let me go so I can finish hanging out with my new friends."

I push her up against the pool table. "You mean the ones who said they want to take turns fucking you? I don't think so, baby girl.

That privilege belongs to us. Don't make me bend you over in front of all these people and remind you how wet I make your pussy."

"We'll wait for you outside." Aries snickers as he and Bones drag the three douchebags out the front door. Duff actually helps them for once. I'm guessing he doesn't want to mop our mess up off his floor again.

Mia's pulse beats fast against my fingers, her chest heaving as she struggles to catch her breath. "You can't have me, Draven. I'm never going to be yours."

There's a wistfulness in her tone. Almost like it's out of her control. I ignore it. "You've been mine since the second I decided I was going to destroy you."

She tilts her head up until our noses almost touch, our lips are close enough to kiss. "First, you think you can steal my land, and now me? All you care about is that poison. And you don't even own that. So don't treat me like shit and then expect me to obey your every command."

This fucking woman is wrecking me. I can't eat or sleep or even fuck random strangers in bathrooms anymore. And she has the fucking audacity to try and remove herself from any blame?

I tighten my grip around her throat as I press my hips into hers. "*I own you*. I. Own. Everything. You hear me, Mia? And I'll decide what I want to do with the *things* I own." My cock stiffens, tenting my pants. Threatening her is my new fucking foreplay. "I think you love being treated like shit. It's the only language you know... the only thing that makes you cum."

Her throat bobs as she attempts to swallow with my hand still around it. "Shut up. You don't know me. I might be depressed and sleep-deprived, *and* I may have made some questionable choices in the last few weeks, but that doesn't give you the right to assume that I have a fetish for your toxicity."

I want to kiss her so I can taste the ache on her tongue. "There's a saying, 'When someone shows you who they are, believe them...'

I think I'm only beginning to learn the extensive list of fetishes you have. I eat toxicity for breakfast." I brush my lips across her cheek and whisper in her ear, "You like it when it hurts because pain is the only thing that lets you know you're still alive."

She whimpers as I nuzzle my nose against her temple. "Stay away from me, Draven. Stay away from Harker Mansion. You have no idea the depths of its darkness."

A sinister memory threatens to resurface, but I push it down and grit my teeth. "This whole town is cursed, Trouble. Every wretched inch of it... *I know about your nightmare.*"

Her body stiffens as she gazes up at me, her eyes wide and full of fear. "What do you mean?"

Oh, no, you don't get to act like a brat and then get answers out of me.

I let go of her neck and step back. "Exactly what I said. Now you really need to get home, Mia. I still have to take care of something outside."

She shakes her head. "I'm not going anywhere until you tell me what you know."

I let out a deep sigh, masking my amusement. "Fine. But you're going to have to watch me murder your new friends first."

Her gaze remains fixated on my face as I drive. It's unnerving. I keep my eyes on the road, my jaw clenched, only glancing in the rearview mirror every few feet to make sure Aries and Bones are still following close behind.

"How far are you going to take this?" The venom in her voice falters between the ache.

I light up a cigarette and roll down the window. The icy wind whips through my SUV like a slap in the face. "There is no line with me. You're going to learn that tonight."

She huffs and looks away. "You know kidnapping is illegal, right?"

"There are no kids here. *This*—I wave my finger in a circle between us—"is what I call consequences."

She folds her goose-pebbled arms over her chest. "And what about the guys from the bar? They did nothing wrong."

The audacity astounds me. She still doesn't get it. "Nothing wrong? I'm guessing you didn't see the toxin they slipped into those tequila shots, then. I gave them a chance to walk away, and they refused. You're lucky I showed up when I did. Fuck. I should've left you there to learn your lesson."

She gasps. "What the fuck? How in the hell did you see them slip something into our drinks? You were on the other side of the room."

I loosen my tie and take a deep breath. "You forget, I drink poison, Mia. I can spot a toxic chemical in liquid from a mile away. You're welcome."

I still don't look in her direction. Her beauty is villainous. I'm already suffocating as it is. I'll never get the scent of jasmine out of my SUV now. Or the taste of her cherry fucking lip balm off my lips. Fuck. I can see her clenching her thighs together in my periphery, and it's driving me wild with need. The ache that lives in her body fills the space between us, begging to be satiated.

All I want is to keep my family's company from falling apart. And the only thing standing in my way is that fucking baneberry. The only one preventing me from having it all is her. So as much as I want to bury my cock inside every single one of her crevices, I can't. It feels too fucking good.

The best scenario is for her to see us for who we are. Monsters. Villains. Fucking depraved psychos who show no mercy to anyone who crosses us. It's the quickest way to get her to sign over the deed and run her out of town. The sooner I get this woman out of

Ever Graves, the sooner I can get her out of my system. And then I'll burn every single jasmine bush to the ground.

As I drive through the rusted iron gates, she rests her head against the window, defeated. "The graveyard? How morbidly poetic."

"They're going to end up here anyway," I grumble as I park and kill the engine.

There's a part of her that still thinks this is a game. That I won't go through with it. I can see it in her eyes.

"Then what? You drive me home and walk me to my door like a gentleman after a first date?" She snickers.

Oh, poor, little lamb. She really has no idea.

"Something like that." I exit the vehicle, stalk around to the passenger side, and open her door. She moves to get out, but I box her in. "Don't you dare scream for them. Or I will do things so unspeakable, it will give you a real reason to scream over."

She sighs, and her eyelids flutter. Her blue eye hungers while her brown one darkens, her pupils swelling from adrenaline. "What do you know about my nightmare?"

A tinge of jealousy twists in my gut. The thought of him getting to touch her whenever he wants... I press in closer. "I know enough."

She looks down at her hands. "You don't know shit." Her voice is a whisper, raspy, and full of shame.

Good.

Ever since she moved here, the darkness has thickened—expanded like a balloon about to pop. She may not have chosen this curse, but she could resist it. Not everyone has that luxury.

Aries and Bones wrestle two of the jocks out of Aries's SUV and drag them over, breaking the psychotic energy between us.

"Where's the other one?" I snap.

Aries smirks. "Dead. In the back seat."

Mia's eyes widen. "Please tell me you're joking."

"You just couldn't help yourself," I quip.

Bones shrugs. "He wouldn't stop screaming, so I hit him. I forget my own strength."

The other two are gagged with their wrists bound, their faces as white as ghosts. I light another cigarette and sigh through the exhale. "Let's finish this so we can go grab a bite to eat. I'm starving."

I stretch out my hand toward Mia. "Come on. Time to face your consequences."

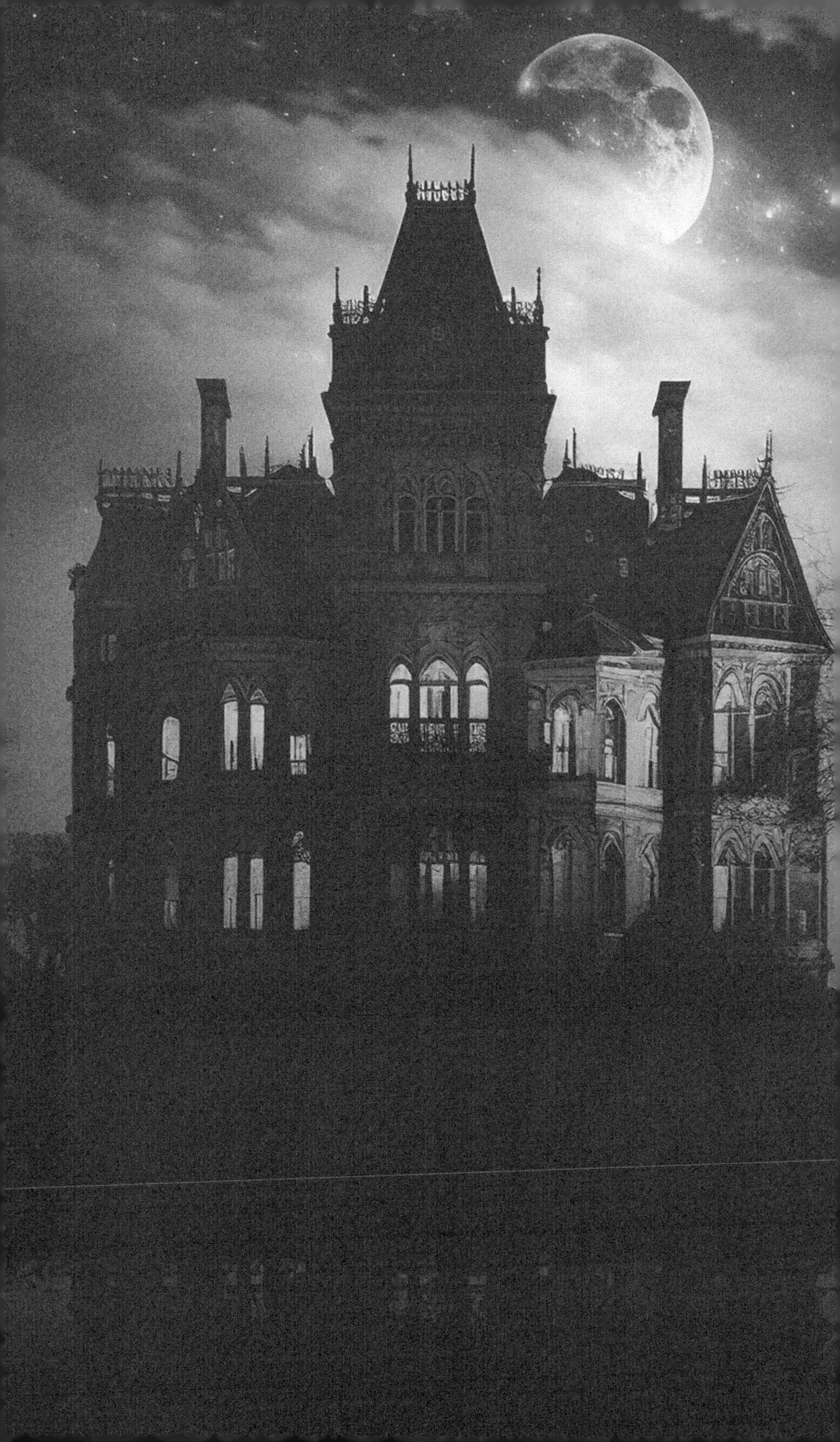

CHAPTER 17

Mia

I SHOULD HAVE LEFT THE BAR WITH LETTIE.
"You brought this on yourself, little lamb," Aries murmurs in my ear. His breath on my face does something wild to my senses. I gaze up into his blue-green eyes and get dizzy. It's enough to make me momentarily forget that I'm in a creepy graveyard with three psychos who just murdered someone and are about to murder two more.

The crisp autumn night air strokes the back of my neck like a warning. I shudder. "You're out of your fucking minds."

Bones pinches my hips and pulls me toward him. The weight of his chest against mine sends a shiver rippling between my legs. I imagine the tight cords of his muscles flexing and constricting when he fucks. Ferocious yet elegant like a wolf. All three of them are a cacophony of exquisite violence, beautiful yet deadly.

I take shallow breaths as his fingers dig into my hip bones. "Of course, murder turns you on."

He tilts his head down, his gaze resting on my cleavage. "I want them to watch you cum while they die."

Fuck.

I was being sarcastic, but they really are sick as fuck. What does that say about me? *My panties are fucking soaked.*

Aries stands behind me, his hands around my neck. "That sounds like a fun game. You in, little lamb? You gonna let me and Bones play with you while Dray butchers those bastards?"

I swallow hard as I look at Draven. He's tightening their ropes around two skeleton trees, grunting over the gurgled cries of his victims.

My cheeks flush, and my belly knots. "I'm not your toy to play with."

I try to wiggle out of their grasp, but they press in closer. I'm sandwiched between them, two immovable forces who only get more excited the more I try to break free.

"Let me go," I growl.

"Shh, relax and enjoy the show." Aries pins my arms to my sides.

I can't stop shaking. I don't *want* to want this.

Bones unbuttons my jeans before pulling the zipper down. He slips two fingers inside my panties, sliding them down my slit. His eyes widen. "Mmm, you're so wet. *Fuck.*"

I bite my lip to stifle a moan. He inches his fingers inside my pussy, and I almost crumble.

"That's it, nice and easy." Aries leans over to watch Bones thrust in and out at a pace so slow, I think I might die from lack of release.

"Eyes on me, Mia," Draven commands.

I bite my lip so hard, I draw blood. I can't let this whimper free. That's what they want. I can only give them so much.

The moonlight glints off the blade of Draven's knife. He caresses my cheek with the flat of it. "For good luck."

Bones adds a third finger, and it takes all of my mental fortitude not to scream from pleasure.

He chuckles. "The more you resist, the harder you're gonna cum."

My chest heaves as I struggle to catch my breath.

Draven stalks over to the two jocks. He approaches the one who touched me first. "Let's talk about your bad choices. You tried to drug *our* little lamb. Then you put your hands on her. But you wanna know what your biggest mistake was?"

The blond man is sweating so profusely that it looks like someone dropped a bucket of water on him. He shakes his head and groans through his gag.

Draven points to Bones. "See that man? That psycho who is finger fucking *our* girl to the sounds of your pathetic whimpering…" Draven drags the tip of his blade down the man's cheek. "That man is the older brother of the *other* girl you were going to drug tonight. So after I kill you, he's going to desecrate your corpse."

The man's eyes bulge with fear right before tears stream out of them.

Fuck.

Bones's gaze turns feral as he shoves a fourth finger inside my aching pussy. "Motherfucker," he growls.

"That's it. Use her," Aries coaxes.

I can't hold back anymore. I let out a deep moan as Bones stretches me. He thrusts harder and deeper, rocking my hips back into the tops of Aries's thighs.

"Oh, now you're having fun. You like it rough, don't you?" Bones barks at me.

I stagger back, my knees turning to mush. His fingers curl up into my G-spot. But he doesn't coax it. No he's flicking it, pressing so hard I can barely breathe. He wants to punish me.

The joke's on him.

I cry out and thrust my hips up. "*Harder*," I beg.

Aries chuckles. "Be careful what you wish for, little lamb."

Bones pinches my jaw with his free hand and shoves me back into Aries. "Get her on top of that grave."

As they drag me over to a cracked and dirty headstone, Draven uses his knife to cut away the blond man's shirt, ripping it off to expose his sweaty chest.

He laughs and points to one of the man's tattoos. "I love when white boys think that inking someone else's cultural symbol on their bodies makes them more interesting. You don't even fucking know what this means. How fucking dare you. I think I'll remove it."

"Draven," I plead. While I agree with the intention, my stomach turns at the thought of him carving a chunk of this man's flesh out.

Bones yanks my pants and panties off before setting me on top of the gravestone. "Too late for begging now, baby girl."

Aries hugs me from behind, pinning my arms to my sides again. The cold stone rubs against my ass as Bones shoves my legs apart and stands in between them.

"Eyes on me, Mia," Draven repeats. "You will watch what you made me do tonight."

Bones shoves four of his fingers back inside my pussy without warning.

"Fuck," I cry out as I buck against Aries.

But my screams are drowned out by the man who tried to drug me. Draven makes his first cut. He digs the tip of his blade deep into the man's flesh and pulls down, splitting him open from his nipple to his ribs.

I jerk my head away, bile rising in my throat. Bones thrusts harder, snapping me like a rubber band. I'm caught between horror and ecstasy.

"What did I say, Mia?" Draven roars.

Aries nuzzles my neck from behind. "You've been such a good girl so far, don't spoil it now." He squeezes the back of my head and forces it back toward Draven.

"Fuck, you're all crazy," I say on a shaky breath.

Bones presses his thumb against my throbbing clit. "Yeah, that's what you like about us the most."

I arch my back into Aries's chest as a crescendo of spasms builds in my core. "Oh, shit. *Bones, please.* It's too much."

"It's not enough." He snickers. "Relax for me."

He pulls out, and my heart races. When he slides back in, my stretch deepens without warning. My belly tightens. Oh, fuck. I look down to see Bones's entire fist inside me.

"Wait—"

Aries forces my head back to Draven. "This is it, little lamb. The slaughter."

I lock eyes with Draven. His lips curl up into a sinister smirk. The man lets out a bloodcurdling scream just as Draven twists the knife into the man's gut and pulls up, splitting him open.

I can't stop myself from rocking back and forth on Bones's fist. My climax is building, climbing toward release. Aries wraps his arms around my chest and tilts me back so I'm almost suspended in midair.

I can't breathe. I'm so fucking full. I'm overstimulated, close to passing out, as he fists my pussy raw.

"Thatta girl, cum for us," Bones growls.

Covered in blood, Draven is the most unhinged I've ever seen anyone. His designer clothes are tainted, his hair disheveled, and his brow is soaked with sweat. He stalks toward us, a wild look in his eyes.

I am stuck between them, drowning in their depravity and degradation. I can't hold on to my sanity any longer. My clit swells like it might explode. A rush of tingles and spasms erupt in my core and span out, gripping my entire body.

"Fuck!" I jerk back, arching my hips forward, and the back of my thighs slam against the icy headstone.

"Oh, you are a beautiful sight," Aries murmurs.

It feels like flying. Like falling and drowning and being lifted all at the same time.

Bones smiles as he milks me. "Every time you tell me it's too much, I will give you more."

I whine like a cat in heat as my juices drip down my thighs. The ache rolls into another spasm as he keeps thrusting. It's everything. I feel like an animal, flailing my arms while Aries tries to keep me contained. I ride Bones's fist so fucking hard it's impossible to discern who is doing what to who now.

When Bones stills his hand inside me, Draven presses the bloody flat of his blade to my neck. My eyelids are heavy, fluttering as I look up at him. I don't dare move another muscle.

"My turn," he growls.

Bones slides out of me and steps back. "That was just a warm-up."

Oh, dear god.

"We're done. You're covered in blood. Take me home," I plead. And yet all the darkest parts of me are on fire, aching to be consumed by him.

Draven steps in between my legs. "That's not what that spark in your eyes is telling me you want." He takes his time wiping the blood off his blade before sheathing it. There's a thick silence between the four of us. An ominous quiet that threatens to scare me out of my own skin.

He flips the covered blade around and presses the hilt against my nub. "*Are* you done, Mia?"

I tremble as he slowly drags the hilt up and down my slit. "You shouldn't do that."

He chuckles and inches the tip of the hilt inside my pussy. "Oh? You afraid you're going to like it too much?"

I bite back a moan as he pushes in farther. I'm going to fucking hyperventilate. It feels so fucking dirty. But I'm a glutton for his punishment. Because it's *him*. He's in control of my pleasure and my pain.

"I want you to cum on my knife." *Thrust.* "You owe me your cum." *Thrust.* "Every fucking drop."

I gasp as he pushes the entire length of the hilt inside my soaking wet pussy. "Draven… oh, fuck. *Yes.*"

Aries pins my arms back and looks down over my shoulder. "Mmm, baby girl. You're taking it so good. That knife was made for your pussy."

A deep, animalistic moan escapes my throat, and stars dot my vision. He's gentler than when he fucked me with the poison bottle. That was rough and brutal, but this… This is agonizing. Slow and deliberate. I'm meant to feel every inch of it.

Bones kisses my cheek. Holy fuck, his lips are so soft and warm. My skin tingles when he scrapes his teeth down my jaw.

Draven rotates the hilt in circles, spinning it as he pumps in and out. "Is my dirty little slut close?" *Twist.* "Hmm? You about to unravel for me?" *Thrust.* "I'm waiting, Trouble." *Twist.* "I spilled blood for you. Now spill your cum for me."

Aries squeezes the sides of my neck, pinching them so hard that my vision darkens. And it's the final push I need. Fuck.

I throw my head back against him and release a feral scream. Fuck. Fuck. Fuck. It's like they lit a match inside me and added gasoline. I'm on fire. Combusting into nothing but slivers of the woman I thought I was.

There's dark, and then there's *unholy.* My blasphemous soul will never be redeemed after this.

When Aries releases his hold on my neck, Draven's face inches back into focus. I blink away the sparkles of dust that float in my vision. I try to speak, but nothing intelligible comes out. I can't control it. I soak his knife with my cum, sopping it all over the handle.

Fuck.

Draven rubs his quivering lips across the handle of the blade, licking my juices off of it. "I own every inch of you."

My legs shake as I lean against the gravestone. "I can't keep letting you do this to me."

He plants a soft peck on my lips so I can taste myself on his breath. "Oh, but you will."

After Aries wipes me clean with his handkerchief, Bones helps me back into my panties and jeans. I have to lean on him so I don't topple over.

"What about the other guy?" Bones asks.

I'm a pile of mush as I watch Draven stalk back over to my predators. I don't have the stomach to watch him gut another person tonight.

I'm relieved when he unties him. "Let this be a lesson you won't forget."

The sniveling man can barely stand he's shaking so hard. "Please. I promise I won't tell anyone."

Draven grabs him by the collar. "You better fucking tell *everyone*. Tell them what Draven Blackwell does to those who come to Ever Graves and fuck with what belongs to him. You understand? Good. Now get the fuck out of here and don't come back."

The man takes off in a sprint toward the woods.

"I love it when you talk about yourself in the third person," Aries snort laughs. "It freaks them out more."

How are they all so fucking calm after that? I stagger forward, toward the cars. "Can someone please take me home now?"

Before I reach the passenger side of his SUV, Draven is at my side, opening the door for me. "Do you need help getting in?"

I glare up at him. "I think you've done enough."

His jaw ticks, but he lets me climb into the vehicle without further argument.

As we wind through the back roads of Ever Graves, the dark dissipates, and twilight peeks through the starry sky.

I clench my thighs together to keep my wet panties from bunching. And to prevent another spasm from turning me into a quivering mess. Just being next to him is enough to send my senses into a forbidden place.

When we arrive at Harker Mansion, he hops out to open the newly fixed iron gates before driving me all the way up to the door. I don't want to think this is a nice gesture. Maybe it's good breeding. He can't help himself from being a gentleman. Even with the woman he despises.

"So what now?" I bite on my lower lip. I had my legs spread wide open for him just twenty minutes ago, and now I'm shy? What the fuck?

He lights up a cigarette. "That's up to you. This isn't a game. I will keep making your life hell until you give me what I want."

I snicker. "You're an asshole." Regardless of these stupid poison wars, we had something between us in the bathroom at Duff's that night. Back before he knew who I was. And it's still there. But he says nothing. He won't even look at me.

I jerk the door open and scramble out. For a split second, I hope he comes after me. I fumble with my keys a little longer than I should. But as soon as I turn the lock, I hear the sound of tires on gravel.

I don't know what's worse, him leaving or me wanting him to stay…

Fuck.

I really should've left the bar with Lettie.

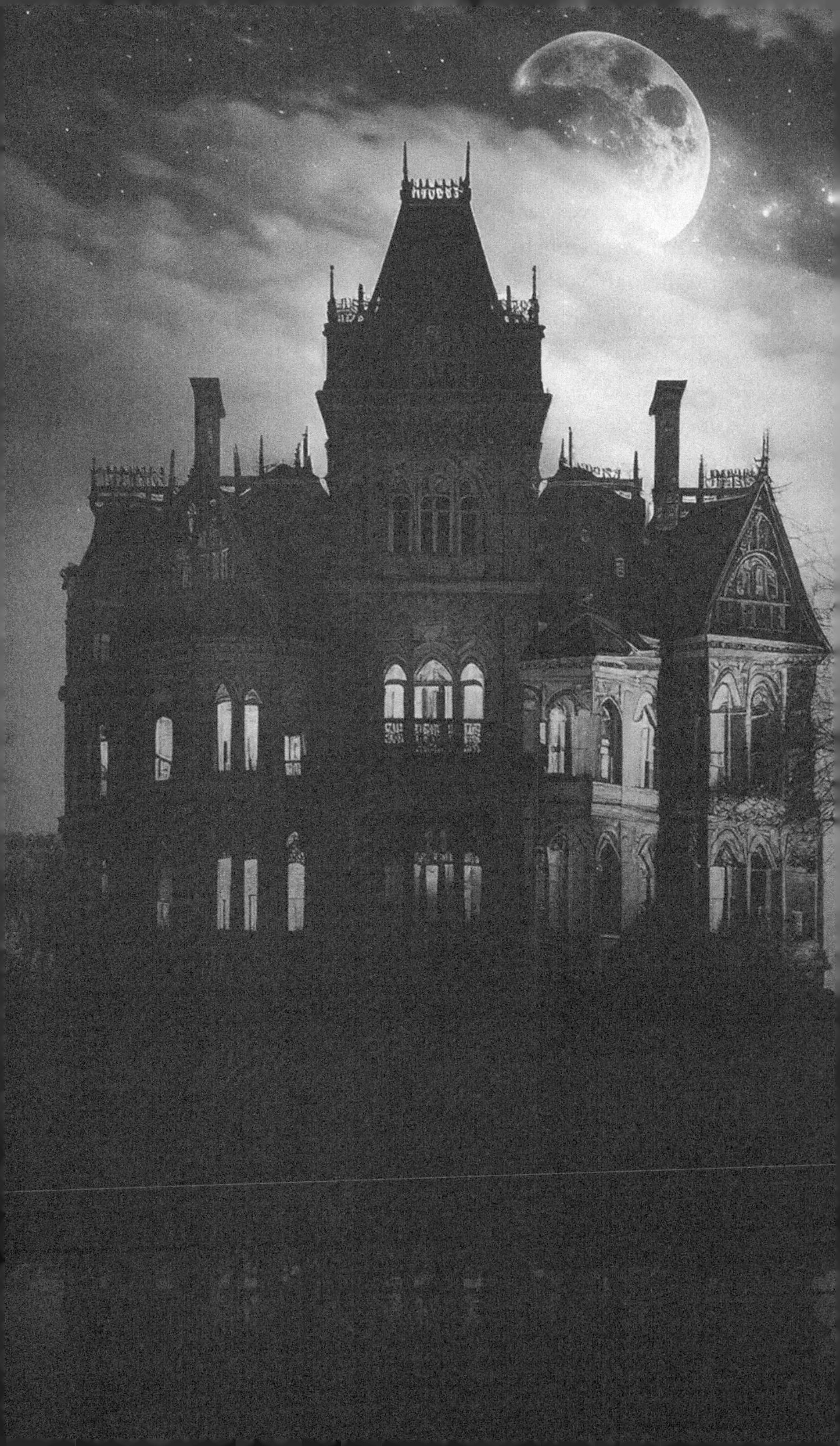

CHAPTER 18

Bones

THERE'S A TINY SHADOW WAITING FOR ME IN THE DARK BACK AT the garage. "Very dramatic, Lettie. I saw your car out front."

She huffs and turns on the light. "What the fuck, Bones?"

My head is pounding and my resolve is fading. "Be more specific."

"Why are you covered in blood and dirt? Please, tell me you didn't do something to Mia again." She folds her arms over her chest, her lips pursed. The fury in her eyes is lethal.

I can't exactly tell her that I fisted her friend after murdering the man who tried to drug her. "You worry too much, Lettie. I was just out doing what I always do."

She crosses the room, rushing toward me with a fire I haven't seen in a long time. "That's the problem, brother. Doing what you always do is why you're a hot fucking mess. Mia told me what you did to her truck. What is wrong with you? You're acting like the fucking devils of Raven's Gate."

I grit my teeth. "I don't know what you're talking about. I didn't do shit to Mia or her truck."

She grips my arm hard. "Liar. You can't even look at me. Why can't you leave that poor girl alone?"

I snicker at the thought. "All right, Lettie. You want to know what I did tonight? I had some fun with your innocent little friend in the graveyard. I bet she doesn't tell you how hard I make her cum."

Her mouth drops open.

"Yeah, that's right," I continue. "Mia Harker acts like she's some helpless little virgin while really she's a dirty little slut who can't get enough of me, Aries, or Draven."

I see the hit coming but I don't dare duck. *Slap.*

"Mia might like it when you call her that but I will not stand here and listen to such fucking filth. And it's no excuse for what the three of you have been doing. Why can't you just take a girl out on a date like a normal person?"

Fuck. I crossed a line.

I sigh. "I shouldn't have said that. I'm sorry. Fuck."

Her cheeks are flushed. "At some point you're gonna have to stop punishing yourself and everyone else for Sonny's death. I'm scared for your soul, Bones."

Her words are like a punch to the gut. "That's not what this is. With Mia... it's different. I can't explain it."

"Well, that girl has been through a lot. Maybe she likes you treating her like shit because it's all she knows." She rubs my cheek. "Sorry I slapped you."

I chuckle. "I deserved it... I promise you, I'm not going to hurt her. It's just the way we are with each other."

"The women in Melancholia are something else," she mutters.

I pull her in for a hug. "Maybe if you got yourself someone

to play with, you wouldn't be so obsessed with my love life. Aren't there any guys at school you're interested in?"

She shoves me away, glaring back at me. "No, Bones. There aren't any *guys* I'm interested in."

I'm not fucking stupid. "So what about the girls, then? Look, *I know*, Lettie. You can't keep pretending. Your old girlfriends here are bitches for what they did to you. Don't let that stop you from falling in love again."

She shudders, her throat bobbing as she swallows. "It was so easy with them at first. I didn't have to force it like I did with boys. I thought it meant as much to them as it did to me. But in the end, I was just a toy for them to play with. So now, I don't want to be with anyone."

My heart actually breaks for her. She's got so much to offer and yet she locks it all away out of fear of getting hurt again. "I don't want to see you alone and hurting forever. You put on a good front for everyone else, but I see right fucking through it. Felix does too. We've talked about it."

She lowers her head. "I'm not ready. It hurts too much."

I pull her in for another hug and this time I don't let her go. "I know. I'll make a deal with you. I'll try to stop punishing myself for Sonny, if you start opening up your heart again."

She sniffles into my shirt. "Fine. But you better hold up your end. I'm sick of seeing you hurt yourself."

I kiss her forehead. "I promise you, baby sister. I will try."

"That's all either of us can do, right?" She murmurs.

After I walk her out to her car and wave goodbye, the guilt settles back in. I really will try but it's easier said than done. The only thing that helps is being around Mia. That girl does something visceral to my soul that makes me forget about any of my own pain. She's my new drug, my new addiction, and my new release.

A dark cloud hangs over me as I kneel down next to the gravestone. I brush the dirt off his epitaph. "Hey, baby brother."

A cold breeze skates across the back of my neck. Just like it did that day. I shiver in remembrance. The sweet scent of freshly potted magnolias wafts up my nose. They're from my mother. She's the only one who still leaves flowers after all these years.

Fuck.

I stuff my trembling hands into my pockets. My grief is suffocating. I feel it like a noose around my neck. I glance toward the woods, my fury growing. I lost count of all the times I've searched for him, hoping he was still out there. But I know he's gone.

A part of me died that day too. I lost a piece of my soul that I will never get back. It haunts me even in daylight. I should have been paying attention. Felix blames himself too but I know that it was my fault alone. I was the one who was tasked with watching Sonny. I'm the one who took my eyes off him.

I fight back the tears as I clench my fists. "I'm so fucking sorry."

I don't deserve to be here.

Furious with myself, I march back to my car. I pace around the newly restored muscle car like a bomb about to explode. Tick. Tick. Tick. FUCK.

I smooth my sweaty palms over the top of my head, my pulse racing. My mouth is dry, my tongue heavy as if it's coated in lead. I see his little face in my mind. I hear his voice begging me to come outside and play with him.

Fuck.

Fuck.

Fuck.

The shadows crawl across my skin, threatening to pull me under. It's too much.

A choked scream unfurls from my throat as I thrust my fists into the passenger side window as hard as I can.

"Ahhh!" The glass cracks, splitting in a thousand directions. Blood drips in between the shattered fragments. *My blood.* I hit it again. And again. Over and over until the flesh around my knuckles look like pulp. Fuck.

I'm sorry. "Lo siento."

I rest my head against the hood of the car while I cradle my throbbing hands to my chest. I promised Lettie mere hours ago that I would try to stop punishing myself. And now here I am doing it again. I'm all kinds of fucked up.

But the pain makes me feel alive. It grounds me and brings me back to the present. I know I have to stop. But how can I when this darkness torments me every waking minute?

"Fucking hell." I rip off pieces of my shirt and tie the strips around my hands before stealing one more glance back toward the woods. "Until next time, baby brother."

The roar from the double exhaust does little to quiet the chaos in my head. So I turn up the music as loud as I can stand without it making my ears bleed.

Without meaning to, I drive toward Harker Mansion. I should keep going and head to Draven's instead. *I should keep going.*

Fuck. Fuck it.

I pull up to her gates and kill the engine. She's the only one I want to see right now. The only one who can comfort me without even knowing that's what I need. I want to bury myself inside her and forget about everything else.

The thrill of being so close to her, the anticipation, is already making me feel better. My adrenaline spikes as I gaze down her driveway. She's not going to turn me away. This I know for sure. Mia might act like she hates me but it's quite the opposite. I see the fire in her eyes when I'm touching her.

I'm her release as much as she is mine. My lust for her has

turned into full blown obsession. She's all I think and dream about. The only one I crave. And it's her who quiets the demons in my head. With her, I'm fully present.

As I stalk toward the front door, I see a light flickering in the window up above. The sweet pungent scent of cedar smoke escapes from the chimney. It creates a stir of butterflies in my belly. Mia is mine tonight. And I'm going to fuck her until she's raw and whimpering.

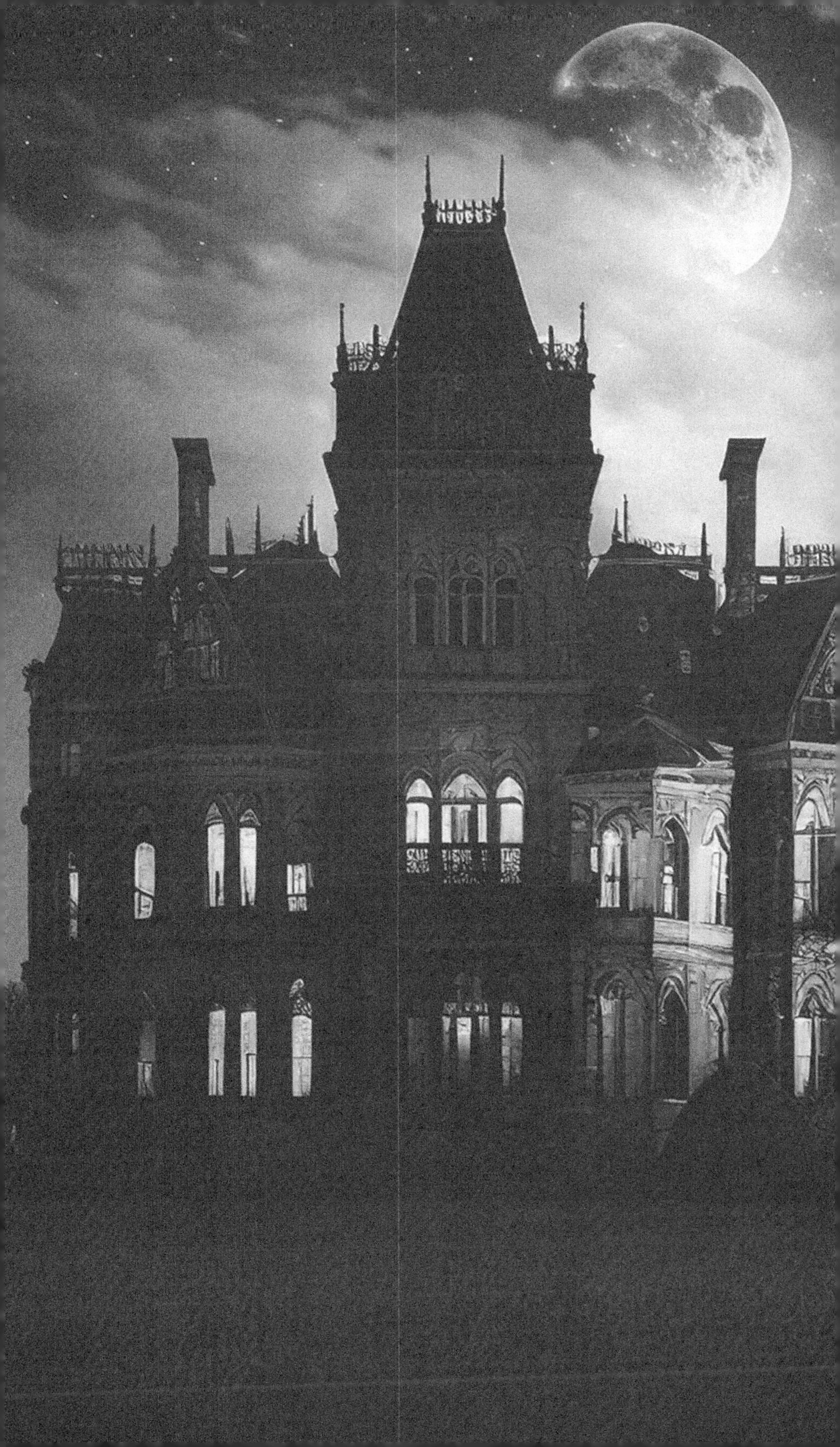

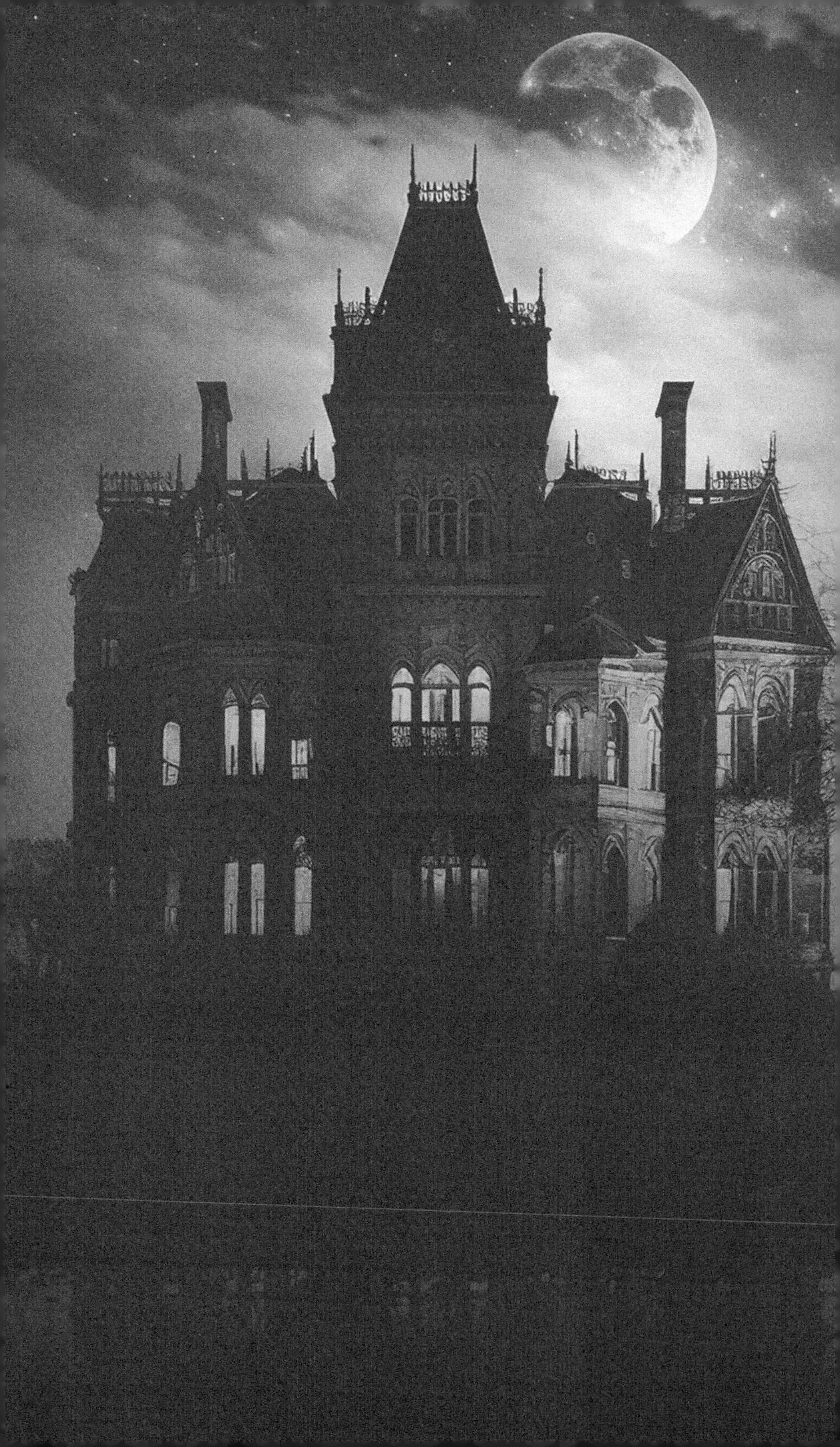

CHAPTER 19

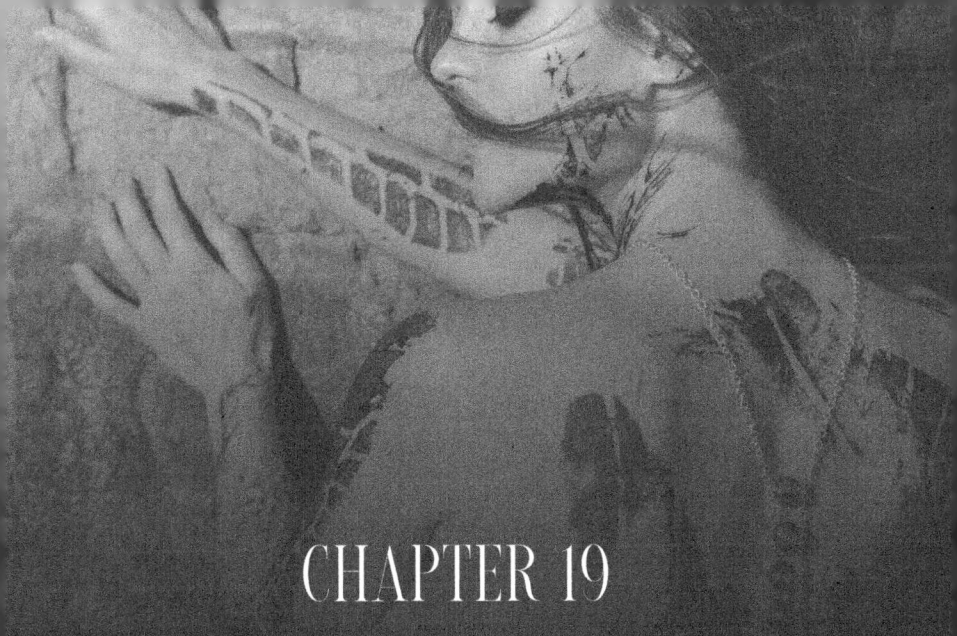

Mia

The whiskey burns my throat. I take another fiery sip and glare at the blank canvas in front of me. I haven't been able to paint since I got here. Every time I try, my body tenses, my heart races, and I can't keep my hand steady enough to hold a paintbrush. My creativity is stifled. And it's all their fault.

I turn my attention to my finished paintings instead, admiring them and fearing them at the same time. The thick swirls of black and purple paint are ominous—foreboding. And then there's the red eyes I've painted on each one. Nox's eyes. They haunt me. On some, they are small and distant, like when he used to watch me from afar. When I was a child, I'd wake up in a dark tunnel. He hid in the shadows then.

But every year I got closer to becoming a woman, he inched closer until he was so close I could feel his breath on my face. I painted that tunnel over and over again. But then I turned eighteen and woke up in another room. The one I still wake up in now. I painted that one too. And his red eyes got bigger in those paintings.

The room is as dark as the tunnel but with a bed in the center. It's his stage and his prison. And mine. The unspeakable things I've let him do to me there…

I shudder and throw the paintbrush at the canvas. It leaves a splotch of black paint on the easel before it falls to the floor. "Fuck," I rasp. I down the rest of my whiskey on my way out.

I'll try again tomorrow.

On my way to the library, I snatch another bottle of whiskey from the cabinet in the foyer. After Aries showed me where the cellar was, I took a handful of bottles to keep up here on the main floor. The cellar is dimly lit and it gives me the creeps. Not to mention how easy it was for Bones to slip in.

The library is almost a mile away from the kitchen, so I make sure to stop there first to grab a snack. This house is so fucking big there are still some rooms and hallways I haven't explored yet. Certain ones give me goosebumps when I pass them. But the longer I'm here, the more I'm settling in, and the less I fear the unknown. It's like the house is finally remembering me, night after night.

The library lights flicker a few times when I flip the switch. Old wiring. If Draven hadn't forbidden every electrician in Ever Graves from working for me, I'd call someone out to take a look at it.

Fucking Draven. Ugh.

I light a fire in the stone hearth before curling up on the overstuffed leather couch in front of it. I pour another glass of whiskey before picking up the copy of *Grimm's Fairytales* I'd left on the side table. Maybe reading about fictional monsters will distract me from the real ones who stalk me.

I forget time as I read, losing myself in the pages. I sip my whiskey and munch on mini ham and cheese sandwiches, content for the first time in a while. All of this grandeur is nice, but it's these simple comforts that ease my anxiety. It reminds me of the nights I'd scrounged up enough change to get a hot cup of tomato soup and grilled cheese at the diner in Raven's Gate. When I was on the streets, sometimes people would pay a few dollars for one of my paintings. It fed me and kept me warm for half the night. The server would keep refilling my coffee so the owner wouldn't think I was loitering.

I breathe in a deep sigh. Now I have more money than I know what to do with, and I'm still searching for something or someone to make me feel whole. I may never find it. But I do know that I want to help others like me. Maybe I *should* sell to Draven and move back to Raven's Gate. I could buy the diner and turn it into a soup kitchen for the unhoused.

I'm so lost in my thoughts that it takes me a few minutes to realize I'm not alone. I draw in a sharp breath as the hairs on the back of my neck prickle. My eyes dart around the room, searching for something I can use as a weapon. I notice the fire poker first. Can I reach it before they reach me? Fuck.

I throw the blanket off and bounce off the couch. As I scramble toward the poker, I'm shoved hard. My feet twist underneath me, and I topple to the floor. I hit my back hard against it, knocking the breath from my lungs.

"You barricaded the back door to the wine cellar? Come on, little lamb. Where's the fun in that?" Bones towers over me, his knuckles bloody.

I fight to catch my breath as my adrenaline races, threatening to give me a heart attack. "What... the... fuck?"

He grabs my wrists and pulls me to my feet with a smirk. "To be fair, I actually knocked this time. You should install one of those doorbells that you can hear from any room."

Now he's being polite? I'm getting whiplash from these boys' mood swings. I lean back against the arm of the couch. "So because I didn't answer, you broke in. Again. You know that's not normal, right?"

He shrugs. "You didn't answer your phone either."

"It's still not an excuse, Bones. What the fuck do you want?" I'm pissed that he's interrupted my quiet, but more pissed about the tingling between my thighs. It's like the three of them have mind control over my pussy.

He runs a hand over his shaved head and looks at me like I'm a glass of water in the desert. "We need to talk about this property. I, for one, am fucking sick of it, but Draven and Aries will not let it go. So what can I say or do to convince you?"

"I don't want to talk about it. You're bleeding by the way." I watch as blood seeps through the gauze around his knuckles.

"I always bleed." He sits in my spot on the couch and pats the spot next to him. "Come sit."

I swallow the lump in my throat. "You need new bandages and ointment." *Why do I care?*

He smirks. "Aw, are you worried about me, baby girl?"

"I just don't want you getting blood on my floors," I bite back. But the heat in my body is rising by the second. The way he looks at me like I'm some puzzle to solve. The way his chiseled arm is draped across the back of my couch. It's all I can do not to give in, to nuzzle up next to his hard body and let him do vile things to me again.

"Well, go get them then." He settles back against the couch and props his feet up on the coffee table.

I could fucking slap him. I ball my fists at my sides. "I don't know where they are," I grit out.

His eyes light up with amusement. He's enjoying every second of my discomfort. "Most of the old houses in Ever Graves have an infirmary. Back in the Poison War Era, they needed to have their own medical supplies and equipment on hand. If I remember correctly, yours is on the third floor. At the end of the first hall. They kept those rooms away from windows and entrances. They didn't want their sick or wounded being too vulnerable."

My mouth gapes open. "How do you know where *my* family's old-timey infirmary is located?"

He shrugs again in that way that he does where he acts like he doesn't care or is bored but he's actually enjoying pushing my buttons. "We are trying to buy this house, Mia. Of course, we have the blueprints to it."

I feel my cheeks flame. I ball my fists tighter. I might actually take a swing at him. "We can discuss how that's an invasion of privacy on the way up there." I shove his feet off my table. "Come on. Up. I'm not your fucking servant."

He laughs and springs up, nearly knocking me over as he steps into me. He thumbs my lip as he gazes down. "I like it when you're bossy."

A breath catches in my throat. A vision of him pinning me to my breakfast table flashes in my mind. The way he fingered the edges of my panties, teasing my entrance and edging the fuck out of me. "I'm just trying to get you patched up and out of *my* house as quickly as possible."

I spin on my heel before he can dish out another smart-ass response. My pulse seems to echo in my ears, throbbing violently with every step I take. He follows close behind on the stairs. Too fucking close. The scent of musk and motor oil waft up my nose. *Fucking pheromones.*

When I reach the top of the stairs, my knees wobble, and I misjudge the last step. I stumble back into his chest.

"Easy, little lamb. You're supposed to be patching *me* up, remember?" He chuckles in my ear. "Do you need me to carry you?" He grips my waist firmly, holding me upright.

I blow out a deep breath and wrangle free. "I'm fine. I've had too much coffee." I don't dare turn around yet. I know my cheeks must be bright red. I can feel the heat emanating off them, spreading to my neck and chest.

The third floor is as dark and musty as I remember it. I've been avoiding coming up here ever since I found that invoice from Absentia Asylum in the office.

He breezes past me and leads us the rest of the way to the infirmary. I was picturing some creepy, sterile operating room straight out of a horror movie, so I'm surprised to find a cozy room resembling a kitchen instead.

The light flickers on to reveal a few cots, a sink and cabinets surrounding it, and a rolling caddy. There are three trays with medical implements that look like they've never been touched. And along the wall, bottles of alcohol, hydrogen peroxide, and iodine line the shelves.

Bones plops down on the edge of a cot. "You gonna fix me up now, Nurse Harker?"

His gaze is unnerving. Fuck. I roll my eyes at him. "Everything's a joke to you, isn't it?" I rifle through the drawers in the cabinet until I find some cotton pads, gauze, and tape. I set those on the rolling caddy before grabbing a bottle of hydrogen peroxide.

I have no fucking clue what I'm doing, but I saw someone clean a wound on a TV show once. It's not like I have to sew a stitch or take a bullet out. How hard can it be?

I sigh as I wash my hands in the sink. The only challenge will be keeping my legs closed while I'm doing it. This man makes me fucking feral.

"All right. Give me your hands," I demand.

He smirks as he studies my face, watching me as I unravel his bloody gauze. I wince when I see his marred flesh. "Fucking hell, Bones. Were you punching a meat grinder?"

He clucks his tongue. "Glass, baby girl. That window had it coming."

Fuck. I pause for a second, contemplating on what to say next. I shake my head and continue, pouring the peroxide onto a cotton pad. "You wanna talk about it?"

He doesn't even flinch when I press the pad to his first knuckle. "You want my sob story. Is that it?" He snickers.

I swallow hard as I make my way down the line of bloody knuckles. "I didn't think assholes had sob stories."

He bursts out laughing. "Damn. I really fucking like you. You don't bullshit. My abuela would love you."

I shrug and feel the tiny hint of a smile pulling at the corners of my lips. "She's a smart woman then."

I gaze up at him for just a second, and it sends butterflies to my stomach. Fuck.

"I like your eyes. They're different," he murmurs.

His hand flexes around mine as I press a fresh piece of gauze around it. "Yeah? Well, it's another reason why people think I'm strange. At least that's what they told me back at the orphanage."

As soon as I tape his hand, he presses it to my cheek. "You are strange, but that's not a bad thing. It makes you more beautiful."

My breath catches in my throat. I'm not good with compliments. "Thanks." I look down and get to work on his other hand. "Are you and your abuela close? I... I've never had family."

Bones spreads his legs and shifts forward, closing more of the gap between us. "We used to be closer. Before my brother died. It's hard to go back to normal after something like that."

I look up to meet his gaze. "I'm sorry. Lettie never mentioned another brother."

Bones's eyes darken. "She was too young to remember Sonny. And it's a sore subject."

I nod. "What happened to him?"

His fingers tremble. "It doesn't matter. Next subject."

Fuck. "I'm sorry. It's not my business." I feel my cheeks burning. I sometimes forget I have zero social skills. Why can't I just keep my mouth shut?

He strokes my cheek again. "It's okay. I brought it up. So, what's *your* sob story, little lamb?"

Great. My turn. The subject I've been avoiding at dinner parties since I was first able to even attend one. I blow out a deep breath. "It's pretty basic. My parents died when I was a baby, but I think you already know that part. I was sent away before that. No clue why. They were rich as fuck and could have easily raised me. Anyway, I grew up in Wickford Hollow Orphanage. On my eighteenth birthday, they handed me a bus ticket and kicked me out. I went to Raven's Gate, slept on the streets for a while until I met my ex-fiancé, got dumped for being strange, and then rich granny died. And now I'm here."

"You left out a lot, baby girl." His gaze burns a hole in my face. I shrug. "So did you. We all have our secrets. Our shame. I don't care to talk about mine either."

"Fair enough." His hand falls to my shoulder.

His touch is electric. Fiery. It ignites sparks in every nerve in my body. I finish wrapping his hand and stand up. "Done. Now at least you won't get an infection."

"You're sweet. I don't think most people know that about you." He leans back on the cot. The edge of his ripped T-shirt shifts up, revealing the V shape of his abs. Fucking hell. *Don't fucking look, Mia.*

"I could say the same thing about you. When you're not breaking into people's houses like a psycho." My belly flutters at the memory.

"Yours is the only house I ever want to break into. I like the way your fear turns into something else. Something… visceral." He slides his gauze-wrapped hand over his belly, inching his shirt up even more.

I don't want to look, but I can't help myself. "What are you doing?"

He undoes the top button of his jeans. "Watching you play nurse is a fucking kink I didn't know I had. Indulge me, Mia. Let's keep this game going."

Tingles spread like wildfire through my core. It's like having chills and heat stroke at the same time. I could leave. I could turn around and walk away. But I inch forward instead. Fuck me.

He unzips his jeans. "Come here, baby girl. Lie next to me."

My limbs are shaking. I can't resist him. The memory of his fist inside my pussy has me so fucking wet… I sit down on the edge of the cot. "We shouldn't…" I murmur.

He pulls his jeans down and off. "Look how hard you make me."

I turn toward him, and my lips salivate. His cock is fully erect, hard and veiny with a barbell pierced through the tip. It's fucking beautiful. "Fuck," I say on a breath.

He rolls his thumb over the barbell, and a little precum oozes out. "Your turn." He rolls on his side, wraps an arm around my waist and scoots me forward until I'm fully lying next to him. "I want to play with your pussy again."

I bite my lip to stifle a whimper. I let my eyes wander his body, admiring black and gray ink that swirls over every inch of him. He's hot as fuck, and I have no willpower against him. With trembling fingers, I unzip my pants and shove them off.

He sucks in a sharp breath as he traces his finger around the edges of my white cotton panties. "Mmm… fuck."

I gasp as he pulls them to the side. "*Bones…*"

"Relax, baby girl."

I clench my thighs, my juices trickling out before he's even touched me. I'm about to cum already.

He pulls my panties slowly down my legs and tosses them to the floor. "Such a pretty pussy. Fucking glistening."

I arch my back. "Fuck. The things you make me do…"

He gets on top of me, spreading my legs wider to accommodate his large, muscled frame. He rolls his barbell over my clit. "Mmm, you're shivering. Don't play shy now…"

I let out an eager whine, ready to let this man do whatever he wants to me. I tear off his shirt in my frenzy. "Get inside me."

He chuckles. "There you go, being bossy again. I fucking love it." He slides his cock into my pussy. We both gasp as he enters. "Oh, fuck."

"Ooh, you're tight. Damn. But so fucking wet. I'm sliding all the way in." He slips in deep, caressing my walls with his ridges. He rolls his hips as he thrusts. "Mmm, I bet you'd look so good with another cock inside you."

I let out a deep moan as he presses against my most sensitive nerve. "Yeah…"

He grinds against me. "Hmm? Will you let us fuck you together? One in that pretty mouth of yours." *Thrust.* "One just like this." *Thrust.* "And another in your tight little ass."

I moan again. Sweat beads down my body as he speaks the filthiest things to me. "I don't know… Maybe," I rasp.

He grunts as he pulls all the way out and then thrusts back in so deep I buck. "Yeah, we're going to do that soon. I can't wait to see your mouth and your ass and this sweet, filthy pussy full of all our cum."

I can barely breathe I'm so fucking turned on. I roll my hips up to meet his as we increase our pace, pumping and thrusting like wild animals. I grab his neck and yank his head closer to mine. "I'm going to cum all over you right fucking now."

His eyes blaze with hunger. "Thatta girl. Give me every fucking drop." He kisses me hard. I open my mouth to devour him. His tongue lashes out at mine. He tastes so fucking good. Fuck.

All the blood rushes to my clit. It's building, spasm by spasm. I clench and then release. "Fuck," I scream.

I feel his hot liquid burst inside my pussy as he growls in my ear, "This is my pussy now."

I jerk my hips and rock against him, riding out a wave of ecstasy so intense my toes curl. "Don't fucking stop."

He rides me hard and fast, milking me for every drop. Unleashing everything he has into me. "That's my little lamb. Letting the big bad wolf slaughter her pussy."

I struggle to catch my breath, my chest heaving as he slows his rhythm. My thighs tremble as he slowly slides in and out, dragging our orgasms out until we are nothing but a sticky mess of cum and sweat.

He stills inside me, his shaft pulsing against my tender flesh. "I want you even more feral next time."

My mouth is dry from moaning. "We can't keep doing this. Not when we're supposed to be enemies."

That flicker of amusement returns to his eyes. "You just gave me a very naughty idea, baby girl."

Oh, fuck. I'm falling deeper and deeper into their twisted games. "Oh, yeah, and what's that?"

"It will be a surprise," he whispers.

I lay on the cot, still trembling, while I watch him clean that beautiful cock of his. I'm actually sad when he puts his clothes back on. "Sorry I didn't sign the papers. I just can't."

He smirks. "Don't worry. I got exactly what I came for tonight." He hands me a wet rag. "But I'm not leaving until I get to watch you clean yourself."

I feel my cheeks heat again. "You're going to make me cum again if you do that."

He pulls up a chair and straddles it. "Even better."

I spread my thighs back and already feel a little spark reigniting in my core. "You think anyone's ever fucked in this room before?"

He licks his lips as I caress my thighs with the rag. "In times of war, people fucked anywhere they could. Guaranteed there's some ghost dick energy up in this room."

I nod and slide the rag down my slit. It tingles, and I can't help but whimper as the rough fabric rubs against my clit.

"Thatta girl. Don't hold back. Clean that pussy good."

I bite my lower lip and moan as I drag the cloth from my clit down to my taint. There's something so fucking hot about the way he watches me. "I need more."

He stalks over to me, wedges a thick pillow under my hips, and returns to his chair. "That's better. Now I can see deep inside. Use your fingers, baby girl. Peel that pussy open for me to see how you mop up all that cum."

A deep spasm rolls through me. "Fuck," I whine. I scissor my pussy lips back with one hand and rub the wet rag in circles against my folds with my free hand. The pressure builds in my core as I thrust up and down against the pillow.

Bones hangs over the chair, his mouth watering, his eyes glazing with lust and hunger. "Yeah, just like that."

His words torment me and send me over the edge. I scream as my orgasm bursts and explodes like fireworks through every inch of my body. I palm the rag, thrusting against it while also using it to mop up my mess. "Holy... fuck." I gasp.

I'm a disaster. A heap of bodily fluids and trembling limbs.

He winks as he stands up and reaches behind me for his phone. "Thanks for patching me up, beautiful. Until next time."

I don't have enough breath to respond. So I just lay there and watch him leave. If this is how they think they're going to torture and intimidate me into signing those papers, then they're going to lose this game real fast.

I'm too fucking greedy for their depravity. Too sick and twisted to be afraid of masked men breaking into my house or chasing me through the woods. The only thing that scares me is how far each of us are willing to go.

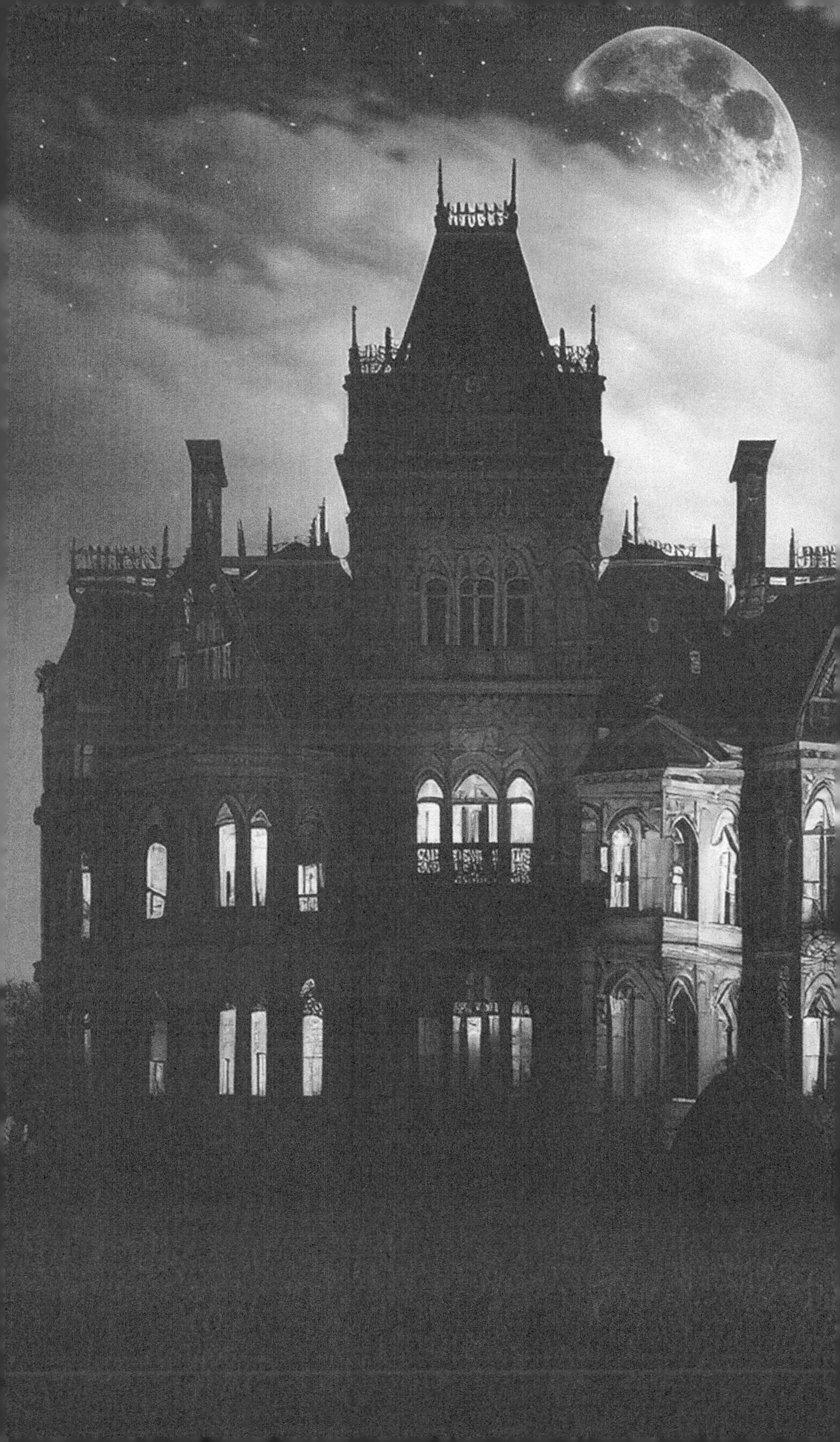

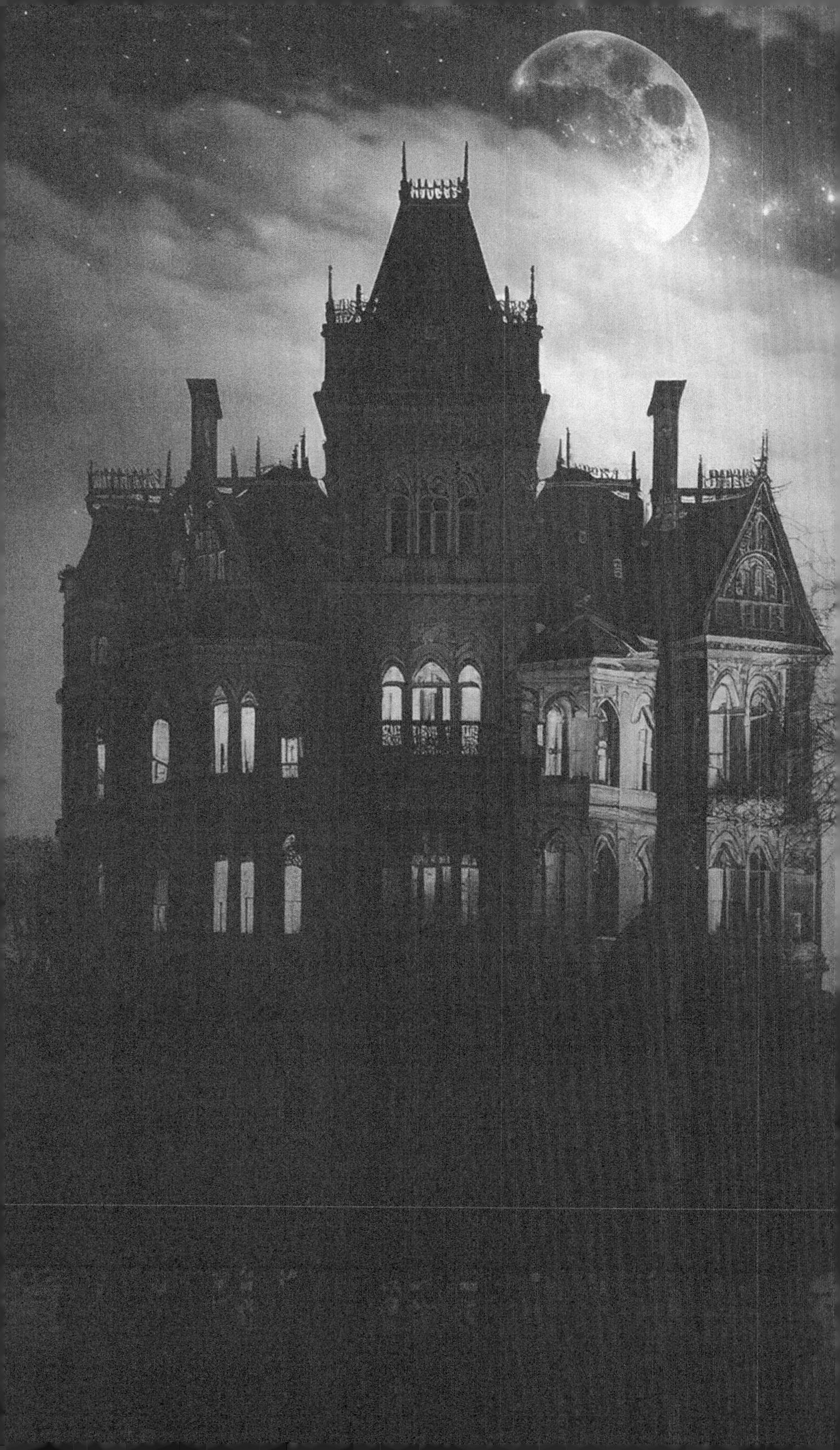

CHAPTER 20

Aries

My phone buzzes with a text from Bones. *This was after I fucked her*, he writes. I scroll down to click on the attached video and almost fall out of my chair. Mia's got her legs spread wide as she rubs herself with a wash rag. Bones sits on a chair watching her, salivating. Fucking hell. Her pussy is so pink and wet. So raw after he fucked her with his thick cock. And now I'm fucking hard.

You're an asshole, I reply back. *I'm guessing she didn't sign the papers with her pussy.*

Bones texts back, *Nah, her pussy was too busy choking on my cock.*

Fuck.

It's time to do things my way.

I see the chat bubbles appear and disappear for a good thirty seconds before he replies.

Don't have too much fun torturing our little lamb.

He wants to join, but he knows I need to do this by myself. Bones turns into a big softie around her and Draven acts like a jealous boyfriend. I'm the only one who can make Mia break. I have no limits, no boundaries, and no fucking empathy. It's a classic Thorn trait. It's how my family built our empire. And it's how I intend to keep it.

I'm banking on her sleeping tonight. After weeks of stalking her house, noting when she turns her lights on and off, I've gathered that she's an insomniac. I figure she's avoiding her nightmare man, resisting him until she can no longer fight him off.

But after what Bones did to her tonight, she's gotta be fucking exhausted and content to crawl under the covers and drift off.

I put on my best suit, grab the toxin I've been working on, and hop in my SUV. My adrenaline spikes as I wind in and out of the back roads. As I pass Draven's house, I shoot off a quick text.

Seeing Mia tonight. Stay home.

He replies with a thumbs up.

The grin on my face widens as I near Harker Mansion. I haven't been this excited in a long time. My tastes have always stretched far beyond my friends' kinks. They let me subject them to it from time to time. But even they have their limits. But Mia is different. I've seen the fire in her eyes when she's doing something dirty. The way she practically begged for it in the woods and then again in the graveyard.

She's the perfect prey. But she's about to find out what a real predator looks like.

I park outside the gates and let myself in with the code that Draven copied from the workers. As I hoped, all the lights in the mansion are off. Bones was nice enough to snoop around before ambushing her in the library and let me know exactly which room she sleeps in.

He also made sure to remove her barricade in the wine cellar. The door creaks open after I unlock it. I wait a few minutes, my heart racing, as I listen to hear if there's any movement.

Satisfied that my little lamb is fast asleep in her bed, I keep going. I stalk up the stairs, taking my time as the blood in my veins tingles. I get to the second floor and take a right as Bones instructed.

I don't have to go far before I see a door cracked open with a thin stream of candlelight flickering against the wall. My cock swells as I enter the room and find her writhing on the bed. She looks possessed. The way her body twists and contorts on the mattress. My little lamb is playing with her nightmare man. *Fucking her nightmare man.* And I get to watch.

She moans like an animal in heat, clawing at herself. She pushes her panties off and spreads her legs.

Mmm, fuck. *Yeah show me again how you touch yourself.*

I almost cum in my pants when she dips her fingers inside her pussy. She pinches her nipples with her other hand, arching her back as she fucks herself.

I bite my lip as I unzip my pants and free my cock. This wasn't part of my plan, but I can't resist stroking it while I watch this delectable creature pleasure herself.

I roll my thumb over the tip as I coax my pre cum out.

She circles her clit furiously as she whines. Fuck.

I scoot closer for a better view as she jerks her hips up and down, riding her own hand with three fingers wedged deep inside her cunt.

She's so wet I can hear her juices sopping against her tender folds. There's a pink flush over her entire body. A glistening sheen of sweat coats her as well. I want to play too. Fuck.

I take off my clothes, climb onto the bed, and nestle up next to her. "I hope you're nightmare man doesn't mind sharing because I'm about to violate you in the best fucking way, little lamb."

The deviousness of this makes me harder. I press my lips to one of her nipples, caressing it back and forth, my breath hot.

Her body jerks, and she freezes. And so do I, my heart beating fast. Did I wake her already?

She lets out a deep breath and begins working her fingers back and forth again.

Mmm, thatta girl.

I chuckle to myself as I lash my tongue out, swirling it around her swollen bud. Fuck, she tastes so good. The scent of jasmine is strong as if we're lying in a bed of it. I continue down her body, dragging my tongue across her rib cage.

She moans, her breath hitching.

I inch down her belly, stopping only when I reach her mound. I move her hand, but she puts it back, whining at the intrusion.

I shift in between her legs, pushing her thighs back farther. I watch as she thrusts in and out, her delicate fingers sliding through her wet folds like butter. Her back arches again as she lets out a deep gravelly whimper.

"You hit your sweet spot, didn't you?" I move her hand again and line up my cock to her entrance, blocking her from touching herself again. "Let's see if I can too."

I push inside her tight, wet pussy, nearly shattering inside her instantly. She's like a fucking oven. Holy fuck.

She moves her hands back up to her nipples, pinching and twisting them as the flush across her skin deepens to a rosy red.

I slide in deeper, slowly, savoring the way her folds feel against every single ridge on my thick cock. Her juices bathe me, soaking me like a warm bath. I grunt as I pull her hips up to angle in deeper, pushing all the way back until I fill her to the hilt. And then I still myself. I close my eyes and take shallow breaths, my cock twitching and pulsing against the inside of her pussy.

Fuck. I could come in seconds.

She would look even better tied up. I was going to save this for later but fuck it. I reach for my necktie and quickly wrap it around her wrists.

She lets out another moan as I use her bound wrists like reins on a horse while I thrust in and out.

Fuck I want her to wake up and see me like this so badly. I pinch her clit as I buck into her hard.

"Fuck," she cries out.

"Yeah, let me hear you scream, little lamb."

She tosses her head from side to side as she writhes underneath me. "Nox," she whispers.

I still myself again. So that's the fucker's name. Oh, hell no. She will not call his name while I fuck her.

I lean over her and give her a little slap on the cheek. "Wake up, Mia."

Her eyelids flutter before they open. She lets out a gasp, her eyes as wide as saucers. "Aries? What the fuck?"

I slide out then drive back in with violent force. "That's better, little lamb. Say my name while I fuck you,"

The look of horror turns to anger but also lust. "Untie me right now," she murmurs.

I roll my hips and aim for her G-spot. "Only if you keep your hands where I can see them."

I know I've hit it when she bites down on her lip to stifle a moan. "How dare you!"

Even as her anger grows, so does her desire. "Tell me to stop then." I rub her clit in circles while I slide in and out, my cock swelling and ready to burst.

Her legs tremble with need as she tries to hide another whimper.

"No? You don't want me to stop?" I chuckle as I grind against her. She feels like fucking heaven. Sometimes being a sick bastard has its rewards.

"Untie me," she growls.

I nod, but I don't stop fucking her. Within seconds, I remove the necktie from around her wrists.

And in the next second that follows, she slaps me hard against the cheek. Fuck. I burrow in deeper. "Hit me again. I'm about to fucking cum."

Her eyes widen then darken as she hauls back and slaps me again.

I let out a deep moan, my cock twitching. All the blood rushes down my shaft. "Yeah, little lamb. I knew you were hiding a feral wolf inside you."

"Oh, fuck," she screams. "Fuck you. I'm… cumming."

Mmm. There we go.

She clenches her pussy around my cock so tight I can barely move. I press her thighs back against the bed and flatten myself against her so I can rub my belly against her engorged clit while I grind my cock in circles on her most tender spot.

And that shatters us both.

She pulls my hair as a deep moan erupts from her throat.

I growl into her neck as my cum shoots forward, filling her like a fucking volcano erupting. I release her legs so I can wrap my fingers around her throat. I wanna feel her pulse in my hands.

She wraps her legs around me and fucks me back as she rides her orgasm, taking out all her anger and rage on me.

"Yeah, Mia. Fuck me like you hate me." There's so much cum from both of us, it drips down our legs, soaking the sheets.

She whimpers and clenches one more time before going limp. "I do hate you. Get off me so I can kill you."

I give her a wink as I slide out. "Relax, little lamb. My cum looks good on you." I drag a finger down her slit, making her quiver. "I bet it tastes good in you too."

Her chest heaves, but she doesn't stop me as I lower my head between her legs and run my tongue up the length of her pussy. "Mmm. Yep. Delicious."

She lets out a shaky sigh. "You can't just break into my house and fuck me while I'm asleep, Aries."

"But isn't that what you let Nox do?"

"Fuck. I said his name out loud…"

I nod. "Don't ever say it again when my cock is inside you." A wild possessive streak flares up as I look down at this exquisite beauty. And now that I've had her, I want more.

She narrows her eyes at me. "Well, you wouldn't have been if you hadn't forced yourself on me like a heathen. This is my house. And I didn't invite you in."

I slam my hands on her pillow, boxing her in. "But you didn't ask me to leave either."

"Yes I did."

"No. You asked me to untie you, so I did. And then you fucked me like a rabid animal."

She grunts and tries to twist away from me, but my cock springs to life, and we both feel it pulse against her entrance. "Let me hear you say, please fuck me again, Aries."

She hisses. "I will not."

I tease her pussy with the tip, knowing she wants me just as badly. "You will if you want to cum again." I inch in a little more, enough to elicit a gasp from her.

She shakes her head. "I'm not going to beg for sex from you."

"I didn't say beg. I said say, please. There's a difference between desperation and fucking etiquette."

She sighs. "What makes you so sure I want to fuck you again?"

I look down between us and smirk. "Baby girl, you are wetter than the leaves on a tree after a thunderstorm. Hate me, slap me, but don't be a fucking liar."

She huffs and slaps me again. "Fine. I agree."

I arch an eyebrow as I give her my ear. "What was that? Hmm? Ask me nicely, little lamb."

She grunts in frustration, her jaw clenched. "*Aries*, put your cock back in me before I fucking kill you."

With the tip of my cock between her folds, I stare hard into her eyes, wanting to somehow drown in their variance. "Good enough."

She screams as I plunge inside her with full force. "As long as you ask nicely, I'll fuck you all night long."

By the third time she cums, a little flicker of panic starts to stir in my chest. With each spasm of pleasure that rolls between us, I'm getting more and more addicted, more obsessed. Each time I pull out and think about going home, the thought makes me crazy. I woke her up with my cock, and now I just want to fall asleep inside her pussy.

Bones and Draven aren't the only ones in trouble. I feel foolish for even giving them shit about it. Because Mia Harker is getting under my skin too. It's the salty taste of her pussy, the sweet scent of jasmine, and those damn mismatched colored eyes. Her long black hair, those fucking beautiful tits with their perfectly red nipples the taste of her cherry lip balm. Everything about this girl is like a fucking drug.

And that is exactly why I have to take things up a notch.

I reach for my pants and pull out the vial of my latest concoction. "I've had fun playing with you, Mia. You fuck me so well. But the games are over now. I need to make you understand how serious I am about that baneberry."

She wrinkles her nose at me. "That better not be poison, Aries. You know I'm not immune like you are."

I snicker. "Another reason for you to sell it, silly girl. But no, this isn't poison." I pour some out onto my monogrammed handkerchief. "It's chloroform."

Her eyes widen, and she gasps as I come for her. I press it over her nose and mouth. "Shhh, you're just going to sleep for a bit. But I won't let you go to your nightmare man, little lamb. No, this is going to be a deep slumber for you. And when you wake up, we'll have a proper chat."

She writhes underneath me, fighting the sleep toxin every step of the way. She's strong, and I like that, but I need to transport her without her making a scene.

Her eyelids flutter, and her limbs go slack.

"Good girl. Breathe it in. Surrender," I whisper in her ear. I wait a few minutes to make sure she's fully out before wrapping her up in her bed sheet.

"Time for a field trip, little lamb."

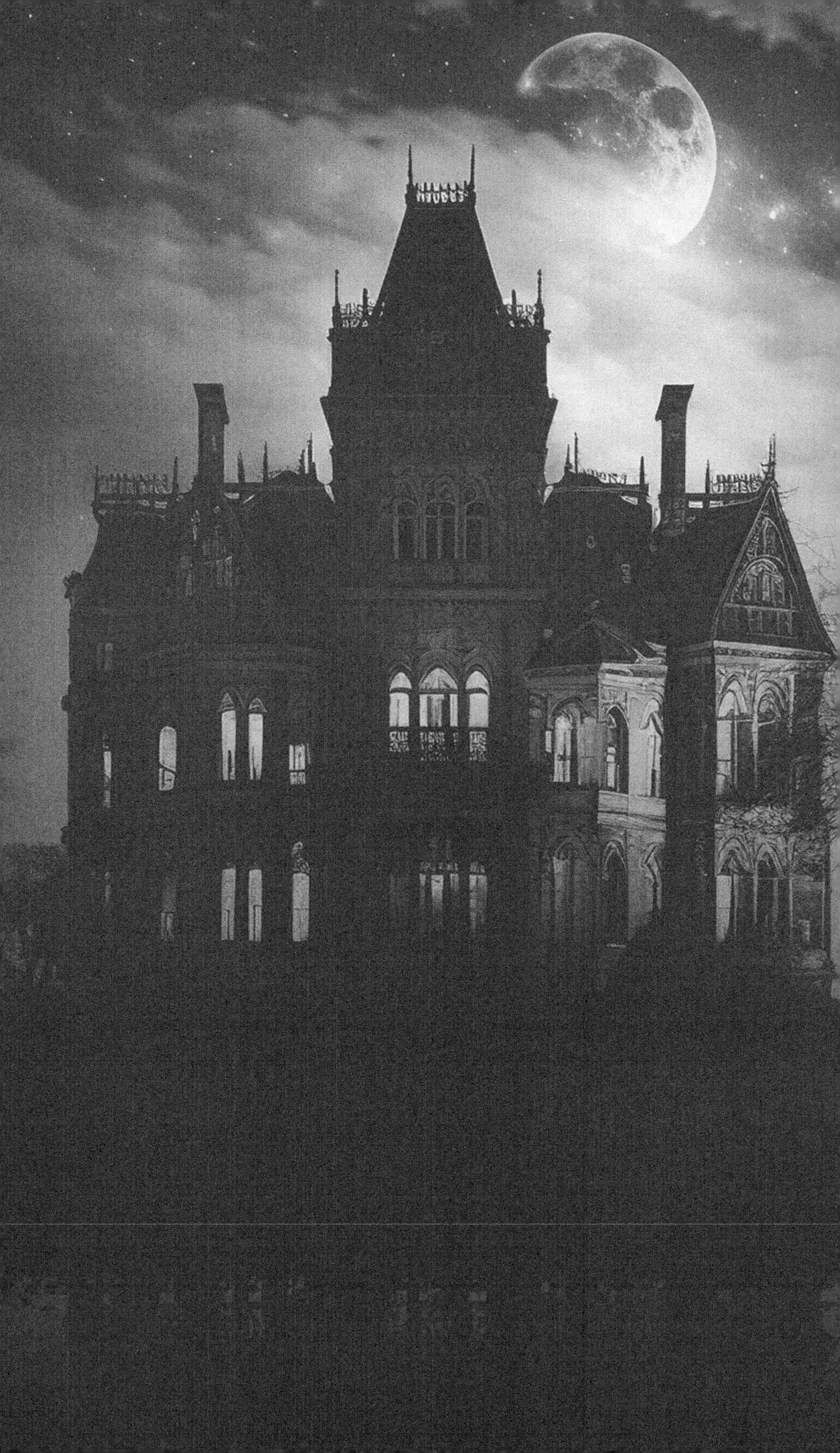

CHAPTER 21

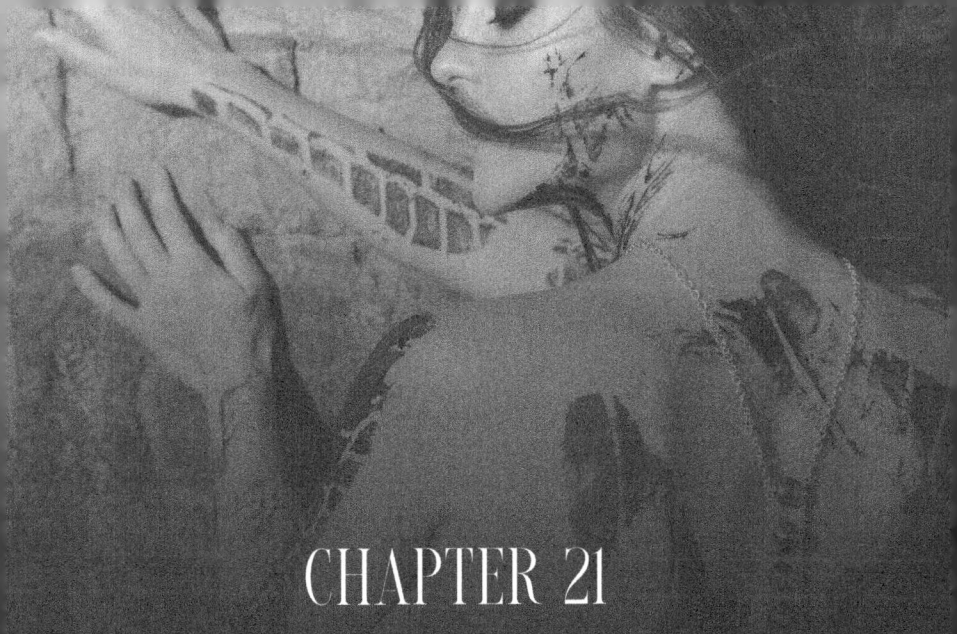

Mia

My throat burns. Fuck, how much did I drink last night? My eyelids are so heavy. I blink a few times, but everything is fuzzy. I reach for my covers, but I can't find them. Cold metal presses against my skin. I must be dreaming, but I'm not with Nox. Where am I? I need to wake up. Fuck.

My head is pounding. Something feels cool against my cheek. I can barely lift my head.

"Wake up, sleepy head."

Aries?

He was in my bed. I fucked him last night after I fucked Bones. Ugh. I need serious help. I blink again and try to wipe the sleep from my eyes, but my wrists are pinned. Oh, no. My adrenaline spikes as my surroundings come into view.

Panic fills me with dread.

I'm in a fucking cage. Naked. "Aries," I rasp, my voice hoarse.

I look up to see my wrists shackled to the bars.

"Shhh, no one can hear you." He's dressed in nothing but a pair of gray sweatpants.

"Aries, what are you doing? You have to let me go." This can't be happening.

He smiles like the devil. "I'm not letting you out until you give us what we want. Your hands stay shackled until you're ready to sign. And you're mine to do whatever I want with."

Chills sweep my body. I knew he was sadistic but not like this. I look around the room and my stomach knots. It's a sex dungeon. "Please, be rational. This isn't the way."

He opens the cage door and slips inside, pressing his body against mine. "I am so fucking excited you like to play hard to get."

I try to raise a knee between his legs only to find that my ankles are shackled as well. "You sick bastard."

"I warned you, little lamb. You brought this on yourself. But I think you're going to have fun too." He slides his hand in between my thighs. "Let's get you wet for my toys."

I suck in a deep breath as he scissors two fingers in my pussy. "You're a monster."

He smirks as my juices leak out. "Thatta girl. Nice and wet." He shoves his finger deep inside my pussy and stills it. "I'm going to play with you all night." He takes one of my nipples between his teeth and sucks while he thrusts another finger inside my core.

"Open wider for me."

"Fuck you."

He nudges my leg, and that's when I notice the bar between them. Fuck. It slides out and locks, forcing me to hold this stance. "You will obey." He pulls me forward so I'm sitting on his hand.

"Damn you." The movement shatters me, and I cum on his fingers.

"Good girl." He exits the cage and locks it.

"Aries, please. You can't keep me like this forever."

He holds up his phone. "You've been a naughty girl, Mia."

He presses play on the screen and my mouth drops open. It's me playing with myself in front of Bones in the infirmary. "He filmed me?" I'm fucking livid.

Aries laughs. "I think you've gotten a little too comfortable in our town. You forget that we are in control, not you." He pushes play again.

"Stop. Turn it the fuck off," I growl.

"But it's my new favorite show. Should we make another one?" His eyes glow in the poorly lit dungeon. And when I say dungeon, I don't mean the kind you see in fantasy movies about dragons and knights. No. This is a room with red lighting, velvet furniture, and contraptions that look like torture devices.

I take a deep breath and count to ten. "If you don't let me go, I will make you regret it."

He hisses. "Why are you so hellbent on keeping that property? We aren't stealing it. Draven has made you an offer that will keep your family line rich until the end of time. You don't even remember this town. Why would you want to be in a place that didn't want you?"

His words are like a knife to my chest. I blink back tears. "Fuck you, Aries. It must be nice to grow up privileged. To have people dote on you your whole life. I, on the other hand, have clawed and fought for every breath. Every moment of peace." I turn my head as the tears stream down. I don't cry for what he's doing to me; I'm mourning the life I never got to have.

He sighs. "Fuck. You're supposed to be scared, not sad. I hate it when women cry."

I choke back another sob. "You think you can break me like this? You have no idea the things I've gone through. I've slept on the streets, had to barricade myself in dumpsters just so I could fall asleep without the fear of someone fucking with me. I have sold my art for pennies so I wouldn't starve. Some nights I did. Do your worst, Aries. Nothing you can dream up will be worse than what I've endured and survived."

"Yet look at you now. All grown up and one of the richest women in Ever Graves. Things turned out just fine for you." He reaches into his pocket to retrieve a stack of papers and slams them against the cage. "Now sign the contract so we can all get back to our privileged fucking lives."

"It's not about the money," I rasp. "Harker Mansion isn't just a house. It's my family's home. *My* home. I'm not giving it up, Aries. It's all I have left of them." I look away as more tears stream down my face.

He stares at me for what seems like forever, his expression unreadable. Until he finally stalks back into the cage. I draw in a sharp breath when he presses his body against mine, my lips quivering as he drags his thumb across my jaw.

"You are going to be the death of us," he whispers. "Fuck." He reaches up and unlocks my shackles.

I pull my arms to my chest. "Thank you."

"I wasn't going to hurt you, you know." He kneels down and releases my ankles. "I was just trying to give you a little scare. But I'm not enjoying it anymore."

"Not much scares me in this world."

He steps aside, allowing me to leave the cage. "You're free to go, but… could you stay? I'd like to share something with you."

I should make a run for it while I can. This could be another trick. Another game. But he's so beautiful, so desperate in his plea for me to hear him out. I can't tear my eyes away.

"I can't stay long."

He hands me a pair of black leggings, a tank top, and sneakers. They're almost my size. I arch an eyebrow as I quickly put them on.

"They belong to my sister, Libra. She always keeps a set of clothes here." He sits down on the bed. "She is the reason I need control of the poison fields."

Lettie has told me some of their story, but I'm curious to hear it from him. I sit down next to him on the bed and try not to think about how much I'm drawn to him. It's his scent, his eyes, his physique. Everything about this man is seductive and inviting. He's made me cum more than a few times tonight, and I can't help but crave more. Even though he's chaos personified, his brand of desire is addicting.

So much so that I'm sad when he pulls on a hoodie, covering up that chiseled body of his.

"Tell me. What happened to her?"

He leans forward, resting his elbows on his knees. "So many fucked up things. And I couldn't do anything to stop it. I didn't know until it was too late. My father was trading her for favors from business partners. From the time she was sixteen. He's a real fucking monster."

My heart sinks. "I'm sorry, Aries. That's horrible. No girl deserves that. Especially from her own parent."

He hides his face in his hands. "Lib is tough. But it hardened her. People think she's a spoiled brat. A bossy rich girl. But it's just a front. She's broken inside. Money and sex and drugs is how she copes. Or at least how she used to until she got locked up."

I can't help myself. I reach over and rub his back. "I heard a little about that part. Draven's grandmother had her committed to Absentia Asylum, right?"

He nods. "Yeah. We thought she was dead for six months. But she's a fighter. She found a way out, and now she's literally running the place. But she wants nothing to do with the poison business. Not after it took her childhood and her freedom. She gave me her ancestral shares in exchange for Draven's permission to murder Penny Blackwell."

And I thought I had issues. These people are more fucked up than me. "Why are you telling me all this?"

He lifts his head to look at me, his watery eyes the color of sea glass. "Because I need you to understand this isn't a game. We aren't just some greedy assholes. We have money, Mia. Lots of it. For Draven, it's about power. The power to stop being at the mercy of our parents. For me, it's about revenge and redemption. I will never let Gemini Thorn have control over me or my sister ever again."

Fuck. I don't want to know their sob stories after all. I don't want to feel sorry for them. "What about Bones? What's in it for him?"

Aries chuckles. "Nothing. He loves us. The three of us have been best friends since we were born. If I ask Bones to murder someone, he will. No questions asked. That's just what we do for each other."

"Like family," I murmur.

"Something like that. Except Bones and I… well we have our own shit going on too." His gaze veers away from me, lost in some distant memory.

They love each other as more than friends. I've never had anything like that. And now I feel even more pathetic. Fuck. Which is why I can't sell the only connection I have to my family. The only home that's ever actually been mine.

"I'm sorry you've dealt with so much, Aries, but… I can't help you. I don't care how much Draven is offering. Like you said, it's about family. And Harker Mansion is the last place mine was."

He sighs. "I know. I'll take you home."

I look around the room again, puzzled at what half of the stuff in here even is. "You're into some dark shit, aren't you?"

His eyes light up, and that charm slips back into place. "You're welcome to play in here anytime you want, little lamb. You have no idea all the ways I can make you cum."

I swallow down the lump in my throat. Everything this man says and does is like fucking catnip for my pussy. "You're insatiable."

He leans over me. "So are you."

My heart races. "You drugged me and kidnapped me. What makes you think I still want you?"

"Oh, sweet, baby girl. You couldn't stop wanting me if you tried. And you're doing a shit job of trying by that look in your eyes." His tongue lashes out across my lips.

Fuck. I'm a whore for these men. I tilt my chin toward him and do the same to his. He tastes like whiskey and something else I can't place. Something bitter. Probably poison. "I guess I'm a glutton for punishment."

He slips his tongue between my lips, and I part them for him. We both gasp as our tongues touch and intertwine. His lips are so soft, like pillows. I whimper as we kiss each other with desperation, with ache and passion and hunger.

I'm losing myself to him.

"Mmm, I want to swallow all your darkness, little lamb," he groans between kisses.

I shift to get on top of him when a loud bang erupts. We both jump and Aries moves in front of me as the door to the dungeon room flies open.

"You're getting soft on me, Ries. Playtime is over." Draven is unhinged. Sweat coats his face as he stands there with his shirt unbuttoned, no necktie, and no jacket. His sleeves are rolled up, showing off his thick black tattoos.

Aries nods. "She's all yours."

I gasp. "What the fuck?"

Draven runs a hand through his disheveled hair. "Good. Because your father called a meeting. And I'm not walking in there without that baneberry."

Fuck.

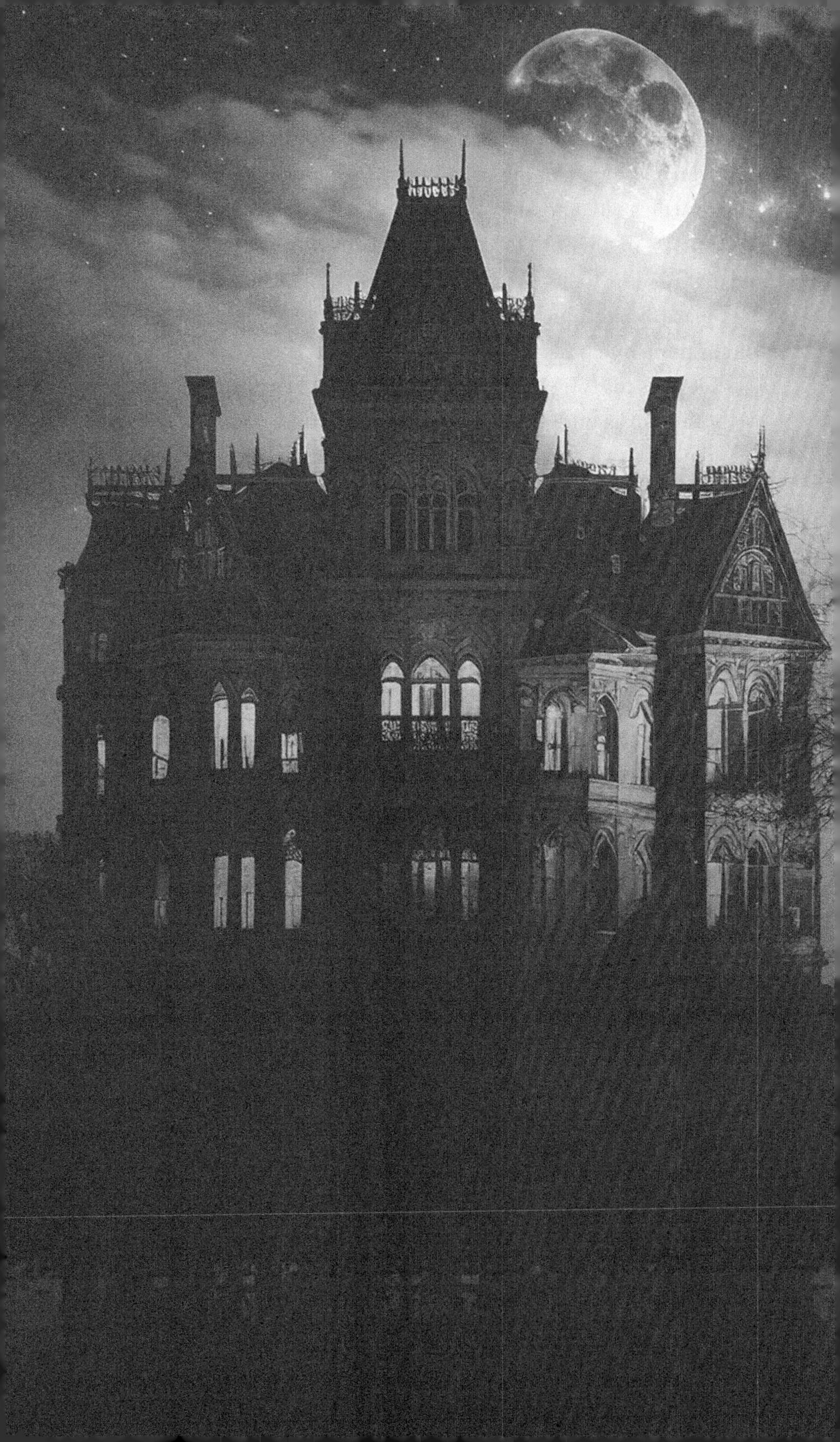

CHAPTER 22

Draven

I'M GOING TO FUCKING KILL HER.

"Let's go. You're moving out of that house tonight." I grab her by the wrists and drag her up the stairs, leaving Aries to take care of his hard cock on his own.

She screams. "You are out of your fucking mind."

I yank her across his marble floors, her slippers sliding easily over the slick surface. "Yeah, I am. Because of you," I scream back at her.

As we near the door, I pick her up and toss her over my shoulder. She kicks at my stomach and pounds her fists on my back. "I'm going to kill you!"

My driver-slash-only father figure I've ever known arches an eyebrow at me. "Sir?"

"Pop the trunk, Rodrick."

He sighs but does as I say. He knows me better than anyone. Even more than Aries and Bones. He knows when I'm in this state it's best not to argue with me.

I toss Mia in. "I warned you. This is what happens when you don't take me seriously."

She screams again as I slam the trunk down.

I slide into the back of the town car and undo another button of my shirt. "Drive. Harker Mansion. Now."

As we wind our way there, he glares at me in the rearview mirror.

"What is it?" I snap.

"You don't have to be like your father or your grandmother. You don't have to be like any of them. You're still a Blackwell."

I snicker. "You know better than that, old man. This is who I am. Who I was always meant to be."

He shakes his head. "You can still fight the darkness. It doesn't have to consume you."

"It already has."

As he nears Harker Mansion, he slows the car. "There's still time to let her out and drive away."

I shoot daggers at him, my silence giving him all the answers he needs.

"I'm grateful you've kept my secret all these years, but you will never understand what it's like to have a soul like mine. To have this part of you that is always stretching toward an empty abyss."

He blows out a deep breath as he turns down Mia's road. "And you think forcing this woman to give you her land is going to ease that burden? Control is an illusion. That poison is a temporary high and when it wears off, your soul will be far darker for having done this."

I don't fucking care. "I'm not trying to ease my fucking burdens. I'm embracing them." The Harkers are the reason I even fucking exist. It's time for them to answer for their sins too.

He looks back at the road and nods. "Very well."

I hate it when he dismisses me. I can feel the disappointment oozing off him, and it stings worse than nightshade.

When we pull up to the gates of Harker mansion, I lean out the window to punch in the code. A breeze of jasmine envelops me, and my heart flutters. The creaking of the iron stretching and shifting to beckon us forward sends my pulse racing even more. I curse under my breath, dreading the hold that this place has on me. That *she* has on me.

"Stay in the car, and do not move, no matter what you hear."

Rodrick nods but says nothing. It's far worse than when he scolds me. But I'm glad that he remembers his place. Despite his help raising me, he is still under my employ.

I hop out and gaze at the baneberry fields for a moment. Even in the dark of night I can see their silhouettes dancing in the wind, illuminated by the moonlight. And for a split second, I wish that they belonged to anyone else but her. Not that it would make any difference. Monsters like me don't deserve love or kindness or romantic gestures. I drink, I fuck, and I wallow. No woman would ever choose to endure that.

I motion for Rodrick to pop the trunk.

"Motherfucker!" Mia swings both her legs out and kicks me in the chest.

"Fuck," I grunt out as I stumble back.

She barrels out of the trunk and breaks into a sprint toward her front door.

The black sludge in my veins swirls, fueling my rage. "You can run, but you can't fucking hide, Mia," I yell back at her.

If I wasn't trying to stifle this woman, I might be impressed by her fire and determination. Her stubbornness. I never have liked a demure, helpless woman.

I chase after her, reaching her before she can turn the key. I embrace her from behind, pin her arms to her sides, and yank her back. "After you sign the papers, I'm going to bury you in the crypt with the rest of your wretched family," I growl in her ear.

She kicks up her legs and uses the door as leverage to push

against. We go flying back and land hard on the wet ground below the stairs. All the air whooshes out of my lungs, and I lose my grip on her.

"Bones isn't the only one who knows how to fight, fucker." She scrambles up the stairs and manages to open the door this time while I'm still wheezing on the ground.

Our little lamb's been holding back.

I glance back to see Rodrick watching from the car. "Wipe that smirk off your face, old man."

Fucking imbecile. And I mean me, not him. I should be more on guard with her.

"Mia!" I charge after her, wedging my foot in the door before she can close it behind her. She slams it against my foot and takes off running again.

This house is massive. There are hundreds of places to hide. But she forgets that I know the layout better than she does.

I catch a flash of her dark hair flying around the banister toward the wine cellar. "I've got you, little lamb. I'm coming."

The heat in my body rises with my adrenaline. Along with my traitorous cock. This game of predator, prey is fueling the ache, the need to be buried inside her tight pussy. Fuck. I hold onto the top of the staircase railing while I adjust myself. The scent of jasmine is so thick I can barely breathe. I need to calm down. *Stay focused.*

I barrel down the stairs, my anger growing with every step. "Mia, stop trying to ruin my life," I call out. Her silence is pissing me off.

I round the corner between the shelves just in time to see her slip out the back door and make another run for it. Fuck. She's going to get herself lost on her own damn property.

The fog is thicker than usual tonight—a bad omen. But through the heavy mist, I spot her running toward the field.

Oh, no.

She's heading straight for the baneberry.

Fuck.

"Mia, come back here," I yell but my voice gets lost in the wind. When she reaches the third row of bushes, she finally stops and turns around. As I make a move to bum rush her, my stomach sinks.

"Mia, what are you doing?" She holds a bottle of liquor in one hand, a cloth sticking out of it, and a lighter in the other.

Her blue eye is almost as dark as the brown one. She smirks back at me. "If I can't have this land, neither will you."

She's lost her fucking mind. We did this. I did this. I fucking broke her, and now she's out of control.

"Put the bottle down and come back to the house so we can talk about this."

"Fuck you, Draven. For the last time, stop telling me what to do." She flicks the wheel of the lighter and the flame sparks to life.

Now she's riding my last fucking nerve. "Did your nightmare man tell you to do this, Mia? Hmm? For fuck's sake come to your senses. Everything will burn if you light that. Including your house."

She laughs and holds the flame closer to the bottle. "Oh, *now* it's *my* house? Go fuck yourself. All you do is torment me. You act like you care one minute and then dismiss me the next. At least be honest. Admit that you don't really want me. That all you care about is your greed. That's the real reason why you won't fuck me."

Fucking hell. My stomach knots. I've done too good a job of pushing her away. She believes I hate her. That's what I wanted. So why the fuck is it breaking my heart to see her look at me with the same hate?

I take another step closer, praying she doesn't set us both on fire. "Think about your family's legacy. I shouldn't have put you in the trunk. We can still figure this out. Just please, put the lighter away."

Tears stream down her face even as her smile remains. "What fucking legacy? They didn't want me. No one wants me. Except him. Only Nox." She lights the rag that hangs from the bottle.

Fuck. I get it. I understand why she won't sell. How could I be so blind? I'm fucking stupid. "Mia, I want you to walk very slowly to me. It doesn't have to be this way. I take it back. You can keep everything. I'm begging you, and I don't fucking beg anyone. Please, come to me."

She shakes her head. "I don't believe a word out of your mouth. You're lying to get what you want. Just like you always do. Well, fuck you, Draven. You can't have me or my land because I'm burning it all down."

She tosses the Molotov to her left and the first bush it hits ignites instantly.

"Mia!" I yell.

She darts out of the bushes as the first row catches. "Enjoy the show," she yells.

"Fucking hell." I sprint back toward the side of the house and grab the hose. "She fucking did it. I can't believe it," I mutter to myself.

As I run back, hose in hand, my heart sinks from my chest. She's on the ground, hunched over. Fuck. I drop the hose and run to her. "Mia?"

On all fours, she gasps for air.

The fumes. Shit. I was so worried about the poison burning, I forgot what happens when it burns. I forgot that she's not immune. Fuck.

She coughs and heaves, her eyes bulging, as she claws at the wet grass.

Panic rises in my chest. My palms sweat, and I can't swallow. "Mia," I whisper.

Rodrick darts out of the fog. "Take the keys. Get her back to Blackwell Manor before the only woman you've ever loved dies."

My stomach turns. Love? No. That can't be right. But she will die if I don't get her out of here. I look back and forth between her and the fields.

"Draven, *now*. We don't have time. I'll clean up this mess. Go." He starts walking toward the flames.

"Don't let it burn," I plead. The fumes are so strong it makes even my throat burn.

I scoop Mia up into my arms and sprint toward the car. I slide her into the back seat and peel out as fast as I can. *Thank fuck my house is just up the road.*

"Damn you, Mia." I slam my hands against the steering wheel. "I get to decide how you die. Not you or anyone else."

Her cough deepens as she twists and contorts in the back seat. *She can't die.*

I don't know what this is between us, but I'm not ready for it to be over.

<hr />

"Everybody out," I roar as I charge into the kitchen with an unconscious Mia in my arms.

My staff scrambles out without hesitation. I set Mia on the center island and rifle through the apothecary cabinets like a mad man. I grab all the herbs I need and a bottle of Blackwell gin. I tear the cork out with my teeth and take a big swig to soothe my throat.

As I mash all the ingredients together to form a paste, I pray that it's not too late.

"All right, little lamb. Time to shed your coat and become like the wolf." I rip her shirt open and slather the paste all over her neck and chest. That should shock her system into consciousness and start to pull the toxin out of her skin.

I fly back over to the cabinet and grab a vial full of liquid. As soon as I found out that *she* was Mia Harker, that she's not immune to the very poison that surrounds her property, I had Bones make an antidote.

I tilt her head up off the counter. "Come on, Trouble. Drink for me."

She whimpers and murmurs something I can't make out.

I slap her cheek. "Drink, Mia."

She parts her lips, but her eyes remained closed.

"Good girl." I pour the liquid into her mouth and tilt her head back, forcing her to swallow.

She whimpers again as I lay her back down. "*I hate you… Slick.*"

I press my finger to her pulse and breathe a sigh of relief as her heart rate slows back to normal. "I hate you too. But you're not allowed to leave me."

When there's a normal rise and fall to her chest, I wipe off the paste with a warm cloth. She's fast asleep now, her body fighting to heal itself. I've never seen anyone who isn't immune to poison survive a blast of toxin like that before.

I watch her sleep for a while, afraid to move her just yet.

The thought of never getting to gaze into her eyes again makes my stomach clench. I take another swig of gin and dial Rodrick.

"How is she?" he asks.

"Alive. And you?"

"Just finishing up. You only lost three rows. They'll grow back in time."

I only lost three rows?

Even Rodrick placates me. It seems trivial now. She almost died for those three rows. Because of me. Despite all my threats, I never meant to hurt her.

"Thank you. I'll send another car to pick you up."

"You did a good thing, Draven. You didn't let the darkness win tonight. I'm proud of you, son."

Chills sweep my back. That's the first time… I swallow hard to choke back a sob. I can't fucking break now. Not like this. "Yep." I click off before he can pry any more sappy emotion out of me.

I carry Mia up the stairs to my bedroom, relishing the way

she feels against me. I suck in deep breaths of jasmine and traces of honey left over from the paste.

When I pull back the covers and lay her down on my bed, that familiar ache returns. The pain from not touching her. I gently remove her slippers and leggings, then the remaining fabric from her ripped tank top before pulling the black satin sheets and comforter up to her neck.

The blush has returned to her cheeks, but I can't risk her freezing to death after I just saved her from poison. I pull a chair next to the bed and sit.

She whimpers softly as she sleeps. I wonder if she is with him now. With Nox. I pray he allows her this one night to rest. Because no matter what my feelings are right now, I'm not done being angry with her.

My troubled little lamb needs to feel my wrath. To know that she does not get to scare me like this again.

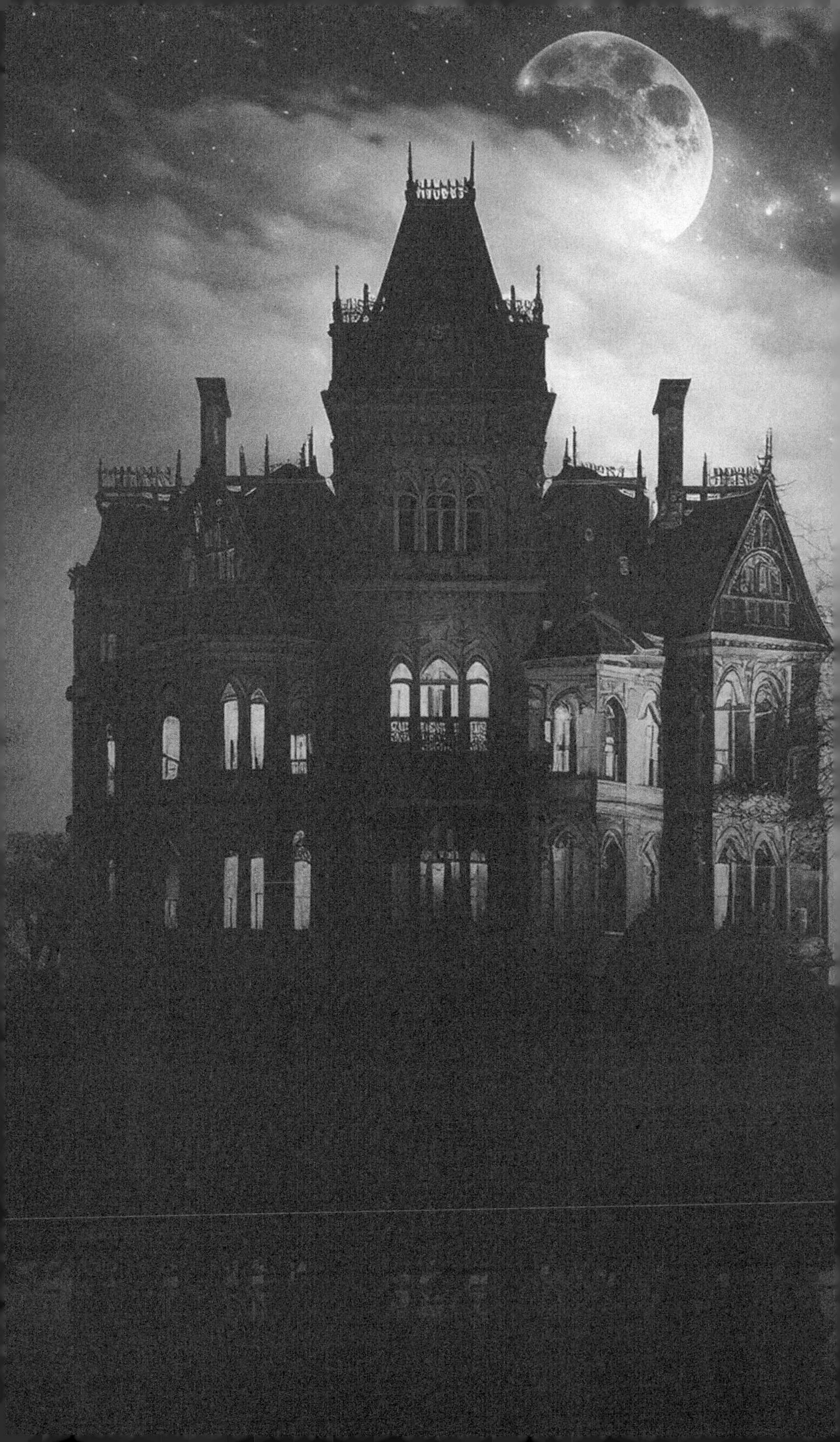

Chapter 23

Mia

"Oh, my sweet, dark one. You are not well. I can sense it."

"Nox?" I don't remember falling asleep. I don't remember anything from last night.

"Yes, my love. I'm here. Tell me what happened." He lies next to me, stroking my hair.

"I-I don't know." There's this gap in my memory. The last thing I can recall is sitting with Aries at his house. We were kissing.

"Something's happened to you. I can feel it. Are you hurt?" Nox tucks me into his chest.

I curl onto my side and bask in his warmth. But there's a chill in my bones that I can't shake. I shut my eyes and try to remember.

"I don't feel hurt."

He kisses my forehead. "That's because you're sleeping. But I sense you are hurt in the other world."

Aries and I were kissing and then we were interrupted by… *Draven*.

I gasp and bolt up. Fuck.

"Draven put me in a trunk. He's trying to make me sell the house to him. I ran away from him. And then… I lit the poison fields on fire."

"What were you thinking?" Nox growls.

I look down at my trembling hands. "I-I wasn't. I was just so angry. That baneberry has caused me nothing but grief. I made a split decision to burn it all down."

He pinches my chin hard between his clawed fingers. "And now you might die, Mia. The fumes from the poison… it can kill you."

Tears stream down my face. "I didn't think about that. He makes me so angry."

Nox releases his hold on me and goes back to caressing my hair. "That's because you love him. Did you ever think that he's using the poison as an excuse to get to you? Embrace your darkness, my love. Embrace his. You need someone to care for you up there. Because I cannot."

Is he right? Do I love Draven? Do I have feelings for all three of them? After everything they've done to me… I couldn't. But I feel something for each of them. I'm drawn to them like an addiction.

"I'm sorry. I know it was stupid. But if I'm here, that means I'm not dead, right?" The chills in my spine deepen. I pull the sheet up around me.

"You are still alive. But you need to rest, so you stay that way." He pulls me back to his chest. "Sleep now, my love. Return to me when you're healed."

I cry myself back to sleep on Nox's beautiful chest. It's these tender moments between us that strengthen our bond. He's my nightmare, but he's also my savior. The only one who has never abandoned me.

"I know that I love *you*, Nox," I murmur as he coaxes me back to sleep. I feel safe in his strong arms.

"Shhh, sleep."

Panic fills my chest when I open my eyes. I'm in a room I've never seen before. In someone else's bed. Where the fuck am I?

My throat burns. Fuck. I can barely swallow. I turn my head, and my stomach knots. I shrink back against the pillows.

"You're awake. Good." Draven lounges in a chair next to the bed.

The scent of honey wafts up my nose. It's sweet but stings to breathe in. "Did it all burn?" I rasp.

He blows out a deep breath, his brow furrowed at me. "No. My driver spent all night hosing it down. No thanks to you."

Fuck. I went too far. *He makes me this way*. All I see is red every time I'm around him.

"You saved me. Why?" I'm under no assumption that he still doesn't want to kill me, but he could have left me for dead in the fields last night.

His eyes darken. "I don't know."

"Thank you." There's something he's not telling me. He's holding back.

He unbuttons his shirt and takes it off. The quiet rage coming off him is palpable. "You do not get to decide when you die. I do." He unzips his pants and steps out of them. "You almost fucking died last night because of your impulsivity."

I'm too weak to argue. And I know he's right. For once, I agree with him. But the way he undresses is stirring an ache in my core. "What are you doing?"

He gently climbs on top of me, careful not to put his weight on my fragile frame. "You have no idea how fucking terrified I was. To see you choking on the ground, desperate for breath. I hate you for making me feel that way."

Fuck. He does feel something more for me. "I'm sorry," I murmur.

He gazes at my lips. "Don't you ever put yourself in harm's way like that again."

I tilt my head closer to his. "I won't."

He pulls back the sheet to get underneath it. The heat from his body sends a spark straight to my belly. "Are you warm enough now? You've been shivering all night."

I nod, not trusting my voice.

"Good." He shifts more of his body weight onto me. I whimper as his cock twitches against my panties. He boxes me in with his arms, one resting on either side of me.

"You did more than save me. You took care of me and watched me sleep all night." I part my legs so he can settle in closer.

He slowly shifts his hips up and presses his length against me. "I did."

We are locked in now, holding eye contact like our lives depend on it. "Tell me how. What did you do?"

He places his hand on my chest. "I applied an ointment here." My breath hitches as he grips my throat. "And here."

I bite back a moan when he rolls his hips again, putting more pressure on my aching nub. "What else?"

He slides his hand up my jaw and drags his thumb across my lips. "I made you drink the antidote. The one we created for you just in case…"

Fuck. *My panties are soaked.*

I lick his thumb, my lips quivering. "Let me show you how grateful I am, Slick."

A low growl rumbles from his chest into his throat. "You need to know something… I'm half-nightmare, Mia."

I let his words sink in. The weight behind him. But I'm not surprised. It's been staring me in the face this whole time. Deep down, I think I knew that about him. I sensed it. It's why we are drawn to each other's darkness.

I roll my hips up to meet his. "I don't care. Now come get your peace."

His eyes widen, sparking with lust and hunger. He pulls my panties to the side and presses the tip of his cock to my wet entrance. "Are you sure?"

I reach down in between us and grab a hold of his shaft, guiding him inside. "I've always been sure. You're my peace too."

We don't break eye contact as he slides inside me. "Oh, fuck. Draven…"

"Mia. Fuck, you feel so fucking good." He rocks into me gently, making sure I feel every ridge.

I wrap my legs around his middle, urging him in deeper. "Does this mean we have a truce, Draven?"

He draws in a deep breath, his cock throbbing against my inner walls. "No. I still hate you."

"Liar," I whisper in his ear.

A soft moan escapes his lips as he thrusts in deeper. "You're still healing. I don't want to hurt you."

The irony is not lost on me. He's been trying to hurt me since I moved to town. But this is different. He's being tender.

But I want his brutality.

"It will hurt me more if you hold back." I grind against him, desperate to feel every inch of him. "Fuck me like you own me."

His eyes darken as he grabs my throat and squeezes. "*I do own you.*"

I scream as he slides out and slams back in. "Yeah, like that. Fuck…"

"Mmm, you make me so angry, Mia." *Thrust.* "But I can't get enough of you."

We're spiraling, crashing together like waves against the shore. Like a storm that's been brewing for centuries only to finally unleash, threatening to wipe out everything in our path.

He made good on his promise to destroy my soul. I welcome

it. I crave it. I need his darkness to seep into my bones, into every crevice of my being.

"Oh, fuck," I whine as he presses against my most sensitive spot.

"I want to die inside you someday. Promise me you'll keep fucking me after I'm gone. Use my body until you've fucked it to dust." He rubs his balls against my taint as he fucks me harder.

This man is beautifully psychotic, twisted, and deranged. I'm obsessed with him. Addicted to his melancholy and madness. "I promise. You're mine, Draven. In this life and the next."

He rides me harder, pulling me into a rhythm that's as agonizing as it is cathartic. "You're not allowed to leave, Trouble. Ever. I'll burn this whole fucking world down and everyone in it."

I cry out and clench around his swollen cock while my juices spill out. "I'm not going anywhere."

"Fuck. Mmm, Mia…" His hot thick cum unleashes into me, filling me so full I can't contain it all. It drips out of my pussy and down my ass. He grabs onto the bedpost as we convulse against each other until we finally collapse.

His chaos craves my peace, chasing it like a storm. And I embrace both his light and his nightmare. Like I'm a vessel for his darkness.

I wake up in Draven's bed alone. I stretch out, my muscles relaxed for the first time in a while. Even though my throat still feels like sandpaper, it's the best night of sleep I've ever had. Nox didn't send for me. He let me rest. I'm grateful but a twinge of guilt sits in my gut.

When I finally drag my ass out of bed, I spot a fresh change of clothes draped across the chair. The same chair that Draven sat in while he watched over me. A flurry of butterflies swims in my belly. It takes me back to our first encounter at Duff's all those months ago. Except last night, he didn't look away. He held my gaze the whole time.

And in his soft expression, I learned more about him than any conversation we've ever had. He's like me in a way. And also like Nox. I knew he was different from Bones and Aries from the start. I just couldn't figure it out. But when the poison fields were burning, and I saw his eyes glow through the smoke, it was the last thought I had before I passed out. *Draven is half-nightmare.*

It makes more sense now than anything else.

I finish dressing in the pair of jeans and cashmere sweater he laid out for me. I tug on my black motorcycle boots, chuckling as I imagine Draven rifling through my closet to try and put together an outfit for me to wear.

It takes me ten minutes to find the staircase. Blackwell Manor is even larger than Harker Mansion. The décor is similar with dark walls, marble floors, and velvet curtains. There are ornate mirrors at the end of each hall and old paintings of people I assume are ancestors. When I get downstairs, I find Draven, Bones, and Aries waiting for me in the foyer.

My stomach flips under the heated stares of all three of them. "Good morning," I murmur.

Bones shakes his head at me. "You promise not to set any more fires if we take you home?"

My cheeks flame. "I-I don't know what got into me."

Aries snorts. "You might be crazier than all three of us. I'm going to start calling you little pyro from now on."

Draven stares at the floor, his shoulders hunched. He's holding something back again.

"Hey, is your driver okay?" I ask. In the chaos of everything that's transpired, I forgot to check on the man who saved my house.

He grits his teeth. "Rodrick is fine. He's worked for my family since before I was born. Putting out fires is what he does best."

I nod, still concerned with what's eating at him today.

"We have that meeting with my father later," Aries quips. "So do we have any of *this* figured out?"

My stomach knots. Aside from the fragile bonds we've threaded between us, there is still the matter of the enormous field of baneberry my property sits on.

"Not entirely," Draven grumbles.

"What if we compromise? I could sell you the poison whenever you want. But I get to keep my land and my house."

Bones arches an eyebrow at Draven, his eyes lighting up. "That could work, Dray."

"You think I haven't already thought about that? It still doesn't give us the control we need. Gemini Thorn will try and get to her somehow."

Okay now I'm getting pissed again. "Hello? I'm still in the room. We could sign an exclusive contract or something. Why are you making this difficult?"

He glares at me. "Are you prepared to be tied to us forever, Mia? If I have that contract drawn up, it's for life. It will require your unwavering loyalty. A deal like that carries more weight than any other. It's like a marriage except there is no divorce if you change your mind."

He's angry again. Scared maybe. "I said I wouldn't leave, and I meant it. Who are you trying to reassure, Draven, me or you?"

Aries snort laughs again. "I'm down for whatever you two lovebirds decide. But I want my share." He stalks over to me and snakes an arm around my waist. "You belong to all three of us, little pyro."

I roll my eyes, but there's a spark flickering in my chest. "Stop calling me that. I was pyro adjacent." Although, it does sound more badass than little lamb.

He fixates on my lips. "It's a turn on for me. I'll happily watch you set fires all over town."

"Don't encourage her," Draven growls.

Bones slips his arm around me from the other side. "If we agree to your deal, you'll have to be a good girl and do exactly as we say."

I know he's talking about contracts, but my dirty mind immediately heads somewhere else. Fucking hell I am way too needy for these men. "The baneberry is all yours, just so long as my name stays on the property title."

Draven finally looks up, his eyes dark and stormy. "And you. I want to hear you say it."

My heart skips as the three of them surround me. They want me to admit surrender. To give them complete control over my body and my soul. But I come with a lot of fucking baggage.

"I need to talk to Nox," I rasp out, my throat still sore.

The three of them exchange a look before Draven pulls out his phone. "Rodrick, I need you to drive Miss Harker home."

He's pissed at me. Fuck. "You're not taking me?"

"No. We have work to do. I'll let you know later what we decide." He turns his back and stalks out of the room.

Aries playfully slaps my cheek. "See you later, little pyro."

I roll my eyes at his back as he heads for the doorway Draven disappeared through.

Bones kisses me on the cheek. "You do what you have to do, baby girl."

I pull him to me before he can walk away. "How did your brother die?"

His eyes darken. "Mia—"

"Does it have something to do with all of this?" I've had a nagging feeling about it since he first told me. The pieces of Ever Graves are like a puzzle I'm slowly putting together.

He sighs. "I was supposed to be watching him, but I was hopped up on poison. He wandered off into the forest and never came home. The search party found his bloody clothes. They figured he was mangled by an animal. My father has never forgiven me. My mother says she does, but I can see the pain in her eyes every time she looks at me."

I squeeze his hands. "Fuck. I'm sorry, Bones. But it's not your fault. You were just a kid yourself."

He clenches his jaw. "My brother Felix and I both fell into depression. While Felix coped with poetry and meditation, I have been actively punishing myself ever since it happened."

"Punishing yourself, how?" I think I know, but he needs to talk about it. He can't keep bottling this pain inside.

He presses his forehead to mine and blows out a deep breath. "I'm reckless. I don't care if I live or die. I do everything to the extreme, drinking, fighting, riding my bike at night with the headlights off. I tattooed my whole body, so I can't cut myself anymore. Don't want to fuck up the art. I will do anything that takes me to the edge. It reminds me that I'm still here, and Sonny is gone forever."

I wrap my arms around his neck and pull him closer. "You're allowed to be upset, Bones. But you have to stop hurting yourself in his name. Do you think he would want that for you?"

He holds me tight and breathes heavily into my ear. "I know, baby girl. I'm working on it."

We stay like this, holding each other for what seems like forever, until I spot Rodrick waiting at the door. He's as still as a statue, with his hands behind his back, and his eyes averted from us.

I slide away from Bones. "I guess I should go home and let you get back to work. Come find me later if you want to talk."

He nods at Rodrick before planting another soft kiss on my cheek. "You have a way of taming beasts. Thank you for pulling that out of me."

"I know what it's like to feel alone. It can be suffocating. But you're not alone, Bones. Remember that."

He gives me a wink. "I'll find you later, little pyro. Stay away from anything flammable until I get back."

I groan. "Ugh, not you too." I shake my head as I follow Rodrick to the car.

"Thank you for putting out the fire. I have no excuse for what I did."

The gray-haired man nods before shutting my door.

We ride in silence until we arrive at my gates.

"Draven told you his secret, didn't he?" he says after he punches in my security code.

"Yes," I murmur. Does everyone have the passcode to my front gates? Fucking hell.

He drives all the way up to the porch before letting me out. "Perhaps lighting a fire is exactly what he needed to wake up."

A chill crawls up my back. "Maybe we all need to wake up."

He nods. "I put my number in your phone. Call if you need anything."

My heart skips. His light-blue eyes are kind and genuine. I'm not used to anyone caring about me. Even my long lost uncle, who freed me from Absentia Asylum, couldn't wait to get as far away from me as possible. He paid my way out and dropped me off at a shelter. I cried for three nights straight until I checked my bank account and realized I had enough money to buy the whole town of Raven's Gate.

And even then, I didn't trust it. I bought myself a used truck and drove here to Ever Graves, half-expecting for it all to be some cruel joke. But I'm starting to believe it more and more. This is my life now. I don't have to be alone. I can choose to let people in.

I surprise myself when I throw my arms around the man's neck. "Thank you, Rodrick. That means more than you can ever know."

He softens his stiff stance slightly to pat my back. "Well, um, it's no bother."

To my right, the fields are blackened. I scrunch my nose as the acrid stench of poisoned ash wafts between us.

He waits for me to get all the way inside before driving away, and my heart melts again. It's nice to be looked after. But now I'm alone in this strange big house that I need to make feel more like my home.

But I can't do anything until I see Nox. Nightmares aren't meant to last forever.

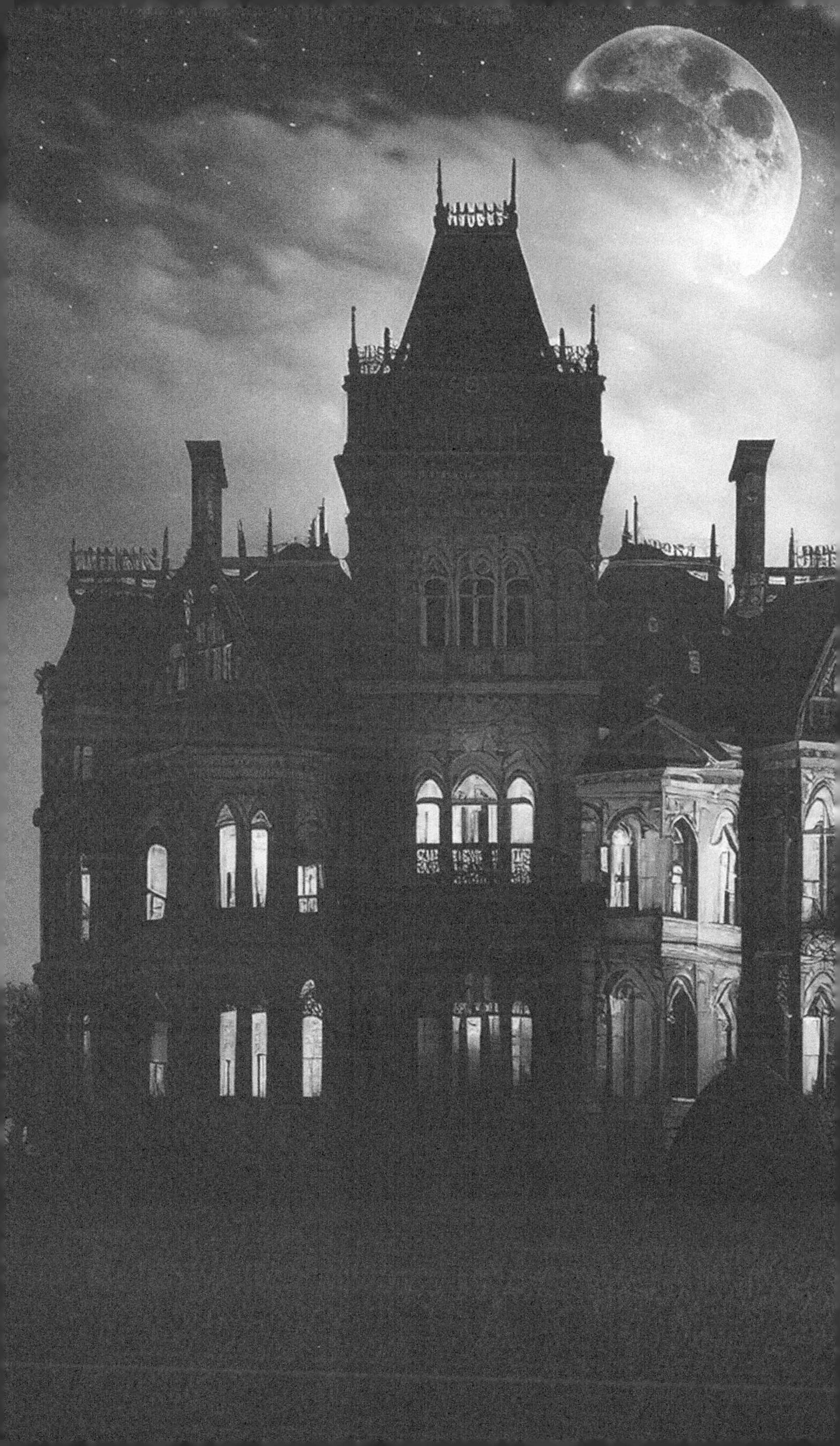

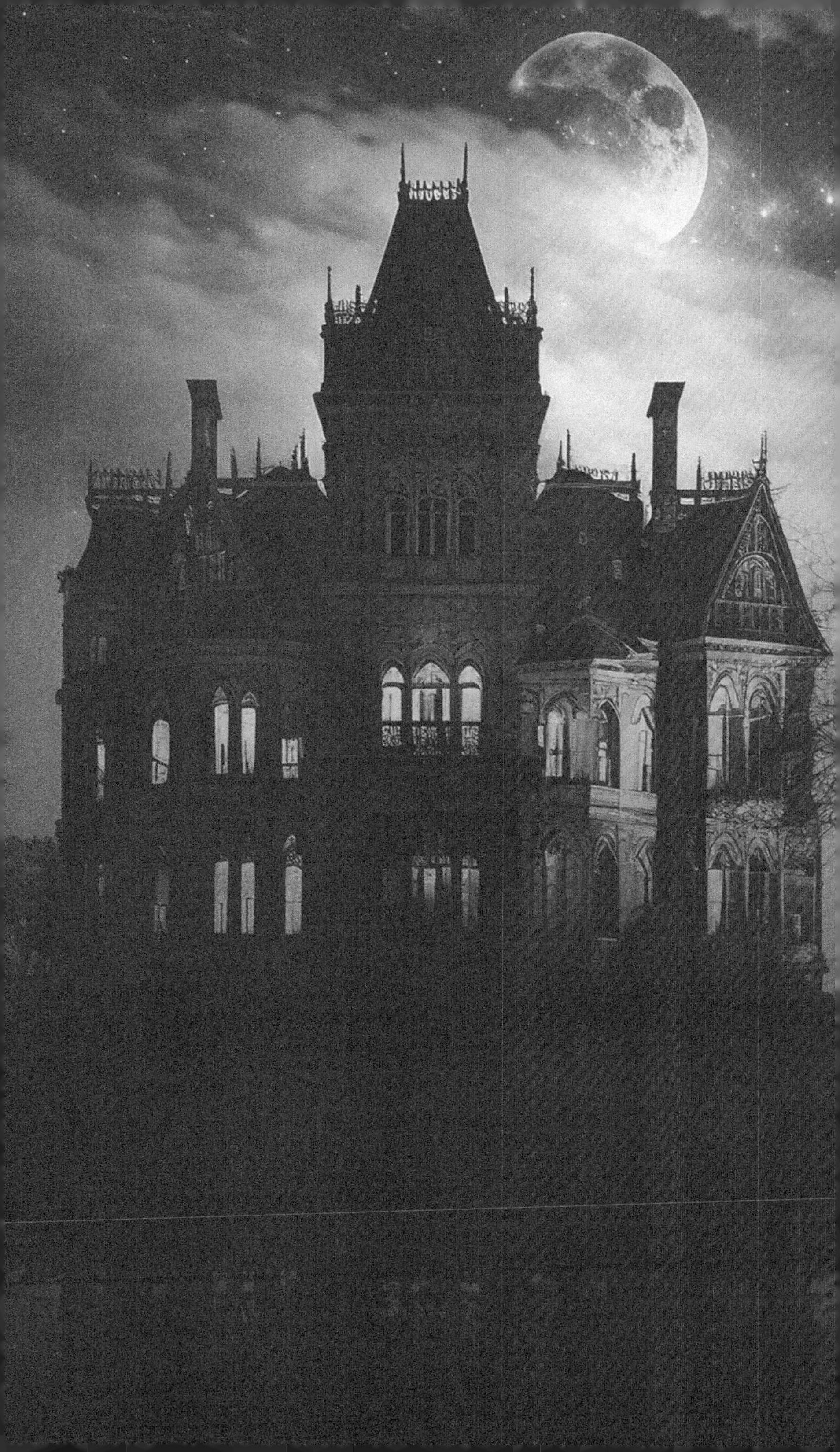

CHAPTER 24

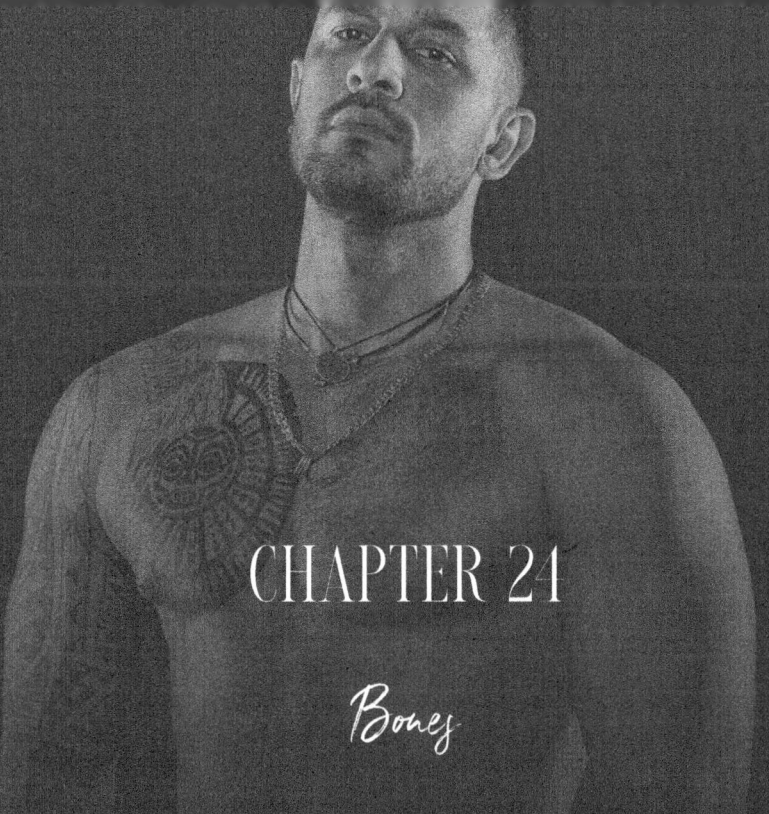

Bones

WE ALL HAVE OUR SECRETS. THINGS WE KEEP INSIDE OUR MINDS, things that are so dark, so inexcusable, that we're afraid to tell anybody. We also tell little white lies, holding back from each other out of fear of changing our dynamic. But after the fucking bomb that Draven just dropped… It's time we all bring our forbidden shadows out into the light.

The terrace at Blackwell Manor is illuminated by torches and flickering candles. We sit around a glass table that's covered in various bottles of booze, vials of poison, and ashtrays full of cigarette butts and half-smoked joints. The tension is as thick as the morning fog, heavy as it swirls in between us.

We haven't slept since leaving Aries's father's house. We drove all night from the top of the mountains of Ever Graves just to get back here before sunrise. It's in these twilight hours where we're most at ease. When the devil's hold on us is at its weakest.

"I can't believe you waited this long to tell us. You know we never would have judged you." I stir the ice cube in my whiskey with my finger before sucking it off.

Draven lights another cigarette. "I know. It wasn't about that. I couldn't bring myself to say it out loud… until last night."

Aries runs a hand through his blond locks, tousling them. His tie is off, his shirt unbuttoned halfway down. It's the most unkempt I've seen him look in a long time.

"You told her before us. Why?" he asks.

The lines on Draven's forehead crease as if he's wincing from pain. "Because of what she is. The nightmare world is familiar to her. It wasn't planned. I wanted to be inside her. But I couldn't do it with this secret between us. I looked into her eyes, and it just came out."

Aries nods, satisfied with his answer. "The Harkers have had a hold on this town for a long time."

"And everyone in it," I add. They were the original sin. The family that started the curse. The reason why every woman born in Ever Graves is saddled with her own nightmare man. But they are just fragments of a greater whole, extensions of the devil himself.

Aries throws me an expectant look. My pulse races. I take a deep drag of my joint. His eyes tell me what his mouth isn't. No more secrets or holding back. I exhale a huge puff of smoke and blow it slowly in his direction.

Draven raises an eyebrow. "What was that?"

Aries leans forward and places his hand on my knee. "Me and Bones are more than friends. We've kind of had this thing between us since we were kids."

Draven smirks. "I think it's adorable that you thought I didn't know."

Fuck. I blow out a deep breath. "You've known?"

He chuckles. "You're not as discreet as you think. Of course, I know."

"But you never said anything," Aries quips.

Draven shrugs. "It wasn't my place to. That's between you two.

I hoped that it would never fuck up the friendship for all our sakes, but it's never been my business to meddle in."

Relief fills me. The last thing I want is for Draven to think we would ever put our friendship in jeopardy. Aries and I promised each other a long time ago that love and sex were a bonus but the bonds between us are forever. Nothing can break them.

"Cool," I say on a breath.

Draven bursts out laughing. "And you say I'm the serious one. Both of you, relax. We're the sons of Ever Graves. Us against the world. Remember?"

I nod. "By the Wishing Tree." When we were just twelve years old, we made a blood sacrifice together in the forest, pledging our loyalty to each other for life.

"So we're all half-nightmare then, I guess. Thanks for disclosing that now. I might not have gone through with it if I had known back then," Aries teases.

Draven snorts. "It doesn't work like that, Ries. I'm still the only one with ties to the devil."

'I know but I enjoy riling you up." He flashes a grin before downing his third vial of nightshade.

"You and Mia," I add. "The devil haunts her every night."

The muscle in his jaw ticks. The mere mention of her name, does something wild to all of us. "That's why we need to keep her close. The curse was created out of spite. The devil wanted to make sure that no woman in Ever Graves would ever know peace. That they would never receive love from another. Not without a nightmare hanging over them."

That dark tone returns to his voice. I didn't realize he knew so much about the curse. I guess I'd learn everything I could, too, if I was half-nightmare though.

I take a swig from a bottle of Blackwell gin. "Are you saying we can break the curse?"

Draven shakes his head. "No, it's too late for that. But maybe there's a way to release her from his hold. If that's what she wants."

Aries nods. "According to the old legends, a Bishop witch gave a blood sacrifice at the Wishing Tree. She let the devil out of hell in exchange for immortality. But he saw Willa Harker in the nearby field and became obsessed. When she rejected him, he created the curse. But he also cursed the Bishop woman and all her future descendants. He made sure they can't ever get into the After. So when they die, they become ghosts, stuck in between worlds."

What the fuck? I must've missed that class in school. "How the fuck do you know all this?"

He grins, proud of himself. "I'm a Thorn. We keep excellent records."

The threads on these hallowed grounds keep burrowing deeper. "I used to think that's all they were, legends."

Draven shakes his head. "My grandmother kept records as well. If she knew what I was, she never let on. But my father knew I was definitely not his. He suspected my mother of cheating, but not with a nightmare man. That never crossed his mind. Rodrick guessed it early on. It was unspoken."

There are so many memories that make more sense to me now. All of that weight was on Draven's shoulders, this secret he had to hide so his family wouldn't send him away like they did with his cousin Maureen. I only wish he hadn't shouldered it alone.

I take another puff of the joint. "We are from some fucked up families."

"And a fucked up town," Aries adds as he rolls a fresh joint for himself.

Draven holds up his glass of gin. "But now we control the poison. I'm surprised that your father relinquished his hold so easily though. I thought Gemini Thorn would've put up more of a fight. What did you say to him when I left the room?"

Aries's eyes darken as he licks the rolling paper. "The truth. That he's lucky I haven't murdered him for what he did to Lib. And that I still might. I told him to sign everything over to us or sleep with both eyes open instead of one."

My cock twitches in my pants. I love when he gets like this. Threats of murder and mayhem are my fucking foreplay. I hold his gaze, revealing all of my ache and pain and hunger for him with just a look. A look that only he and Mia understand.

"Should I give you two a minute?" Draven snorts.

And apparently Draven understands it too.

I give him a wink. "Nah, we can wait. Besides, we'll need more than a minute."

"Thatta boy," Aries quips back.

I am hard as a rock now. "Careful, Ries, I might change my mind and bend you over this table right now."

He leans back in his chair, his cock tenting his pants. "I want our little lamb between us."

Draven's eyes glaze with lust too. "I'd like to see that… I'm not done punishing her for what she did. Let's make it another game."

I lick my lips, my glands salivating for another taste of her. "She is fun to play with."

Aries stares at my crotch. "Show me how hot she makes you."

Now I'm going to fucking burst. I glance over at Draven.

He pours another glass of gin and leans back. "I don't mind watching if you don't."

Fucking hell these two are going to give me a fucking heart attack. I look back to Aries as I unzip my jeans and free my swollen cock. I wrap a hand around it and squeeze.

Aries spreads his legs open and palms his own cock. "Slide your hand up and down, nice and slow for me."

Having Draven watch is somehow making me hotter. More unhinged. I want to fuck Aries so bad. I do as he says, taking my time as I finger every ridge on the way down to my tip. I squeeze and a little dribble of pre cum spurts out. "Mmm, I want to fill all her fucking holes."

"We'll fill them together," Draven confirms.

"A little faster now," Aries orders, his voice breathy.

I let out a soft whimper as the blood flows down, pulsing with need.

"Yeah, just like that," Aries praises. "You look so fucking good."

My balls tingle as my blood pumps faster in a race against my heartbeat. I roll my hips up as I squeeze and pull on my cock. "I want to scare the fuck out of her. Her fear feeds me."

Draven stalks over to my chair and stands behind me. He rests his hands on my shoulders. "Close your eyes and cum to the vision of her screaming in fear."

Oh, fuck.

Aries sucks in a sharp breath. "Fuck. Now I'm gonna cum." He pulls his cock out of his pants and fists it. "We should have invited you a long time ago, Dray."

"Aw, fuck. You've done it now..." My cum bursts out, coating my hand in thick, hot ropes.

Knowing how much I love pain, Draven pinches the tissue between my shoulder blades hard. "There you go. Let it all out."

I open my eyes just as another orgasm rips through me, a wave of flutters that zaps every nerve in my body. I pump harder and faster, milking myself while Draven digs his fingers into my back.

Aries growls and moans as he watches me, a sopping mess of white cream soaking his swollen cock. "Mmm, fuck. The things we're going to do to her..."

Draven releases his hold on me but smooths his hands softly over my back one last time. "I'll be right back."

Aries and I stare hard into each other's eyes, our chests heaving as we both struggle to regain control of our breath and our heartbeats. We've never done anything like that before. Not with anyone watching. But it was especially hot because it was Dray. Fuck, he's intense, and having his eyes, then his hands, on me was what gave me the final push over the edge.

He comes back out a few minutes later with a towel for each of us. "Thank you for letting me watch."

"Anytime you want," Aries rasps.

As I clean myself off, I spot something else in Draven's hand. He tosses three black ski masks on the table. The eyes and mouths are covered with a thin mesh lining so we can still see and breathe, but she won't recognize us. Plus, I texted her earlier that we wouldn't be back in town until tomorrow.

A rush of adrenaline races through my veins.

"You say you want to scare her. These will help."

"Tonight?" Aries asks.

Draven smirks. "Right fucking now."

Sunrise is still at least two hours away, but we know Mia isn't sleeping. All three of us have been watching her long enough to know that she makes herself stay up for days in between nightmares. She'll be delirious, exhausted, and easy to trap. Especially since she still doesn't even know the way around her own house.

I put on one of the masks, the snug fabric already making me feel like an unhinged predator. "Let's go hunting."

It takes me less than five minutes to flip all the breakers to Harker Mansion, enshrouding it in darkness. Masked and dressed in all black, the three of us slip in the back door off the kitchen.

I almost laugh out loud when I hear Mia cursing and stumbling around in the dark. But as soon as I get a whiff of jasmine, my primal instinct kicks in. My belly flutters knowing she's so close. So vulnerable. We are the monsters tonight. Awake or asleep, there's no escaping us. But I prefer her awake. I want to see the look of fear mixed with lust in those pretty mismatched eyes.

Draven points to the ceiling, and I nod. We're going to herd her upstairs. We could grab her now, but where's the fun in that? No, I want my little lamb to run. To feel the beasts at her back, breathing down her neck.

We split up and take various dark corners to hide in on the first floor. My heart races as I wait. After a few minutes, I hear her scream from down the hallway. Bare feet slap against the marble floors as she rounds the corner in a full sprint. She's coming right toward me. I step out, blocking her path to the wine cellar.

Gotcha.

She smacks into me and stumbles back. Her eyes widen as I walk her back against the wall. "Get out of my house!"

I don't touch her. I don't speak. I just box her in and tower over her. The anticipation has me hard as fuck.

Wearing nothing but a thin, white cotton T-shirt that barely covers her ass, her body trembles. "I-I have three psychos who are about to walk in here any moment," she lies. "They're gonna kill you."

My adrenaline spikes. *That's right, baby girl. We will kill anyone who dares to touch you. But it's us that you should be more afraid of tonight.*

I step to the side and let her put space between us before stalking toward her again, flanking her on the right so she's forced to go up the stairs.

"Please, I have money. I'll fucking pay you to leave me alone." She still hasn't realized there are three predators in her home tonight.

Sweat soaks through her shirt, plastering it to her body, showing me the outline of her pink nipples and that *sweet fucking pussy*. She walks backward up the stairs, keeping her eyes trained on me the whole time.

Good girl. No sudden movements, or I might attack.

I slow my pace, trailing behind her by at least four steps. When she reaches the second floor, she makes a run for it again. And I let her. Aries is up next. And soon, we'll have her right where we want her—bound, naked, and at our mercy.

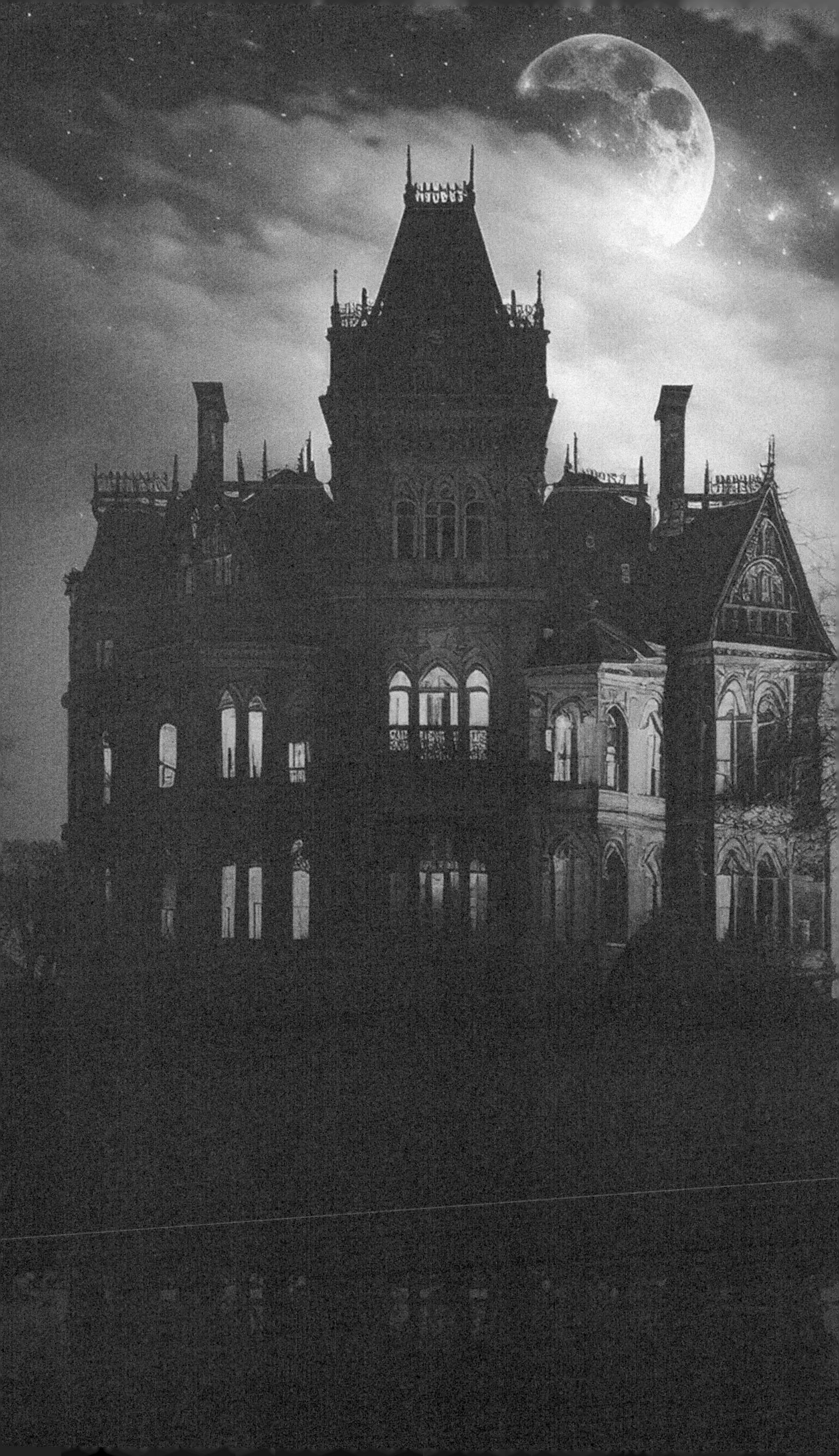

CHAPTER 25

Mia

If Bones, Aries, and Draven think I don't know that it's them behind the masks, they don't give me enough credit. But I'll play their little game. I'll act scared and scream for help. It turns me on as much as it does them. I am not their helpless victim. I never have been. Even when Aries locked me in a cage, deep down, I enjoyed it. Every depraved fucking second.

But I didn't survive this long on my own by being naïve or stupid. Do your worst, boys. Your little lamb has come to play tonight.

I run away from Bones and sprint down the hall. As I slide around the first corner, I smack straight into another wall of solid muscle. With broad shoulders and a puffed out chest, he towers over me by at least a foot. *Aries.*

I scream in his face as he grabs my arms and pins them to my side. "Please, don't hurt me," I pretend to plead.

He slams me against the wall and presses his body into mine. I feel his cock pulse against my middle, and my juices trickle out.

This is more fun than I thought it would be. It's hard not to grin up at him. But I keep the horror frozen on my face.

He tilts his head toward my neck and takes a full breath, breathing deep as he laps up my scent like a hound dog. It sends shivers down my back. *The anticipation is fucking killing me.*

In a split second, he drops my arms and steps back. And I make a run for it again. He stalks me down the hall, slow enough to make me think I'm going to get away. My adrenaline spikes as I reach my bedroom door. As soon as I enter, the door slams behind me. I spin around to see the third masked man blocking my only way out.

He creeps toward me, forcing me backward until I'm pressed against the window. I know the darkness that hides behind the mask. And I want it. I crave it.

He pins my wrists over my head and sniffs my neck the same way Aries did. I quiver as the mouth of his mask brushes my cheek.

"Stop edging me, Draven, and come get your peace." I nuzzle his face with my own.

He stiffens and then releases a deep breath. "I knew as soon as I looked in your eyes… Now I'm not sure who's hunting who."

"I will always know it's you. All three of you. Our bodies know each other even when our minds are confused."

His grip tightens on my wrists as the door opens behind us and Aries and Bones walk through.

"Welcome to the party, guys," I breathe out.

"She's known this whole time," Draven rasps. He lets go to pull his mask off but I stop him.

"No, leave it on." I clench my thighs together. "I wanna keep playing."

"Take off your shirt and get on the bed."

The three of them watch me like snakes about to strike. I take my time peeling off my T-shirt, letting them get a full view of my hard nipples and gooseflesh. In nothing but my white cotton panties,

I crawl onto the four-poster bed and slither back against the black satin sheets.

"Take off your panties," Aries orders.

With trembling fingers, I push them down slowly and toss them onto the floor.

"Spread your legs." Bones adds to the list of demands.

I'm on fire, my pulse racing. This is different from the woods and the graveyard. This is sexy and sensual and intimate. I part my legs for them.

"Wider," Draven growls.

As I unfold for them, more of my juices leak out. "Please," I whisper. "Destroy me."

They let me suffer in silence as they each remove their own clothes save for the masks. Their bodies are beautiful, smooth, chiseled, and tattooed.

Bones's black and grey ink stretches over every inch of him from the bottom of his chin all the way down to his feet. Including his thick cock. Aries's chest and back are covered but low enough to hide under a suit. And Draven… fuck, his tattoos are black and intricate with thin lines of filigree woven in between. They swirl across his chest, down his arms, and across his thighs. The three of their bodies are works of art. Psychotic canvases ready to devour and swallow me whole.

They join me on the bed, Aries and Bones on either side of me while Draven takes the spot between my legs. He runs his hands down my thighs until he reaches my apex. He slides a slender finger down my slit. I whimper as he teases me.

Bones circles his knuckle around my taut nipple. "You're ours now, little lamb. You belong to the wolves."

"And we're going to tear you apart limb from limb," Aries groans in my ear as he pinches my other nipple.

I let out a soft moan and arch my back. "Yes, please."

Draven thrusts his finger deep inside my pussy and pumps back and forth. The pressure increases in my belly as I spasm around him. "Please," I beg again.

"I want you to get on top of Aries and slide this tight little pussy down his cock," Draven orders.

I whine when he pulls his finger out, but I do as he says. There's nothing that I want more in this moment than to be defiled by all three of them.

As I climb onto Aries, he yanks my hips down and fills me. I gasp at the size of him stretching my walls. "Rock back and forth, baby."

I move my hips in a circle as I struggle to accommodate him fully inside me. He's long and thick and hard as fuck. I take deep breaths as I sit all the way down on him. Until I can feel him in my lower back.

"Thatta girl. You're doing so good," he coaxes.

Bones caresses my lips. "Mi amor… I can't wait to cum inside your pretty mouth."

Fuck. The only thing that terrifies me now is how I could get used to this. They are slowly becoming an addiction. And unlike the baneberry, there's no antidote to them. If they shatter me, I'm dead. If only Nox were here, it would be a perfect kamikaze of love and destruction. I swallow down the guilt of his absence, heartbroken that he can't be here.

Draven slaps my ass. "Don't wander off, Mia. Stay with us in this moment."

I nod and work my hips forward and backward. I clench as I slide up and down on Aries's cock. "I'm so tight. Fuck."

"Mmm, yeah you are. But we are going to get you nice and stretched for all of us." Aries swells inside me, his cock growing even more. *Fuck, I thought he was already fully erect.*

I suck in a sharp breath as I rub my clit against his abdomen. "Fuck…"

Draven probes at my entrance from behind. "Relax for me, Trouble. You're doing so good." He wedges a finger inside my ass.

Oh, fuck. Another spasm erupts from my core. "What are you doing?" I can't hide the panic in my voice.

"Shhh, I know you can take two of us at the same time. I'm going to get you nice and wet. Do you have any lube in the bathroom up here?" Draven eyes dart around the room.

Of course I do. It's in a drawer next to my vibrator. I point to the bedside table. "You better give me all of it."

Aries thrusts up hard, reminding me who's in control. Reminding me that this is what I signed up for. That I want whatever they give me. I moan louder as he hits my G-spot over and over again until I'm on the verge of cumming. Then he stills himself, edging me to the point of blacking out.

My teeth chatter, and my legs shake from the buildup. "I need to cum. Please."

Bones rubs my lower back. "Not yet, baby. Deep breaths."

Fuck. My head is spinning. I gasp as a burst of liquid shoots into my ass. "Oh, fuck."

Draven dips two fingers inside my anus, pushing the lubricant deep inside. "See how slick you are? Now, relax and open up for me. I don't want to hurt you."

I lean forward to give him a better angle. "Go slow, please."

Bones caresses my lips again. "He'll be gentle at first, baby girl. You just gotta let him in."

Draven lines his cock up to my entrance. "Be a good girl, and give me a deep breath."

I force myself to relax as I lock eyes with Aries. He stirs inside me again, and it takes everything I have not to fall apart. I want us all to cum together. So I unclench and take a deep breath.

Draven nudges my hole. I gasp as he pushes the tip of his cock inside. Fuck, I'm already so full. May the devil have mercy on me.

"Good girl." He spreads my ass cheeks apart and burrows in another inch. "Almost there. Fuck you feel so good."

I'm a whimpering mess as the girth of his cock stretches me. I've had Nox in there before but not like this. Not with my pussy already full to the brim. Fuck.

Aries pulls me forward until I'm lying flat on my stomach against him. "Mmm, you're the first woman we've done this with," Aries coos. He tugs on my hips, urging me to grind on him. "And you'll be the last."

Another burst of liquid seeps into my ass. It sends a shiver up my thighs. But it's what I need so he doesn't rub me raw. I take another deep breath as Draven slides in another few inches.

"Thatta girl. I'm so fucking deep. Just a couple more inches now. Mmm…" He pulls my hips up, angling my ass toward him for leverage.

"One more deep breath for us, baby girl," Bones coaxes with his hand around my throat.

I've never felt anything like this. The pain is masked by the spasms in my core. Every time he pushes in deeper, it hurts for a few seconds and then an obscene wave of pleasure rolls through me.

"Come get your peace, Draven."

He growls as he thrusts his entire length inside my anus. "Mmm, I could cum right fucking now."

An animalistic whimper escapes from my throat as I'm stretched as far as I can go. They are both deep inside me now, their cocks pulsing with need.

Aries lifts my hips. "Now we're going to do this together, little lamb."

I cry out as I'm see-sawed between them. I'm lifted up and back onto Draven's cock and then back down to Aries. My eyes roll back as tingles erupt from both of my tender holes. They take turns thrusting so I always have one of them fully inside me.

Bones shifts to his knees next to us. "You're doing so good, but you're not full enough." He fists his cock and presses it to my lips. "Open up so I can fuck that pretty mouth of yours."

Oh, fuck. I'm crumbling, shattering all over their cocks like a fucking junkie. I don't think I can handle one more.

"It's too much," I whimper.

Bones pinches my chin, yanking my face toward his cock. "It's just right, baby girl. Now part those lips for me."

I moan softly as his thick cock enters my mouth. He tastes so fucking good.

He grabs my head and thrusts to the back of my throat. "Oh, yeah. Mmm. Just like that, little lamb. Swallow me whole."

My eyes glaze, tears filling them, as they fuck me senseless. I'm a rag doll, limp and defenseless against their hunger to destroy me. But it's what I asked for. And my juices are spilling out like from a faucet.

Aries rubs his abdomen against my clit as he pumps in and out, backing me into Draven's torturous cock. It's unearthly, depraved, and so fucking hot.

Bones swells, punishing my mouth with his pierced cock. The metal of his barbell clanks against my teeth. I can't stop moaning and whining like a greedy slut for them. He thrusts harder, slamming into the back of my throat. My belly twitches as I gag on him.

"Breathe through your nose, baby girl." Bones wipes the tears from my cheeks as he looks down at me.

Aries squeezes my hips and yanks them down hard. "I'm cumming. Don't you dare fucking move."

Draven growls and burrows himself to the hilt. "Oh, baby. Stay nice and still between us. We're going to fill you up together."

I cry out as I feel the rush of liquid bursting into me. The two of them moan like wild animals, growling like rabid dogs.

"Make her cum with my cock in her throat," Bones snarls, his expression darkening.

They push and pull me, rocking me back and forth on their sticky cocks. The tingle starts in my nub and spreads like wildfire. I try to cry out but Bones thrusts to the back of my throat again. I'm overstimulated, cumming all over them while he unleashes inside my mouth.

He holds my head tight in his hands, his fingers threaded through my sweat-soaked strands. "Drink it down, little lamb. Mmm, fuck. Swallow every drop."

My orgasm grips me as I clench around both Aries and Draven. I moan as Bones's hot salty cum shoots down my throat.

"That's my fucking good girl," Bones roars. He moans and thrusts harder, using my mouth as his own personal fuck toy.

It makes me cum harder. The way they all use me, the pleasure and pain that they promise and deliver is everything I yearn for.

Bones finally pulls out of my mouth and wipes my lips with his thumb. "This mouth is off limits to anyone but us now. Do you understand?"

Draven slides out and pulls me with him, lifting me off Aries. He wraps one arm around my chest while his other hand encloses around my throat. "Your mouth, your pussy, your ass... all ours."

My chest heaves as I struggle to steady my breath. I can't deny that being possessed by them sends butterflies to my belly... But they are asking me to make a promise that is impossible to keep.

I climb off the bed and throw on my silk robe. My heart is pounding. My body wants more from them. But they are forgetting that my soul has been bonded to someone else since the moment I came into this world.

"I can't do that to Nox."

I finish towel drying my hair as I walk downstairs. The shower helped soothe my muscles, but I'm still sore. Even with the ointment Draven rubbed on me, my flesh is still tender and raw. But it's a small price to pay for what I let them do to me. It's the aftermath I'm more worried about.

I find the three of them in the library, their masks off. Bones lounges on the sofa with this feet up while Aries and Draven lean over the fireplace, basking in the warmth from the flames. While they were destroying me upstairs, a storm has been ravaging the grounds outside. It's extra chilly tonight, especially with the icy draft slipping in through the cracks and crevices.

"What did you decide about the baneberry?" I ask. "Do you accept my terms or are we going back to you trying to bully me into selling?" I hope for the former, but Draven is hard to read, and I wouldn't put it past him to want full control.

Aries ruffles his blond locks, smoothing back the fallen strands off his forehead. "My father conceded. We control the poison fields now."

"I will accept your offer under one condition… Pledge your loyalty to us forever." Draven grabs my hand. "Swear you'll never leave."

It's never been about the money with them. They have enough to foster generational wealth for decades, even centuries maybe. This has always been about control and leverage.

"Only if you promise to accept Nox. I am his too."

"I thought you were plagued by him, Mia. I don't understand," Bones protests.

"We are trying to find a way to free you from him," Draven adds.

My stomach knots. Maybe I've realized that I don't want to be free. "He's the only one who's never abandoned me. Through my birth and my time at the orphanage, then when I lived on the streets, and when my ex broke things off… Nox is the one who has always been there. He's part of me. I won't let him go."

After a long pause, Aries blows out a deep sigh. "Very well. Then we have to find a way to bring him to our world. You can't keep slipping into a coma for days on end, Mia. I've seen the toll it takes on you. You're exhausted and over-caffeinated all the time."

"I know," I murmur.

Draven, still grasping my hands, presses his forehead to mine. "No matter what happens, we will not abandon you either. *You are ours.*"

Bones chuckles. "What he means to say is you have all three of us in a chokehold. The baneberry is yours. We are yours. You can have everything, baby girl. We finally met our fucking match."

I nod. "I have to talk to Nox tonight."

"Will *he* accept us?" Aries asks.

"Yes. He's the one who told me to embrace my feelings. He just wants me to be happy and cared for." I choke back a sob.

Draven wipes my tears. "I have something I need to tell you…"

"*Dray, don't,*" Bones warns. "It doesn't change anything."

"Well, he's already started now. Can't walk that back." Aries snickers.

My stomach is in knots. I don't know if I can handle any more family secrets getting dropped like bombshells.

He pulls me to the couch and sits down next to me. "Your parents ignored the curse and decided you would be born here. That part you know. What you don't know is that it was *my* grandmother who had your mother committed to Absentia Asylum. The price of her freedom was you. Your grandmother Emma sent you to Wickford Hollow Orphanage in exchange for your mother's release. She was wracked with grief and took her own life shortly after coming home."

All the blood in my body rushes to my feet, dizzying me. "What the fuck? Penny Blackwell made them give me up?"

Aries takes a seat on the coffee table across from us. "Your father drank himself to death a few years later. Emma spent the rest of her life with deep regret. In the end, this is your legacy. Nightmare man or not, she knew you deserved to be here."

Draven nods. "She left the entire Harker estate to you as a fuck you to Penny and as a way to make amends with you. What sickens me even more is that my grandmother would have done the same to me if she found out my secret."

The more I learn about Ever Graves, the more I understand why everyone here is so fucked up. Penny Blackwell was so afraid of the devil that she became one herself.

I think Emma always knew I'd come back here. She wasn't trying to protect me from a fate that had already been decided; she was just trying to prolong it until I was ready.

"What if my mother didn't ignore the curse? What if she had me here on purpose to make sure I'd always have someone watching over me?" I find it hard to believe that a Harker woman would intentionally turn a blind eye to a curse that has been plaguing our family for generations.

Bones taps a cigarette against the table, packing the tobacco down tight. His upper lip twitches when we lock eyes. "We can't know for sure. That's why I said that it doesn't matter. We can't change the past. Trust me, I wish we could…"

My heart breaks for him as I see the sadness haunting his eyes. I know he's referring to the death of his brother and the blame he still carries for it.

Aries clasps his hand. "It's not your fault, Bones. You have to let it go before it eats you alive."

A nagging feeling in my gut tells me that this darkness inside us isn't going anywhere. We will always carry these burdens and secrets. They've been forged into us, branded into our bones like tattoos. We hide our scars from the rest of the world but not from each other. Because our scars all come from the same place. Ever Graves. We have to learn to live with them. To embrace our dark flaws and shadows.

"It's who he is," I murmur.

Draven nods. "It's who we all are."

Aries is the last to give in, refusing to accept the things his father has done to their family. But he knows we're right. We should hold zero shame for what has been done to us. Our trauma doesn't define us, but it took part in shaping who we've become.

I move toward the fire, warming my trembling hands in front of the flames. "I already know how to bring Nox here. I've always known. I've hesitated because I don't know what will happen if he's no longer in my nightmares. He is darkness personified, an extension of the devil himself. He won't hurt me or you, but it could either break the curse or make it stronger."

Draven lights a cigarette and blows out a slow stream of smoke. "Do it. I'm ready for whatever comes."

A shiver races up my back as Aries and Bones give their approval as well. After tonight, Nox will be here in this house. There's no taking it back.

I nod. "Then it's settled. Tonight, I will sell the rest of my soul to the devil."

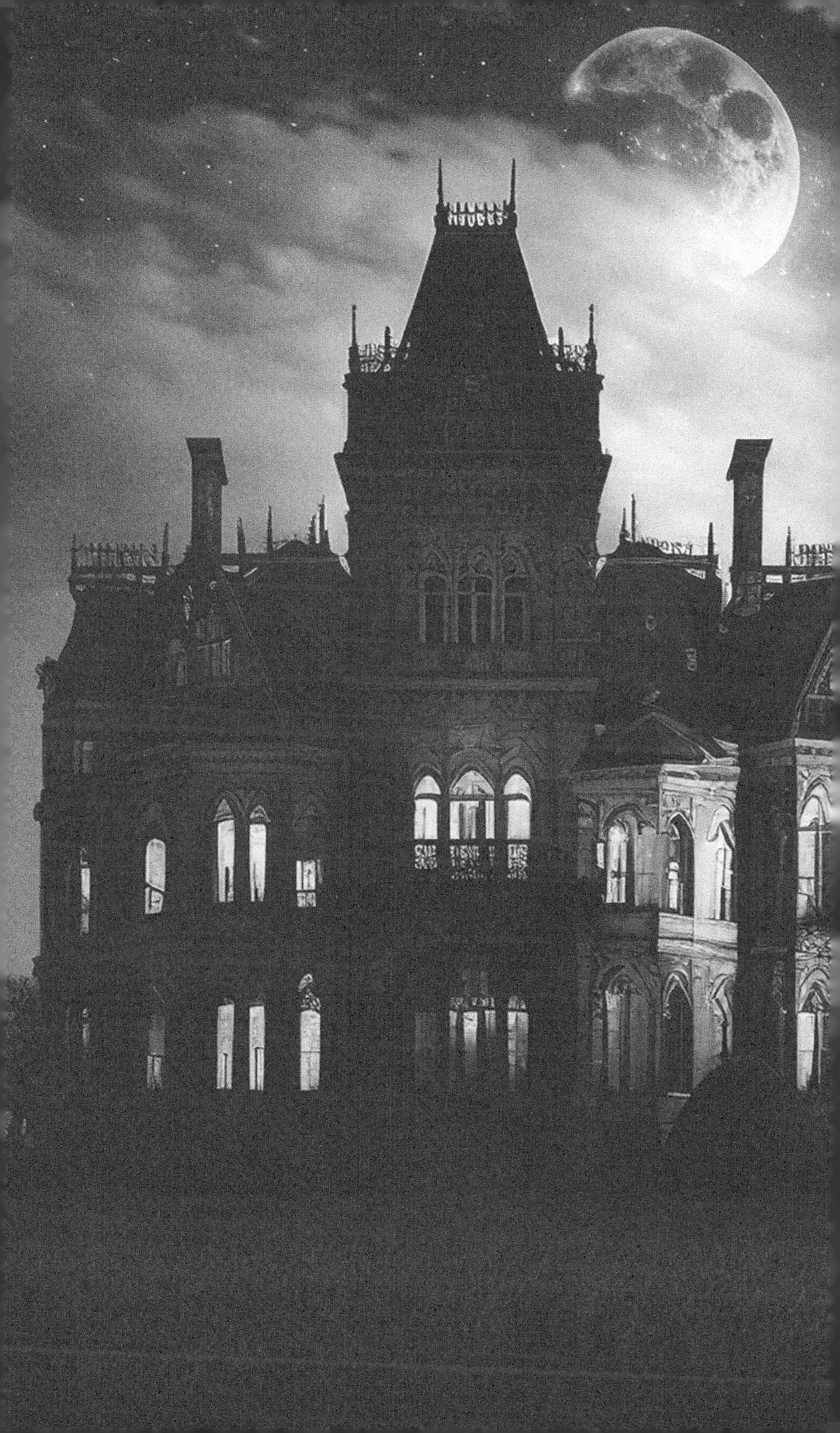

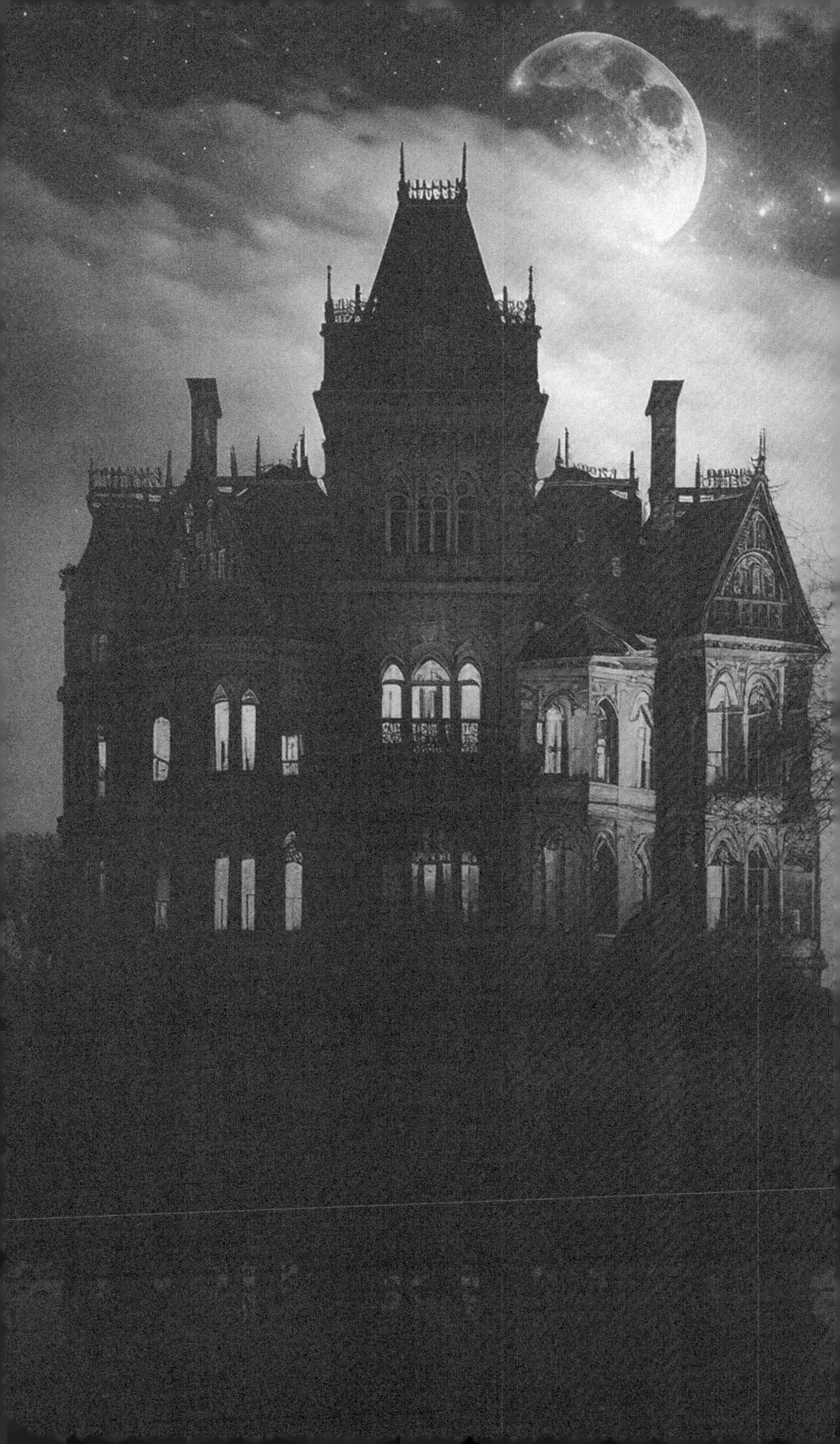

CHAPTER 26

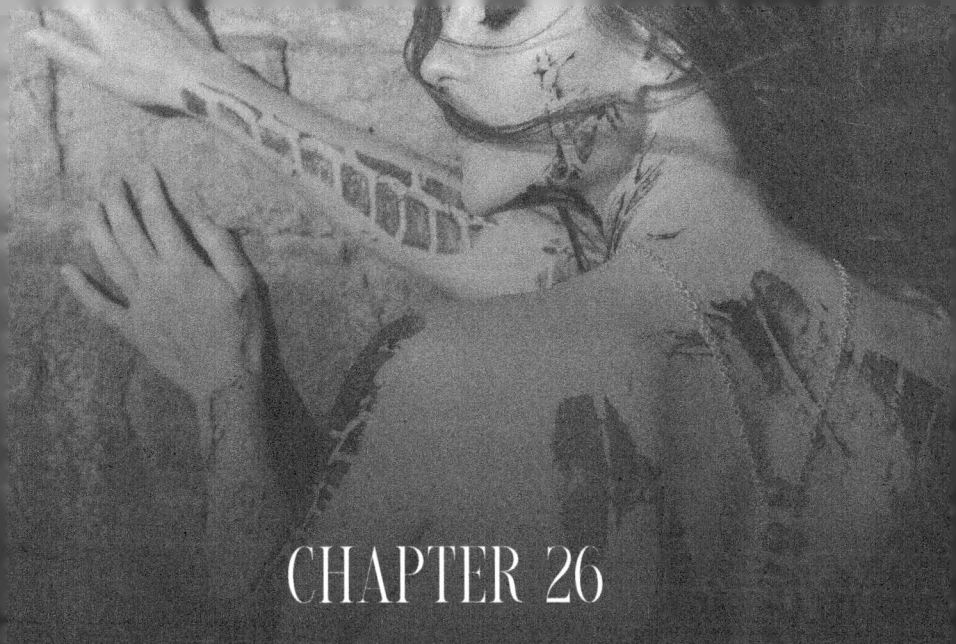

Mia

"I know what I want now," I whisper into the dark room. "I'm ready."

Nox towers over the bed, his red eyes glowing back at me. I see him for all his beauty, his black horns, sharp claws, and long ravenous tail. He may look like a monster, but his heart is more human than most. His depravity exists because of me. From what I have craved and needed from him for all these years.

I rest my cheek against his taut belly. "I want you with me always. It's time for you to leave this prison."

He caresses the back of my head. "I did not think I would ever hear those words from you, my love. Are you sure?"

I nod and nuzzle my nose against his warm skin. "Yes. You're mine, and I am yours. This room shouldn't contain us anymore. I want us all to be together… You, me, Bones, Aries, and Draven."

"It will not be easy for any of us. You know that, right?" He cups the back of my head with both hands, his claws tangled in my messy strands.

"Nothing has ever been easy for us, Nox. But I don't want to live like this anymore. And I won't give you up." There is no me without him. Neither of us knows a life without the other. I can't imagine mine without him.

"You must make an oath at the Wishing Tree. A soul for a soul."

"I know. I remember," I murmur.

"Then you'll go to sleep, and when you wake up, I will be there. Forever. As if we were never here."

I choke back a sob. More curses, more bargains, and more ties that bind. But I can't keep him trapped here any longer.

"Shhh, dark one. Don't cry. How can I make you feel better?" He tilts my chin up. The look in his eyes is tender yet hungry. His forked tongue slithers out as he licks his lips.

I shake my head. "I want to make *you* feel better." I wrap my lips around one of the heads of his cock and suck while I grip the other head tight in my hand.

He lets out a gravelly moan. "I don't deserve you…"

His foreskin is as smooth as silk and saltier than any other I've tasted. I've spent many nights with him in my mouth but tonight feels different. It could be the last time we defile each other in this room. And I want it to be special.

I take a deep breath before pushing his other head into my mouth. The stretch of my cheeks almost makes me gag. I blink back tears, breathing deeply through my nose with both of his heads filling me.

"Oh, my dark one… You devour me so well." His eyes roll back in his head as he rocks his hips gently back and forth.

His heads weigh heavy on my tongue, pressing all the way to the back of my throat. It stirs a fire in my belly, tingling my nub from the rawness of the act. This act of service I give him as a token of my love and adoration.

I gaze deep into his red eyes as I suck. Those red eyes I've painted a thousand times but which can never be fully captured on canvas. In the flesh, they are stronger, brighter, and more seductive. I wonder if he will change on the other side.

"Mia, my love. I am close. Pull back now if you think you can't handle it." He pets the back of my head softly.

I take more of him down my throat, determined to swallow every drop of him. I whimper as he twitches against the inside of my cheeks, the ridges on his cock protruding out with violent force. I relax my throat and tilt my head back as I wait for the devil's nectar.

"Mmm. Alright, then." He cradles my head, holding it firm between his palms as he jerks into my mouth.

His tail slithers around my body, finding its way between my legs. I gasp as it slips inside my pussy. I rock back and forth on it, trembling as it penetrates deeper, stimulating every nerve in my core.

A stifled moan erupts as the first gush of liquid shoots down my throat. I grab onto his waist, anchoring myself to him as his tail slides in and out of my throbbing pussy. I squeeze and release, coaxing my own pleasure as I milk him.

"I love how you worship me, dark one. So devout," he praises.

I shudder as he shatters me, and I cum all over his tail. His words sound like a holy hymn to my ears. I lap up every drop of him until I've licked him clean.

He fingers my swollen lips. "Delicious."

I kiss his stomach. "I like being on my knees for you."

He lifts my chin. "You're exquisite."

We curl up next to each other on the bed. I don't want to sleep yet. If the ceremony works, this will be the last time we are safe from the outside world. The last time I will ever see this room. As much as I've loathed it at times, it's been in my head for so long, it's hard to imagine it gone.

And if it doesn't work, it will remain like this, yet half of my heart will always be somewhere else…

"Whatever happens will be. Don't worry, my love." He draws light circles on my back with the tips of his claws as I drape a leg over him.

"I know. That's what scares me. Everything feels out of my control. Am I greedy for wanting you all?"

He chuckles, a rarity from him. "No, *we* are the greedy ones. We want to consume you every second."

I sigh against his chest, hoping that there will soon be an end to this madness. We lie like this for hours, listening to each other's breath and heartbeat. I didn't think I'd ever find comfort like this again. Not from anyone other than the entity who has been shadowing my soul since the beginning. But now I have to let some light in. And this is the only way I know how.

I press my lips to his shoulder, kissing him softly. "I need to go back now."

A soft whimper, almost inaudible, escapes from his lips. "Yes, my love. Sleep now."

As I drift off, he recites his poem. The first time I heard it, I was afraid. But I didn't understand what it meant. Not until now…

Down, down, down
Winter's bony fingers pull me down
Night never ends
Sleep is forever
I wear the nightmare crown

Don't make a sound
Silent as the howl less wind
Down, down, down
Back to his web again

Honeyed fingers, poisoned tongue
Sharpest is the kiss that feeds

There is no dream in which I'm from
Lost between the Wishing Trees

Down, down, down
Crushed by devil's rocks
Bound, bound, bound
To an eternity of Nox.

I kind of like the smell of motor oil now, I realize as I sit cross-legged on the ground next to the 1962 Super Beetle that Bones is working on. Hunched over the trunk, he looks gorgeous in his grease-stained muscle tank. In the days when these cars were originally built, the engines were put in the back. Another thing I learned from Sister Mary, the mechanic, at the orphanage.

"She is such a classic. What are you going to do with her after she's all fixed up?" I've always had a soft spot for this model.

He pokes his head out from behind the hood and winks. "What color do you want her to be?"

I nearly choke on my cherry cola. "Um, what?"

He grins as he wipes his hands on a dirty rag. "She's yours if you want her."

I bite my lip to stifle a cheesy grin. "Is that a trick question? I absolutely want her."

"What color then?" He plops down across from me and steals a sip from my soda.

I salivate over the way his throat bobs when he swallows, glancing back and forth between him and the can. "Red. Cherry red."

"You got it, mi amor. Mmm, this drink tastes like your lips." He takes another sip before handing it back to me.

I fidget with a loose thread on my jeans, my anxiety building.

There's so much I still don't understand. But I'm grateful my path has led me back here. *To them.* "What will happen to me?"

He leans back against the car and sighs. "You'll be tied to him and this place forever. Cursed. Forbidden to enter the After. That's the deal. He gives you Nox, and, in return, he gets to do whatever he wants with your soul."

I peel back some of my chipped nail polish, making it worse. "That might happen anyway…"

He nods. "We've got you, either way, mi amor."

"Whatever happens will be," I murmur, repeating Nox's words.

"That is the way it's always been." He kisses me on the forehead before standing up. "I'm going to get cleaned up, baby girl. Don't lose that vial. It's the only dose."

I tap on the outside of my jacket pocket. "I won't let it out of my sight." I guess I'm going full macabre tonight, poison, sacrifice, and a blood oath. *Just a typical Saturday night in Ever Graves.*

Bones had offered to bring it to me at Harker Mansion, but I needed to get out of that house. I've been pacing the halls since I left Nox yesterday. There's something about the smells and sights of Bones's Garage that ground me.

"Thanks again. I'm off to go meet Lettie for a drink." *Hopefully, she doesn't try to kill me for sleeping with her brother.*

"Give her my love. I'll see you later tonight." He pulls me up from the ground and presses his lips to mine for a long kiss. "Mmm." He licks his lips. "Sweet like candy."

I feel my cheeks flush. I could kiss this man for hours if he'd let me. "Go, before you make me late," I tease.

He flashes me a sloppy grin before charging upstairs.

I hop in my truck and head toward town, still giddy. Each of them knows how to distract me in their own way. Draven's methods rile me up and make me want to break something in between ripping his clothes off.

Aries likes to wind me up like I'm his favorite toy, coaxing me to give in to my darkest kinks.

But Bones is just raw and pure. He's a ferocious fighter one minute and a shameless flirt the next. Despite his past trauma and the ghosts that haunt him, I feel so much lighter in his presence. I hope I can convey that to Lettie in a way that doesn't make her feel weird. I don't have any siblings, but I can imagine you wouldn't want your brand new friend dating one of them.

Lettie is already waiting for me outside of Duff's when I pull up. I bounce out, happy to see her but also nervous to confess. She embraces me, and that warm sugary scent of vanilla surrounds us. *How is this girl single?* She's gorgeous and sweet and always smells like freshly baked goods.

"Hey, girl. Thanks for meeting me. I have a lot to fill you in on," I say on a shaky breath.

"I would never miss getting a chance to hang out with my new favorite girl in Ever Graves." She winks as she holds the door open for me.

Happy hour at Duff's is just as busy as late Friday nights are, apparently, but we find a table in the corner by the front window. We order two of the house specials, The Petite Poe, which is a flight of martinis made with Blackwell gin.

"Mmm," I take a sip of the first one, a chocolate gin martini, and almost orgasm. Duff's might not look like the kind of bar you'd find anything other than cheap beer in, but it's a hidden gem full of premium cocktails.

"Right?" Villette nods. "I knew you'd like these. Wait till you get to the lavender one. It's transcendant."

I giggle, almost euphoric to finally have a close female friend whom I can do these types of things with. *I hope she never goes back to Raven's Gate.* "I need to tell you what's going on. And I'm trying to find the right words…"

She puts her hand to her mouth, feigning a gasp. "Let me guess, you're falling in love with my brother and his friends. Story of my life."

I feel my cheeks heat. "Lettie, I'm sorry. I should have told you sooner."

She bursts out laughing. "Relax, it's not the first time. My best friend, Maureen, is with my brother Felix. That one was a hard pill to swallow, but I got over it. As long as you and Bones are happy, I give you my blessing."

I let out a sigh of relief, but I'm still uneasy. "Are you sure this doesn't bother you at all?"

The one thing I've picked up about Villette is that she's a people pleaser. She holds things back. *No one can be that bubbly all the time.* I worry that one day she's going to explode from being so nice.

She squeezes my hand. "I promise, Mia. It doesn't bother me. Bones has never had anyone except for Aries and Draven. If he's letting you in, that means he really fucking likes you. And that makes me happy."

"Okay, cool. I don't want you to stop being my friend."

"That will never happen. Now, what else is going on? I overheard Bones talking about the Wishing Tree. That place creeps me out."

My stomach twists in knots as I gulp down the third martini, a sweet concoction of blood orange and honeysuckle. I might need three more flights of these to prepare me for tonight. "I'm bringing Nox here... Are you sure you still want to be friends with me?"

Her face slackens, and she downs another martini. "You mean your nightmare man? Bring him here, to our world?"

I nod and fidget with the stem of one of the glasses. I spend the next hour telling her the plan. I explain the oath I have to make, how I will be forbidden to enter the After, and the agreement that the guys made to stand by me. All in exchange for Nox's freedom so we can be together. So I'm not tormented by my sleep anymore.

We finish our flights in silence. I can see the storm brewing in her eyes. Her expression is conflicted, her brow furrowed.

Finally, she shakes her head. "Fuck. I'm gonna need another round, chica."

I jump up from the table to go order. "Yes, I'll buy this time."

Fuck. I can't read her. She's not angry, but the bubbliness is gone. Great. Maybe I'm going to be the one to make this girl finally unleash. I have that effect on people.

I return to the table and wait for Duff to set our drinks down. Villette and I stare at each other quietly until he leaves.

"Please, say something," I plead.

She lets out a deep sigh. "We are from some fucked up families, aren't we?"

I release the breath I'm holding. "Yeah. And from this cursed fucking town. But we are the ones in charge now. I don't know much about your parents, but mine are dead. Aries's are cut off, and Draven's moved as far away as they could get. I have to take back some control of my destiny."

"My parents are superstitious. They live here, but they keep to themselves. My family made a fortune in tobacco. They've never wanted anything to do with poison or ravens or ghosts. Especially after my brother Sonny died. I'm surprised they even let me go to Tenebrose Academy." Her gaze is distant, her voice trailing off as if she's forgotten that I'm sitting across from her.

I grab her hand. "Bones told me a little bit about that. I'm sorry for your loss."

She shrugs. "I was a baby when he died, so I don't remember him. I'm sad for my mother and my brothers, though, for having to carry the burden of his death. I grew up with that unspoken tension always hanging in the air. It's suffocating sometimes."

Everyone has their own shit to deal with. Their own burdens to carry. Being isolated for so long, I convinced myself that I was the only one suffering. That my problems were the worst. I feel shame for being so selfish.

"You don't always have to put on a happy face, Lettie. At least, not with me," I offer.

She flashes me another warm smile, but sadness pulls at her eyes. "I know. I sense that about you. Thank you."

"Here's hoping I don't make this curse worse tonight." I down the next martini in one gulp.

"No matter what happens, we've all got your back. You're stuck with us now," she quips. Now that the glasses lined up in front of us are empty, the knots in my stomach twist. I'm tempted to lick the rest of mine clean. Or order another round.

But the sun fading into the horizon reminds me it's almost time to go. Draven, Bones, and Aries are meeting me at Harker Mansion. And soon, Nox will be there too. *If all goes according to plan.*

Villette squeezes me into a tight embrace, and I instantly crave chocolate chip cookies. "You're going to be okay, Mia Harker. I promise you that. Cursed or not, you are strong, resilient, and come from a very long line of badass bitches."

I laugh as we say our goodbyes, but a tinge of longing sits in my belly. I wish I'd known some of my ancestors. Once I pledge this oath, I for sure never will.

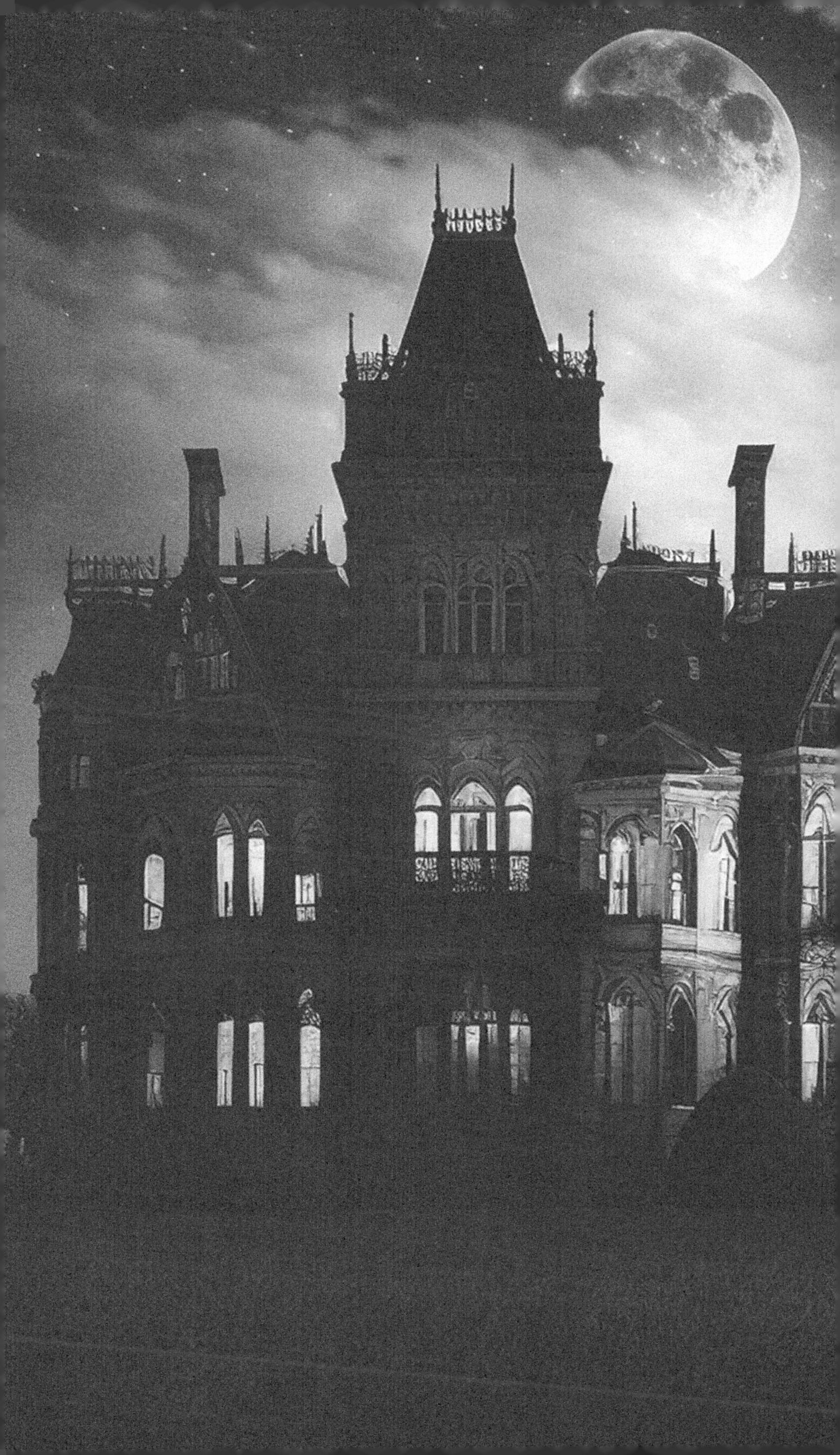

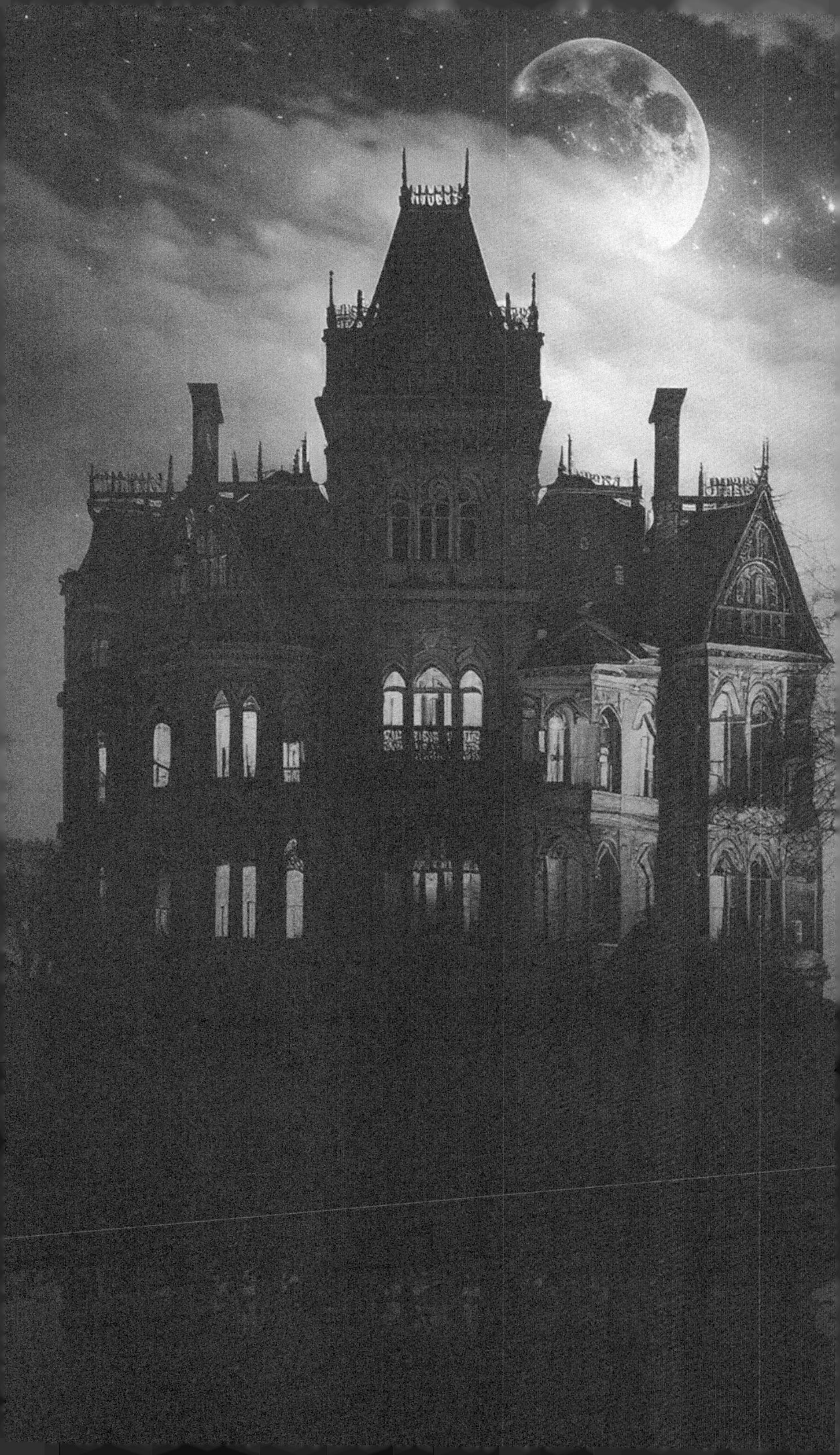

CHAPTER 27

Draven

If you cage a bird long enough, they will never fly away, even with the door open. They become loyal, loving, and devoted. I never locked mine. Maybe I'm the one in the cage.

I kept Gunpowder a secret from my family for so long. The only raven left in Ever Graves. I found him wounded in the woods when I was a boy. Rodrick helped me mend his wing and then hid him in his cottage at Blackwell Manor. None of my family would ever step foot in the servants' quarters.

I visited him every day. Even after I became a man, I would crawl in drunk and pass out by his cage. Rodrick would somehow get me back to my room by morning. My grandmother hated the ravens as much as she hated the devil. As much as she hated me.

Deep down, she must've known what I am. But I was the only heir left who she hadn't sent away. Maureen's mother was her biggest disappointment aside from mine. In the end, Penny died a bitter, nasty woman, and no one cared.

I reach into the cage and gently pull Gunpowder out. He cocks his head and caws at me.

"I know you like your cage, but we don't have to hide anymore." I set him on my desk. "You're free to go or stay. It's your choice."

He flies around the room before settling back into his cage and turns his back to me. I let out a sigh. "The door has always been unlocked, my friend. And it always will be."

I can't say the same for myself.

Or for Nox.

But tonight, Mia will fly free from her own cage. She's always been able to, just like Gunpowder. That woman is her own worst enemy. I know because I'm the same way. We have both punished ourselves for the hands we were dealt. We punish each other. But no more.

If she can accept her nightmare, I have to accept mine. That I'm the devil's son.

I take a deep drag off my cigarette and pour another shot of gin as I study the package on my desk. It's from Riot Graves, the head of Nocturnus in Raven's Gate. We haven't spoken much, and I wasn't very pleasant to him when he last came to town. So I was surprised when he answered my call.

In order for Mia to make a proper blood oath, she needs the raven's blade, a sacred dagger that has forged many bonds since the beginning of the devil's first pact. I was even more surprised when Riot agreed to temporarily part with it.

But the last year has taken a toll on us all. I'm guessing Libra influenced him as well. She kind of owes me one. Not that I'm keeping score. I'd do anything for Aries and his sister.

I promised him he'll get it back, unscathed, but with a little more blood on it. Lettie is returning to Tenebrose Academy in the Spring and has promised to deliver it straight into his hands.

Now we have our means, our will, and our little lamb. It's time to drop the veil. To bring the darkness into the light. And maybe it will ease some of my burden as well.

I open the box and unwrap the silver dagger from its velvet cloth. A tingle shoots up my wrist when I latch onto the hilt. It reverberates in my chest, tickling the hairs on the back of my neck. So many sigils have been carved with this blade. Thousands of bonds forged. It's a testament to Riot's confidence *and* cockiness that he knows he's getting it back. Anyone who holds it in their hand will think twice about pissing him off.

He doesn't intimidate me, but we've come to blows in the past. And I prefer to have him as an ally rather than an enemy. Not to mention that psycho Valentin Erebus never leaves his side. Not much is known about *his* family, and that is something that scares me a little.

I wrap the dagger back in its velvet cloth, slip it into my inside jacket pocket, and down the rest of my gin before heading out the door.

Rodrick already has the car running when I get outside. I look up at the dark sky and search for stars like I've done every night since realizing what I was. But it's still pitch black. A shudder passes through me.

"Ready, son?" Rodrick holds the limousine door open for me.

"Let's go. Trouble's waiting."

Mia sits between Aries and Bones in her signature ripped jeans, black motorcycle boots, and black zip-up hoodie. Rodrick closes the partition, giving us privacy as he drives us deep into the woods. To the Wishing Tree.

I breathe in deeply, desperate to consume every trace of jasmine that wafts between us. I want to bathe in it. Thoughts of slipping into her bathroom while she's showering fill my head. I swallow hard, almost choking on my own need.

Her mismatched eyes watch me with caution. She can always sense when I'm at my most unhinged. Her nightmare calling to mine. "Count the trees, Draven," she commands in a soothing voice.

I loosen my tie and feel the weight of the raven's blade practically burning a hole in me. I take a deep breath and gaze out the tinted window. It's too dark to see, but I count in my head, bringing myself back to the present.

Bones moves to my side of the limo. He slides his hand behind my neck, kneading his fingers into my tight muscles. "Tranquilo," he coaxes. "Everything's all right, Dray."

I grit my teeth. "I'm fine."

Aries loosens his tie as well. "You're making me nervous, man."

"Nox won't hurt anyone," Mia rasps.

"You don't know that." Just because Nox loves her it doesn't mean she will be able to control what he does. We are unleashing a nightmare man. Once he's out, he can't be put back.

She nods. "You're right. But I have to believe that everything's going to be fine."

Rodrick parks the limousine in a clearing in the woods. He gets out and opens the door for us. We leave him there as we go the rest of the way on foot.

The woods are so dark, Bones uses a flashlight to direct us there. He walks arm in arm with Mia while Aries and I follow. The knots in my chest tighten as we approach the sacred tree. Its roots extend out by at least four feet in every direction, swallowing up the ground.

Mia lights five candles around the base of the tree, her hands shaking the whole time. I watch as the flickering flames cast shadows on her face, illuminating her beauty. In the quiet stillness of night, when we aren't screaming at each other or ripping each other's clothes off, I can appreciate how exquisite she truly is.

I had wanted her to be mine since that first night at Duff's, but I was in denial. I've been fighting it, afraid to admit to myself that I need her. But I won't let her go now. I don't care that I have to share her. *She's still mine.*

"Did you bring the vial I gave you?" Bones asks.

She nods and fishes it out of her pocket.

"Good. Drink all of it," he tells her.

He made her a small dose of baneberry, diluted with healing herbs found on her property at Harker Mansion. Along with helping her sleep, the poison will keep her connected to this world.

I hand her the raven's blade. "Make five cuts in the palm of your right hand and then smear your blood on the Wishing Tree. Speak your intention as we practiced."

Mia's breath hitches as she downs the rest of her vial. "It burns," she croaks.

"The pain will pass. Just breathe into it." I squeeze her hand, attempting to comfort her.

The three of us form a protective circle around her. This part of the woods is forbidden, a place no sane person would dare enter. Whether you believe the legends or not, you stay away just in case.

Mia shivers, her fingers trembling around the hilt of the blade. "It's like it has electricity running through it."

"It holds a lot of power," I whisper as if the blade might hear me.

She winces as she draws the first cut. "Fuck, that hurts."

We draw in closer, encircling her like soldiers protecting their queen on the battlefield. By the third cut, her knees are wobbling. "Guys... I feel weird."

Aries whispers loud enough for us to hear, "Relax, little lamb. It's just the power of the raven."

"So many sigils were carved with that dagger," Bones adds.

She's on her knees now, facing the tree. She takes a deep quivering breath and makes the final cut. "I offer my soul in exchange for Nox. Free him from my nightmares, let him walk amongst us. And in return, I will let you feed on my soul for eternity."

That last part makes my stomach turn. Someday, when the time comes, I will sell my soul as well. If she is locked out of the After, forced to roam this land forever, I will be by her side.

"Fuck," she cries out as she rubs her blood over the splintered tree. She bites her lip and closes her eyes, her face paling.

"I can't believe we have to leave her here all night. What if something else comes for her?" Bones's eyes dart around the woods, his shoulders tense.

Aries shakes his head. "Nah, she'll be fine. Even the animals know better than to come near this tree."

I snicker. "We are the foolish ones, then."

Mia whimpers, her eyelids fluttering as she curls up on the ground. "I can't keep my eyes open."

I lean down next to her tiny frame. "Good. That means it's working. We have to go now, Trouble. But if you're not back by morning, I will find you."

"I want you to stay," she pleads.

"Shhh, sleep, little pyro," Aries coaxes. "He'll be here soon."

The poison burns through my veins as we walk away. I keep telling myself we aren't abandoning her, that this is what has to be done for her to get what she wants. She assured me earlier that she understands we have to leave. It's between her and the devil and Nox.

But if she doesn't come back to us by sunrise, I will burn that tree to the ground.

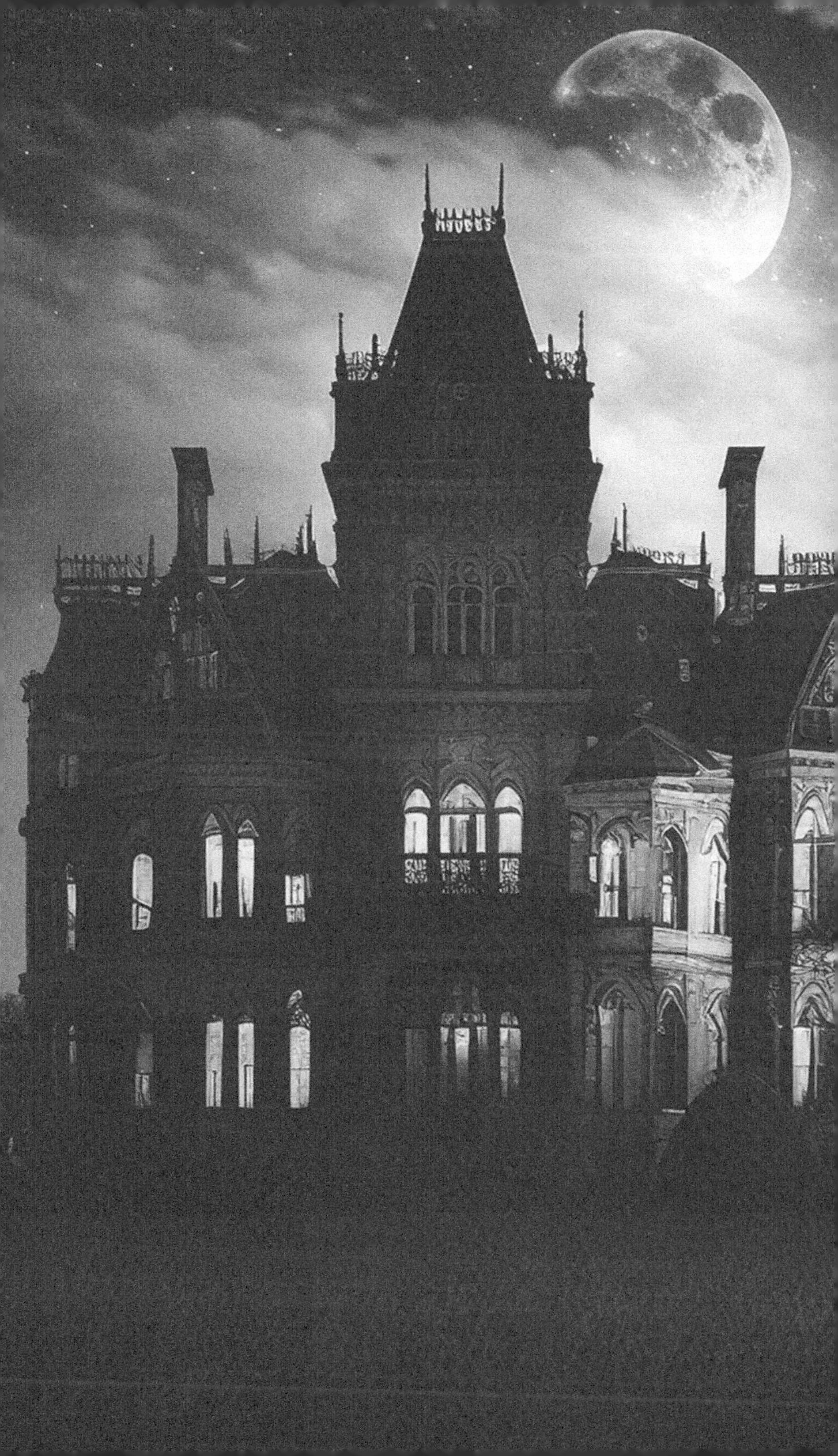

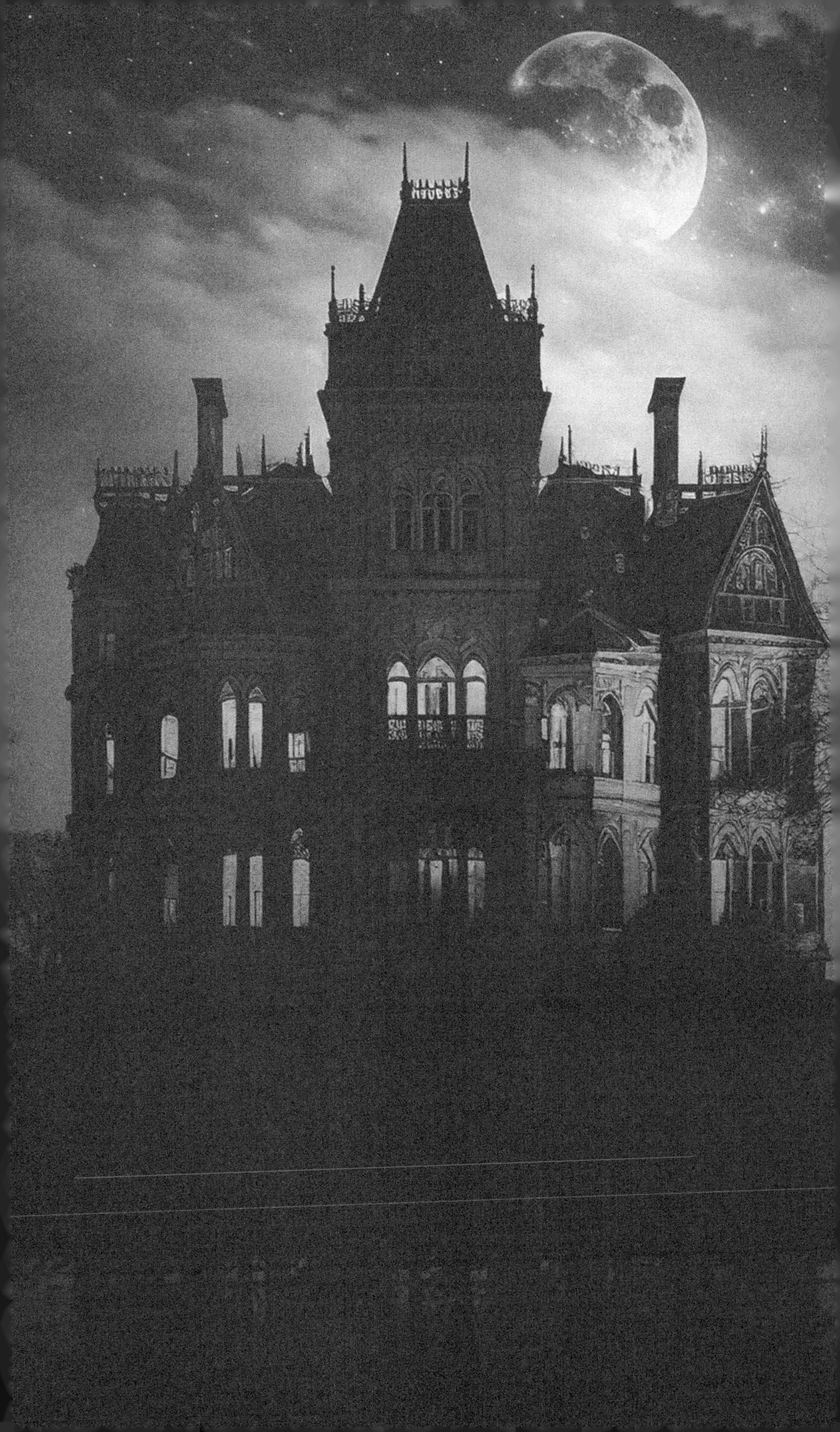

CHAPTER 28

Nox

I SEE THE TREE. HER. THE NIGHT SKY. THE AIR IS CLEAN, EARTHY, and thick with the freshness of wet leaves and soil.

I remember.

There was a before. I was in these woods. Not me. A part of me. They aren't my memories. But I feel them as if they are.

Mia looks as peaceful as she does when she's in my bed. In our nightmare world. But the colors are sharper and brighter. Her skin glistens from the morning dew.

It worked. My dark one kept her promise. She sacrificed her soul to save mine. I kneel down beside her, my limbs shivering for the first time. The wind chills me. A sensation I only have a distant memory of.

I caress her cheek, thankful that I still have my claws. I wasn't sure what form I'd take in this world. I touch my horns and my tail, making sure they are still there as well. We have crossed a dangerous line. My form is not supposed to be here. So, I will be confined to another prison, but at least it will be a waking one. I'm content with being bound to her home. As long as I am with her.

"I must get you back before anyone sees us, my love." I scoop her up gently in my arms and lift her off the wet ground. I'm certain that a naked monster carrying a woman through the forest would not be taken well.

She whimpers against me. "Nox…"

"Yes, dark one. I'm here." I continue down a narrow path, remembering the way to Harker Mansion as if I've been there before. It's a shared memory, a collection of fragments that belong to other damned souls.

With each breath of this new air, my lungs expand. She seems tinier in my arms today. In the great expanse around us, I feel smaller as well. Even at nearly seven feet, I am but a speck in the great space that stretches beyond us in every direction.

I spot the back of the house a few feet ahead. I tuck her tight to my chest, afraid she might disappear if I'm not touching her.

She stirs in my arms. "Nox…" she repeats.

"We're almost there, love. Almost home." I choke back a sob as the words spoken aloud seem too good to be true. But as I round the back steps to the terrace, it couldn't be more real. More tangible. I'm flooded with emotions as I carry her inside the mansion.

My heart races as I take in the colors and textures of the walls and the floors. Everything is more vivid than I imagined. I want to breathe it all in, but my love is shivering, and her hand needs attending to.

I follow the sound of voices. The ones who wait for her. *Them.* The other men I will have to share her with. I fight back the urge to revolt and steal her away. That wouldn't make her happy.

I climb a flight of stairs to another level of the house, and I'm in awe. The tapestries are rich in deep shades of red and black, surrounding the painted portraits that decorate the walls. Portraits of Harker women who all look like my Mia.

A warm draft calls to my senses, urging me forward. I spot a flickering light from a room up ahead. The voices grow louder as I near.

Mia nuzzles her face against my chest. "I have to wake up. It's time for me to go back."

I stand in the doorway of the room with the voices. It's a library. The light comes from a fire in a stone hearth. "You are back, dark one. I am here with you. No more nightmares."

She gasps as her eyelids fly open. "Nox," she rasps.

Three figures stare back at us, their eyes wide. A smirk pulls at the corners of my mouth. I snake my tail possessively around Mia. "Hello."

They are beautiful in their own right, tall and muscular, with smooth skin and soft lips. The blond one is almost as tall as me, while the other two exude strength and power. They can't take their eyes off us. The ache and desperation in their expressions are palpable. There is a synergy between them.

"Set her down on the couch so I can clean up her hand," the man with jet black hair orders.

I'm not used to taking them, but I do because Mia is my only concern. I lay her down and tuck her into a soft blanket. Her cheeks are pale and clammy, her forehead sweaty. She shivers as she clings to my hand.

"Y-you're here. It... worked," she murmurs.

"Yes, my love. Rest now."

The black haired man approaches with caution. I step back to show him I have no intention of hurting him. He sits next to her and cleans her hand before applying an ointment.

"Draven... are you okay?" Mia asks him.

She looks at him with so much longing, I feel it as if it were my own.

He nods. "Better now that you're here."

"Bones." She reaches for the shorter, stockier man with tattoos.

"I'm here, Mia. Are *you* okay?"

"Yes, I don't feel any different," she murmurs.

The tall blond one stares me down. He studies my face, then my chest and finally his gaze lands on my cock.

"You must be Aries, then." I make a point to lock eyes with each of the three heathens. "I am Nox because that is the name she gave me. That is what you can call me too."

"I brought you some clothes, but now I'm thinking they aren't gonna fit." Aries snorts.

"I've never had any need for clothes, but I will wear them if it makes you more comfortable." I look to Mia. Hers is the only opinion I care for.

Her eyes are wide as she gazes back at me. "Whatever you want, Nox."

"I prefer you put something on, actually," Draven snaps.

I nod and smile as Aries hands me a soft black sweater and black pants. I have to rip a hole in the back to allow my tail to fit through. They watch me like hawks, curious and leery of me at the same time.

"It's snug, but it will do for now." I pull down the fabric of the sweater. It just barely reaches my hips.

Draven glares at me. "She needs to rest now. Everyone out."

I don't like him telling me what to do. But he's right. I prefer to watch over her, but I'm sensing that isn't going to happen tonight. Not with them here.

"Come, let's get you your first drink." Aries pats me on the back, and I almost toss him into the nearest wall. No one has ever touched me except Mia. But I refrain.

"I'll be back later, dark one." I kiss her forehead before

following Aries, Bones, and Draven out into the hall. "What are we drinking?"

Bones lets out a deep sigh. "Fucking everything."

"That might not even be enough," Draven huffs.

His aura is dark like mine. It's odd to stand so close to another being that exudes the same energy.

"Lead the way, then."

I chuckle as they exchange exasperated looks.

This is going to be a very long day. *For them.*

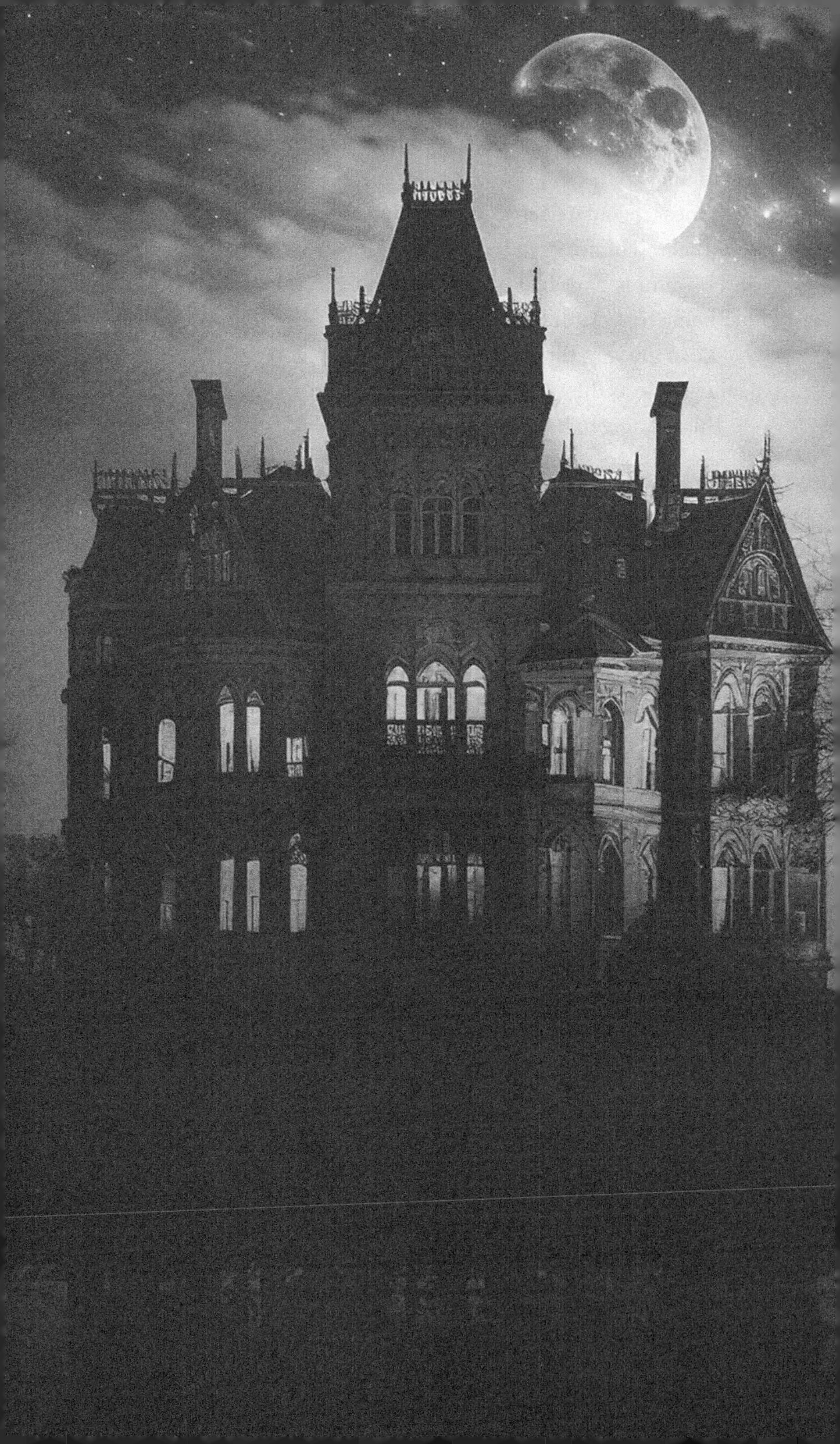

CHAPTER 29

Aries

Mia's monster is bigger than I thought he'd be. Not that I'm jealous. I'm not. But fuck… he even has a forked cock and tongue. The things he can do with both…

"Ries, where'd you go, man?" Bones snaps his fingers in front of my face.

I take a swig of my whiskey, breathing into it as the spicy liquid sloshes in my mouth. Nox smirks as I eye him over the glass. This fucker knows the effect he's having on me. He was literally designed for sin.

"I'm good, just processing," I rasp as the whiskey burns my throat.

Draven snickers. "Right. Sure you are. Anyway, we need to discuss some rules."

Nox presses his shoulders back and curls his tail around his legs. "Shouldn't we do that when Mia is awake? I think she'd like to have a say in her own life."

I nearly choke on my next sip.

Draven glares daggers at him. "No. These are the rules amongst men. I'd say gentleman but I don't think there's anything gentle about us. I'm sure we'd all like our own time with her so let's be civil and figure that out."

The way Nox sizes him up is hysterical. This nightmare man could literally knock Draven out just by blowing in his direction. But I have to give my broody friend credit. He's vicious and violent in his own right. And he's not backing down to anyone. Horns or no horns.

Bones clenches his fists as he takes a step between Draven and Nox. "Everybody chill. My hands have barely healed from the last fight. And I don't think Mia would appreciate us getting blood all over her kitchen floor."

Now Bones might be shorter than all of us but he's the only one I'd bet money on against this towering monster. His strength lies in his recklessness and obsession with pain. He'd probably get off on Nox tossing him around the room a bit.

Nox flexes his jaw and takes another step toward Bones. "Shhh. You're embarrassing yourselves."

Fuck.

I slide in between them and place a gentle but firm hand on Nox's chest. "Easy, big guy. Everyone is tired and a little too fired up. Let's all just take a second to breathe and calm down."

He licks his lips as he eye-fucks me. "You're going to be fun."

My cock twitches in my pants. The heat emanating from his chest onto my hand stirs a longing in my gut. I just hope Bones doesn't mind me playing out this new fantasy. "I'm all kinds of fun. You have no idea."

He slithers his tail around my ankle, sending shivers up my back. Fucking hell. I almost let out a moan when he snakes it up my thigh, nearing my entrance.

Bones hisses. "He's teasing you, Ries. Can we get back to focusing on Mia?"

"Is someone jealous?" Nox chuckles but withdraws. He steps away and leans back against the wall. "I think she'll rather enjoy watching all of us... get along."

I don't get flustered often. Probably never. But the thought of having our little lamb sandwiched between all four of us gets the blood in my dick pumping so fast I feel like I could cum just standing here.

Draven loosens his tie. I've never understood why he bothers to wear one. He always acts like they're choking him. He lets out a deep sigh of relief when it no longer touches his neck. "You're right. We'll let her decide. If this is going to work, we have to try to not kill each other."

"How diplomatic of you, dark one." Nox smirks like we are the most amusing things he's ever seen.

Bones relaxes his shoulders and unclenches his fists. "Dark one? You call him that because he's half nightmare. You can sense it."

Draven shudders and downs the rest of his gin.

Nox nods. "Yes. Our souls are damned. Cursed. And forever connected. No matter where you go, Draven. You will crave me *and* her."

Something tells me that we all will. I break free from his hold and another shiver trails up my spine when his tail slithers away from me. "Our little lamb has sacrificed a lot to bring you here."

"Indeed," Nox drawls. "I plan on honoring that sacrifice by giving her *whatever* she pleases." He looks down at my crotch and smiles.

Fucking hell. I get why Mia couldn't resist him. He's the epitome of carnal desire. Everything he says and does is dripping with delicious blasphemy.

Bones and Draven can deny it all they want, but I see the way they are looking at him too. It's unavoidable. We don't just want to fuck him. We want to be fucked *by* him. And he knows it.

"Did you tell her to burn down the poison fields?" Draven snaps.

Nox stalks toward him, his tail slithering behind his legs. "No. I would never have put her in danger the way you have."

Draven tilts his chin to glare up at him. "You're blaming me for her almost dying?"

Nox's eyes darken. "Yes. You forced her hand. Mia was never this reckless until she met the three of you. Be very careful what you say to me next."

It's Bone's turn to diffuse the situation. He places a hand on each of their arms. "Tranquilo. He's right, Dray, it was all our faults for her setting the baneberry on fire. And *you*, Nox, it's your fault she's so fucking sleep deprived that she wasn't thinking clearly. Now, can we all get over it and concentrate on making our little pyro happy?"

I laugh out loud at that. "Don't let Mia hear you call her that again."

"Fine," Draven grits out. "Consider it water under the bridge."

Nox's smirk returns. "Agreed. We can save our anger for the bedroom."

And my cock twitches again. Fuck. This man, er—nightmare, whatever, is quickly becoming the new shiny toy I want to play with.

Bones blows out a deep breath as he side-eyes me. "Good. Now let's make our girl a pot of coffee and at least pretend to enjoy each other's company."

Nox goes back to his post against the wall by the breakfast table while Draven lights up a cigarette and glares out the window. The tension has simmered for now, but it's only day one. I have a feeling we have a lot more to work out in the days and weeks to come.

"Here, let me help you," I murmur to Bones who is unsuccessfully trying to grind coffee beans. "You have to plug it in first."

He snickers. "I know. Fuck. I'm distracted."

I lean into him. "I will always want you more than I want him."

He turns his face toward me, his lips almost brushing mine. "I know. I just have to get used to this new dynamic. As long as we still have our own private moments, I'm cool."

I inch forward and plant a soft kiss on his lips. "I promise. You're mine before you're anyone else's."

He nips my lip with his teeth. "And don't you ever forget it."

When I look up, Nox is watching us with that look of amusement again. He may not understand our bond, but it's no different than the way he feels toward Mia. The possessiveness he has toward her… it's the way we all feel toward her, but especially with each other. Maybe in time, he'll be included in that as well.

At least for now we have an understanding. Once Mia wakes up, once she's in the same room with all of us, the dynamic will change once again. Hopefully she can handle the four of us without losing her mind and killing us herself.

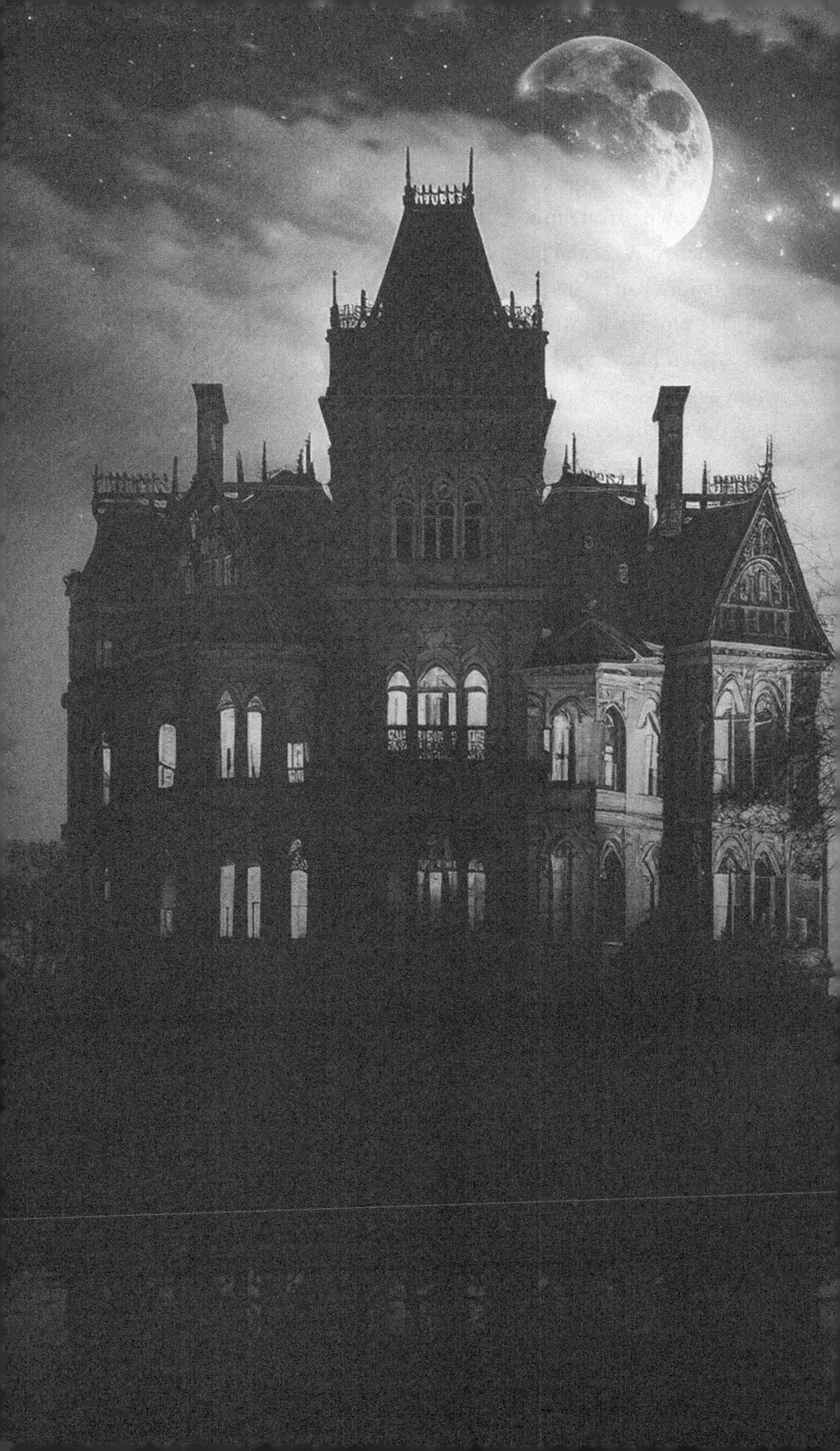

CHAPTER 30

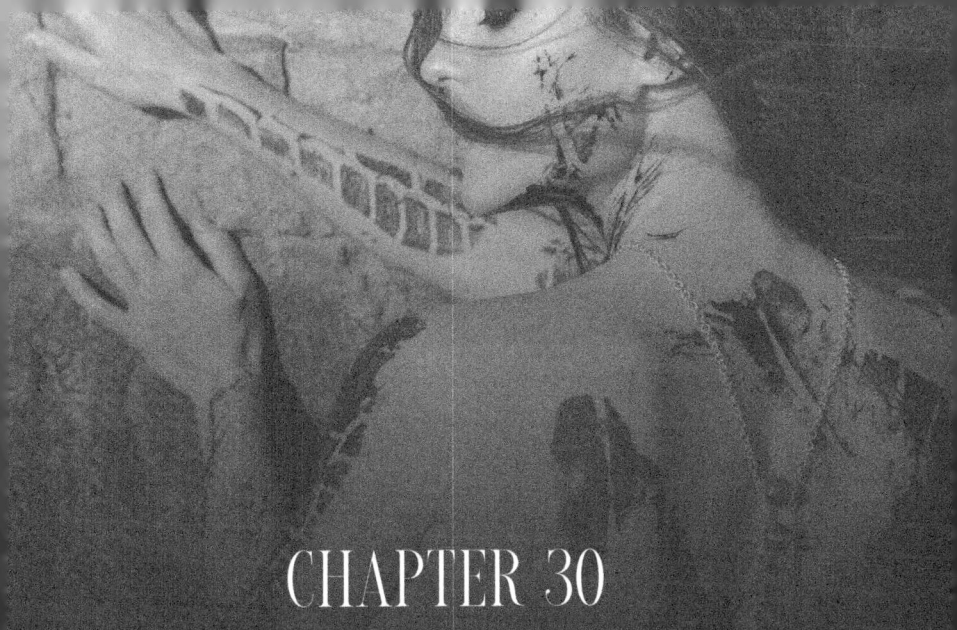

Mia

Honeyed fingers, poisoned tongue. Sharpest is the kiss that feeds. There is no dream in which I'm from. Lost between the Wishing Trees.

My hand throbs as I drift in and out. He's here…

Roses bring thorns. Night is ever black. When the raven comes, the Crane will attack. Heads will roll when the shadow plays. Stick close to the trail of unmarked Graves.

They're all here. My four beautiful monsters. I wince as I roll over onto my side and attempt to sit up. A sharp pain shoots down my wrist. Fuck. My head buzzes from the poison still swimming in my veins.

"I hope this is what you meant in your letter, Emma," I whisper. The fire crackles, startling me to my feet. I wrap the blanket around my arms and creep toward the door. I listen, my heart racing. Are they getting along or trying to kill each other? It's too quiet. Maybe I dreamed the whole thing up.

But as I make my way downstairs, muffled voices sound from the kitchen. I take a deep breath before entering.

"Holy, shit," I say on the exhale.

Nox is fucking here.

His black hair hangs loose around his horns, the tips of his strands grazing his enormous shoulders. I drink in the sight of him with fresh eyes. He looks the same but different here; his skin's more golden under the track lights.

And he's wearing clothes. The black cashmere sweater and black slacks barely fit him, accentuating his ripped muscles more. He winds his tail around his legs, reminding me of all the things he can do with it.

Aries, Bones, and Draven lean against the counters, drinks in hand. Whiskey and gin before noon seems appropriate after last night.

I swallow down the lump in my throat. "Hi."

"Good morning, beautiful," Bones murmurs.

Aries hands me a steaming mug of black coffee. "I can make you breakfast, too, if you're hungry."

I take a sip of the hot liquid, and my stomach growls. But I'm too nervous to eat. "Maybe later. Thank you."

It's hard not to look at Nox. "Your eyes... they're black."

He nods in response.

"Let's give them some space," Draven demands.

Before they file out, I grab his hand. "I'm still yours," I whisper.

His eyes darken. "I know. We've already discussed a schedule."

I almost laugh out loud at the absurdity. "Not with me, you didn't." I pull his waist toward me so our chests are touching. "Of course, we're going to have our alone time. But I want you together too."

He presses his forehead against mine. "I'll give you whatever you want, Trouble."

Nox tenses at our display of affection. I kiss Draven on the cheek before he follows Aries and Bones out into the foyer.

"They worship you as I do."

He looks strange in my kitchen. After all these years, my whole life, of only ever seeing him in a fever dream… to have him standing here in front of me, in my house, is jarring.

"I can't believe you're here. Can I touch you?" I feel like a nervous teenager again, unsure of how to connect with him.

He blows out a deep breath. "I want nothing more."

I cross the room to him and place my hands on his chest. He's more solid—sturdier. Nothing can break him.

He bows his head. "What's wrong with my eyes?"

I cup his face in my hands. "Nothing. They're beautiful. *You are beautiful.*"

He wraps his arms around me while his tail slithers around my waist. "You kept your promise. I would have kept loving you anyway, but now I love you even more. I'm yours, dark one. Use me. *Fuck me.* Tear my skin apart with your teeth if I ever anger you. You own me."

I rest my head on his chest. "I want to serve you, Nox."

He threads his claws through my hair. "You will serve all of us well, my love."

We hold each other for a few more minutes before I break away. "I need to talk to them too."

"I'll wait for you here."

My heart almost bursts at his words. He's not my nightmare anymore. I don't even know what sleep will bring for me now. But I'm euphoric just knowing that he will be *here* every time I wake up.

I find the three of them lingering by the front door. The tension and anxiety are so thick I'd need the raven's blade to cut it.

"We have to go to work now, little lamb." Aries slips on his jacket before planting a kiss on my cheek.

"Our team will be arriving later today to start harvesting the baneberry for production. They've been instructed not to bother you," Draven huffs. He won't look at me.

I block his path. "Hey, don't shut me out. We've come so far."

Without warning, he grabs my face and kisses me hard. Our tongues swirl hungrily around each other in response, ravenous and desperate. It sends butterflies to my belly. "I never want the taste of cherry to leave my lips... I'm not shutting you out, just processing."

I nod, relieved that he's not having second thoughts. "See you here later tonight, then?"

"You're never getting rid of us, Trouble."

Bones inspects my hand again. "Keep this wrapped. I'll change it when we get back."

I tease him with a salute. "Yes, sir."

"Ooh, I like hearing you call me that." He flashes me a grin before heading out the door.

As I peer out the window, I spot Rodrick waiting for them in the limousine. He's a good man—loyal, dutiful, and he doesn't judge.

Nerves mix with excitement at the thought of sharing myself with all four of them. There's so much I want to explore and experience. And I hope in time, they will share each other.

I return to the kitchen to find Nox exactly where I left him. "You know you're free to go anywhere you like. This is your house too now."

"I want to see your artwork. The ones you've told me about. Show me."

My stomach knots. I don't know why I'm so nervous. "Okay," I squeak out.

We head upstairs to the study. When I switch on the lights and reveal all the canvases, another flicker of nerves eats away at me. I fold my arms over my chest, watching him as he takes his time looking at each one.

"They're all of *me*." His voice is richer than I remember, deeper and full of ache.

I fidget with the zipper on my hoodie. "Um, yeah. It's always been you."

He strips out of his clothes and sprawls out on the floor. "Will you paint me now?"

"I-I haven't been able to paint in a long time." I feel sick. What if he hates it?

"Will you try? For me. Please. I want to see you in your element." He spreads his legs and rests his tail to the side.

He's so beautiful. So perfect. This is the first time I don't have to paint him from memory. I nod. "Of course. I've always wanted this."

As I dip my brush in the paint, butterflies dance in my belly. *This is Nox in the flesh.* I touch the brush to the empty canvas and begin. I wince slightly from the ache in my palm. The bandage makes it awkward to hold the brush at first. But I soon adjust and find my grip.

Our love flows through me as I work, almost as if I'm in a trance. No one has ever watched me paint before, let alone the subject I'm painting.

My body comes alive as I furiously switch between colors, my fingers tingling under the heat of his gaze. And I don't stop until it's a masterpiece. All the other paintings of him from before are ominous, thick swirls of black ink with red eyes.

But as I stand back to look at this new piece, a smile plays on my lips. He's a man with horns, a tail, claws, and a forked cock. His skin is golden brown, and his eyes are black. There's nothing dangerous or sinister about it. This new version of Nox is so pure it's almost human.

His gaze lingers on the canvas for what seems like an eternity before he breaks the silence. "Thank you, my love. I wanted to know how you see me now. This makes me happy."

I stifle a giggle as I watch him squeeze back into the clothes Aries gave him.. "Sorry. We'll get some custom things for you to wear."

He smiles back at me. "Whatever you wish, Mia."

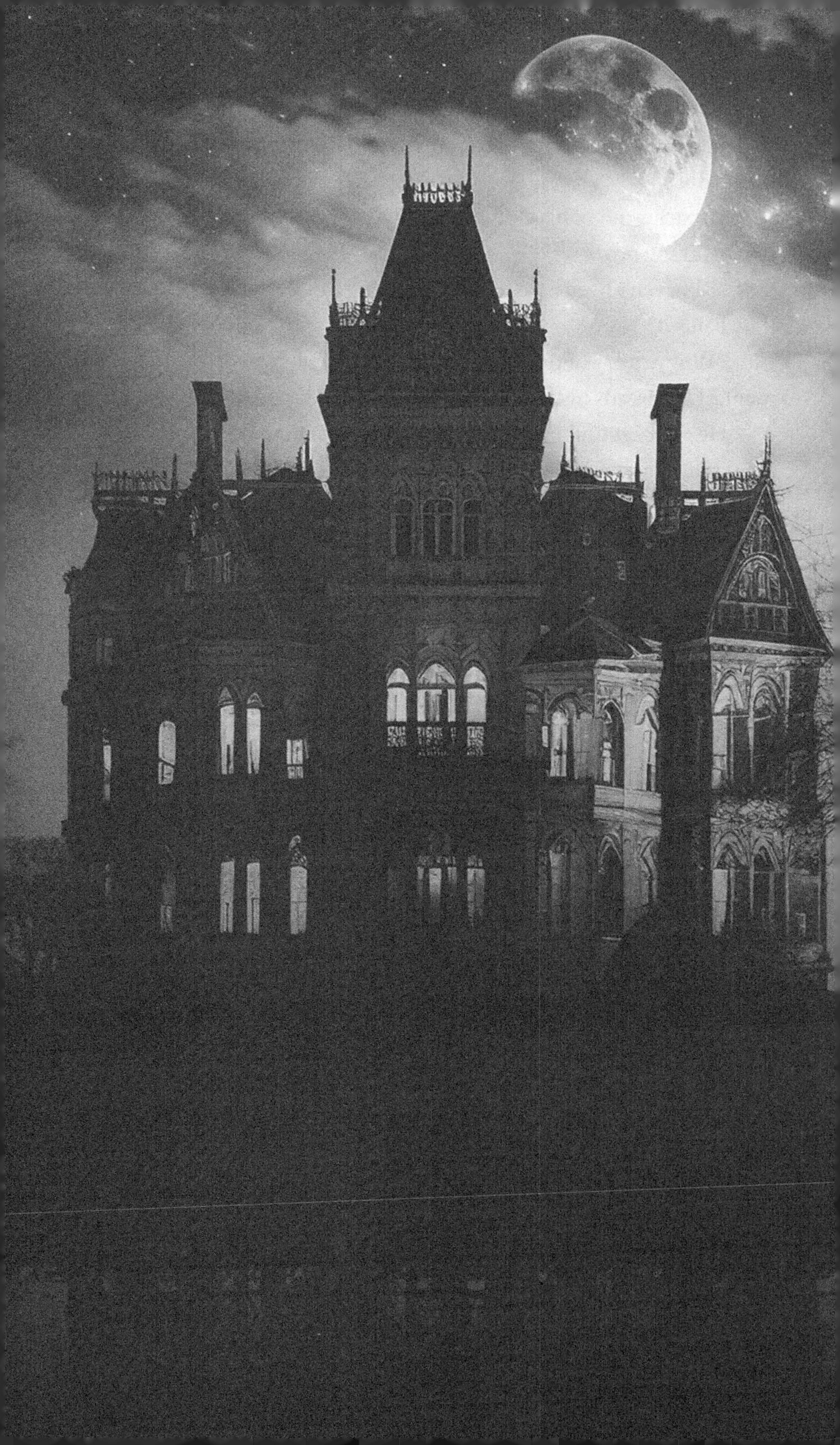

CHAPTER 31

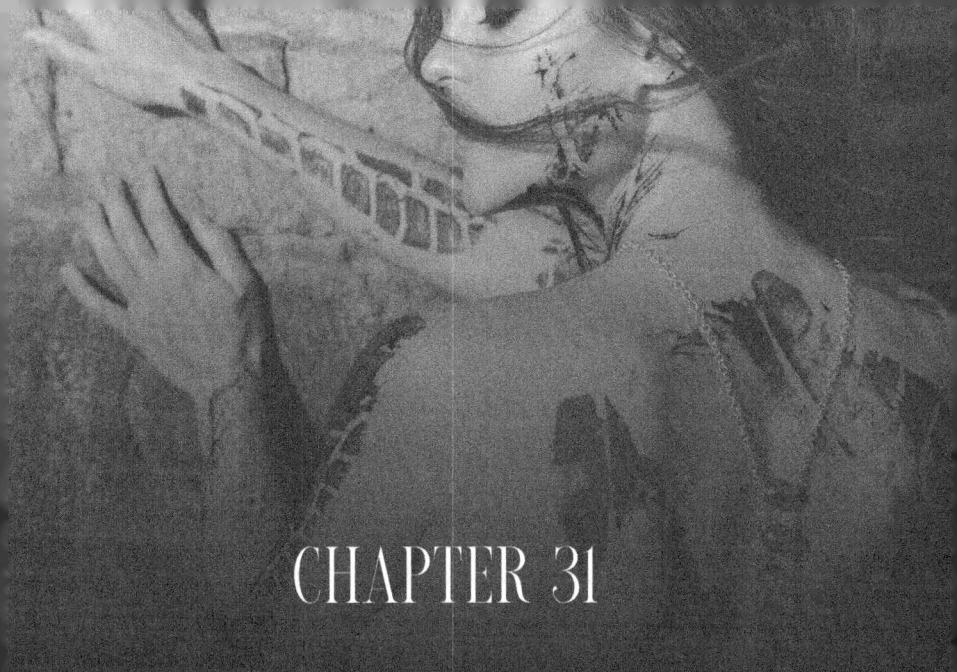

Mia

"Are you sure no one will notice?" Nox asks as I finish tucking his horns inside the black hood of his sweatshirt.

"Who the fuck cares if someone does?" Draven loosens the knot on his tie. "This is our town. If anyone upsets our little pyro, I'm breaking their face."

Aries and Bones nod in agreement, almost giddy at the thought of brutalizing someone in my honor.

It's been almost a week since I brought Nox out of my nightmares and into our world. A week since I sold my soul to the devil. Oddly enough, I don't feel any different. But the cuts on my palm have left scars that don't seem to have any intention of fading. A reminder of my sacrifice. I will display them proudly as I don't have a single regret.

I've spent time with each of them separately over the past few days but there's still this unspoken tension. An uneasiness that none of us want to verbalize. This new situation will take some getting used to. Nox seems like he's the least bothered by it. He's intrigued more than anything. And I can't help but notice a tiny spark between him and Aries.

So when Lettie called me to suggest we throw a party for Nox, I was all for it. We need a night to let loose, throw back some drinks, and just have fun. Then maybe I can get the three of them to open up to Nox more.

With blue contacts, a hood covering his horns, his claws retracted, and his tail pinned against his leg under his new custom jeans, he looks like a dark angel—haunting, ethereal, mesmerizing. Caught between something human and otherworldly.

But while Nox may tower over all three of them; Draven, Aries, and Bones are formidable. And ever since we've stepped into this new version of reality, their energy has oozed even darker. Draven especially.

He takes my hand, lacing his fingers through mine. "You look beautiful."

I feel my cheeks heat under the weight of his stare, his gold-flecked eyes rich and warm like burnt honey. The first time I went to a party at Bones's Garage, I scolded myself for showing up in a tight dress and stiletto heels. I almost fell flat on my face in the dirt. But tonight, I hold my head up high.

Dressed in a short denim skirt, a black lace camisole, and motorcycle boots, I feel sexy and practical. I throw on my cropped leather jacket and flash them each a grin. "Let's have some fun tonight, boys."

Aries grabs my hips and anchors me back into his chest. "Boys? We are grown men with ravenous appetites, baby," he teases, his breath hot in my ear.

A warm sensation starts in my belly and quickly spreads through my core. "Mmm, you'll have to prove that later."

Nox approaches, hovering over both of us. "Yes… I'd like to see that."

Draven takes his tie off and tosses it on my kitchen table. He undoes the top three buttons of his shirt before unbuttoning his cuffs and rolling his sleeves up. "Maybe we start now."

He presses into me, sandwiching me between him and Aries. Nox draws in closer, a low growl erupting from his chest. All I can feel is the heat between us. Beads of sweat roll down my back as I clench my thighs together.

"Fuck," Bones rasps. "As much as I'd like us to take turns eating your pussy out right here on this table, my sister is going to kill us if we don't get back to the garage. She's already blowing up my phone."

Draven chuckles. "She might be the sweet Crane but she's still a Crane, nonetheless. I'm not trying to piss her off."

We all laugh at that except Nox. He stares at me, his lips quivering. It's hard for him to shut it off. To exist in a capacity that isn't sexual or affectionate.

I wrap my arms around his waist and press my cheek to his chest. "Later, love. After the party. I'll let you do whatever you want to me."

He holds me tight. "Be careful what you wish for, dark one. You forget just how brutal I can be."

My belly does a little somersault. It's the times when we are at our most vile and depraved that I crave. His little threats only make me more aroused. "Promise?"

He chuckles in my ear, finally relaxing his tense muscles. "You were literally made for me."

Nox whispers his words, but I know Draven can still hear him. He flashes me a pained look, his eyes full of questions and hesitation. I know I'll need to appease him with answers tonight. The last thing I want is for there to be any confusion between us.

We've gone to hell and back since that first night in the bathroom at Duff's. I need him to know that my feelings for him have only deepened. I've become just as obsessed with him as he is with me.

"Finally!" Lettie shrieks as she barrels toward me. I inhale a deep scent of her cookies and cream scent as she wraps her arms around me. "I should've known you'd all be late to your own party."

I arch a teasing brow at her. "Have you ever tried to wrangle the three of them? And I had Nox to dress on top of that."

She smooths her hair. It's tied loosely into a low ponytail at the nape of her neck. She looks gorgeous as ever in a green and white striped romper. "You have your hands full it seems. So where is your mystery nightmare man?"

I nod toward a corner of the garage, the one spot in here that's not illuminated by Bones's industrial lights. Nox's eyes are glazed, his chest tight. No doubt he's already overstimulated. "This is a lot for him."

Lettie's eyes widen. "He's fucking huge. Holy shit. Good job, Mia."

I chuckle. "Yeah, I never thought about it much on the other side. But seeing him here… he's a beast." I lick my lips, my belly fluttering again. All four of them make my glands salivate and my pussy twitch.

She fans me with her hands, giggling. "Okay, simmer down."

I flash her a devious smirk before we wander over to the makeshift bar she set up. The hired bartender pours us a couple shots of whiskey before I can even open my mouth to order. From the DJ in the center of the room, to the tables full of delectable snacks, she's really outdone herself.

"How are the guys handling everything?" She wrinkles her nose as the first sip of bourbon rolls down her throat.

I do the same, my eyes watering. "On the surface, fine. But Draven is off. Well, he's just his usual broody self. But he's been more distant. I'm giving him space."

Lettie's eyes bulge. "No. That's the opposite of what you should do. I know Draven well. He'll just keep retreating inside himself. Force him to deal with it, Mia. Reassure him that you're still into him."

She's right. I've been avoiding it. Dancing around the fact that I'm in love with him. As fucked up and twisted as that is. I fell in love with him the second he crashed through my gates. I knew in that moment that his brand of toxic matched mine.

I nod and take another sip. "I'll find him."

She rubs my arm. "Good. I'm going to go introduce myself to Nox. I've never met a nightmare man before."

Imagining the look on Nox's face as he listens to Lettie ramble on at full speed makes me laugh out loud. "Go easy on him. I don't want his head exploding."

She sticks her tongue out at me before bouncing off with an extra pep in her step for my benefit. Fuck, I've really grown to love that girl. I'm going to miss her when she goes back to Tenebrose next semester.

I spot Draven over by my newly restored cherry-red Super Beetle. He looks out of place next to it in his designer suit. What's even stranger is watching him sip Blackwell gin out of a red Solo cup. I'm surprised he didn't bring his own engraved flask.

"Hey, Slick. Penny for your thoughts?" I don't know why my palms are sweating. I've let him do some of the vilest things to me. But now I'm suddenly shy. Go fucking figure.

He places his hand on my chest; his fingertips dance across my collarbone. My breath hitches. The movement is delicate, gentle, and electric. We're simmering with need. I tilt my head up toward his, meeting his darkened gaze. "Dray…"

His hand goes from gentle to firm as he wraps it around my neck. "Meet me in the bathroom upstairs."

I nod as his fingers dance away and he leaves me standing there breathless. I slam another shot of whiskey on my way up, my belly a bundle of nerves. I never know what version of him I'm going to get. His anger looks a lot like desire. And vice versa. Either way, I'm desperate for his darkness. His toxicity and pain.

As soon as I enter the bathroom he slams the door shut with me up against it. He boxes me in with his arms, his palms flat against the wood on either side of my head.

"I'm feeling nostalgic, Trouble." He rubs his cheek against mine before stepping back. "Turn around and face the mirror."

My pussy twitches under his command. Those are the very same words he said to me that first night at Duff's. I grip the counter and angle my hips back, giving him access.

He runs his hands up my thighs, pushing my denim skirt up around my waist. He draws in a sharp breath when he discovers I'm not wearing any panties. "That's my good fucking girl."

My knees shake in anticipation. I need him inside me so fucking bad it hurts. "Draven, please."

"Shhh, relax." He drags his finger down my ass crack and underneath until he finds my entrance. I'm a sopping mess by the time he pushes two fingers inside my pussy.

I let out a deep moan and double over the counter. "Fuck." I press my cheek against the linoleum tiles, my body heat rising with every jerk of his hand.

He yanks me up by the hair. "Eyes on me, Trouble."

I meet his gaze in the mirror. He brushes my hair to the side and presses his lips to my neck. His tongue darts out, licking the sweat from my skin. But he never looks away from me.

My juices run down my legs. I widen my stance and whine. "*Please.* Fuck me. Fill me with your cum."

He growls in my ear as he unzips his pants and frees his cock. He thrusts it inside my pussy with so much force I lurch forward, almost smacking my face against the mirror. "*Uhhh,*" I cry out. Fuck. I squeeze my eyes shut, remembering how he didn't want me to look at him the last time.

He slides out then slams back in, grunting as he stretches me with his girth. "I said eyes on me, Mia. Fucking look at me."

I return my gaze to his and when we lock eyes this time, an explosion erupts in my core. He reaches around and rolls his thumb over my clit. "That's it. Bend for me. Break for me. Shatter to fucking pieces for me."

I take shallow breaths as the pressure builds in my clit. The tip of his cock taps my G-spot and it takes all of my strength to stay upright. Sensing my shakiness, he wraps an arm around my waist to anchor me.

"You've always been mine." *Thrust.* "Every," *thrust,* "inch of you," *thrust,* "is mine."

"*Yes,*" I say on a breath. Mascara runs down my face and my cheeks are bright red. His gaze unravels me. But I still don't look away. I pull down my straps, inching my top down until it's around my waist. Just like my skirt.

My nipples are hard and swollen. I squeeze and pinch them taut between my fingers as Draven fucks me harder, ramming my hips into the hard counter.

"You're so fucking beautiful." He drags the tip of his tongue across my jawline. "I love how you take me. How you fucking clench around me." He jerks his hips up, hitting a spot so deep inside of me that my mouth drops open and I scream.

"Thatta girl. Fucking cum for me."

I grind back against him, urging his cock in deeper. "Harder," I beg.

"Mmm, fucking hell." He slams into me again. It's violent and cruel and so fucking erotic. I squeeze my nipples harder as he pinches my clit between his fingers.

"Oh, shit. I can't… Fuck. I'm cumming." Stars dot my vision as an orgasm crashes through me. I press his palm to my mound and grind in circles.

"Mia. Fuck." His cum invades my core, thick and hot. He holds my hips still against him while his cock throbs inside me, pulsing against my walls.

"Fuck," I rasp. My pussy trembles around him while his cum drips down my thighs.

Neither one of us dares to move, our eyes locked, unwavering.

"I love you, Mia." He kisses my ear.

I gasp. It's hard to say when our obsession with each other became more. When it became tangible. I don't think either of us were prepared to get attached. But here we are again, fucking in a bathroom like two sex-starved teenagers. "Dray… I love you too."

He wraps his arms around my chest, his cock still inside me. "You better."

I smirk at him in the mirror. "Do I still fuck like a slut?"

He holds me tighter and his cock springs to life again, eager for another round. "You fuck like you're *my* slut. As you fucking should."

I rock my hips back, causing him to get even harder. "I'm not done yet. Make me cum again."

He arches an eyebrow at me. "Aren't we bossy tonight. Now I'm going to have to remind you who's in charge." He pulls out and slides his cock up my ass crack until he finds my other entrance. "I own you, remember?"

I whimper as he nudges my anus with the tip of his cock. "Oh, fuck. Yes."

He chuckles as he rustles a drawer open and pulls out a tube of lubricant. He squirts a big glob of it inside my ass. "Come here. Open up for me."

He spreads my ass cheeks apart as he pushes in. And I almost black out. The pleasure mixed with pain drives me wild. And the sound that he unleashes once he's buried all the way inside me makes us both feral.

"Do you take *him* like this?"

I inch forward but he yanks me back. I'm not sure what he's asking. If he's angry or turned on or both. "Yes," I stutter out.

"I want to watch." He thrusts hard inside me and I scream. "Next time, I want to see how his forked cock destroys you." He thrusts deeper, rubbing me raw. "I want to see how his tail slides in and out of your tight cunt."

I want to be angry but I'm too fucking hot for this man. I'm too aroused. My juices leak out of my pussy as he fucks my ass so hard my cheeks go numb. "I'll give you whatever you want, Dray. Whatever makes your dick hard."

He slaps my ass. "You make my dick hard, Mia. And the sight of the ones you crave fucking you senseless. Violating you. Doing vile and disgusting things to you. That's what makes me hard."

And I'm a goner. I clench as a different kind of orgasm shatters me. One that starts in my ass and spreads to my clit. I shudder around him, a deep moan leaving my throat as he once again fills me with his thick cum. We climax together as he guides my hips forward and back, grinding against me and the counter. I fall apart. My knees buckle but he catches me.

"You can have two more drinks. Then we're going home to live out your darkest fantasies." He pulls out and I whine over the absence of his perfect cock.

I bite my lower lip to stifle another whimper. My ass is tender but not sore. I can definitely take more tonight. I'm a greedy little slut who wants all of them. I bat my eyelashes at him. "Yes, sir."

He thumbs my lip. "Keep talking like that and it'll only be one drink instead of two."

"Don't threaten me with what I want," I purr.

"Fucking hell, Mia. You really are going to be the death of all of us."

While we finish cleaning ourselves up, I can't keep the grin off my face. For the first time in my life, I have people who actually love me. Who care about me and aren't going to run away when things get weird. Because they're just as fucking weird as I am.

As I suspected, Lettie is still talking Nox's ear off in the corner.

Bones and Aries rush to my side, each with a drink for me. I laugh and take both. Draven did say I could have two more drinks.

I sway my hips to the music, content and happy. *I have a family.* A twisted and toxic one, but it's mine. Draven drapes an arm over my shoulders. "Bottoms up, Trouble. The sooner we get home, the sooner we can get you naked and on all fours."

Fuck. My belly flips. I shoot the rest of my drinks back, say goodbye to Lettie, and climb into Aries's SUV. With the five of us inside the vehicle, my heart skips. There's a knowing look on each of their faces. It's finally happening. We're going to solidify this bond tonight.

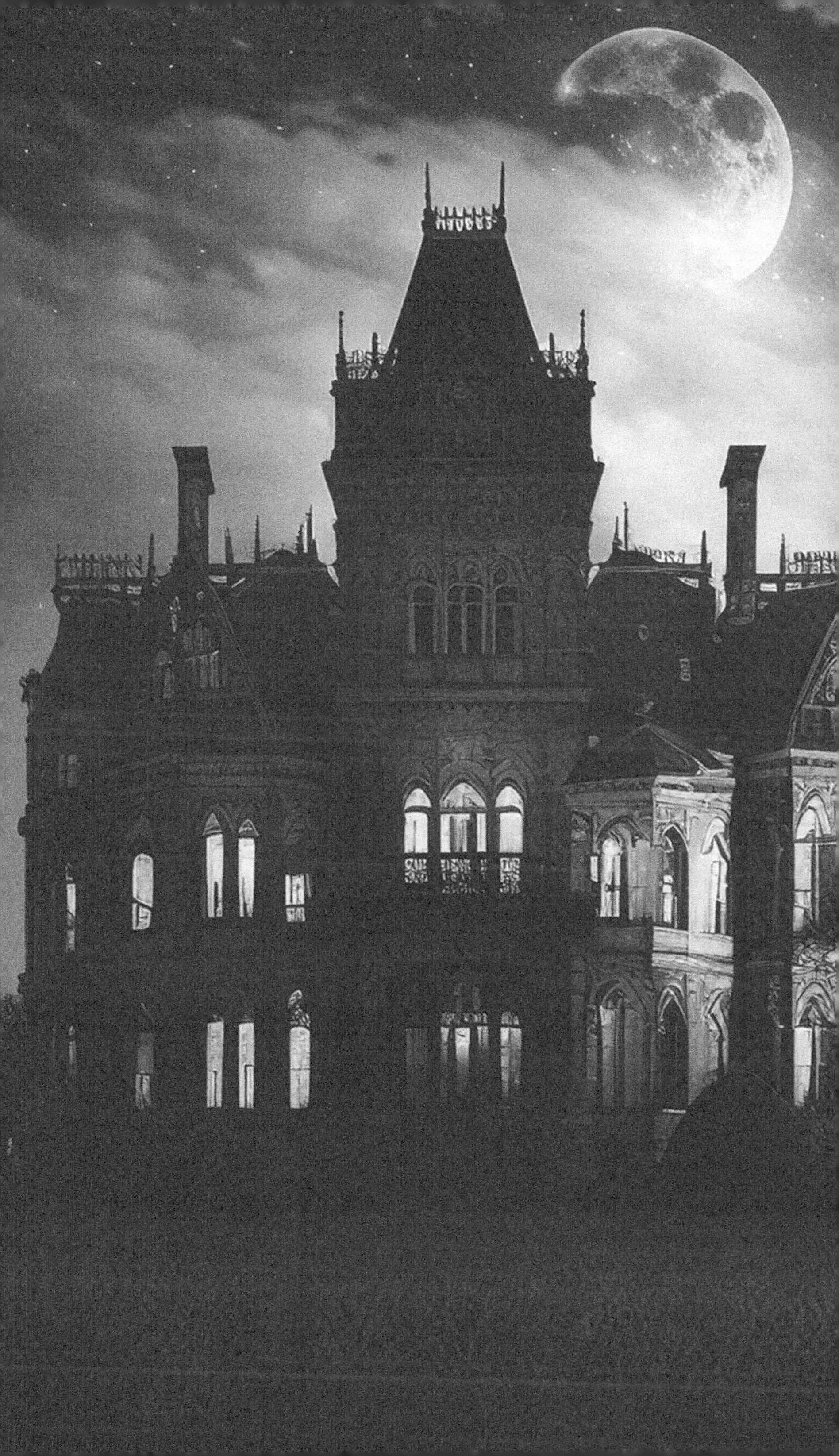

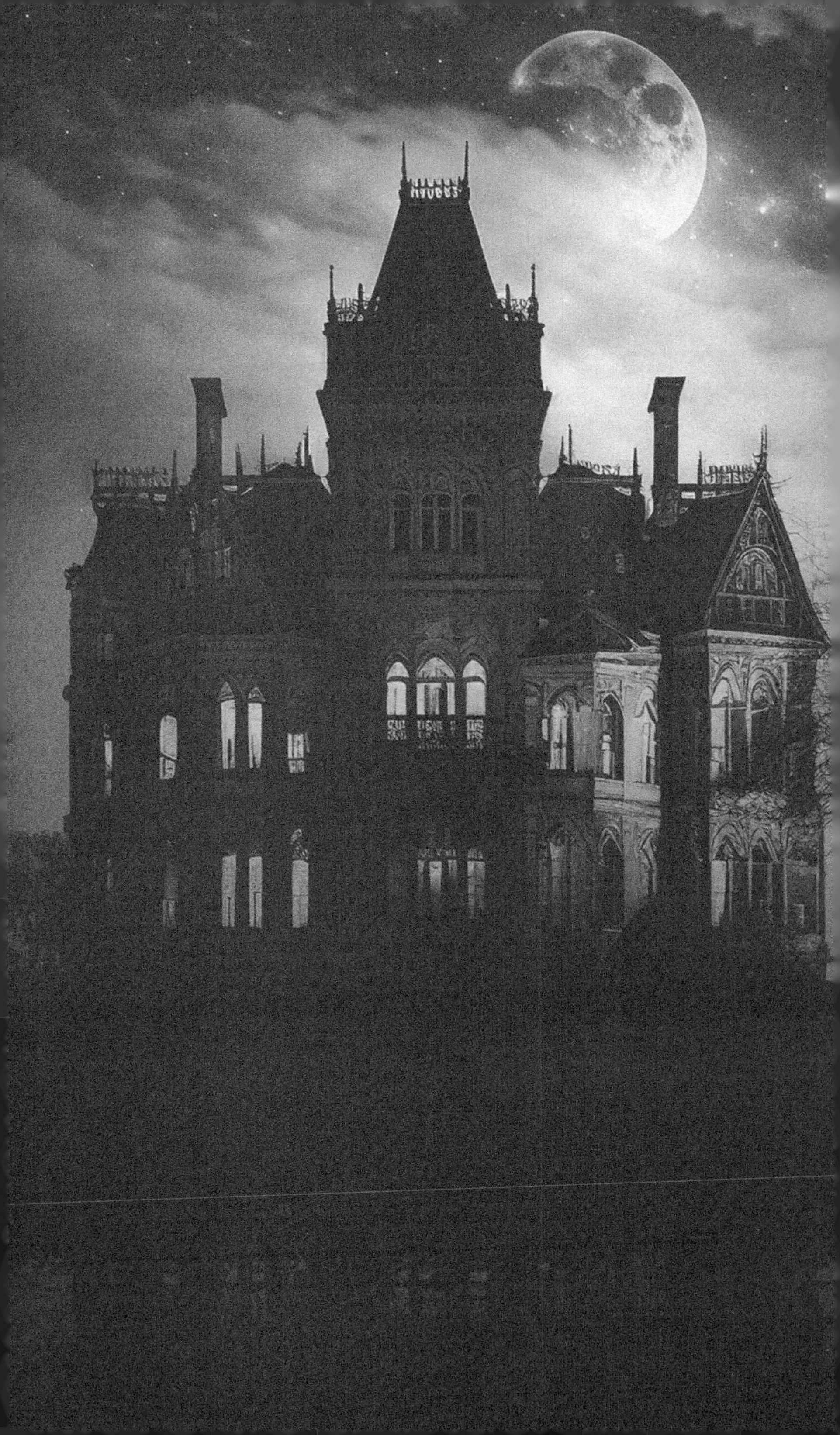

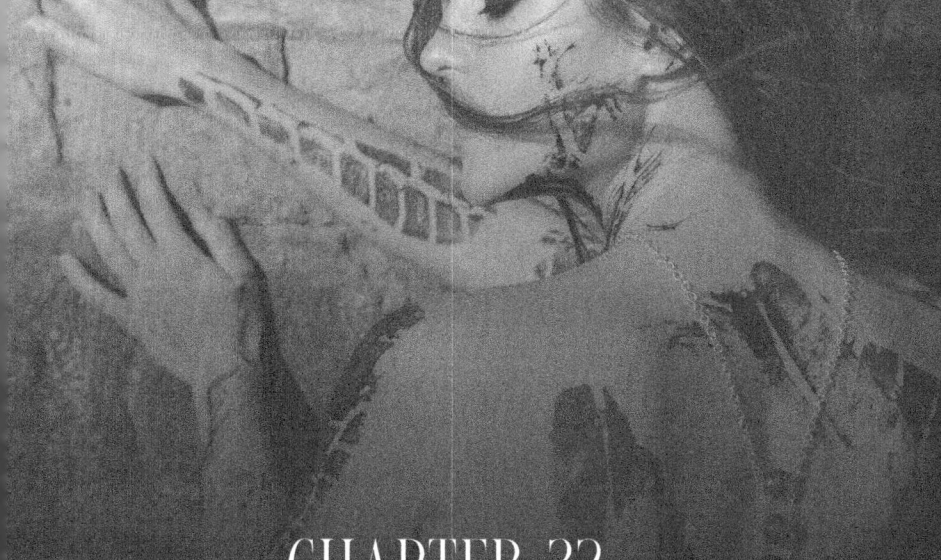

CHAPTER 32

Mia

I LAY ACROSS MY BED AS THEY OGLE MY NAKED FLESH, THEIR EYES glazing with lust and fire.

Draven, Aries, and Bones undress while Nox and I watch. My pulse is racing so fast I'm shaking.

They climb onto the bed. Draven lies on my other side, while Bones and Aries perch at my feet.

Nox slithers his tail toward Aries. "We can do all sorts of naughty things if you want."

Aries's eyes light up. "I want to fuck our little lamb with your tail in me."

A spasm shakes my core as they stroke me while gazing at each other. I've wanted this for so long.

Nox scrapes his claws against my nipples. "Open your legs for him."

Aries mounts me as soon as I spread my thighs apart. I gasp as he shoves his cock inside my pussy. "Oh, sweet little lamb…"

Nox licks his lips, his tongue forking. "That's it. Get deep inside her. Show me how you slide in and out."

I buck as Aries pushes in so deep, he hits my most tender spot. "Oh, fuck."

Draven rolls his thumb over my clit while he stares at Nox. "I want to feel your tongue."

Nox leans over and nudges Draven's nose with his. "Open your mouth."

I almost cum watching them kiss. Nox licks his lips, then thrusts in his mouth. Draven lets out a deep moan and rubs me harder. They embrace the darkness between them, devouring each other with a need I've never seen either of them display.

Bones kneels beside Aries and fists his cock at the base, jerking him off while he thrusts inside my pussy. A gurgled cry unleashes from my throat. I can barely breathe. Every inch of me tingles.

Nox pulls back and wraps his tail around Aries's waist. "Relax and let him in."

Aries moans as Nox's tail penetrates his ass. He thrusts down hard on me, shattering my core. The spasm spreads through my pussy as I clench around him. "Aries, fuck."

Bones slides a hand underneath me and pushes two fingers inside my ass. "I love how fucking tight you are, baby girl."

Nox plays with my nipples, pinching and scratching them without mercy. "Unfold for us. Surrender."

Draven shoves his cock into my mouth. "Swallow it all, Trouble. Choke on me."

I blink back tears as he stretches me. I'm being teased and groped from all angles. It's a dark ecstasy meant only for us. A sinful melody that only we know the notes to. I cum over and over again as they take turns filling me and each other.

Nox rolls me onto my stomach and pulls me to my knees. "Let me show you what she begs me for."

He thrusts one of his cock heads in my pussy and the other in my ass.

Aries rubs my back. "Ooh, fuck. Thatta girl. Rock your hips back and forth."

I whine and whimper as they slide their hands all over me. Bones forces his cock in my mouth. "Let's cum together," he tells Nox.

I feel his claws digging into my ass. Draven and Aries play with the outside of my pussy while Nox's cock head pierces me inside. I sway back and forth between Nox and Bones. I'm almost to the point of blacking out when another orgasm takes furious hold of my body. I twist and writhe against Nox's massive frame.

Bones pinches my chin. "Breathe through your nose, little lamb." A burst of hot cum fills my mouth. "Mmm," I moan and swallow it down like it's holy water.

Nox slaps my ass, shattering me again. He lets out a scream as he cums inside me.

We collapse how we are, in a heap of tangled limbs and heaving chests.

Whole. Sacred. Bonded to each other for life.

And when I finally fall asleep against their arms and legs, for the first time, I don't dream. I stay right here with them. No more nightmares. Just sleep.

There is darkness in all things. Some more than others. Twisted, rotting things that snake through your bones and take a hold of your soul. Monsters that crawl up from under your bed and slide between your sheets. These monsters have staked their claim on me. And they are all mine. Forever.

An eternity of Nox...

And Bones. And Draven. And Aries.

Even with the curse looming over my head, we'll find a way to stay together.

Like poison, they've seeped into my veins. They are my addiction. My obsession. There is no cure for them. I belong to them like the moon belongs to the night.

Lost and found between the Wishing Trees.

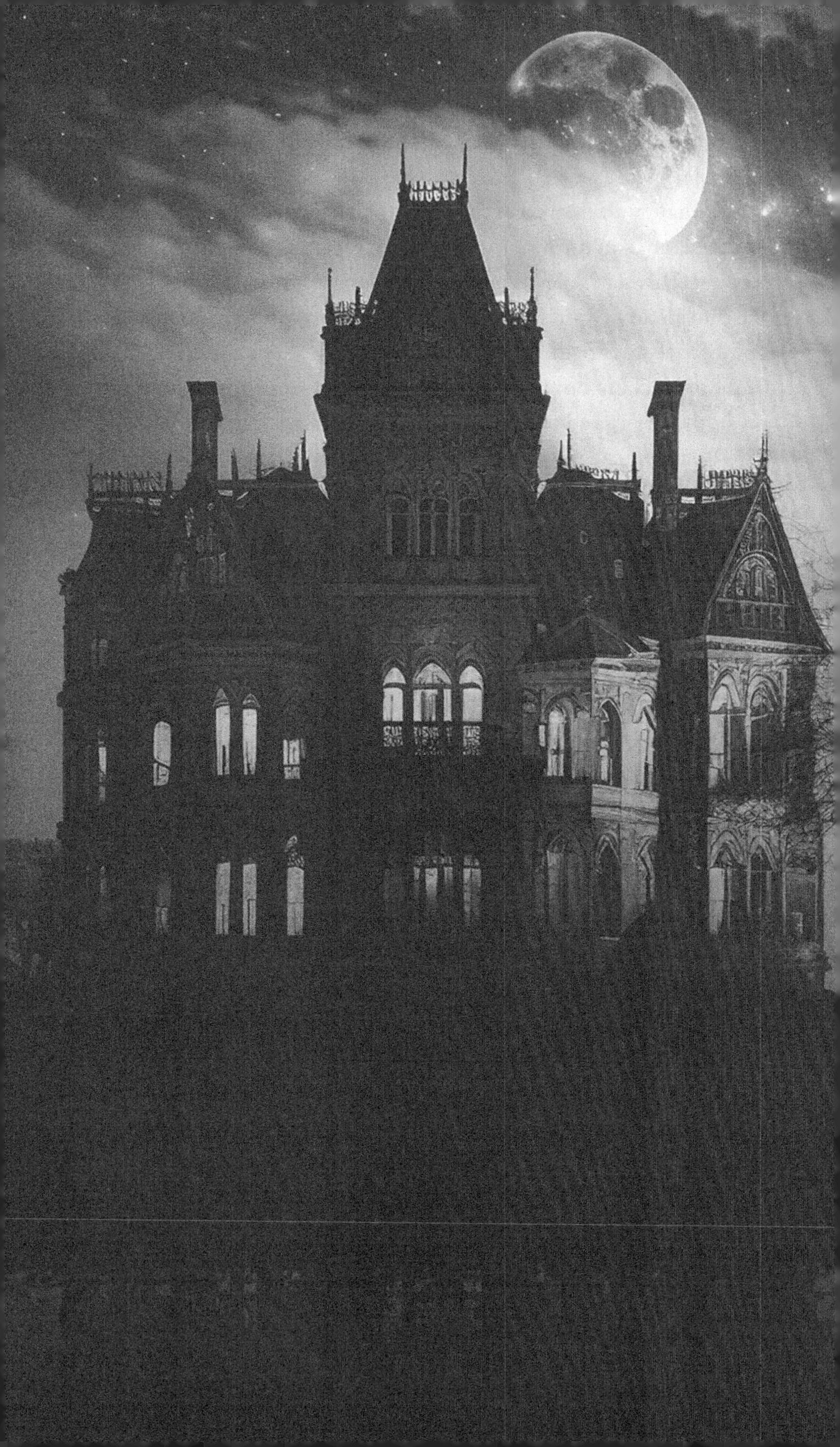

EPILOGUE

Draven

Gunpowder perches on Nox's shoulder. He gently strokes the raven's feathers as he gazes out at the fields of baneberry. The wind is warm for the first time in months, signaling the end of winter.

From inside Harker Mansion, the sound of maniacal laughter rings out. Mia has been trying to teach Aries and Bones how to paint. They suck at it and it's the most amusing thing she's ever seen. I chuckle every time Bones curses at the canvas in Spanish, and Aries throws his paintbrush to the floor like a child having a temper tantrum.

Mia knows I can't sit still long enough so luckily I dodged that bullet. I have no desire to pick up a paintbrush. Besides, I've been too busy staffing her house and watching over the poison fields. I've always been the more serious one out of the three of us, anyway.

Now that things have settled, I've been urging Bones and Aries to have more fun. I've kept them suffocated in my darkness for so long, it's only fair that they finally get to exhale.

"Take off your clothes," Nox murmurs.

I'm so lost in my own thoughts, I don't realize he's watching me until now. "Excuse me?" We've fucked each other senseless in the last few weeks but it's the middle of the afternoon and we're outside. A dozen or so workers harvest the fields just a few yards away from us.

"You need to relax. It's a beautiful day. Take off your shirt and pants and come sit by me." He pats the spot next to him on the stone bench.

I'm dumbfounded. My suits are my armor. "Don't be ridiculous. I'm not as big of an exhibitionist as you are."

He laughs. "Flowers cannot grow without sunlight. You're shielding yourself from demons that live inside you. Not out. Take off your clothes so you can feel the wind at your bare back. Scrunch your toes in the grass."

Maybe I don't wanna fucking grow. But I already have. Day by day, Mia and Nox bring me farther out of my toxic shell. I sigh as I unbutton my shirt. "This is childish. We are grown men."

"I've never been a child. Only this. But innocence lost can be found again, Draven." Nox jerks his head toward my pants. "Off."

I strip down to my boxer briefs and shudder. I don't think my body has seen the sun since I was a teenager. Back when Aries, Bones, and I used to swim in the lake. "If this is some sick joke where you run off with my clothes, I will murder you. Devil or not."

He laughs with his whole chest. "I see why she's so enamored with you. Your grumpiness is charming. Now come sit and enjoy the day with me."

The stone bench is cold against the backs of my thighs but it doesn't take long to warm up. Gunpowder caws and makes his way over to my shoulder. He hasn't done that in years. I let out a deep sigh and close my eyes. He's right. The sun feels good on my skin.

"Your darkness is self-inflicted. It's who you are because you chose it to be that way. It's okay to let the light in sometimes." Nox covers my hand with his.

"How did you get to be so wise? You've been living inside Mia's pussy for twenty-five years," I growl. I'm half-teasing but also annoyed that he's almost never wrong.

He shrugs. "Consciousness is a mystery, is it not? Even for a devil like me."

Mia's shrieks of laughter grow louder. I turn to see Bones and Aries chasing her through the yard. I can't stop the grin from forming on my face. I love all three of them so fucking much. *We fit.* And my affection for Nox grows by the day. Aside from the carnal lust we have for each other in the bedroom, his soul is like mine. We are two fragments from the same whole. Two pieces of a puzzle that remains hidden.

I turn my hand and lace my fingers through his. "I'm glad you're here."

He pulls his lips into a smirk. "Don't worry. I won't tell anyone you said that."

A euphoric wave of laughter billows out of me. My fingers spark and tingle as he squeezes my hand. Mia, Aries, and Bones freeze. They look at me like I have two heads. Like I've gone mad. Maybe I have.

I keep going until my belly hurts and I can barely breathe. It's orgasmic. Exquisite. I feel young again. Free.

They see it too. They feel it.

And soon we're all laughing and chasing each other around the yard like children. We kiss and dance and hold hands as we rediscover that one last sliver of innocence we still have left. A ray of light, faint as it might be, that loosens that shadowy grip around my neck.

We let ourselves feel everything.

Tragically beautiful. Still vulnerable. Ever dark…

MORE BOOKS BY M VIOLET

Good Girl (Wickford Hollow Duet Book 1)

Little Fox (Wickford Hollow Duet Book 2)

Wickford Hollow Duet (includes Good Girl, Little Fox, and an exclusive bonus chapter of Riot and Maureen)

Pretty Little Psycho paperback (Pink Pages Edition)

Dirty Little Saint paperback (Purple Pages Edition)

The Devils of Raven's Gate Duet

Absentia Mori (A Dark Asylum Romance)

Wicked Midnight
(A Dark Why Choose Romance Retelling of Cinderella)

Unholy Night (A Dark Why Choose Holiday Romance)

ACKNOWLEDGEMENTS

Thank you for reading *Ever Dark*! I've been plotting this story for almost three years. For those who have read all the way back to Good Girl, you know that I mention the town of Ever Graves from the start. But the story wasn't ready to be told until now.

Mia Harker was a complicated character to write. But I enjoyed every second I got to live in her head. Bones, Aries, Draven, and Nox were the icing on the cake. These heathens were so much fun to play with. I hope you have been enjoying your trip through Melancholia thus far and I can't wait to bring you more stories from this world in the future!

I first have to thank my amazing editor Kat Wyeth of Kat's Literary Services. During the process of writing Ever Dark, I experienced some major life changes and family difficulties. It was hard for me to get words out some days and I got behind. Kat was an absolute angel in my corner. Kat, I cannot thank you enough for moving deadlines, for your unwavering support, and for your encouragement when self-doubt crept in. I am forever grateful for you!

Thank you to my incredible PA, Darcy Bennett! You go above and beyond for me and I am so appreciative. You are a rockstar and I adore you!

Thank you to Artscandare for another gorgeous cover! I'm in awe of your artistry and talent! (Even though you've enabled my book cover buying addiction LOL)

Thank you to the lovely and talented Stacey of Champagne Book Design for formatting Ever Dark! You never cease to impress me again and again. Thank you for making this part of the publishing process seamless and stress free!

Thank you Stephanie Thomas of Jade Love Designs for creating another gorgeous NSFW art piece for me! At the time of writing this, she is still putting the finishing touches on it. And I can't wait to share it with you all!

Thank you to my VIXENS!!! Whether you're on my Street Team, ARC Team, or hang out in the group to support me and books, I am so lucky and happy and grateful and blessed to have you all on this journey with me. Thank you STREET TEAM for your support, your enthusiasm, and your loyalty. It means so much. Thank you ARC TEAM for your excitement to read every book I release. Thank all of you for just being a really awesome group of humans. I love you so much!

Thank YOU. Yes, you, dear reader. Thank you for picking up this book and reading it. It makes my dark heart so happy to share Ever Dark with you. Thank you for taking the time to read it. I appreciate you!

Thank you to all my BADASS AND BEAUTIFUL friends! A.L. Maruga, Cassie Fairbanks, Candi Scott, Renee, The Smutven, and Write Club! I'm obsessed with all of you and I love you so much.

And last but never least, Thank you to my family for all your support. I would not be able to do this without you. Especially Mama Vixen, Dad, my sister Jen, and Mr. Violet. Thank you for never judging me or what I write. I am so blessed to have you in my pod.

Until next time, lovelies.

M Violet
XOXO

ABOUT THE AUTHOR

M Violet is a dark romance author with a flair for the dramatic. She likes whiskey, rainy nights, and writing by the fire. When she's not creating scorching hot villains for you to fall in love with, you can find her eating chocolate and binge watching her favorite shows.

Facebook: Authormviolet
Instagram: Authormviolet
Tik Tok: Authormviolet
Website: mvioletbooks.com

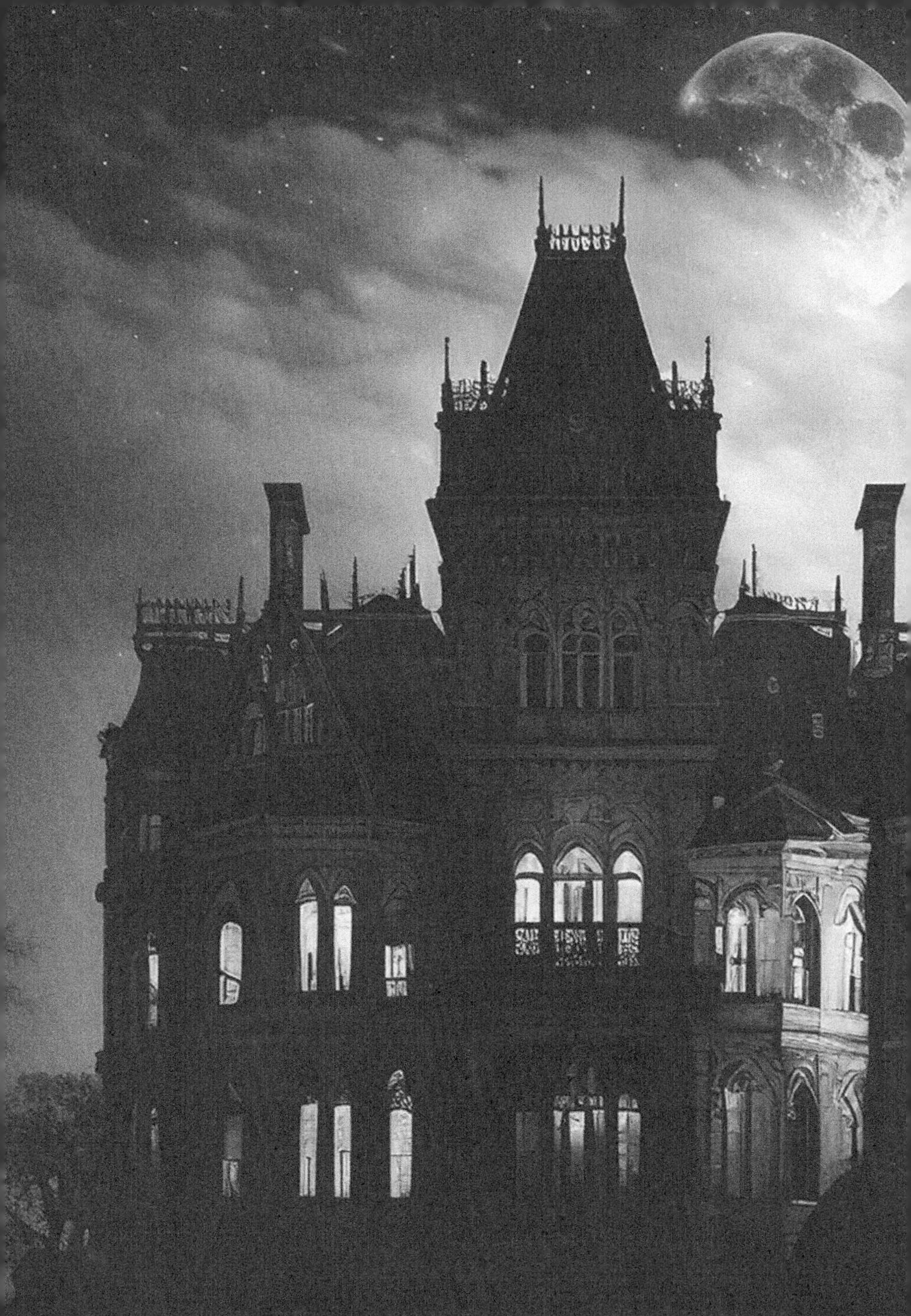

Made in United States
Orlando, FL
24 March 2025